PRAISE FOR DARKEND

"*Darkend* is the thoughtful conclusion of The Gateway Trilogy. Our two heroes, a son of darkness and one of light, are faced with the consequences of their weaknesses and the need for full submission to the Lambiant (God). Filled with compelling side characters and rich world-building, *Darkend* will satisfy readers looking for a fantastical spiritual journey."
—AMANDA WRIGHT, bestselling author of *Darkfell*

"Grant has created a true epic fantasy with interesting magic and internal battles we can all relate to, even if we've never fought in a war. *Darkend* perfectly accomplishes what Christian fiction does best, shining light into dark places. This series is ideal for fans of *Lord of the Rings* and *Star Wars*, or for those who simply love stories full of human heart."
—RACHELLE NELSON, Christy Award winning author of *Sky of Seven Colors* and *Embergold*

"*Darkend* is a fantastic final book for this epic and sprawling trilogy! Truly a satisfying ending to a beautifully told fantasy! I highly recommend this series!"
S.D. GRIMM, author of the Children of the Blood Moon series and *A Dragon By Any Other Name*

DARKEND

Quill & Flame
PUBLISHING HOUSE

CRYSTAL D. GRANT

*Dedicated to those who fear they've gone too far to dream again.
Don't worry. You haven't.*

CAST OF CHARACTERS

Mason Grey – former Shadowman of the Dark Army; now allied with the Steward Army

Seria Gayle – former healer of the Gateway; now a servant of the king

Eric Passion – prince of Paladin

Aden Passion – king of Paladin

Braylee Wright – Second Captain of the Steward Army

Dudley Nells – First Captain of the Steward Army

Jervis Planks – Third Captain of the Steward Army

Aladee Planks – Captain of the Stewardess Army

Lionel Percy – Lieutenant in the Steward Army

Lena Carwright – Seria's friend

Graulik Jader – Emperor of the New Realm

Bruin Pralus – Commander of the Dark Army

Dreeya Faybe – scout in the Dark Army

Areem Kanen – former student of Mason's; member of the Dark Army

Crue Vancer – Mason's former servant boy

Dakim Walston – cadet in the Steward Army

Zakkias Pole – Private scout in the Steward Army

Naomi Ponce – staff member of Daymont

Rossi Evans – Lieutenant in the Stewardess Army

Frakes Bolson – member of the Steward Army once controlled by Mason

Timothy Halk – member of the Steward Army once controlled by Mason

Hiram Stein – member of the Army Reserves once controlled by

Mason

    Feegan Hames – Captain in the Dark Army

    Luron Furvor – physician in the Gateway Stronghold

    Nola Pharris – head cook in the Gateway Stronghold

    Marcus Wain – Nola's employee

    Barry Lewis – blacksmith in the Gateway Stronghold

    Kullen Hendrix – Lieutenant in the Steward Army residing in the Gateway

    Mavis Derron – Sergeant in the Steward Army residing in the Gateway

    Griselle Wright – Captain Braylee's wife

    Shayna and Ella Wright – Braylee and Griselle's daughters

    Ayna Carwright – Lena's mother

    Cal Carwright – Lena's grandfather

    Ira Dankton – former client of Seria's

    Byron Jayes – peasant boy living in the Gateway

    Michael and Keeli Jayes – Byron's parents

    Liam Grey – Mason's brother (deceased)

    Shon Larson – Mason's friend and scout in the Dark Army (deceased)

    Ollen Knavis – Sergeant in the Steward Army (deceased)

    Uralis Faunt – former Grand Marshal of the Steward Army (deceased)

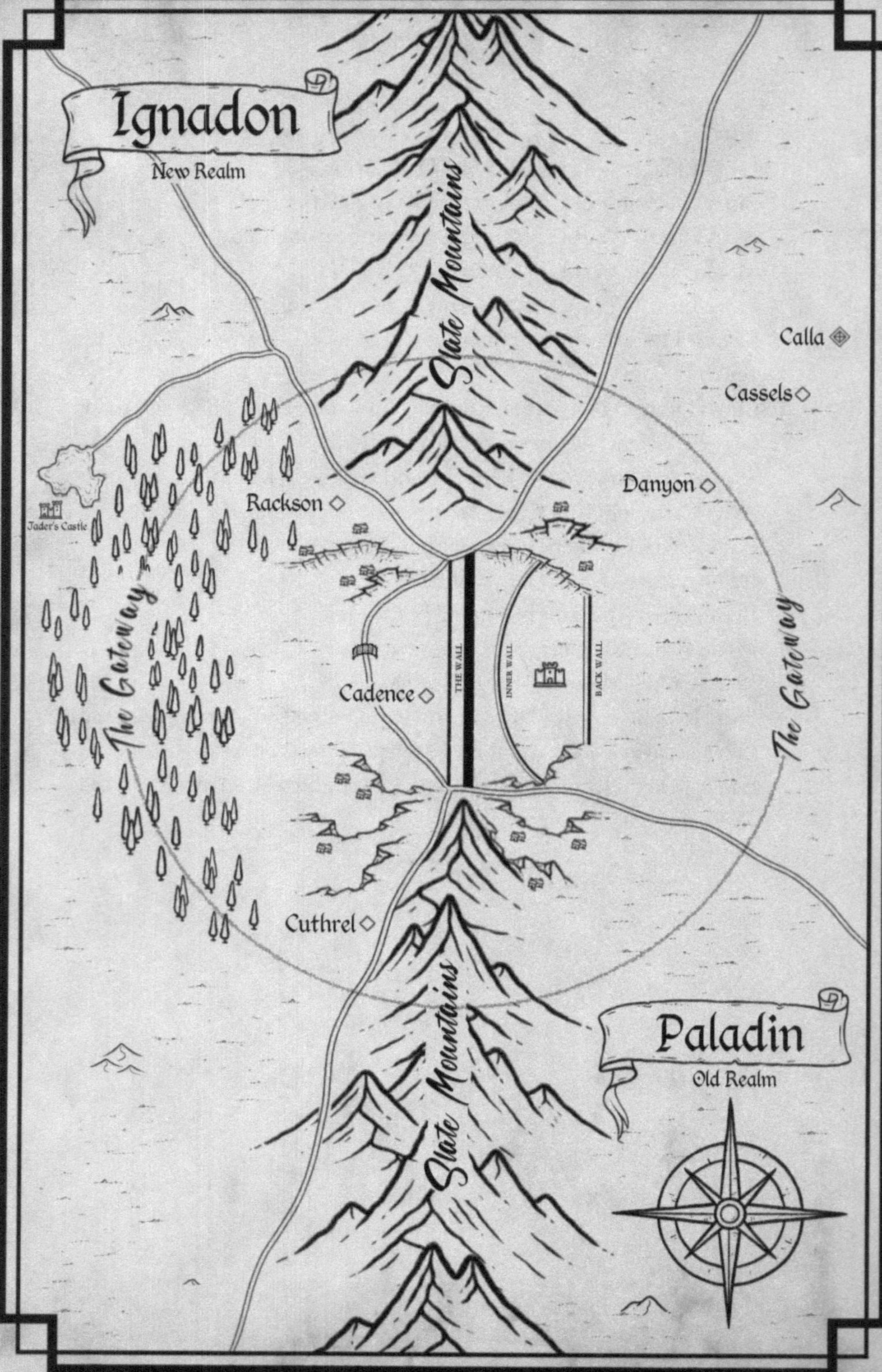

Ignadon
New Realm
Slate Mountains
Calla
Cassels
Danyon
Rackson
Jader's Castle
The Gateway
Cadence
THE WALL
INNER WALL
BACK WALL
The Gateway
Cuthrel
Slate Mountains
Paladin
Old Realm

The Massacre

Graulik Jader sat astride his stallion, unseen as the battle played out in the woods before him. Stewards on horseback charged at a group of civilian males—most under the age of eighteen, though the heavy rainfall and added shadows made that detail impossible to detect. The boys tried to fight back with their hand-me-down weapons but stood no chance against the trained knights. One by one, they fell.

He resisted the urge to lean forward or fidget and waited for the message that after months of planning, the objective had been carried out without fail. The success of this operation would decide his next course of action.

His horse stamped his hoof, and Jader checked him with a sharp tug of the reins. The animal snorted but lowered his head submissively.

The screams grew dimmer. Weaker. After another moment, the Stewards rode away, and silence fell. The stillness settled deep in his spirit, the chill of it invigorating him. He peered out at the darkness that rested over the woods ahead of him, willing it to lift. Soon, the shadows disintegrated, leaving only the rain and dusk.

Hoofbeats approached, and Jader straightened. His commander, Bruin Pralus, appeared, his dark hair plastered to his head in the rain. But he appeared at ease with the downpour he had created. Not a drop of water reached Jader. By the time Bruin reined his horse in, the rain had stopped.

"It's done, my lord."

"And the boy?"

A frown drew Bruin's thick brows down. "He got away from Baris and ended up on the battlefield. He was injured, but he lives."

Jader leveled a hard look at the commander. "And Baris?"

"Dead, sir."

"Good." If the fool could not keep the boy from harm, he did not deserve to return to Jader's fold. "How bad is the boy?"

"He was shot in the chest, but he managed to hit a couple of soldiers with his crossbow."

"That so?" His mind moved ahead. "That could work in our favor, providing he does not die first."

"The healer is tending to him, but it doesn't look to be a fatal wound. He will take some time to heal though."

The wrinkle in his plan rankled, but as Jader contemplated the future, he relaxed. "This might work out for the better." He yanked the reins of his horse. "Take me to him."

A medical tent had been erected at the edge of the battle site. Jader rode by the dead bodies with nary a glance, concerned only with the one survivor. He dismounted at the door, where a Darkman held back the flap. As he stepped inside, the pungent smell of willow bark hit his nostrils with a force that dried his throat.

"How is he?" he asked the physician.

"Holding his own. He's young and healthy, so he'll heal completely." He wiped his bloody hands on a towel. "He's starting to stir."

Jader moved to the bed, his good eye scanning the young patient before him. The boy had no shirt. A tight bandage wrapped around his thin chest. His brown hair was wet and tousled, his cheeks pale and scratched. He groaned, blinking up at the ceiling of the tent. Then he sucked in a breath and let out a yelp.

"You are safe, my boy," Jader said, bending down on one knee. "No one can hurt you here."

The boy sat up in his cot, gasping. "Liam!"

Jader patted his arm. "Calm yourself, son."

"My brother!" The boy's voice shook. "Where is he?"

"Are you speaking of one of the orphans?" Jader knew the answer before the boy replied. Baris had shared his disdain for the protective older brother.

"Aye." The kid swung his desperate gaze to Jader. He recoiled at the sight of the scar that ran down over his right eye but pressed on. "He was—he was stabbed!"

Jader released a sigh. "I am sorry, son. All the boys are dead. Including your brother."

The boy cried out, his fists crumpling the blanket that lay over him. "They killed him! The Stewards killed him!" he screamed.

The depth of rage in one so young was a sight to behold. Jader reveled in it. That anger would be useful. "I regret that you came to see the truth of the Stewards' brutality. It is a reality long covered by many."

"I hate them!" His words ended in a sob, and he covered his face with his hands. Then he moaned and lay back on the cot, his skin washing out even paler.

"What is your name, son?"

There was a long pause, and Jader waited, not wishing to pressure the youngster at this vulnerable time. He had too much riding on this.

"Mason Grey," the boy finally whispered.

"I am sorry for the loss of your brother, Mason, but if you will allow me, I would like to invite you to join my household. I will see you have everything you need from here on out."

Mason squinted up at him. "Who are you?"

Jader gave him a smile. "I am Graulik Jader, Master of Hagnok."

The boy gasped. "You're Jader?"

"That is right. I happened upon you after..." He grimaced. "I could not bear to leave you alone, so my men brought you to camp. I would be honored if you would accept my invitation." When Mason still hesitated, Jader went on. "I can give you whatever you want."

"I want the Stewards to die."

Jader rested a hand on Mason's hair. "Together, we can make that happen." It would be exciting to watch this boy grow and develop his Gifts.

There was another long pause while Mason made up his mind. "Then I'll go with you."

1

For where darkness dwells, light will not inhabit.
-The Sacred Code

The Gateway
Thirteen years later

Darkness and light didn't mix.

The thought pounded in Mason Grey's head as he zigzagged a trail through the sparse woods.

Night and day. Darkmen and Stewards. Shadowstones and Beacons. None of them coexisted peacefully.

He sucked in a breath and picked up the pace, listening for the multiple footsteps trailing him. His lungs and legs burned as he ran, the branches grabbing at him when he passed. Sweat streaked down the sides of his face, pouring down his back. His boots pounded the shadowed dirt path before him.

Out of habit, he reached for the Shadowstone around his neck, but instead of the cool, dark stone, his fingers met the rough fabric of his leather vest. His Shadowstone was gone, resting in the bottom of the ravine where he had tossed it.

Even now as he sped through the forest, in a race against time, he almost wished he had never let it go.

He stifled the thought and focused on the pursuers behind him. Two pairs of Stewards on his right and left. Another pair behind him. They were persistent; he had to give them that. With every direction he turned, they stayed after him, but they were losing ground.

The thrill of the hunt throbbing within him, Mason peered ahead, willing himself to go on, despite the exhaustion weighing him down. He would not let them overtake him.

It seemed he was always running these days. Running from memories and regrets. Avoiding people. He had always been a loner, but these days, he kept to himself even more than he used to.

His pursuers had fallen behind again, so he ducked behind a thick oak and waited, holding a hand against the stitch in his side. After a while, they approached.

"Do you see him?" a voice called out.

"I thought you had him!" a second replied.

Mason snorted as they argued amongst themselves. As good as they were, they still could not track him on a sunny day, much less one draped in evening shadows. He waited for them to get a bit closer before stepping out into view, his crossbow up.

The boys halted, gaping at him. One muttered under his breath and kicked at the ground.

"We almost had you," the leader said, putting his hands on his hips.

Mason lowered the bow with a smirk. "You were closer this time."

The grumbles grew into groans. "That's what we get for letting Dakim take the lead."

Dakim scowled. "One of these days, I will catch you."

"We'll see." Mason moved through the midst of the six greenhorns—none of them more than eighteen—to get back within the walls before nightfall. Before he was caught fraternizing with the cadets, breaking the most recent stipulation added to his probation.

The list scrolled through his mind again.

No association with cadets and juveniles.

Stay within the boundaries of the fort, unless supervised.

Complete all tasks without question.

Attend all chapel meetings.

Report to his superior officer daily.

Absolutely do not *use his Gifts.*

He made no attempt to control anyone, but no one could stop him from helping himself to other people's thoughts. Sometimes it happened without him meaning to, but it proved to be quite entertaining at times to learn what people really thought of him.

The cadets followed close behind, debating what went wrong.

"You move too fast," he said. "You have to stop and get a feel for where someone might go. You can't spot a footprint and go barreling in that direction. Pay attention to the depth of the print, the weight of the toe and heel."

Dakim nodded. "I'll remember that."

"You better if you want to pass the trials," another boy jabbed.

"I'll pass," Dakim said, his chin jutted at a stubborn angle. Then he grinned at Mason. "Maybe you'll get to have your commencement with us."

Lovely. He'd be the twenty-five-year-old Steward graduating in a class of teens.

Weariness pressed in on him, and he craved his solitude. Trying to appear as if all was well when he felt as out of place as a donkey in a ballroom wore on him. Most of the time, he was left alone, but these boys seemed to be in awe of him. And he couldn't turn them away when they sought his advice. As cadets working for their own Beacons, they craved the glory and recognition of any new soldier.

They were the only ones willing to tolerate the former Shadowman's presence. Mason could handle the Stewards' distance, preferred it even. Most of them didn't give him a hard time, but they clearly were not ready to accept him.

The Reservists were a different story. Many of them followed the Stewards' lead and avoided him. But some took offense that he had been given the title of Steward when they were still mere militiamen.

Mason could have told them that his title meant very little in the sense of rank. Sure, he was a Steward in the simplest of terms. The Beacon had glowed for him. But he had to go through the same training and steps as these wet-behind-the-ears students to get his own light rod and earn his official place in the Steward Army. He was the lowest ranking, unable to claim even the title of private. If he thought about it too long he grew irritated, but it was fair. He had to work up through the levels, like anyone else.

Even if he had been a soldier for years longer than many of the privates and corporals in the whole army.

But, overall, things could be worse. In fact, he could be almost content if it wasn't for—

"What's Lt. Lionel doing here?"

Great.

Gritting his teeth, Mason spotted the young officer riding his horse in their direction. The hard set of his jaw made his displeasure clear. Then again, that was all Mason ever saw from him. Lt. Lionel Percy had made it clear from the beginning that he did not like Mason, which was no love lost, as Mason liked him even less.

Here we go.

"You want to explain yourselves, cadets?" Lionel demanded before he even reined his horse in.

Dakim stood at attention. "We were practicing our tracking skills, sir."

"You're all late to your watch duties," Lionel snapped. "You will prolong your duty to make up for your tardiness. Now get going so you won't be any later than you already are."

"Aye, sir," they all responded and shuffled off. Mason dared not meet their eyes, lest they see his frustration simmering beneath the surface.

Lionel turned his ire on Mason. "This is the second time you've disregarded the terms of your sentence."

Mason hid a snort. Only the second time the nosy lieutenant was aware of.

"You are not to fraternize with the young soldiers, Grey, and you know it." Even after three months, he still refused to call Mason by name. Indeed, Mason could almost hear the silent title of *Shadowman* every time Lionel addressed him.

"They asked me to train with them. Lieutenant." He tacked on the title flatly, earning another glower.

"I do not hold them responsible for the terms of your sentence. One more incident and I'll have no choice but to report it to the Council. I don't have to tell you what will happen then." Lionel gave him another long look, daring him to argue, then spun his horse away.

Mason exhaled through clenched teeth and released his fisted fingers, unsure why Lionel didn't go straight to the Council now with his complaint.

It had only been a week since he had moved past the chaperones tailing his every move. No one had been happy about Mason having the freedom to move about on his own within the stronghold, Lionel least of all. Nothing would make him happier than to have Mason's freedom taken.

He looked up at the darkening sky. *A little help would be appreciated.*

It still amazed him how natural it felt to talk to the Lambient after hating Him for so long. But when one was locked away with nothing else to do, it was easy to fall into the habit of conversing with the only One there to listen. It was especially helpful in moments like these when he wanted to lash out and hit something. Or someone.

The sun's golden rays slipped behind the wall-like slopes of the Slate Mountains as he broke through the woods and into the large clearing designated as the training field, where men were packing up and heading back to the fort. On any other day, he'd wait for the field to clear out and then work out his frustration against a stuffed opponent or a target board. Tonight, he had to report at the livery.

A group of Stewards huddled as he passed, talking amongst themselves. One man glanced over his shoulder at him, but Mason avoided his judgmental scrutiny. Frakes had more reason than most to scorn him, ever since Mason used him to get his Shadowmen allies in the fort. At his side was, Timothy Halk, Mason's first Reservist victim in the fight at Rackson.

No one spoke to him, and he concentrated on the entrance back into the fort and headed for the stables that held the officers' horses. Along the way, he spotted a slim form across the road, watching him.

Mason slowed, wondering if Crue would talk to him now. The teenager had avoided him ever since they both ended up at the fort three months ago. Mason wished he could explain his actions—particularly controlling the lad to remove him from danger—but he had not had a chance to speak with him.

Crue lowered his head and hurried away. Mason's shoulders slumped. He cared very little what most of the people in the fort thought of him, but Crue's friendship had come to mean a lot, and he hated that he had lost it.

There had been a time when friendships meant nothing to him. After losing all the boys at Handan in the massacre, including Baris, the young assistant who had taken him under his wing, he had sworn off anything of the kind. Mason didn't need soft relationships cumbering his mission. It wasn't until a stubborn Shon Larson pushed through the stone walls Mason had built around himself that he could even claim he had a friend. But now Shon was dead, taking with him the last remnants of friendship Mason had shared.

Because he could not call the prince who had interceded for him a friend. An ally, perhaps, though that was even hard to swallow. How did one become allies—much less friends—with the man he had hated for most of his life? It still felt strange, unbalanced. While Mason appreciated the prince speaking on his behalf, he also resented it. Their relationship was miles from anything that could be considered a friendship.

And the only other person he cared about was a long way from the fort, sent away from him by order of the king.

A sharp pain raced through his chest, tightening the muscles in his neck. He let out a long breath, feeling it all the way to his core as he deflated. The walk loosened up his tense muscles and cooled the flames licking at his spirit. He approached the corral behind the barn, drinking in the sight of warm-bodied beasts who cared not who he was or what he had done.

The horses lifted their heads at the sight of him. His roan nickered and trotted to the fence. Mason stopped to pat the horse's neck before entering the cool interior of the barn. He moved to the bar closing off the work donkeys from the horses. It was empty except for one gray, swayback donkey. He caught sight of Mason and flicked his ears forward, showing his teeth so that Mason could almost swear he was smiling. Sanjo plodded over to greet him, his eyes half shut in pleasure. It was the same reaction Mason got every time he visited the old donkey.

"Would you cut that out? The way you act, you'd think I never came to see you."

Sanjo only snuffled and stretched over the bar, rubbing his nose against Mason's stomach.

"All right, all right." Mason pushed his muzzle away. "Don't go slobbering on my shirt." He rubbed the space between the gentle eyes. Sanjo sighed and rested his chin on the bar, staring up at him.

"You miss her, too, huh?" A familiar cloak of guilt draped over him, heavy and stifling. She was not here because of him. Everything that had fallen on her—and so many others—was because of his foolishness, his hatred. And now they were all paying the price for it.

He ran an agitated hand over Sanjo's spiky mane. The Councilmen who taught at the small fort chapel claimed his past had been erased the moment the Beacon lit up in his hand. But he still remembered it. Every act of hatred in the name of justice. Every life lost or destroyed by his actions.

The life of the girl he loved turned upside down because of his deception.

He rubbed a hand over the pain beginning to form in his forehead. Nay, the Lambient may have forgiven his wrongs and accepted his feeble attempts at making things right, but Mason did not see how he could ever fully accept that grace. He didn't deserve it.

There was a shout from outside. After offering the donkey a bit of carrot he had managed to swipe from the kitchen, Mason stepped outside.

Something was afoot. Knights—Stewards and militiamen alike—moved about in pairs, searching for something. A few men stood in a huddle, talking. Some gave him odd looks of suspicion on their way to retrieve their horses. A few outright glared at him.

Captain Dudley strode to the barn with Lionel at his side. Mason's wariness spiked at the soberness on the older man's weathered face.

Lionel shot Mason a sharp look as they drew nearer. "Where've you been?" he asked.

Mason gestured at the barn. Lionel should know that Mason was on duty.

"Did anyone see you?"

"Lieutenant," Dudley cut in, arresting the unspoken accusation that heated Mason's neck.

"What's going on, Captain?" Mason asked.

Dudley sighed. "We've had a prison break."

Mason cut to Lionel. "And you think I'm involved?"

Lionel scowled. "It doesn't matter what I think. Everyone in the fort is going to think you're behind it."

"Why would they think that?"

"Because the man who escaped was another Shadowman."

2

The Lambient gives grace to those who humble themselves.
-The Sacred Code

Calla, Paladin, Old Realm

She was stuck doing laundry. Again.

"It's not that I'm too good for laundry," Seria Gayle said, flicking a glance at her companion. "My sentence could've been worse, and maybe it should've been." She dipped the tunic back into the hot water, swishing it around before dropping it into a large basket at her feet and reaching for another. "But did it have to be the very thing I'd managed to get away from?"

The sun shone warmly on her uncovered head as she straightened to her full height, groaning against the crick in her back. "I know, I know. Disciplinary action is supposed to be unpleasant, or else no one learns from it." And she had indeed learned from the wrongs she had committed. Lessons such as honesty, integrity, and loyalty instead of fraternizing with the enemy.

Or falling in love with him.

"Not sure I'll ever get over that one." Her heart gave a pang.

A titter met her ears, and she looked at the bluebird eyeing her from a nearby bush in the yard. It let out another chirp and flew off, disappearing over the walls.

"Fine conversationalist you are," she called out.

"Are ye talking to yeself again, Seria?"

Seria grinned at the approaching woman dressed in the garb of a maid. "Not at all, Mae. I was talking to a bluebird."

Mae laughed and shook her head as she set another basket of dirty laundry at Seria's feet. "Anyone else caught talking to theirselves or the animals would be seen as mad."

"It's not a good habit, I suppose," Seria admitted as she pulled another garment from the pile and swung it over the rope, giving it one last good wringing. "But I had a lot of time to myself for a while. Until I got my donkey. Now he's a real listener, that one."

"I didna know ye have yeself yer own donkey."

"Unfortunately, I had to leave him behind when I came here."

"I see." The maid picked up the basket of clean clothes Seria had folded earlier. "I'm sorry fer that. I'm sure ye miss yer little pet."

"I do," Seria agreed softly, her heart pulling her back to the fort where her dear Sanjo lived, along with many friends who had become like family. And the man who still held her heart.

Pushing away thoughts of the place that had once been home, Seria gave Mae a wide smile. "Maybe I'll see him again someday."

"I hope ye do, miss." A slight frown creased the woman's forehead. "Best hurry yeself out here. Naomi's complaining about the kitchen laundry building up."

Seria picked up her pace. "Thanks for the warning." She suspected Naomi added to the pile to keep her busy, but she kept the accusation to herself. It did no good to express her grumbles, especially since she had so few.

The summer months had not been nearly as hard as she had expected when ordered to leave the Gateway Stronghold, even with her disappointing laundry assignment. The castle—Daymont, as it was known—already had a healer more than capable of handling matters in Calla, so there was little use for Seria's skills.

Still, Daymont was lovely, with so many rooms that she itched to explore. The grounds were breathtaking. Green hills and perfectly manicured trees and hedges provided a picturesque backdrop for the red rock castle. And the little stone chapel that sat off to the side of the estate had become her favorite spot.

It was surreal at times when she stopped to ponder the fact that she was working in the very place the prince of Paladin had grown up. If only the circumstances that led to her living here had been more favorable.

A warm breeze blew the wet garment against her cheek, and she basked in the coolness before moving on to the next one. The redundancy was almost as bad as the backbreaking labor of bending over a washtub, but one by one, she hung each piece until the load dwindled to the very last one.

During her days working with Nola in the mess hall, she had gotten to know many of the men by name. But it was her work in the infirmary that had won the respect of the Stewards, including their crusty physician. And she had become friends with a lot of them. But that all seemed so long ago now. Here, in the castle of King Aden Passion, the resident physician resided over the care of the inhabitants. Whereas she was a servant, a washerwoman. Unimportant.

Shaking her head at her self-pity, Seria bent down to snatch the final item from the water. *Lambient, forgive me.* She had no call to murmur. It was her own actions that put her there. Her desire to be somebody important—to do something important—had led to decisions that served no one but herself. She could not blame the king for his disciplinary actions. And she owed the Lambient she had served since she was a small girl.

No more feeling sorry for herself. She would pay her dues and prove to the king, the Lambient, and herself that she was truly repentant.

She looked up at the sky, wondering what was happening at the fort. How was Mason doing? She had received no word from him or about him since she had left. Not that she expected any. She shouldn't be thinking of him at all. That door of her life had closed.

But it did not stop her from missing him. Or worrying about him.

"Seria Gayle!"

She jumped at the yell and blinked through the sunlight at the hefty woman scowling at her from the entrance into the back rooms of the castle.

"Quit your lollygagging and go pick up the wash from the kitchen."

"Aye, ma'am," Seria said meekly, picking up the empty basket and hurrying to the door. She slowed as she passed the woman, offering her a sheepish smile. "Sorry, Madam Charlin."

"Madam, nothing," Charlin scoffed, but not before Seria could see the glimmer of humor in her eyes. "I declare, girl, if you don't get your head out of the clouds, I'm going to have you placed somewhere else."

"Is that a promise?" Seria tossed over her shoulder as they walked the hall.

"You won't think it such a good thing if you end up mucking stalls."

Seria cocked her head. "Can't be much worse than some of the laundry we have to do."

"Oh, get on with you now." Charlin waved her on.

Despite the scolding, Seria laughed as she deposited the basket on a table in the laundry room and snatched an empty canvas bag from the large linen closet. She turned down another service hallway and pushed through the heavy portal into the hot, busy kitchen.

Several women moved about the large room, stirring, kneading, or minding the fire. Two large hearths occupied the opposite wall, and three tables were lined up in the middle of the room. The single door in the far corner hung open, letting in traces of the cool breeze.

Seria stepped to the bin where the pile of dirty rags waited for her, all the while peering around for Lena Carwright. She spotted her standing over a table, rolling out a mound of dough. After filling her bag with the laundry, Seria crossed the room to greet her, careful to stay out of everyone's way.

Lena looked up with a smile. "Good afternoon, Miss Seria. How are you this lazy afternoon?"

"Quite bored with nothing to do, Miss Lena."

"'Tis such a bother being women of leisure, is it not?"

"Such a bother." Seria glanced around the room. "This room is always so busy."

"Nonstop," Lena agreed, blowing a strand of hair from her flushed face.

"Are you well?" Seria asked. "You look tired."

"I'm fine. Tired, but not achingly so. This is our bread-baking day, so it's busier than most."

A pang of remorse hit Seria. Lena had dreamed of opening a bakery where she could create pastries and tarts. Now, she was stuck in a sweltering kitchen, baking simple loaves of bread and bumping elbows with a dozen other women to feed the inhabitants of the castle. All because she had helped Seria meet with an enemy of the Stewards.

A tall, thin woman cut into her thoughts, dropping a trencher of tarts in front of Lena with a clang. "Did you bake this?"

Lena straightened and wiped her brow with her arm. "Aye, Arma asked—"

"Arma is not in charge of my kitchen." The woman tossed the pile of tarts into the fire. "They're blasted awful. I'll not have you embarrass this staff with your incompetence."

"Lena bakes the best tarts in the Gateway," Seria blurted, incensed at how the woman treated her friend.

"Seria," Lena cautioned.

"It's about time you show up," the woman addressed Seria with a huff. "We've been tripping over the dirty towels."

Seria bit her tongue. The load of rags was no bigger than usual.

"Now, you quit wasting time and slowing the staff down." The woman dusted her hands off and bustled off.

"Ugh, that awful woman," Seria fumed. "How do you put up with her?"

"It's fine," Lena said, composed and proud.

"But she tossed a whole plate of perfectly good tarts—"

"Naomi is an angry woman who takes her anger out on the world around her." Lena shrugged. "This is her kitchen."

Seria let out a heavy breath. "I'm sorry, Lena."

"I made my choice, Seria, like I've already told you. Multiple times. I knew what I was doing was wrong, convincing myself it would all work out. And it will, someday."

"I wish I had your optimism."

"You'll feel a lot more optimistic when our shift is ended," Lena said, resuming her rolling.

"Can't deny that," Seria agreed as she swung the bag of dirty clothes over her shoulder.

Lena was correct, as usual, and Seria's good humor had returned by the time they joined up for a late supper in the servant quarters. Seria found it ironic that stew was a common dish for the castle staff, but this recipe was much more flavorful than anything she had been able to make in her little cabin in Cadence.

"Shall we go outside for a while?" Lena asked as she pushed her bowl away.

Seria scrutinized her friend. "I thought you'd be too tired."

"There's nothing strenuous about sitting on a hill. Let's go."

They walked arm in arm out the back door and through the yard. An early autumn chill hung in the air. They strolled for several minutes, chatting about their day until they came to the stone wall that bordered the castle grounds. Once they stepped through the double gates, they could see miles and miles of fields.

As one, they turned left and followed a small trail to the top of a small hill with a grove of trees. At the bottom of the hill, a training field was set up, very similar to the one at the Gateway fort.

Settling down in their usual spots, they looked down to where the soldiers took advantage of the last bit of sunlight. The knights were serious and focused, moving through their training with the grace and speed of a cat. And they were all women.

Like their male counterparts, the Stewardesses were devoted to serving the Lambient and the Sacred Code. Strong and proud, they wore the same colors as the Stewards, though their tunics were cut trimmer and longer. But out here, in the field, they wore the standard green, oiled jumpsuits, their bare arms flashing under the sunlight.

Seria was fascinated by the strength and skill of this company. She was also terrified of them. Living in the castle, she had crossed paths with a few of the lady knights, but always with her head down, studying them out of the corner of her eye.

Her friend, Ollen, had once told her about the Stewardesses, not long before his untimely death. Without warning, Seria could see him, showing her how to fire an arrow at the target. His gentle voice filled her mind, patiently teaching her about the Stewards' history and legacy.

Pain swelled in her chest. She leaned back against a tree trunk and sighed. When would it stop hurting so much?

"Are you thinking of Ollen again?" Lena asked.

She nodded. Ollen, her dear friend who had shown her such compassion and grace when she needed it. Ollen, whose life had been ended too soon by soldiers in the service of Emperor Graulik Jader.

"I feel like I let him down." Her heart squeezed at how she had failed him. Ollen had loved her, truly loved her. She knew that now, had known it then, even though she tried to pretend she didn't. But Seria had chosen to give her heart to a Darkman, even after he had taken on the Shadowstone and pledged his service to Jader.

"Did you love him?"

"Not the way I do—*did* Mason. But I did love him."

"You can't punish yourself for not feeling more, Seria."

"Maybe not, but maybe I should've been willing to give him a chance, especially since loving Mason was wrong. Ollen was a good man. He deserved a chance."

"He was a good man," Lena agreed. "But I don't think he would've wanted you to choose him for that reason alone and not for love."

"I think I could've loved him. As more than a friend." Seria's lip quivered. "But by the time I realized that, it was too late."

Lena wrapped her arm around Seria's shoulders. "He died knowing you cared for him. He died doing his duty. Don't take away from that. Besides, there's something you're forgetting."

"What's that?" Seria murmured, blinking back tears.

"Mason is no longer a Shadowman. And Ollen's death played a part in that."

Seria drew in a shuddering breath. It was still hard to believe. Yet the proof had stood before her that day in the fort. Though it did not erase his former life, Mason's loyalties were revealed by the glowing Beacon in his hand. No more evidence was needed.

"You're right." She leaned against her friend. "But I'll never forget him."

Lena gave her another squeeze, then turned her attention back to the soldiers below. "So, you've had some sword training, as well as archery. Think you'll ever be down there?"

Seria laughed at Lena's attempt to take her mind from her sorrow. "Not even close." She wiped her damp cheeks. "Mason taught me a few defensive moves, but I'll never hold up in a fight. And my one arrow did not hit anywhere close to the targets. Nothing like these ladies."

The Stewardess Army was renowned for its archery prowess. To this day, Seria had not witnessed any of them miss.

Three knights stepped up to the line and aimed their arrows. They held their bows steady, then released them. From the cheers around them, their shots hit the mark. Seria shook her head. "Aren't they something? I sure wouldn't want to meet any of them in battle."

"Especially their leader." Lena pointed to the lone figure standing to the side. Her ebony black hair and dark skin glistened under the fading sunlight.

"I think I'm more afraid of her than any of them," Seria said. "She looks so fierce."

"Even back at the fort, I heard the Stewards talking about Aladee Planks. She's very respected."

"And scary." Seria had met the other woman shortly after arriving in Daymont, as the Stewardess was in charge of overseeing the castle staff. Ever since, Seria had done everything in her power to avoid her.

"Maybe someday you'll get to tell her about your training," Lena teased.

"I don't think so." Seria adjusted her skirts and hugged her knees to herself. "I would look plumb foolish. Here, I'm not even a healer anymore. I'm a washerwoman." To the captain, Seria would be nothing more than a silly girl. Maybe even an enemy.

They watched until dusk made it hard to distinguish between woman or target, then made their way back up the hill to the single side door that led to the servant's wing. A maid met them there.

"Did you hear the news?" She was almost bouncing with anticipation. "The king just collapsed!"

3

A sound of battle and great destruction is in the land.
-The Sacred Code

The Gateway, Old Realm

Prince Eric Passion bent over his stallion's neck and whispered, "Go, Oakley."

The dappled gray stallion lunged forward, picking up speed and streaking ahead of the man to his right. Eric could not stop his grin as he left his companion behind. At the base of the last hill before they could see the fort, he reined in and waited.

Captain Braylee Wright soon caught up on his big bay steed. "We both know Beast doesn't stand a chance against Oakley, so there's no point in boasting."

Eric laughed. "Who's boasting?" He patted the gray's sweaty neck. "Oakley was born to run, that's all."

"And Beast was born to eat," Braylee grumbled.

The two men urged their horses up the hill at a steady walk. A small company of Stewards and militiamen followed a few paces behind.

"It'll be good to be home," Eric said.

"We were gone but one night."

"But it could've been worse. Thank the Lambient all was well."

"I wish we could say the same for the rest of the Gateway."

The words rang true. The Dark Army had kept them busy over the summer months, ever since Eric's Stewards had shut down Jader's kidnapping operation in Joshun and returned the children to their homes. The Darkmen never approached the fort, but they hit Gateway towns up and down the mountain range, striking back against the growing resistance.

On top of the trouble on that side of the wall, rumors had flown for weeks about various towns and cities of Paladin. Reports of insurrection and rebellion against the king kept the Stewards on edge. It was hard to know what was true and what was not. The last thing they needed was another civil war in the Old Realm.

When Eric had received word about trouble in a nearby town, he led a small company to check it out, anticipating the worst, especially so close to the fort. But this time, fortunately, the rumors had proven unfounded, and all was peaceful, giving him no reason to believe the town had revolted against their king. He left a few Stewards there for a few days, just to be safe, while he and the rest of his men returned home.

But Eric had not sat by idle during the emperor's attempt to weaken the defense. Every chance he got, every potential bit of news he received, he sent men out in search of the Shadowpit, the source of Jader's dark power. If they had any hope of winning this war, that pit had to be destroyed.

And they *would* win this war.

The incline leveled out beneath the horse's hooves, and soon they could see the wall of the Gateway in the distance, stretched out between the gaps of the Slate Mountains. It would take more than an hour to reach it at their unhurried pace, but the sight of it—solid and strong—brought a sense of relief.

Even as Eric reveled in that peace, however, his stomach twisted. Jader would not let that wall stop him from gaining power on this side. Indeed, the rumors of rebellion were a result of the work of his Shadowmen, loosed into the Realm months ago. Shadowmen who knew how to manipulate the truth and turn good people away from it. Even his home city of Calla wasn't untouched by it, as people on the northern border began to protest.

"What was the last you heard about the riot at Baynet?" he asked.

Braylee shook his head. "Nothing new since this morning. A few dozen civilians ransacked a town loyal to the crown. At the time, Jervis said he had soldiers on the way."

Eric stroked Oakley's mane in an attempt to ease the tension from his body. "Hopefully, it will amount to very little."

"Jader knows what he's doing, creating chaos throughout both sides of the Gateway." Braylee's brows bunched. "Keeping the Stewards stretched thin."

"He's never been accused of being a fool. At least, not in ways of warfare." Eric's mind moved to the most recent member of the fort. "But at least he no longer has the power of a Reader in his grasp."

Braylee agreed, but he still looked troubled. "How much good it will do us is still dependent on whether or not he can learn to coexist with the Stewards."

Eric exhaled. "We knew it would be difficult."

"Unfortunately, we don't have a lot of time to spare."

Again, there was truth in the statement, which did nothing for the tightness in Eric's middle. "No one knows what to do with him."

"He's an enigma, to be sure." Braylee scratched the dark whiskers on his jawline. "By all evidence, he's a Steward, but his demeanor hearkens back to his Darkman days. It doesn't help that they remember all he's done."

"Especially the militia. Have you noticed?" Eric asked. "Most are honorable men, but they lack the faith in the Lambient to take the Beacon at face value."

"Which is ironic, considering they are more vulnerable to Mason's Gift."

"And the Stewards are distant, at best."

"Not all of them," Braylee said. "Most of the younger ones are fascinated by him."

"But others are downright angry about him being there."

"Like Lionel?"

"Aye." Eric shook his head, thinking of the young lieutenant. "He's changed in the last few weeks. Hardened."

Beast lowered his head to sneak a bite of grass, and Braylee tugged him back up. "He's had a lot to deal with, especially in light of Ollen's death."

Sadness raised its head. "That was a hard blow for everyone. Not only to lose a well-loved Steward officer but an entire squad, as well."

"Zakkias still struggles," Braylee said. "Being the only survivor is not easy for a man to live with."

For a while, the only sound that could be heard was the soft clomping of their mounts' hooves over the thick grass. Eric thought of the young scout, the lone survivor of the squad that had discovered the location of Stonehard, Jader's secret hideout where he hid and trained captive children. If not for Zakkias, by direct order of Ollen, Eric would never have found it.

But Mason had already begun the act of liberating them by the time the Stewards had arrived.

He took a breath and broke the silence. "I wish Mason would make more of an effort to connect with the men."

"He clearly prefers to be left alone. And don't forget that he's done much to earn their distance. He can't fully erase the wrongs he has done with the rights he is doing now." Braylee adjusted his position on the saddle. "That's the bad thing about choices. You can realize your mistake, even make it right. But it does not remove the consequences of those choices or erase the scars."

"I know," Eric sighed. "As much as I would like to fix it for him, Mason has to work through this on his own. He has to earn their respect."

"Much like you had to when you first took command."

Eric glanced down at the horse Braylee rode. The big bay had belonged to the former Steward commandant, who had also been Eric's mentor. "Maybe that's why I find it so easy to accept Mason being here now. I bore the brunt of his anger, and I knew why."

"You also witnessed him turning against his own army," Braylee added. "Which none of the rest of us saw. So, it makes it easier for you to see him as a changed man."

"I don't think he's fully forgiven himself," Eric mused. "He doesn't feel worthy. So, he's pushing everyone away, holding on to his usual distrust."

"He sure is uneasy around me."

"Can you blame him?" Eric deadpanned. "You're quite intimidating.

Especially in the mornings."

Braylee gave him a light glare.

The sky darkened in the west, a soft shade of violet that would soon spread across the sky like a ripple. The sun had lost its intensity and chose to bathe them in its soft, warm glow.

But Eric's skin tingled, and a chill went down his spine as a familiar sense of urgency filled him.

"What is it?" Braylee asked, always sensitive to Eric's moods.

Eric shook his head and waited a moment, determined not to act impulsively on the merits of the famed Passion intuition he and his father shared alone.

Lambient, guide me.

The feeling intensified, leading him on. He looked to Braylee, who met his gaze steadily. "Something's wrong."

"The fort?"

"Aye." Eric shortened Oakley's reins. "Let's ride."

Braylee called to the men behind them. "Pick up the pace!"

Soon, the peaceful evening was broken by the sound of galloping steeds as they rode to the fort. Eric, with no idea of what he was praying for, sent a plea up to the Lambient for whatever was before them.

4

What communion or unity does light have with darkness?
-The Sacred Code

Mason could feel the stares of the men as he followed Dudley and Lionel on horseback to the gates of the outer wall. Suspicion and doubt pierced his skin like needles. A Shadowman had escaped, so naturally, everyone would assume he was involved. Despite the fact that he was supposed to be a Steward now.

A Dark Steward. That's what some of them called him. He had heard the whispers.

The captain pulled his horse to a stop at the gates. "Lieutenant, take your men and scour the area between here and Cadence. I'll see if I can see anything up higher."

Mason spoke up. "If he's already out of the fort, he'll be making for the woods. And with the sun setting, he's got plenty of shadows to hide in. Not even your vision could see him."

"Are you suggesting we let him go?" Lionel scoffed.

"Nay." He looked to Dudley. "Let me search for him." Even as Mason said it, a part of him rebelled against the idea of volunteering to go after someone who had once been an ally. But he knew what he had to do.

"It's getting dark," Lionel said. "It's already too late."

"Not too dark yet. We still have some time, especially if we can catch him before he gets to the woods. But not if we keep standing around here." Mason did not bother telling him that his night vision was still as sharp as when he wore the Shadowstone. Somehow, he suspected that bit of news would not be well received. But if he could recapture the escapee, maybe that would deflect some of the blame people would cast his way.

But Dudley shook his head, shooting down Mason's slim hope. "Nay, I don't like it. It's almost as if it was planned. I don't want to send anyone into an ambush."

"Isn't that what the Beacons are supposed to be good for?" Mason asked.

"You're verging on insubordination, Grey," Lionel said.

Mason swiveled to respond, but Dudley cut him off. "Stand down, you two. Lionel, take some men to scour Cadence." He looked at Mason. "You go with them. Maybe you'll notice something they don't." Then he left, climbing the steps with long, hurried strides.

Lionel was anything but pleased to have Mason along, but he said nothing as he led the way through the opening gates.

The search in Cadence produced nothing, just as Mason had suspected. He scanned every shadow of every building, his ears peeled for the sound of silent footsteps that only he would catch.

At the very edge of town, he caught something on the ground and dismounted. Too slight for anyone else to notice was a shallow indentation in the dirt softened by the early autumn rainfall the night before. It did not look like a Steward boot, and it was too fresh to be one of the Cadence civilians who used to live here.

His breath caught, and he peered into the landscape beyond. A Shadowman could blend in with the terrain, seek out any crevice or rise that cast the slightest shadow. Pulling himself back in the saddle, he glanced around, saw that everyone was preoccupied, and left the dust of the street behind.

Tracking him down and returning him to the fort would go a long way in earning the people's trust. A Shadowman on the loose would do nothing for what little reputation he had here.

The tracks were almost nonexistent, but every few steps, he caught another one, leading to a cluster of bluffs. He urged his horse faster, his pulse racing with anticipation.

Help me. The request was a bit more desperate than he had intended, but he let it be what it was.

He looked up at the sky and grimaced. The sun was half hidden behind the Slates already. Ahead, the forest looked black in the gathering dusk. All around him, the shadows gathered against the bluffs.

Just a little more time. That's all he needed. The Shadowman seemed to be on a straight trek west out of Cadence and to the woods. If Mason could get to the hill ahead, he might be able to spot him in the distance, even if no one else could. His gelding could easily outrun him.

"Grey!" Lionel's enraged call did not slow him down. Mason pushed the roan into a gallop. Behind him, he heard horses approaching.

Almost there. He did not bother to look at the ground now. All he needed was a glimpse before darkness fell.

But the night was advancing with a swiftness that stifled any hope he dared to hold on to. He pulled the roan to a stop on a small rise, able to see for miles from his vantage point. There was nothing but fields and more woods in the distance, edged by the Slates on one side, all slipping into twilight. There was no sight of anyone running for the woods.

The Stewards caught up to him, but it didn't matter. The pursuit was over.

Lionel appeared beside him, red and blustering. "What were you thinking?"

"Trying to spot him before he got too far," Mason answered.

"And did you?" the knight asked, his frown evident. When Mason did not respond, he nodded. "Of course you didn't. Because it's too late, like I said." He motioned to the approaching dusk. "We'll never catch him in that."

The rest of the Stewards joined them, peering down into the valley from horseback. The growing shadows encircled them.

"I thought you said you could catch him," one of them said.

"I said I wanted to try," Mason returned.

One of the militiamen trailing them spoke up. "Maybe he didn't try hard enough on purpose."

Mason twisted in the saddle, ready to lash out, but Lionel reacted first. "Enough." But it wasn't clear who he was talking to.

Fisting his hands, Mason struggled to keep the anger from spilling out. It would do him no good to lose control.

Of course, they would suspect him. What little bit of acceptance—if not trust—he had gained shattered with the news that a Shadowman had broken free from his dungeon cell and fled the fort.

"Any idea where he went?" another Steward asked.

Mason ran a stiff hand through his hair. "Back to the closest camp he could get to, no doubt."

Lionel huffed. "And you don't know where that is."

"Seeing as I've been holed up in the fort for three months, nay, I don't. They don't stay in one place for long."

Lionel looked like he wanted to say more, but he shook his head and moved away. "We certainly won't find him now. Let's head back to the fort."

Mason looked up at the skies, feeling as isolated as the lone star that peered down on him. As he turned his horse to follow, something flashed in his peripheral vision. "Lionel," he called out in a low voice.

The Steward swiveled around. "*Lieutenant—*"

"Shut up and get your blasted Beacon out."

Lionel whipped the rod out, casting light in a circle all around them. The other men tensed, reaching for their weapons, searching the shadows that stretched towards them from the bluffs.

Mason gripped the hilt of his sword, a chill running down his spine, cursing himself for his stupidity. They were surrounded by soldiers that only he could see.

The path before Eric cleared as he circled the mess hall and cut through the center of the courtyard. The inside wall's gate was already open, and they continued through the lower bailey. He could feel the stares of soldiers and civilians alike as he rode past, but he kept his focus on

Dudley descending the steps ahead.

Eric tightened one rein to ease Oakley into a tight circle. "Is everything all right, Captain?"

The older man put his hands on his hips, his expression sober. "No surprise to see you arrive right at this moment."

"What's going on?" Eric asked as Oakley finally eased to a stop. Braylee and Beast halted beside him.

"We had a prison break a little while ago."

"A prison break?" Braylee repeated.

"Only one man," Dudley hurried to assure them. "But it was a Shadowman."

"How did he get out?"

"We're still looking into that. Some of our men are in Cadence. They should be back any moment."

Eric turned Oakley around. "Let's go."

Questions took shape and multiplied, but he would deal with them later. A growing uneasiness spread through his middle as they left the fort behind and entered the empty town of Cadence. Seeing no sign of his men, he rode on.

There, in the distance, he spotted them. Stewards and militiamen engaged in combat with mounted shadowy figures that did not take full shape under the setting sun.

"Circle them on both sides!" he called out.

The Stewards split into three groups. Braylee circled to the right with his men. Another band cut to the left, and the rest stayed with Eric.

As he neared, he pulled Lavrynth from the sheath and urged Oakley on. The big gray, still running strong, surged ahead.

Mason and Lionel were on horseback in the center of the fighting, their horses facing opposite directions as they tangled with two Shadowmen. Eric guided Oakley straight through the middle, his arrival upending the advances of the Shadowmen, who tried to turn and run for the darkness that edged them. But they were cut off by the Stewards who circled them.

Eric lifted a hand and, with his Gift, wrenched the weapons out of the Shadow Soldiers' hands.

And just like that, the fight was over, before Eric had to lift his sword. The Shadowmen quickly raised their hands and surrendered, cursing all the while. Eric noted the hate-filled glowers they sent Mason's way.

There were thirteen of them in all, including the prisoner who had escaped. Eric gave orders for them to be bound, then addressed Lionel. "What happened?"

"We almost got ourselves blasted killed, that's what happened," Lionel burst out. He jabbed his sword in Mason's direction. "He went running like a crazy man for the woods, and by the time we caught up to him, they had us surrounded."

Mason's expression was set like stone, but he did not deny the accusation. Both men were too angry to get a decent report, so Eric changed the subject. "Was anyone hurt?"

A couple of men reported only minor injuries, to his relief. The Shadowmen's hands were soon bound and tied to a mounted knight's horse.

"Let's get these men to the dungeons," Eric ordered.

Lionel still looked ready to start swinging at Mason, but he gave a sharp nod and followed his men.

Mason did not look at Eric as he rode past, his shoulders set in dejected lines.

Eric sighed as he picked up Oakley's reins and guided him back to Cadence.

5

The announcement of the king's illness rumbled through the servant wing of the castle throughout the evening.

"How serious is it?" Seria asked when she got a chance to talk to the girl who had shared the news.

She shrugged. "I happened to be working in the grand hall when he nearly passed out. Land sakes, you should've seen the scurry of bodies to keep him upright! I suppose that's what comes from being the king, though."

Seria quit listening to the girl ramble on, her mind skittering to Eric in her concern. Though relieved she had never had to cross paths with the king since he had brought her here to serve, she did not wish harm on him, especially for Eric's sake.

The maid went off to spread her news to other willing ears. Seria suppressed her irritation. Sickness should never make up fodder for gossip.

The door to the staff common room opened, and to Seria's surprise, Aladee Planks stepped in, still wearing the green training suit. Her presence seemed to fill the room as her piercing hazel eyes probed the group of women.

All conversation faded away as the tall woman stepped further in. What would the head of the Stewardesses be doing in the servants' wing?

"Seria Gayle?" Aladee called.

Seria stifled a gasp and stepped away from the back door. "I'm here." Apprehension wrapped around her as Aladee's focus fell on her. What had she done this time? Had Naomi complained about the confrontation in the kitchen? Surely that incident was below the interest of the Stewardess captain.

"Come with me, please." Without waiting to see if her order would be followed, Aladee turned and exited. Stunned, Seria had to force her feet to move and run after her.

They walked without speaking for a few steps before Aladee slowed her brisk pace so that Seria could catch up. "We are in need of your service, Miss Seria."

"M-my service?" What laundry need was so dire that she would be summoned by a captain?

"Aye." A shadow of concern darkened Aladee's eyes. "You may have heard already that King Aden has fallen ill."

"Oh, um, aye, I did hear something."

"Calla's physician has been called away, so there is no one to see to the king's condition. Would you care to look at him?"

Seria almost tripped over her own feet. "You want me to treat the king?"

"I'm asking you to treat a man who needs a healer."

The words convicted her. "Begging your pardon. Of course, I will. I was taken off guard, that's all."

"I understand." Aladee hurried on until Seria almost trotted to keep up with her long-legged strides. "And I also understand you are quite efficient. All I ask is that you treat him as you would any other patient."

"Of course." Seria had no intention of giving him any more or less care than she would to anyone. But the idea of being in the presence of the king made her insides quake. She swallowed her qualms to ask, "What seems to be ailing him?"

"For one, he works too hard," Aladee said in frustration. "He pushes himself to the point of exhaustion. After laying out plans for tomorrow, he tried to stand, then went very pale and sweaty and fell over. My husband had to catch him before he hit the floor. He's complaining of chest pains."

"Where is he now?"

"Still in the hall. We were unsure of moving him. It happened less than an hour ago. He insisted he just needed to sit for a bit, but he's not improving. They fetched me from the fields, and then I came for you."

Seria ran all the information in her head, contemplating some possibilities and dismissing others. "Most likely, he'll need to be put to bed."

"We'll see it done as soon as you take a look at him."

It was surreal, carrying on a conversation with this intimidating lady about the king of Paladin. She, a launderer from Cadence, had been called to treat the highest level of royalty in the kingdom.

Lambient, please give me a steady hand and a clear mind for this task that has been placed before me.

At the end of a long hall, they approached a set of tall, wooden doors with a guard on either side. The men opened the doors without a word being spoken, and Aladee led Seria into an office just to the side of the throne room.

The office was larger than her cabin in Cadence and much grander. But Seria looked past the red carpets and tall bookshelves until she found the king, who sat in a large, cushioned chair by the fireplace. Thankful he was still upright, Seria noted that his face was washed out and sweat beaded his lined brow.

A tall, muscular black man stood beside him, his hand on the king's stooped shoulder. The man exchanged a quick look with Aladee before addressing Seria.

"Miss Seria, have you met King Aden?" Despite the concern that weighed his introduction down, there was a trace of good humor there as well.

"We've spoken on a couple of occasions," Seria answered, standing before the king. She did not disclose when and where.

The silver-haired man's breathing was heavy, but not labored. His soft blue eyes—so much like Eric's—lifted to study Seria. After a moment, they twinkled dimly. "I guess I'm about to see what everyone else says about those healing hands of yours," he said softly, his words halted by his breathing.

"I'm sorry you're not feeling well." Seria cocked her head, trying to forget who he was. Right now, he was a suffering gentleman who needed a healer.

He frowned and tried to straighten. His hand went briefly to his chest, then back to his lap. "I hate for people to fuss over me. I'm just an old man who can't keep up with my younger captains." He gave the couple beside Seria a wink.

"Can you tell me what's bothering you?"

"Can't catch my...breath. And my chest." He winced. "It feels tight."

Alarms rang through Seria's head as she stretched a hesitant hand out to Aden's forehead. It was warm and clammy, but not feverishly so. His eyes looked dark and pained, and he held himself stiffly, as if trying to ease his breathing while maintaining his proud posture.

"I think the first thing we need to do is get you into bed, Your Majesty," she said. "Then, with your permission, I'll see if I can ease some of that discomfort."

He drew in a deep breath. "I don't suppose you're going to let me walk there myself, are you?"

"There's a flight of stairs to his chambers," Aladee supplied.

"I'm sorry, but that's not a good idea."

Aden gave a resigned smile, then addressed the man. "Well, then, Captain Jervis. I suppose you better put me to bed."

Jervis lifted the sick man from his chair as easily as if he was a child. With a gentleness that touched Seria's heart, he bore him through the halls. Doors opened before them without a word, as Aladee went ahead to clear the way.

The last portal opened, and they moved into a sprawling suite of polished wood and red and blue furnishings. A huge four-poster bed dominated the floor, and several doors led off from the room.

Seria hurried to the bed and turned back the thick coverings. Jervis laid his burden down carefully and stepped back, giving Seria room to work.

"We should change his garments into something more comfortable," Seria said.

Another woman appeared out of nowhere, already bearing a linen gown over her arm. "I will help all I can, miss," she said, her anxious gaze on the sick man.

"This is Daslyn, the king's personal maid," Aladee said.

"I would greatly appreciate the help." Seria looked to the king, trying not to give him any cause of embarrassment. "Will you grant us permission?" She held her breath, hoping he would be cooperative.

"I will," he said. "A man of my age has no call to be proud anymore anyway."

Aladee waved her husband off. "We don't need to be here for this." Then she spoke to Seria. "I'll be outside if you need anything."

Seria thanked her and turned her mind to the business at hand.

A while later, Seria spoke to Aladee and Jervis in low tones before the hearth. Aden rested against the pillows, not quite as pale as before.

"How is he?" Aladee asked.

"A bit more comfortable now. I managed to get him to eat some soup with all-flower seed."

Aladee blinked at her. "All-flower?"

"It's a type of wildflower," Seria explained. "Something my mother showed me. The seed has properties that ease pain and regulate the heartbeat. And I gave him some chamomile tea to help him rest."

"What's wrong with him?" Jervis asked, looking at the king from where they huddled in a corner.

Seria could not be anything but honest. "I believe it's his heart. It's very weak, which makes everything, even breathing, much more difficult."

Aladee's dark face pinched. "He's been very anxious since the riots started in Baynet. Even before they broke out yesterday, he seemed troubled."

Seria pressed her palm to her forehead. "Of course. His intuition. No wonder he's uptight."

"It's not something he can put off," Jervis said, his voice deep.

"I'm sure," Seria agreed. "And I suspect he's very much like his son in that he deeply feels any potential trouble."

"That is correct."

"So, what does that mean?" Jervis asked. "Will he get better?"

"It's hard to say. This could be nothing but a passing spell, and he could be back on his feet in no time. But I fear the pressure he is under is causing his body a lot of physical stress, especially considering his age. Whereas Er—the prince is young and strong..."

"King Aden has more than a few years on him." Jervis sighed. "It's no more than what we all knew would happen eventually."

Seria watched the couple study the king, their expressions mirror images of worry and sadness. "He's not at death's door yet," she assured. "I believe with good rest and care, he can continue to run his castle."

That seemed to put them a little more at ease, and Aladee gave her a grateful look. "Daslyn will look after him tonight, and we'll see he gets what he needs. We won't keep you any longer."

"The physician will return soon, I'm sure," Jervis added.

Seria took that to mean she was dismissed and stepped to Aden's bedside one more time. His easy, steady breathing assured her again that he was in no immediate danger, so she exited the room, trying not to feel let down.

It was silly to feel so. She had little desire to be in the presence of the king for long, and not because he was the highest-ranking monarch in the land. He made her uneasy. He saw her as a criminal, someone who had fraternized with the enemy—the very one who had tried to kill his son. She was here out of punishment. Nothing more.

But it had felt good to use her healing skills again, to touch someone in a way that made them feel better. She had missed it these past few months. How she hoped she would be able to do it again someday.

She let out a sigh and straightened her back. Now was not the time to wish for what was not hers. She was here to make amends for her wrongs against the Steward Army. There was no cause or right to expect anything more until that was done.

6

My adversaries have prepared a net to entangle my steps; they have dug a pit for me to fall in; my soul is low.
-The Sacred Code

Mason pushed through the doors of the Council Hall and headed for the barn, working to tamp down the heat that wrapped around him. He should have known Lionel would report his actions to the Council. After all, he had gone against the hotheaded young officer's orders.

It did not matter that Mason had openly defied Emperor Graulik Jader or that he had abandoned the Dark Army's mission. It made no difference that a Beacon had lit up in his hand to reveal his loyalties. In their eyes, he would always be a Darkman, a Shadowman. The enemy.

He had spent a good chunk of his morning explaining his actions to Gaynor and the other white-haired old men who served as the justices over the Gateway. Then he'd had to endure Lionel's report on all his misconduct from the way he kept his bed to disobeying orders in Cadence. The only thing he missed was Mason's fraternizing with the cadets, but Mason didn't bother to remind him.

By the time Lionel was finished, Mason had a slim hold on his temper. The Councilmen scolded him for not following Lionel's direct orders. Then he was expected to take Lionel's Beacon and prove, once again, that he was a Steward. The rod had glowed brightly, bathing Mason in warmth and bringing peace. The feelings it elicited never failed to amaze him, and in that moment, he was filled with hope, reassured once again that the Lambient was with him.

If only it could last. If only it could purge him of his past.

But, as always, the heat sank into his skin, shooting up his arm and into his chest. He had held it as long as he could, then thrust it back at Lionel.

Satisfied, the councilmen dismissed him, and the meeting was over.

To his relief, Lionel was nowhere to be found, so Mason headed for the barn, where Barry, the blacksmith, would be waiting for him to begin his shift.

Throughout the summer, Mason had been relegated to kitchen staff, liveryman, errand boy, maintenance, and a host of other mundane jobs in a variety of venues from the barns to the chapel and even the Great Hall. The assignment as liveryman was the one he most preferred, even if the demotion grated on him. He, a prominent scout and newly appointed sergeant of the Dark Army, had been reduced to a stableboy. But as he would rather spend his time with the animals than most of the people of the fort, that suited him fine. And it kept him out of reach of nosy spectators for the most part. Most days, he worked in the barn until dark, then slipped away to the training fields after everyone else was gone.

Tonight, he appreciated the manual labor even more, as it gave him a way to work out his frustrations. He threw his back into shoveling each pile of soiled hay into the cart, piling it high before dumping it outside, where the gardeners would use it next spring. With each trek back and forth, he worked to bring his temper down, but every time he thought of the way those people looked at him, his blood heated all over again.

On the last trip back to the barn, the door was blocked by one of the Reservists. Hiram, the man Mason controlled into showing him around the fort months ago so Shadowmen could infiltrate it later, had an especially sharp dislike for Mason.

"Move it, Hiram, I'm busy," Mason said as he neared, ready to plow right through him if necessary.

"You gonna make me?"

"Do you realize what a stupid question that is?"

Hiram grunted but stepped out of the way.

The man stood several inches taller than Mason and did not hide his attempt to look down at him. His thick lips were frozen in a sneer under his wide nose, and bushy hair stuck out all over his head. "You go ahead and use your *Gift* on me. I'll have you back in your cell so fast, it'll be like you were never out."

Mason did not bother to answer as he positioned the cart up against the wall beside the door. He picked up the shovel where he had left it in the straw and turned to find Hiram standing inches from him. His irritation flared at the man's nerve.

"You wanting something?"

Hiram narrowed his eyes. "Everyone knows you're the one who let that Shadowman loose."

Mason wanted to retort with a "Tell me something I don't already know," but he kept quiet, gripping the handle of the shovel with white knuckles and drilling his glare into the other man. It was on the tip of his tongue to give an order, control him into leaving him alone or walking into a tree. Instead, he helped himself to Hiram's thoughts.

A more messed up jumble of arrogance, resentment, and immaturity he had never seen. Mason snorted. "You're going to have to rethink your future, man, if you think you have a chance for the Steward army."

Hiram's ugly mug reddened. "You think you're so much better than me that I can't outdo you?"

"I don't think it works that way." Mason started to turn away when Hiram grabbed his elbow. Acting quickly, Mason jerked his arm out and jabbed a well-aimed thrust into the man's side. "Touch me again, Hiram," he challenged.

Stumbling back a step, Hiram's look became murderous. "I'll have you thrown out of here, you filthy Shadowman," he spat. "I'll prove you let him out."

"And then promptly caught him again with his friends. Sure, you make sense of that."

"Everyone knows the prince got you out of that mess. If it wasn't for him, you would've had that whole band of Stewards slaughtered by your shadow friends."

Mason took a quick step forward, ready to pound his fist into the man's thick skull, when Eric made a sudden appearance. "Is there a problem, gentlemen?"

Mason turned away as Hiram stammered. "Nay, sir, Prince Eric."

"Glad to hear that."

Hiram gave a short nod and hurried out of the barn, his bravado dissipating in the presence of the prince.

"I don't know how a man like that ended up a soldier," Mason muttered.

Eric spun on him. "How on earth do you expect to build goodwill with these men if you continue acting like an outsider?"

The reproach fanned his emotions even hotter. "I *am* an outsider."

"And you will continue to be if you don't try to make your place here."

"They will never see me as anything but a Shadowman."

"And what have you done to make them think anything else?"

The question infuriated Mason, and he turned his back on the prince, throwing the shovel he still gripped to the ground. "I've only given up everything, turned on the man I believed in, and told you everything I know about their future plans." He stalked down the aisle, tempted to drive his fist into a wall. "Nearly got myself killed in the process. But none of that's good enough for them."

"And ever since then, you've been stewing and grumping about."

"Because no one wants me here!" Mason spat.

Eric crossed his arms. "It's going to take time, Mason."

"And in the meantime, Lionel is breathing down my neck, waiting for me to trip up."

"Don't let him get under your skin; he's just trying to prove himself. But remember, he's your supervising officer. Making him your enemy won't do you any favors."

Anger loosened Mason's tongue. "Lionel may be my supervisor, but the lousy assignments all come straight from you."

Eric's gaze did not waver. "If I show any weakness or preferential treatment toward you, I will lose the confidence of my men. And we cannot afford that on the brink of their toughest assignment ever."

Resenting how petty the comparison made him sound, Mason gritted his teeth.

"Not long ago, you were on the opposite side, working against them. You can't expect them to shrug everything off."

"All they see is what I used to be."

"Come on, Mason." Eric held his hands up. "Tell me to my face that you don't still burn with resentment against me for your brother's death."

The challenge disarmed him, too close to the truth. He had thought he had beaten the bitterness, but it still crept up on him at times. The anger drained from in him a rush that left him exhausted. He slumped against the wall and rubbed his forehead.

Silence stretched between them until Eric let out an exhale. "I can't fix it for you, Mason. I can't make them accept you, and I can't make you want to be here."

"Hiram isn't the only one who believes I let the Shadowman escape."

"I know. The militiamen don't hold the same faith in the Lambient. The Stewards know what that Beacon means, but they're watching you now to see how real it is."

"They still don't believe it." Mason stared down at the ground. "Every week, I have to prove it by showing them the Beacon."

"Mason, all cadets have to show the Beacon regularly."

That caught his attention. "What?"

"It's part of their regular training. During this early stage, they are sincere, but also young and impressionable. They can choose to reject the light just like anyone else."

Startled by the revelation, Mason looked up.

"It's true," Eric said. "Surrendering to the Lambient is a choice we make. He sees when we truly mean it, and He gives us His favor, shining forth from the Beacons. But He also gave us free choice, and we can choose to walk away."

"Has any Steward done that?"

"Unfortunately, aye. Not many, but anyone can be pulled away from the truth when they allow themselves to be surrounded by too much darkness. And it's most likely to happen in the early years, before they've had a chance to grow their faith."

Which meant Mason could shine a Beacon for the rest of his life, and some people would still expect him to fall.

"I think some people are scared." Eric rubbed his jaw, his expression contemplative. "They know what the Beacon means, may even believe you are a true Steward."

Mason had to bite his tongue at that.

"But they also know men are fallible. If you were to change your mind, it would leave us vulnerable, especially with you right here in our midst."

"Is it that easy to cast it off?"

"Nay. It takes one small step and one careless choice at a time."

Is there any hope? Mason could not help but wonder. He had no intention of ever going back to the lies and darkness that had defined his life for so long. But would he ever truly be accepted as a Steward? Would he ever feel like one?

"Anyway." Eric straightened. "You were wrong about one thing you said."

"Only one?"

"Ah, the snark is coming back. Must be feeling more like yourself."

He rolled his eyes. "You were saying?"

"You said no one wants you here, but that's not entirely true. The Lambient wants you here. And I believe you do have a place here, even if no one else does, including you."

Not sure how to take the assurance, Mason pushed off from the wall and picked up the shovel, placing it back where it belonged.

"I'm sorry I was not at the meeting. I received word that my father has fallen ill."

Mason waved it off. "You're not my caretaker." His shift ended, he headed for the door. Before exiting, he asked, "How is he?"

"Weak, but holding his own. Thank you for asking."

Talk of the sick man turned his thoughts to Seria as he left the barn and headed for the training fields, where he could finally be alone. Her touch, her laugh. The way she pushed him to be a better man.

His heart bled at the Seria-sized hole in his life. Sometimes he tried to hold on to a fragile hope that this separation would not be forever. But Seria was far away now and, he hoped, establishing a life for herself. And he was glad. She didn't need him, didn't need to be shackled with the burden of his past. She was better off without him.

Ignadon, New Realm

Emperor Graulik Jader turned from the window as Commander Bruin Pralus entered the throne room.

"Word from the fort has come," Bruin informed after a quick bow. "Jeck was recaptured, along with the rest of the party."

Jader made his way to the throne so that he could better see Bruin with his good eye. "Perfect. And what of our wayward son?"

Bruin's face darkened, but his tone remained neutral. "It appears he's getting in good with the prince."

"After all Eric Passion has done to him." Jader tsked with his tongue.

"He keeps to himself most of the time," Bruin continued. "He doesn't seem to be very well accepted by the rest of the Stewards."

"Of course not." Jader brushed his shoulder-length hair back. "They are a proud group of men. They will not allow anyone beneath their grand ranks to associate with them." He rubbed the scar running over his eye, his mind going back to his days working alongside the Steward Army. The isolation. The arrogance. "It is a wonder Mason has lasted this long."

"How much longer do you think it will take?"

Jader ran his fingers over the whiskers on his chin. "He is a stubborn man once he has his mind set on something. And for now, he believes he is actually standing with the Stewards. But the Stewards will not accept him. And soon, he will come running back to us."

7

The desire of the upright is for good, but the hopes of the wicked are for evil.
-The Sacred Code

Seria sat across the table from Lena for a quick midday meal of bread and cheese, a cup of cider at her fingertips.

Lena looked over Seria's shoulder. "What is Captain Aladee doing here?"

Seria turned too fast and knocked the mug to the floor, the impact sending its contents all over her dress and up the wall.

"Good grief, girl, can't you keep from making a mess?" Naomi exclaimed, stopping on her way to one of the hearths, hands on her hips. "We don't got time to be cleaning up after you."

"I'm sure the spill was not intentional, Naomi." Aladee's smooth voice sounded from behind, and both Seria and Naomi spun in surprise.

"Oh, C-Captain, I didn't expect you." Naomi pasted on a sugary-sweet smile. "Can I help you with anything?"

Seria dropped to her knees with a rag she snatched from a nearby table, hoping to hide the redness staining her cheeks. Lena circled the table to wipe the wall.

"Nay, thank you. I actually came to see Seria. Here, let me help." Aladee took another rag and knelt beside Seria. At Seria's protest, she only winked. "I dropped my tea all over Jervis's lap this morning."

The confession wrung a laugh before Seria could stop it. The three women made quick work of cleaning the wall and floor. Naomi lifted her chin and walked away.

"Oh dear, your dress is all wet," Aladee noted.

Seria waved a dismissive hand. "I'll change as soon as I get a chance. How is the king this morning?"

"He seems to be feeling a bit more comfortable, though still quite weak."

"That's to be expected."

"He's the reason I am here. I wonder, could I convince you to come to my quarters for the midday meal? I assume you've not had a chance to eat yet?" Her dark eyes flittered to Seria's untouched food.

"Oh." Surprise robbed Seria of a rational answer. She wiped her hands on her wet apron, glancing at Lena. "I told Lena I'd eat with her."

Before Lena could speak, Aladee said, "Both of you are welcome. I'd love to have a chance to get to know you."

The idea of having a conversation with this tall, beautiful woman scared Seria to death. What would she have to talk about with a Stewardess? The thought of rambling mindlessly had her ready to bolt. "I, um—"

"We'd be delighted," Lena said.

"Wonderful," Aladee said as Seria cast Lena a wide-eyed look of panic. "I'll give you a few minutes to change if you want—"

"Nay, it's only a little—" Seria swallowed as she realized her rudeness. "I apologize. I didn't mean to interrupt."

Aladee only chuckled, and a dimple appeared in one cheek. "You will find I'm not easily offended. Come then. I have stew already cooking."

As Seria followed silently, her mind spinning, one random question stuck out. The captain of the Stewardesses cooked stew?

It did not take long for Seria to realize that her fears were unfounded. Aladee Planks was a lovely lady with an open air about her that put people at ease. Her husband, Jervis, also joined them. He was much like his wife in the way he spoke to the visitors, asking them questions that drew them out and eased them into conversation. Indeed, Seria's new concern became that she would dominate the conversation with her tendency to talk too much. But she found them just as interesting to listen to.

Jervis had served as Aden's captain for about five years. He was the third captain in rank, with Dudley and Braylee holding the first and second positions. Seria learned that there were two other captains, in addition to the Stewardess Captain.

Aladee had held her position only a few months, but Jervis could not speak highly enough of her skill. The Stewardesses had blossomed under her command until there was not a finer shot in all the land, and their prowess with the sword was not to be underestimated. They defended the castle grounds with as much commitment and ability as any Steward in the Old Realm.

It was fascinating, and Seria soaked it all in, though it caused her heart to ache, remembering how Ollen tried to teach her the Steward ways.

"How long have you been a healer, Seria?" Aladee asked at one point.

"My mother taught me," she answered, pushing her empty bowl away.

The stew itself had been a delightful mix of meat, vegetables, and spices—nothing like the bland stuff she had cooked day after day in her cabin in Cadence. Seria relished every morsel.

Lena spoke up. "Her mother was Shasta Gayle's wife."

"Ah, I've heard of them," Jervis said. "I understand they were killed in the New Realm?"

The question was asked with such kindness that Seria's throat tightened. "That's right. I didn't know until much later why they were killed. I wasn't even aware my father was a Steward."

"There are still a few of those Steward spies out there, from what I understand," Jervis said.

"Aye." Seria had met one in the Gateway, when she had stowed herself away on the Stewards' mission. Not her best move.

"And your mother taught you?" Aladee redirected the conversation.

"She did." Memories of standing at her mother's elbow while she patiently explained how to mix the herbs flooded her. "I never had any formal training. Nor did I work in a professional capacity until I began to work under Luron Furvor."

"That's what I thought. Both your mother and Luron are known to be highly skilled. You couldn't have worked under better teachers."

"I doubt many of the best healers received formal schooling in the healing arts," Jervis added. "It takes just as much common sense and hard work as it does book learning to know how to treat people."

"Your skills are actually why I wanted to talk to you, Seria," Aladee said, clasping her hands together on the table. "I'll get right to the point."

Concern chilled Seria's mood, but Aladee did not look upset, just serious.

"The king is feeling better, and his maid is doing a fine job of seeing to his needs. But I—we"—Aladee cast a look at her husband—"would feel better if he had more regular care at this point."

Jervis's deep voice rumbled. "Our physician may be tied up a little longer, what with the uprisings that have started in the north in Baynet. It will be at least another week before he can get away."

"What is causing the uprisings?" Lena asked.

Aladee sighed. "People protesting the war. Declaring they want to be free of the Sacred Code."

"The king has already sent out companies of both Stewards and Reservists to keep things under control. But with trouble building in the Gateway, we can't spread ourselves too thin."

This talk always made Seria uncomfortable. She knew Jader would eventually bring his army to the gates of the stronghold, but the idea of conflict already growing in the Old Realm was troubling. She remembered snippets of talk she had heard after the first Shadowmen infiltration into the fort. The one Mason had helped bring about. "Is this because of the Shadowmen who made it to this side?"

"We believe so, for the most part," Jervis said. "But there's always a remnant who believe they would be better off out from under the protective law of the Code or the rule of the Lambient. They are taking advantage of what's happening to stir up their own agenda."

"We keep getting off track." Aladee straightened in her seat with a smile. "I bring all this up because I would like for you to be the king's caretaker for the time being."

Seria's mouth came open. "Caretaker?" Her heart skipped a beat at having to be in the king's presence every day.

"That's right. I think he needs more care, and you are the perfect one."

She could not deny that regular care would benefit the sick man, but Seria still struggled with a reply.

"We don't want you to think this is an order," Jervis said. "You can certainly turn it down, but I do ask that you consider it, for the sake of King Aden."

Seria looked to Lena, who seemed to be trying to send her a silent reassurance. "I, um...I must admit, being around the king makes me nervous. I would hate to fumble his care because of my nerves."

"You did wonderful with him yesterday," Aladee said.

"Aye, but that was a bit of an emergency. Besides, I'm not sure how much King Aden trusts me." How could he when she had admitted to meeting with a Jader loyalist? "He has reason to resent my presence here."

Aladee's eyes twinkled. "King Aden has already approved the idea."

That stopped her. "He has?"

"He was quite impressed with your thoughtfulness yesterday. And I think he would like to get to know you."

"Surely he knows all about me he needs to know." He was the one who sentenced her here, knew about her dealings with a Shadowman. What more could he possibly want to learn about her? Unless he thought this was a good way to keep her close so he could keep an eye on her.

Aladee rested her hand on Seria's arm. "Don't feel that everyone here is watching you, waiting for you to betray us."

Seria blinked at her. Did Aladee know why Seria had been brought here?

Of course, the Stewardess Captain in charge of the security of the staff and servants would know. Seria bit her lip, humiliation burning her eyes.

"All I'm concerned with is that you have a very skillful hand in the healing ways, and that is what King Aden needs. I would not allow you near him if I had any thought at all that you were anything but a kind, honest woman, who the king placed under my care for a reason."

The assurance eased her mind, but the prospect of facing King Aden every day still left her feeling very small. "I wonder if I can think about it? I won't make you wait long, I promise."

Aladee patted Seria's arm. "Of course. I realize a request like this would come as a shock."

Shock did not fully describe what held her back. Seria could still see the piercing blue eyes Aden had pinned on her when she confessed to being Mason's ally, could still feel his disapproval. What further shame would placing herself in his presence every day submit her to?

8

If a Reader submits to the authority of Shreil, he surrenders control of his Gift to the force of darkness.
-The Lost Record of Gifts

The investigation into the Shadowman's break from the dungeon did little to relieve Braylee's concern. He discussed it at length with Dudley and interviewed the guards on duty. While there may have been a trace of carelessness, there was no sign of negligence.

He even attempted to talk to the Shadowman, a short, skinny man with cold eyes and pale skin who called himself Jeck, but of course, he said nothing. One of the few Shadowmen caught the night Mason had smuggled them through the fort, he and his two companions had been locked up in the furthest cells, under heavy guard and constant lights. It had been enough up until now, so what had changed?

He shared his findings with Eric, whose face drew long at the news. "That leaves us right where we started. We won't get anything more out of Jeck, I'm afraid." Then his head came up. "Mason."

"What about him?"

"He could read Jeck's thoughts, tell us how he got out."

Braylee nodded. "It's a good idea."

"Why didn't we think of it sooner?"

"We didn't need to. Jeck was safely locked away, along with the other two, and Mason gave us everything he could tell us."

Eric's gaze went distant. "He could read the other Shadowmen we imprisoned as well. Find out how they knew to be in that location."

"I'll go fetch him." He raised a hand before Eric could object. "He has to get used to me, Eric."

"I know." Eric rubbed the back of his neck. "He's very distrustful right now."

"I'm sure a lot of that stems from the fact that I took a shot at him at Stonehard."

Eric gave him a grim smile. "That doesn't help."

"I'll bring him in."

"I think he's working the mess hall today."

Braylee left the prince at the dungeon and strode with purposeful steps to the hall, trying not to worry about it all.

Mason's conversion had rocked what little belief he held about Shadowmen, but since then, his faith in the Lambient had only strengthened. He should have known that it could take nothing but the power of the Lambient to turn a man like Mason—an embittered, vengeful Shadowman—around to the truth.

But Mason's presence still disrupted the peace Eric had worked so hard to build among the Stewards. Many of them looked at Mason with resentment, others with confusion. The younger ones seemed fascinated by him, but even that did very little to draw Mason into unity with the army.

The militiamen were a whole other issue. Many of them were much like the Stewards—good men with noble motives. But every army had their scoundrels, and the Royal Army of Reserves was not spared its share. A few jeered and openly mocked Mason's turn to the Lambient. While the Steward Knights struggled to accept the Shadowman's surrender in light of his sinful past, some of the militiamen openly rejected it.

Braylee pushed through the double doors of the hall, thankful it was between meals, so there would be fewer spectators. The first person he met upon entering the long room with rows of wooden tables was the manager herself.

"How goes it, Nola?" he greeted the robust woman.

She put her hands on her plump hips. "Captain, please tell me Miss Seria will be back soon. I've little decent help since she left."

A clatter punctuated her words, and she threw her hands up. "Marcus, if you break another dish, I declare I will kick your carcass out of here!"

A thin young man with wide eyes ducked his head, hurrying to pick up the scattered dishes.

Nola shook her head. "So, that's how goes it, Captain."

"I'm sorry, Nola. I don't know when Seria will be back." He did not add that he wasn't certain if she would ever be back. There was no predicting what the future held.

"Ah, that's my luck," she sighed.

"Is Mason Grey working? The prince needs to see him."

"Of course, my one good worker today." She pointed to the door that led to the kitchen. "He's scrubbing the floors."

Another crash sounded in a corner, and Nola shook her fists.

Thanking her before she lost her temper, Braylee left her to deal with Marcus's ineptitude. He found Mason in a far corner, on his hands and knees, scrubbing the floor with much more force than necessary. Braylee could not help but sympathize. No soldier ever expects to be demoted to floor duty.

"I'm not cleaning Marcus's mess again," Mason said without looking up at Braylee's approach.

Braylee cleared his throat.

Mason's head came up. The tense line in his jaw tightened even more. "Come to see if I'm getting it clean?"

At the insolence, Braylee cocked a brow, staring him down.

Mason let out a huff and stood. "Did you need something?" he asked, his tone more subdued.

It was not an apology, but Braylee let it slide. "Prince Eric needs you at the dungeon."

"You all decided to throw me back in after all?" Before Braylee could respond, Mason put his hands up. "All right, all right. I'll shut up." He pulled off the dirty apron he wore, tossed the scrub brushes in the bucket of dirty water, and placed everything in a corner, out of the way. Then he stretched a hand out so that Braylee could precede him.

Braylee led the way without a word. The tension rolling off the man behind him was almost palpable, making for an awkward walk back to the dungeon, where Braylee was happy to step aside and let Eric take over.

"Sorry to call you on such short notice," Eric said when he saw them.

"It's not as if I was doing anything important."

Braylee shifted his jaw but caught Eric's eye and stayed silent. For now. Frustrated or not, Mason would have to learn respect.

"It occurred to me that we could get some answers if you are able to read the prisoners."

"Not with their Shadowstones."

"We've removed those," Eric said. "I need to know how Jeck escaped so we can make sure it doesn't happen again, especially now that we've taken in more."

Mason rubbed his jaw and eyed the door that opened up to the darkened hallway leading to the cells below.

It struck Braylee that Mason dreaded the idea but didn't want to admit it. It had to be strange, to read the minds of the men he had once worked with in order to aid the man he had betrayed them for. Eric waited, letting Mason come to grips with the request.

"Now?" Mason asked, though not with his usual impatience.

"I believe it would be best to learn what we can right away."

"Why didn't you ask sooner?"

"It honestly didn't come to mind before now."

Mason massaged a wrist with one hand. "All right, let's get it done."

Pulling his light rod out, Eric led the way to the dungeons. After a brief hesitation, Mason followed, and Braylee brought up the rear with his own rod. The Beacons lit the narrow space easily, casting the shadows to unseen corners. They passed a few empty cells before coming to a sharp turn to the right. A Steward guard nodded as they walked by. The end of the hall was flooded with lights, every torch burning along the walls. The cells each held a prisoner who, upon seeing the man in the middle, approached the barred door with dark frowns.

To his credit, Mason did not look right or left, but his back was rigid.

Eric stopped at the last cell and stepped aside, holding the Beacon up so Mason could see.

Jeck draped his arms through the bars. "Why, if it isn't the traitor himself."

Eric did not acknowledge the statement but looked to Mason, tilting his head in Jeck's direction.

Drawing in a breath, Mason directed his Gift at Jeck. A moment passed, then two. Jeck stared back with a sardonic grin, not bothering to look away. Mason frowned, unease spreading on his face. Something wasn't right. Jeck had to know about Mason's Gift, yet had no qualms about giving Mason full access. With a sharp intake of breath, Mason broke away and stepped back, rubbing a spot on his chest.

"What is it, Mason?" Eric asked.

Braylee glanced back at Jeck, wondering if he had a Gift they had been unaware of.

Mason did not answer, his gaze flittering all around the hall, as if looking for a place to run.

"Go ahead and tell them." Jeck leered. "Tell them you can't read my mind."

Braylee and Eric both looked to Mason. After a moment, he answered. "I can't."

"Hmm…" Jeck leaned between two bars. "Can't? Or won't?"

Eric gave him a severe look. "Your lies won't work here."

Braylee hung back, observing Mason's discomfort grow by the moment. "Maybe it's a Gift," he suggested. "Maybe he can block a Reader."

Jeck snapped his fingers. "Maybe that's it!"

Eric turned his back on the prisoner and urged Mason away. "Then try another one," he said. "One of the new ones."

They withdrew to a second door, where another man threw visual daggers at Mason. "I should've killed you as soon as we had you surrounded," he snarled.

Mason rubbed his mouth, glancing at Eric before meeting the Shadowman's eyes. He shook his head. "Nothing," he murmured. "It doesn't make sense."

Jeck's taunt sounded from down the hall. "Maybe he's not telling you what he's reading!"

"Shut up," Mason growled, still rubbing his chest. It looked to Braylee like he was reaching for something out of habit that wasn't there.

Like a Shadowstone, perhaps.

"Or maybe it's because you can't take away a Shadowman's power by taking his stone off," Jeck continued to mock. "Just because I ain't wearing it, doesn't mean I can't still use it."

Mason shook his head. "Nay," he whispered. His breathing accelerated. He winced and rubbed his temples. "I can't...I can't read them."

Braylee looked to Eric and motioned to the exit.

"Let's go, Mason," Eric said. "We're done here."

"You don't stop being a Shadowman just because you take the stone, you idiots!" Jeck screamed after them.

The other Shadowmen began to yell and curse. Mason bumped past Eric and rushed up the hall.

"Mason, wait!" Eric called.

"Maybe you should let him cool off," Braylee said, putting his Beacon back on his belt.

"What happened?" Eric asked as they left the dungeon, blinking at the lovely, reassuring sunlight.

"They were messing with his head."

"Do you think..."

"Nay, I don't believe he was lying. He truly could not read their minds. And I think that startled him more than anything."

Eric groaned. "I thought this would be helpful. What if I've made it worse?"

Braylee thought about Jeck's last words. "Unfortunately, I do believe what Jeck said about the Shadowstone. Apparently taking it off does not remove its powers."

Awareness dawned on the prince, and he looked down in the direction where Mason ran. "That's what he's afraid of."

"I think so." Braylee ran his fingers over the handle of his Beacon. "Which was exactly what Jeck was trying to do."

"It doesn't matter." Eric's jaw was set in that familiar stubborn tilt. "Mason accepted the Lambient. That does away with Shreil's hold. No matter what they may try to tell him."

"I believe it, too," Braylee agreed. "But I'm afraid it may take longer for Mason to truly believe it himself."

9

It is required of every Steward to be found faithful and pure.
-The Sacred Code

Mason shoved through the double doors of the barn. Panting hard, he cast a quick look around, relieved to see it empty of its human workers. The donkey stall at the end was unoccupied too.

Trying to calm his speeding heart, Mason yanked the back door open and stepped out into the dry lot, where the horses and donkeys were released during the day. A few horses nibbled on some hay in a small corral. Some of the donkeys were gone, but one gray donkey stood at the far side, watching a group of ducks waddling around the barnyard. Gripping the top wooden plank of the pen, Mason bent over, squeezing his eyes shut against the raging headache ripping through his temples.

Not being able to see into the men's minds had rocked him. They no longer wore their Shadowstones; there should have been no wall between his Gift and their thoughts.

Jeck's words poked at him. Was he right? Did the power of the Shadowstone continue, even when not worn? Even if someone had tossed it away?

It would explain Mason's night vision. But he had revoked the power dwelling in that dark stone. Stark fear seeped into his skin, chilling his blood. What did this mean? Would he never be free of the hold of the Shadowstone?

He covered his face with a trembling hand. *Help me,* he silently begged. *I don't want it anymore.*

His fingers tingled and itched for the stone that had hung over his chest. "Nay," he ground out. "I refuse." Lambient had accepted him. The Beacon glowed for him. That was all that mattered.

But no matter how many times he told himself that, he seemed to fall deeper into the well of darkness that had opened up in his mind.

Please. I'll do anything. Just get rid of it.

A soft nose nudged his fist gripping the rail. Mason jumped and huffed out a laugh. Sanjo stood in front of him, hay sticking out of both sides of his wrinkled muzzle, his ears standing straight up and aimed at Mason. "You look ridiculous, you know."

Sanjo chewed noisily, then blew out a breath of straw-scented air into Mason's face.

"Now, don't be doing that, or I'll run you off." Even as he made the threat, Mason wound his fingers into Sanjo's mane. His breathing eased, and the cloud that had threatened him dissipated. The headache still pounded but not as hard now.

"Mason?"

He stiffened and scowled over his shoulder at the prince. "You know how stupid it is to sneak up behind me?"

Unabashed, Eric moved closer. "Are you all right?"

Relaxing his stance, Mason crossed his arms and rested his elbows on the fence. "Just great."

Sanjo kept his position in front of Mason, cocking one hoof and looking ready for a nap.

Moving to his side, Eric looked out at the animals, saying nothing.

It bugged Mason. "I didn't lie to you."

"I don't think you did."

Not sure if he believed him, Mason still frowned. "I'm not sure the captain agrees." His hands fisted as he remembered how he'd fallen apart. It was bad enough to show his weakness in front of Eric, but that Captain Braylee had to witness it gnawed at him. The man had already tried to kill him at Stonehard. How many times did he wish he had not missed?

"Captain Braylee believes what you say."

Again, doubt took root, but Mason did not argue. Just swallowed the bitterness that coated the inside of his mouth.

Eric looked down at the donkey. "Seria's, I take it?"

Realizing he was stroking Sanjo's chin, causing the animal's eyes to close in bliss, Mason answered with a grunt, folding his hands together.

"She'd be glad to know you're looking after him." Eric patted Sanjo's neck.

The last thing Mason wanted to talk about was Seria, but before he could say so or leave, Eric spoke again. "What are your thoughts about the escape?"

"What?"

"I've investigated and interviewed everyone I can."

"So, now you're checking to make sure my story matches?"

"Nay." His tone was stern. "I need your help. You have insight none of the rest of us have. The cell was locked. The guard was in place. How could that Shadowman have escaped?"

He was serious. While everyone else was pointing the finger at him, Eric was asking for his help to figure out who was behind it. He straightened, going over all the angles. His mind went to Seria's friend, Lena, and how she had helped him slip into the fort.

"Are you sure he can't pass through walls?"

"Like Lena?" He frowned, pondering the idea. "I guess it's not impossible, but I don't think so. The lock showed signs of being worked on from the outside. If he could go through walls, he would not have needed to unlock it."

"Then he had inside help."

Eric grimaced. "You mean someone within the fort helped him escape?"

"That's right."

"But who?" Eric began to pace. "Who would want to release a Shadowman?"

"Everyone in this fort thinks I would."

"Not everyone," Eric said absently.

"The ones who don't are going to be vastly outnumbered."

"Well, when their opinion outranks the prince, then they can complain about it."

Mason gave him a quick look. Seemed the prince had some snark to him.

Eric stopped by the corner of the barn and crossed his arms. "Your suspicion is the same one that I came to, unfortunately. Which means we have someone living within these walls who may be loyal to Jader."

All humor fled at what that meant. "Any idea who?"

"I don't believe it's any of the Stewards. I hate to cast doubt on the militiamen, but they're an obvious possibility."

"Civilians?"

"I suppose, though many of them are refugees from the New Realm." Eric sighed. "This means we are going to have to start studying everyone who gives us reason to suspect their loyalty to the Code."

Mason leaned back against the fence. He didn't envy Eric's job, but he also realized that until the mole was found, his life wasn't going to get any easier. What little advancement he had made here could be ruined until people believed he had nothing to do with it.

After a moment, Eric joined him at the fence again. "I apologize if I made things worse for you in the dungeon. That wasn't my intention."

Uncomfortable at the turn in conversation, Mason crossed his arms. "Sorry I wasn't more help," he said, his voice gruff. Jeck's words ran through his mind again. "Maybe Jeck was right."

"About?"

Mason shifted. "Maybe one doesn't stop being a Shadowman just for tossing the stone."

Eric's eyes narrowed. "So, the Beacon lighting up is a coincidence?"

"Nay, but—"

"Mason, you told me months ago that you made a commitment. Are you going back on that pledge now?"

The question irritated him. "Nay, but it doesn't change the truth staring us in the face."

"And what truth is that?"

Mason spun on his heel and walked away, rubbing his forehead. Dare he tell Eric what he knew? What if it got him thrown back in the prison cell with Jeck and the other Shadowmen?

"Talk to me, Mason."

Indecision almost held his tongue, but there was no point in hiding it anymore. "I still have my Shadowman abilities."

Eric tilted his head. "Like what?"

"From what I can tell, all of them. Night vision, muffled sound, blending in the shadows. I couldn't use my Gifts on a Shadowman, but I always assumed it was because of the stone. Now…" He gave a helpless shrug.

Eric looked thoughtful as he mulled over the news. Mason held his breath and waited for the verdict. A man who still held the skills given to him by the Shadowstone still had to be a Shadowman, right?

"That's interesting," Eric said after a long silence. "It seems those abilities are woven more into your being than we realized. Even after rejecting the stone, they stay with you." His thumb tapped his belt as he thought on it. "I can't explain that, but it doesn't change what you are now. You may not be an official member of the army yet, but the Beacon makes it clear that you're a Steward."

"I don't think everyone else is going to be quite as accepting if they find out."

"Maybe not," Eric conceded. "I guess for the time being, it may do well to keep that between us."

Mason agreed. He didn't need anything else for the Stewards to hold over his head anyway.

Eric bid him good night then, and Mason mumbled an acknowledgment to his parting words. Something about keeping his head up and they would talk later. A small part of him appreciated Eric's attempt, even if it irritated him. He wasn't sure why Eric continued to waste his time on him.

He's doing it because he feels guilty. The dark thought was quickly followed by another. *He's using you for your Gifts. Just like Jader did.*

Hard footsteps approached the barn door, and he had to suppress a groan when a stone-faced Lionel appeared. "Grey, what are you doing here? Nola said you didn't finish your shift."

"Did she tell you why?" Mason asked, his defenses springing up.

"She shouldn't have to. You're supposed to finish your job."

"I'll be sure to tell that to Captain Braylee next time he comes for me."

Lionel scoffed. "Why would he pull you from your assigned task?"

Not about to detail what had happened, Mason bristled. "I don't know, *Lieutenant.* Why don't you go ask the prince? He's the one who called for me."

Lionel pulled back slightly. "The prince?"

Mason pressed harder. "Maybe if you'd taken the time to check with Nola, instead of itching to nail me again, you would've saved yourself some trouble."

"You better get off your high horse, Grey. It's a long way to fall."

"You should know."

A muscle jumped in Lionel's jaw. "You may think you've gotten in on the prince's good side, but you will remember that *I'm* still your supervising officer when you speak to me."

Mason held his place, tempted to unload on him. But rationale held him back. His position was on shaky ground as it is, and he would not let Lionel be the one to keep him from taking his place in the army. "Aye, *sir.*"

Lionel glared back at him a bit longer before he stormed back through the barn.

Defeat washed over Mason, making him tired. Sanjo lipped at his shirt, and he tugged it free. The swaybacked, old donkey reminded him of the only person who had ever felt like home to him. But she was far from him now, and if things continued to go as badly as they were, he feared it would be a long time before he felt at home again.

He was losing control, and he knew it. The problem was, there wasn't much in him that cared anymore. Lionel jerked his sword belt off his hips and threw it on his cot. He dropped down on the side of the mattress, his elbows digging into his knees.

"Rough day, Lieutenant?" someone asked.

"Leave me be."

The man did just that, exiting the Steward quarters without a word.

Lionel dropped his head forward and rubbed his neck. The anger was always a part of him now, at the edge of his tongue and in the sharpness of his actions. It scared him a bit. He had always been impulsive, but for the most part, his quick judgment had been borne out of good intentions. But lately, everything he did was seasoned with a good dose of rage. He was a loose wheel, spinning out of control, without a steady hand to bring it back to normal. His outbursts had drawn attention.

He couldn't fight the hot anger raging in him at the way things had turned out. Or this thick resentment against Mason for his role in the Dark Army, and even against Ollen for being the hero until the end. Or the bone-crushing guilt for his failures.

A groan escaped him, as a pain squeezed his chest. How he missed Ollen, the one friend not afraid to put him in his place when he needed it. Lionel had teased and tormented Ollen for his straitlaced way of living. Serious and good. That was Ollen. Lionel was the splash of adventure and humor Ollen needed. Or at least, that was what Lionel had told his friend many times in their early years as Steward cadets. Ollen was too stern. Too focused.

When in truth, Ollen had always been a step or two ahead of Lionel, all the way to his death.

Lionel, on the other hand, couldn't do anything right. The last several months were littered with failure. Getting injured in Thaylor, which laid him up when the rest of the Stewards searched for Jader's secret location. Not getting to Joshun in time to save Ollen. Letting the Shadowmen slip through the gates that night they infiltrated the fort.

Even getting the assignment of supervising the Shadowman did not bring the break he had hoped. Mason Grey was doing everything he could to make Lionel look like an idiot.

You don't need any help with that. Lionel could almost hear Ollen's voice form the statement in his head. So much so that a smile pulled at his tight lips. If only Ollen was here to tell him that in person.

He straightened, stretching his back to relieve the tension. His gaze fell on his Beacon, still hooked to his discarded belt. He took it in his hand, rolling it between his fingers. It lit upon his touch, but even the light did not seem to comfort him as it used to. And that scared him more than anything.

10

Commit all your works to the Lambient, and He will direct your thoughts.
-The Sacred Code

Seria thought long and hard about the job Aladee had offered her. Oh, she knew it wasn't a real job. This was only because there was no one else more suited to care for a sick man. But it still meant that she would be in the king's presence constantly. And the very thought of it made her want to hide.

"You've always wanted to be a healer," Lena reminded her when Seria said as much to her as they readied for bed.

"Aye, but I meant practicing from my own home or working alongside a physician like Luron. Being a private caretaker to the king is not exactly what I had in mind."

"Aren't you the least bit curious?" Lena asked. "I mean, this is Prince Eric's father."

"Lena, this is the man who banished us from the fort," Seria burst out. "How am I supposed to work with him when he obviously hates us, let alone what he must feel about Mason?"

The other woman cocked her head. "I don't get the feeling that he hates us, or I doubt we would have been given positions within his castle. And he's very kind when he visits the kitchens."

"You've talked to him?"

Lena chuckled. "It seems Prince Eric gets his sweet tooth from his father."

Seria thought for a moment. "Fine, maybe he doesn't hate us. But I get the impression he doesn't care much for me."

"Does that change anything?"

"What do you mean?"

"You've never let anyone's feelings about you keep you from helping them. Just think of Mason in his early days."

She chuckled at the bittersweet memories. "Oh, goodness knows he was a most trying patient." Indeed, he had been difficult at the beginning, but soon, his hard exterior began to slip, and she had caught glimpses of the softer side of him.

"You miss him, don't you?"

Seria blinked back tears. "I worry about him. He looked so alone the day we left."

"I'm sure he's missing you, but he's not alone. He's under the Lambient's care now. Besides that, he has a strong ally in the prince."

"If Mason accepts him. I can't imagine it's easy to suddenly be in the same fort as the man he hated for so long. But you're right. Eric will do all he can to help Mason." She said it to reassure herself as much as to agree with Lena.

"I believe so." Lena's answer was thoughtful.

Seria sighed. "But none of this is helping me make my decision."

Stirring from her contemplation, Lena pulled the pins from her neatly wound hair. "You and I both know you've already made your decision."

With another groan, Seria slipped under the covers. "You're right again. Even with the unease, I don't think I could ever pass up a chance to work with the King of Paladin."

With a soft laugh, Lena blew out the candle by her bed. Soft moonlight slanted in through the single, small window between their beds. Seria had been shocked to learn that not only would she share a room with Lena when they had first arrived in Calla, but that they had it to themselves. It was small and sparse, but she loved the privacy it afforded them from the curious eyes and wagging tongues of the royal staff.

"I still wish you had not gotten yourself banished with me," she said aloud into the darkness. "But I am glad you're here with me."

There was a slight pause. "I wouldn't have it any other way, Seria."

Aladee was more than pleased when Seria told her she would accept the position. The Stewardess immediately made arrangements with Charlin for Seria to leave her current position so that she would be available for the king.

As soon as the decision was made, a slew of doubts hit Seria. Was she ready to have the responsibility of his care rest solely on her shoulders?

Lambient, please be with me, she prayed as she headed to his room her first morning. Pausing at his door, where two guards watched her approach, she took a deep breath. Then they opened the door for her, and she stepped into the large suite.

Aladee was there, easing Seria's mind. The awkwardness of the first day would be bad enough without someone else present.

"Ah, here is our healer," Aladee greeted from her position at the foot of Aden's large bed. "I knew she would be early."

Seria made herself speak to the man in the bed who watched her with tired eyes. "How are you feeling this morning, Your Majesty?" she asked, with a small curtsy.

He let out a shallow sigh. "Not too bad, I suppose, but I've had better days."

"I understand you're not sleeping well."

He winced and tried to straighten. Seria was quick to adjust his pillow behind him so that he could sit up. "Sleep has been scarce of late," he admitted.

If he was not sleeping well, then it would make his body too tired to fight off illness. "Can I ask what is keeping you awake?" she asked, to make sure it was not a physical ailment that had been going on longer than they realized.

"These are hard times for a ruler to rest," he said, his eyes on the ceiling above him. "Many things to worry about."

"Are you experiencing any pain since your illness?"

"Occasional twinges in my chest but nothing like before."

Seria clasped her hands in front of her, going over all he had shared, as well as what he had not. His slow movements, the shadows under his eyes, the pallor of his skin—she took notice of all of it. "The first thing we need to do is ensure you get better rest," she said, trying not to react when her statement drew his gaze to hers. "You cannot recover if your body is tired."

He gave a slow nod. "I must admit, rest sounds good." Indeed, he did look ready to drop off at any moment.

"Feel free to get some sleep, if it comes, and I'll go see to getting you some soup and tea."

Seria frowned as she made her way down the stairs to the kitchen. The king really was weak, and she had not even done a thorough evaluation of his condition yet. How was a ruler supposed to lead a kingdom if he was sick in bed, especially in a time of war?

That's why you're here. She had dreamed of being a healer for most of her life, just for times like these. To bring someone back to health. To do something important. How much more important could a king be?

Eric would worry about his father if he knew how sick he was. And he could not afford to have his mind pulled from what was happening in the Gateway.

Never would she be given a more important task. "Help me, Lambient," she whispered. She had little doubt in her ability to treat the older man's condition, only in her ability to work under the king's watchful gaze.

What would happen if Paladin lost its king? What impact would that have on the prince? Eric would make a fine king in Aden's place when the time came, but to have to take that role in the middle of a war would be difficult indeed.

She shut down such thoughts. Her worries were getting out of hand. King Aden was ill but not at death's door. Seria had seen these kinds of conditions before. He could recover and be back on his feet, almost as good as new. Though he would never be a young man again, he could yet have many years in him. There was no reason to assume the worst.

A short while later, Seria carried a tray with some chamomile tea to help him rest, as well as some poultry soup with wild lettuce and all-flower seed to help with the pain. A small bouquet of lavender brightened the tray and let off a soothing aroma.

Aden was awake when she arrived, though Aladee reported that he had dozed for a short time. "My Stewardess Captain is going to spoil me with her constant attention," he said.

"I'm only here to be of assistance to Miss Seria," she said. "I do need to see to some things shortly, but I wanted to make sure you and she got along."

Seria busied herself with his tray when she felt his scrutiny. "I've heard too many things about our healer to assume anything other than that we shall get on quite well."

After helping him to sit up again, Seria set the tray on his lap. "Of course we shall. So long as you are a good patient." She stifled a gasp at the boldness of her own words, but his chuckle eased her alarm.

"I shall do my very best." She forced a smile and moved away to give him space to eat. Aladee circled the bed and met her by the table in the middle of the room.

"You'll do fine, Miss Seria."

"So long as I don't forget I'm serving the king." She put a hand on her hot cheek. "My mouth is going to get me kicked out before the end of my first day, I'm sure of it."

Aladee chuckled. "You'll find King Aden is much more easygoing than you believe. He has a strong sense of humor, and he's very kind to his staff."

Unless his staff has had dealings with the enemy. Then he sentences them to servitude and expulsion. Seria could not stop the thought and promptly confessed her resentment to the Lambient.

"I really must go," Aladee said, looking back to where the king ate his stew. "I know I leave him in good hands. If you need anything, Daslyn will be nearby, as well as the guards by the door. Don't hesitate to call for help."

The idea of being alone with the king sent her pulse to racing, but Seria raised her chin. "I will. Thank you."

Aladee spoke to the king with a slight bow, then left. Seria stood by the table for a moment, looking around the spacious suite and avoiding eye contact with its occupant. When he called her name, she nearly jumped out of her skin.

Get it together, Seria, she scolded herself as she turned to her patient.

"I didn't mean to startle you," he said. "I don't think I can eat any more."

Crossing the room, she took the bowl, noting it was not even half gone. She handed him the mug of tea. "This will help you rest."

"It seems all I do is try to sleep," he said before taking a cautious sip.

"Which is exactly what you need."

Much to Seria's relief, King Aden downed most of the tea and settled in to rest. He was soon sound asleep, soft snores drifting from the bed. She sank into the chair by the bed, already tired. And morning had not even passed yet.

How was she going to make it through the coming days?

11

I am the One who created light and darkness; I make peace and find justice;
I am the Lambient who sees all these things.
-The Sacred Code

"Defend the helpless, uphold what is right, preserve what is good, protect the innocent, regard the pure, honor what is just, and maintain what is true." The instructor's lecture drifted to the back bench of the Council Hall where Mason sat with all the young students for his weekly lecture.

"What does that mean to you?" the teacher asked.

There was a rumble of words as various students answered, but Mason couldn't make any of it out.

"All very good ideas," the man said with a chuckle. "But let's concentrate on one particular part. 'Honor what is just.' What do you think of when you hear that?"

Dakim answered, his confidence ringing. "To fight against injustice."

"Do you think? What if justice can't be found?" the teacher asked.

There was no answer. Mason caught himself leaning forward to hear the point of the question. Was the instructor implying that justice would not always happen?

"I'm not saying we should not fight injustice," the man continued. "That's what our Steward Army is doing each and every day. But things do happen that aren't fair, and while we may be tempted to fight back and demand justice, sometimes the Lambient asks us to wait. Let Him take care of the judgment. Our task is to continue to live in a way that honors Him."

The lesson ended for the day, and Mason slipped out the door before anyone could catch him. He grabbed the pail of soapy water he had left outside the door and took his position on the large veranda. Sweeping the rag up and down the textured post, he ignored the young men who passed him by. Adolescent cadets had more freedom and respect than he had, despite his experience as a soldier.

It wasn't fair.

"But things do happen that aren't fair...sometimes the Lambient asks us to wait."

The words dropped into his spirit, and his stomach tightened.

Are you asking me to quit grumbling about how unfair everyone's being? He directed the disgruntled question upward, but received only silence in answer.

"Hiya, Mason!"

Dakim's greeting pulled him back. A few other teens called out their goodbyes as they left, and even though he wasn't supposed to talk to them, he waved. He finished his cleaning and stepped off the platform, lugging the bucket of dirty water in one hand and the rags in the other. Dumping the water alongside the packed dirt road, he tossed the rags in and headed for the barn for his last chore for the day.

But someone stood in his path, his eyes hooded and his stance uncertain.

"Crue." Mason stopped short, afraid to scare the boy off. But now that he was so close, Mason wasn't sure what to say.

Crue eyed the cleaning supplies. "I never thought I'd see you doing the cleaning."

Mason shrugged. "A little cleaning never hurt anyone."

The boy huffed. "Unless you leave a stain. They get you in real trouble."

Mason stared at him, remembering the fit Dreeya had thrown when Crue left a small oil spot on her saddle. It was her actions that led to Crue working for Mason. Was this an attempt to be funny, or was Crue's bitterness revealing itself?

But Crue winced. "I'm sorry. I suppose that was distasteful."

"Nay, not at all. I was trying to decide if it was safe to laugh or not."

Mason set everything down and dried his hands on his pants. "I was afraid you were upset with me."

"I was, at first." Crue's face shadowed. "I thought I had done something wrong or that you had grown tired of me."

"That wasn't it at all."

"I see that now." Again, his gaze dropped to Mason's tools. "I wasn't sure what to think when you showed up here. For a while, I thought Emperor Jader had sent you in here with a plan."

"I no longer serve Jader."

"It took me a while to realize that. But when you kept working all the jobs—jobs that servants do—that's when I knew you had changed. Because no soldier of Jader's army would lower himself that much."

It was true the Darkmen carried around a sense of arrogance and conceit. Mason had worn his status like a badge. "I learned some hard truths," he said. "About Jader. About the prince. And about myself. It wasn't easy to turn around, but I decided I wanted to do right by the Lambient."

"Even if it meant you had to be a servant boy instead of a Steward?"

"If that's what He asks of me." It was meant to sound humble, but instead, he sounded like a grumpy schoolboy.

"That sounds more like the old Mason."

Mason grimaced. "I'm still trying."

Crue studied him. "You are different, though. I always knew there was something better in you than in the rest. You treated me like I mattered."

"Because you do." A sudden desire to see Crue accept the same path Mason had chosen filled him, but he held himself back. He couldn't overwhelm the boy with his own conversion.

Crue did not acknowledge his statement. "But you also had this anger always simmering inside of you. It scared me sometimes." He squinted at Mason. "It's gone now."

It was surprising to hear when Mason walked around feeling like he was going to explode. He was still angry, but his anger was different now. It wasn't a rage that fed his actions.

Crue swallowed and lowered his head. "I, um, I'm sorry I avoided you for so long."

"There's no need to apologize."

"For a while, I stayed away because I was upset you had controlled me. Then I was afraid you were going to do something in the fort. Then I didn't know what to think."

"So, you watched me from afar. Until you felt safe to approach."

"Aye, I guess so."

Mason crossed his arms. He knew someone could catch him at any moment talking to a civilian, and a young one at that, but he could not turn away from Crue now. "And do you? Feel safe with me?"

Crue did not answer immediately. "I do. But..."

"What is it?"

"Who was he?"

Mason frowned. "Who was who?"

"Who was the man you had me take into Shales?"

Mason's stomach squeezed. In his mind, he could see the young Steward bleeding out before him. Could hear his last words that would forever be planted in his memory. "He was a Steward." He looked down at the ground, remembering the bodies of the other young soldiers. "They all were."

Crue's expression was sober. "I heard you got the kids at Stonehard out."

Mason shook his head. "I helped put them there in the first place. Righting that wrong is nothing to be proud of." He frowned as his memories took him back. "Ollen and his troop died in their search for Joshun. By then, I already knew I was wrong. But it was him...the way he died that finally got through to me." He took a deep breath. "That was why I had you take him back to his Stewards, along with the rest. I'm sorry I took advantage of you like that."

The teen studied him for a long time, but he didn't appear resentful. "I'm not angry about it," he said. "I figured he had to be important for you to go through the trouble of caring for a Steward's body. I know you aren't—weren't fond of Stewards."

"I'm still not." Mason forced a grin to lighten the mood. "But I suppose they're better than most of the Darkmen I knew."

Crue looked around them at the buildings of the fort. "I've been

watching them since I got here. They're very serious about their work."
There was no denying his admiration.

"They are." Mason had to agree.

"Are you a Steward now?"

He barely stifled a snort. "Not officially yet."

"But you will be? Because of the Beacon?"

The very Beacon that burned him upon contact, but Mason did not
share that. "Aye, I suppose."

"Can anyone become a Steward?"

The longing in his question was more than obvious. "I suppose if
a no-good Shadowman like me can become a Steward, anyone with a
willing heart can aim for that goal."

Crue chewed his lip. "I know you sent me here to be safe, but it won't
be long before Jader brings his army to attack, and when that happens, I
need to defend myself."

Mason tried to sort out Crue's rapid words. "So, what are you saying?"

"Can you train me?" Crue's eyes widened with hope. "To fight?"

"To fight?"

"Aye. I don't expect I could ever be a real soldier. But I do want to
fight Jader's army. He's the reason my parents died and why I ended up
a servant boy. I've known for a long time that he was bad, but I had no
place else to go. Here, I have a chance to stand against him."

"Slow down, boy." Mason sighed. "I'm not sure that's a good idea."

Crue's shoulders fell. "But what will I do if they break through the
fort?"

Mason wanted to assure him that wouldn't happen, that he was safe in
the Gateway Stronghold. But reality was too strong to spout off empty
promises. Jader was cunning. He had a way of getting what he wanted.

Crue looked so crestfallen that Mason wrestled the tug inside. This kid
had lost everything to Jader. Wasn't it right that he got a chance? "Why
do you want to fight Jader?"

Crue blinked. "To stop him."

"To stop him or to pay him back for what he did to you?" Mason
lowered his voice. "Because believe me, if that is your motive, it will eat
you up inside."

To his credit, Crue did not answer right away. He looked away, thoughtful. "I do want to see him pay," he confessed. "But I don't plan to go after him myself. I can step aside and let those more worthy take care of him. I don't know that I'll ever be good enough to join the Steward Army, but maybe I can become a Reservist."

"You have as much of a chance to become a Steward as anyone, Crue, so long as your motives are pure."

"Right now, I just want a chance to defend myself, and maybe others, if the fight comes to me."

Mason exhaled, gratified by Crue's honesty. "I wish I would've had your mindset when I was younger." He nodded once. "All right, I'll work with you. But"—he held a hand up before Crue could react—"you have to keep this between the two of us."

"I promise."

"Good." Mason stared at the young boy, thankful he had not cut ties with this young friend. He let a cocky grin slip, anticipation at training again thrumming within him. Only this time, he would be training someone for the right side. It was risky, agreeing to work with a young civilian, but something in him needed to do this despite the risk. "Rest up then, boy. Because you're about to work harder than you've had to work yet."

12

For the Lambient is both a sun and shield to His people; He withholds no good thing from those who walk uprightly.
-The Sacred Code

There were still no strong leads as to how the Shadowman had escaped, and Eric was growing frustrated. No one knew anything. No one had seen or heard anything. But Shadowmen did not escape without help. So, who had assisted Jeck in leaving the cell?

Eric stewed over it that morning as he broke the fast in the mess hall, going over any and all possibilities until he thought he would go mad. When he found himself considering the possibility that Nola had a hand in it, he gave up and headed for the door, colliding with Marcus and knocking the young man's empty tray across the room.

Marcus took a halting step back. "I-I'm sorry, Your Majesty."

Eric sighed and retrieved the tray. "It's not your fault. I wasn't looking where I was going."

"Marcus!" Nola bellowed from the kitchen door. "What are you breaking now?"

Waving a hand to calm the woman, Eric said, "I bumped into him, Nola. All is well."

She gave him a suspicious look. "All right. Marcus, it's your turn to do the dishes. Let's see if you can get it done without incident."

Marcus ducked his head and escaped to the kitchen.

"Don't be too hard on him, Nola. Not everyone can be as efficient as Seria."

She put her hand to her forehead. "Mercies, I know. Makes me wish I'd told her more how much I appreciated her. The kitchen just doesn't seem as cheerful with her gone."

"I know what you mean. Maybe someday you'll get a chance to tell her. Speaking of workers, Nola, how is your newest employee working out?"

"Very well." Nola put her hands on her hips. "I wondered in the beginning if he was going to give me attitude, but Mason's been very cooperative."

"I'm glad to hear that." Eric gave her a bow and took his leave. As soon as he stepped outside, an uncomfortable feeling settled over him, and he paused, looking across the narrow street to the Great Hall and up and down the streets. His perusal fell on two men talking together across the street. Lionel and Hiram. Something about their serious exchange made him uneasy.

Lionel looked up and saw him watching. He spoke to Hiram once more, then crossed the street to meet Eric. "Prince Eric."

Eric gave him a nod. "Lieutenant."

"I need this week's assignment list for the Darkman."

Eric drew in a deep breath. Lionel used to be his most optimistic Steward, eager and cheerful about whatever he had to do. But no more. The young officer's jaw was tight, his posture stiff. And he still refused to accept Mason as a Steward.

"As long as you keep referring to him that way, Lionel, you will never see him as an ally."

Lionel's eyes narrowed. "I'm afraid I still don't see him in that light."

Eric crossed his arms. "Has he acted outside of the expectations of the soldiers of this fort?"

There was a pause as Lionel flattened his lips. "He acts like he's above the rules."

"Has he broken any rules?"

Lionel looked away. "He doesn't follow orders, shows little respect for the officers."

Eric dipped his chin. Mason would never show respect for Lionel, because Lionel did not have any for Mason.

"He still doesn't fit in here."

"It might help if you tried to work with him. Stop seeing him as the enemy."

Lionel's gaze snapped to Eric. "He *was* the enemy, Sire."

"But he isn't anymore. And you know as well as I do what that Beacon represents."

"Yet he does not carry one."

Eric let out a breath. It was true Mason did not carry his own Beacon, but he had not gone through the ceremony yet. The king felt that Mason needed to earn it like all the other new cadets, but Mason had to get through his sentence terms first.

"Your Highness, your father appointed me to be his supervisor. You made your expectations clear that we were to allow him to be among us. But you did not ask me to be his friend." Lionel's voice hitched at the last word, and he looked away, his expression hard.

Eric studied him, his heart heavy. Lionel's grief over Ollen was still sharp and cutting. He would not allow anyone to take his place. Especially a man who had fought against them for years.

"You're right, Lionel," he said. "I didn't. Maybe that would be too much to ask of you." He paused. "But I think you should also remember that it was because of Mason that Ollen's body was brought back."

A muscle in Lionel's jaw twitched. "Do you have his assignment list, Your Highness?"

Eric let it go. "Nay, with the breakout, I did not have a chance to write him up a new one. Keep him on the same schedule as last week."

"Aye, sir." Lionel bowed stiffly and moved away.

Something squeezed in Eric's middle. Lionel had shown so much promise a few months ago, so determined and bold. But ever since they had returned from Joshun—ever since Ollen was killed discovering the site—he had not been the same.

Surely Mason's conversion would not cause them to lose a Steward.

The tension mounting between his shoulder blades, Eric headed for the back gates. He passed by the bakery and caught sight of Ayna Cartwright dumping a bowl of dirty water by the door. At her wave, he felt compelled to stop.

"How are you, Your Highness?" she asked, her cheeks ruddy and plump around her smile. For a while, she had acted rather stiff toward him after his father had sent her daughter away. But over time, she had warmed back up to him. Maybe she had realized that Eric had nothing to do with Lena's exile.

"I'm well," he replied. "How is Cal?"

"Oh, as grouchy as ever, but hale and hearty," she said with a laugh.

Eric could well imagine the old man grumping. He had made it clear months ago that he did not intend to live in the stronghold, even with the danger growing in the Gateway. Funny enough, it was Mason who intervened and got the man within the safety of the fort walls.

"Can I get you anything?" she asked.

"I don't suppose you have any honey tarts, do you?" he asked.

"I'm sorry, I do not. With Lena gone, I've not had time to make any." A frown wrinkled her forehead.

His heart pinched at the sound of Lena's name. "I understand. I don't really need anything anyway. I'm heading to the training fields."

She bid him good day, and he left her to her work. Lena's face, serene and lovely, haunted his steps.

He missed her as much as he did Seria. Maybe more. He had not talked to her much but had grown to appreciate her calm presence. Unfortunately, as soon as he realized that, she admitted to helping Seria sneak out to see Mason, and his father had her sent away as well.

It was fair. Both young women had confessed their wrongdoing. But how he wished Lena could have stayed. And not just because of the honey tarts.

The training field was mostly empty, much to his relief. He did not plan to stay long and had not even changed to his green training suit. Worries and stress cluttered his thinking. He needed some time to focus.

He selected a worn bow and a well-stocked quiver from the weapons shed and took his place at the mark. The target was two hundred yards away, but he faced it with familiarity. He raised the bow and let the arrow fly. Without approaching the target, he knew the arrow had hit the center. Not bothering to retrieve it, he pulled another one and aimed at another spot. He continued with each arrow, pinning them in a circle around the bull's eye.

Though he had nothing on the skill of the Stewardesses, archery had always been a strength for him. The activity had a calming effect on him, though he did not get to engage in it as often as he would have liked.

He lost track of time, but by the time he had spent his last arrow, his shoulders and back were more relaxed. The worries were still there, but he needed to trust Lambient to see him through each challenge. In the meantime, he would keep his body strong and his mind sharp so he would be ready for whatever was ahead.

As he pulled the arrows from the canvas, satisfaction swelled at the two perfect circles that surrounded the center arrow. Not the typical way to practice one's shooting skills, but he liked to change things up a bit. He plucked each one out and placed them back in the quiver. Ready for the day now, he moved to the shed, noticing another man had taken his place at the archery stands.

Eric slowed as he recognized Zakkias. "How are you, private?" Eric asked.

"I'm all right, Prince Eric." He toed the ground, sober beyond his years. "I think everyone is expecting me to fall apart."

"Nay, not at all." Eric swung the quiver over his shoulder. "But you have been a bit quiet lately."

"I apologize if I've seemed distant."

"Any man who's come through what you have needs time to get past it."

"I don't know if I'll ever get past it." Zakkias frowned up at the sky. "I wish I hadn't left them."

"If you hadn't, those kids would not have survived."

"The Dark Steward already had them out." He pointed the fact out with neither resentment nor admiration.

"He would not have gotten them out by himself." Eric met the private's gaze. "There were a lot of people who had a hand in that victory, including you being the one to track the location down."

Zakkias's throat bobbed.

Eric clamped a hand on the young man's shoulder. "You're here for a purpose, Zakkias. Lambient still has a plan for you."

"Thank you, sir."

Eric left him alone, glad he'd run across him. Zakkias had been so withdrawn the past three months. It was good to see him back on the training field.

Being the only survivor of a group that was more like family than coworkers was enough to set anyone back. But as long as Zakkias did not allow the loss to make him bitter, Eric believed the young Steward would become stronger.

13

Walk blameless and harmless as children of the Lambient, without re-proof, that you may shine as lights in the midst of a dark world.
-The Sacred Code

Seria had never talked so little in her life. Her time with the king was spent keeping him as comfortable as she could while she monitored his breathing and his heartbeat, administered herbs that would help with the pain, and help him rest. But she spoke to him only when necessary and no more.

After the first day, Aladee had resumed her usual schedule and routine, though she dropped by periodically, as did Jervis. Seria was always glad to see them, as it gave her a chance to talk to someone. The king also seemed to appreciate the chance to visit.

Aden was polite and compliant to her care, but he did not say much, and Seria did not press him like she would have had the patient been anyone other than the king. The quiet drove her near mad at times, but she was more afraid of him talking to her. His observation followed her when she moved about the room, his judgment burning her skin like a midsummer sun ray. It kept her on edge when she had to work around him, and she had to tamp down the temptation to put him to sleep every time he woke up just for her own sake.

But of course, she would never do so.

Fortunately for her, he did sleep for long periods. He still had not gained his energy or strength back, much to his dismay. She assured him that his body was healing, but it would take time.

She checked her supplies on the table next to the bed. The tea was cold and almost gone; she would need to make more tonight.

Aden coughed, and she nearly dropped the pitcher of water.

Good grief, get a hold of yourself, Seria! She schooled her features to ask what he needed, but he spoke first.

"I was told you were quite a conversationalist."

Caught off guard, she said the first thing that popped into her mind. "If you mean chatterbox, I'm trying to break the habit."

He folded his hands over his chest. "That's too bad. I enjoy a good, stimulating conversation."

Maybe with people he trusted. "I'm afraid my topics of conversation would be dull and disappointing, Your Highness."

"Try me." He angled his head, and a lock of silver hair fell over his forehead. She caught a glimpse of Eric in his appearance. "Anything would have to be better than the boredom of silence."

Maybe he was truly bored, but she still held back. What could she possibly talk to the king about? She certainly couldn't discuss anything she had done recently; that would only draw more of his criticism. And her life before Mason was so simple and uneventful that she would put him to sleep. Which was not a bad idea.

"It's getting rather late," she said. "Are you ready for some tea?"

He regarded her for a long moment, his expression almost sad. "I suppose so," he said.

"I'll have to make some, so you sit tight until I get back." She waited for his assent before she loaded the dishes on the tray and carried them out. A sigh of relief drained from her as she made her way to the stairs.

Aden needed to get well soon so he could return to his usual duties, though a part of her wondered how much he would be able to take on. The man was still so weak, his heartbeat erratic at times. What if he could never fully resume his kingly role?

As uncomfortable as Seria felt in his presence, she genuinely sympathized with him. Lying in bed all day had to weigh on his mind, and there were times she sensed his agitation. She caught enough snippets of his conversations with Aladee and Jervis to know that he worried about the riots and the events happening at the Gateway. His keen sense of perception seemed to keep him awake as much as his discomfort did. But there was nothing he could do while he was ill, so he had to trust his son and his Stewards to protect his kingdom.

Seria mulled over his dilemma as she made her way through the halls. It must be hard for a king to step aside and let others lead. Aden Passion was known to be a good king, one who led his people with a steady hand and a sharp mind. Her father had respected Aden to the very moment of his death, even though he had not been able to serve him openly for the last few decades of his life.

Eric would one day take the role of king. She did not doubt that he would do just as well.

The heavy door appeared before her, and she turned to push it open with her back. Once inside, she stopped short at the sight of the couple sitting at one of the tables. Their chairs were pushed together in the corner, and their heads were bent very close.

Naomi jumped to her feet. "What are you doing here?"

Seria moved to the hearth that still burned. "I don't mean to interrupt. I only came to fix some tea."

The man with her did not look upset at the interruption. He draped his arm across the back of his chair, a smirk twisting his lips. A ribbon of uneasiness wriggled through Seria's chest.

"This kitchen is not to be used after the final cleanup," Naomi said, her tone haughty.

Seria gave her a direct look. "It's for the king."

Naomi narrowed her eyes and crossed her arms over her bosom. "Just because you're the king's personal servant girl does not give you any more privileges than the rest of us."

Swallowing a retort, Seria poked at the fire. Whispers sounded behind her—Naomi's harsh voice and the man's soothing one. Seria did not bother to remind Naomi that the kitchen was also not to be used by the staff to socialize, especially with a man who, Seria was fairly certain, was not a part of the castle's employ.

A creak brought her head around. The man rose from his chair and retrieved his cloak. "I'll see you later."

"You don't have to go, Varon," Naomi said, her eyes fixated on him.

Varon glanced at Seria. "I don't think everyone feels the same."

Naomi flashed Seria a hard look. "She doesn't matter."

Smiling, Varon caressed Naomi's flushed cheek. "I don't want to get you in trouble."

Seria turned back to the pot, uncomfortable to have intruded.

There was a soft swish of cloth then a giggle, leading Seria to wonder if Varon had kissed Naomi. The thought warmed Seria's cheeks, and she wished she had fixed the tea earlier that evening.

Varon's footsteps crossed to the other side of the room, and the back door of the kitchen opened, letting in a draft of chilly air. Seria risked a glance and was startled to find him looking at her.

"Nice to meet you, Miss Seria," he said with a salute. Then he stepped out into the night air and shut the door.

Seria held her tongue lest she say something that would only anger the other woman. But her restraint did not stop Naomi from turning on her.

"How dare you waltz in here like you are above the rest of us."

"I didn't mean to cut your visit short. I was just—"

Naomi slashed her hand through the air. "Oh, save your excuses. Don't think I'm going to tiptoe around you in your new position."

"I wouldn't think of it." Seria stirred the tea in the pot, trying to stay calm. "Your friend seems quite...charming." She hid a wince. Varon had left a bad feeling crawling down her spine, but she didn't think she would get in Naomi's good graces by saying so.

But the woman did not look appeased by Seria's effort and stepped into Seria's space. "See that you keep your mouth shut about seeing Varon here, or I'll make sure you don't go near the king's room again."

Seria gaped. What had caused Naomi to feel so bitter against her? Seria had never done anything to her, but from the first day, Naomi had turned her nose up at any attempt to befriend her. "I have no reason to share what I saw tonight," she said, hoping she was right. Varon obviously meant a lot to Naomi. Just because Seria felt uncomfortable did not mean he was a bad person.

"Make sure you forget about it." Naomi spun away and flounced off.

Good grief. Seria's blood heated, and she paused to collect herself. How that woman infuriated her.

A hiss caught her ears, and she rescued the tea before it boiled over. Lena's words returned to her as she prepared the tray.

Naomi was an unhappy woman who took her unhappiness out on other people. Maybe her relationship was the one bright spot in her life. It mattered little to Seria. Naomi was free to make her own choices. For once, Seria was glad that she had become Aden's caretaker, if for no other reason than to not have to cross paths with Naomi so much.

14

When I have nothing left, I will trust in You.
-The Sacred Code

"Mason!"

The lilting voice halted his movements, and he whirled from the wooden beam he was polishing. His heart leaped at the sight of the familiar smiling face running toward him. "Seria," he breathed, dropping the brush in the dirt. Not caring who was watching, he bolted down the steps to meet her halfway.

She threw her arms around his neck, and he twirled her around, holding her tight. He buried his face in her neck, drinking in her smell of soap and sunshine.

"Oh, Mason, I've missed you so much," she murmured, running her fingers through his hair.

He set her back on her feet and stared down into those green eyes sparkling up at him. Her cheeks flushed in her joy, her smile radiant.

"What are you doing here?" he asked, keeping his arms tight around her waist, determined never to let her go again.

"King Aden had to come to the fort, and I accompanied him."

"So, he approved—"

"It doesn't matter. Just hold me." She clasped her fingers behind his neck, tipping her face up, her lips mere inches from his. Not about to argue, he lowered his head, his blood thrumming in his veins.

Mason bolted awake, his heart pounding, and his arms empty. As the remnants of the dream faded, he struggled to hold on to her, make it real in his mind, if nothing else. But it drifted away in the recesses of his subconscious.

Jerking the thin blanket off, he wadded it up and tossed it to the floor. Careful not to disturb the other occupants of the bunkhouse, he sat up in bed, holding his head between both hands. His chest ached with the longing to see Seria. He needed her light to seep into the cracks of his emotions, holding him together when he was ready to fall apart.

The constant dreams were both a blessing and a curse, so real that he was convinced every time that she was really there, and the nightmare of their separation was over. The feel of her in his arms filled him with hope and courage to tackle the hard task before him. He could do anything with her at his side.

But he always woke up. And the loneliness was a thorn to his bleeding heart, digging deeper with each moment of clarity. He was more alone here than he had ever been in the camp of the Darkmen.

Not liking where that thought would take him, Mason reached for his boots. After lacing them up with short, quick movements, he grabbed his shirt and vest, then stalked outside.

It was not quite dawn, and a few stars winked at him. He stopped outside the bunkhouse, staring up at the sky. It was so calm, so peaceful before the chaos that the sunlight would bring.

How can I be a Steward if I still prefer the night?

Pulling his shirt on over his head, he walked without any destination in mind. He had no place to go. No one to talk to. He gripped the leather vest in his fist. He was no closer to being an official member of the Steward Army now than when he served under Commander Bruin. Maybe a little wiser, but no more pure. His temper was still too hot, his intentions fell too short, and his past held too many regrets.

And now, with him falling under suspicion, he was even farther away from where he wanted to be.

His brisk footsteps led him to the back gate. One lone guard stood at the portal at ground level. Two more would be watching from their posts in the guardhouse.

"Either let me out or move out of the way," Mason snapped.

The man lifted the bar, allowing Mason to push his way through.

The training field lay before him, empty and quiet, to his relief. This had been one of the very few benefits of his sentence. The Darkmen's training fields paled in comparison to the spacious lawns and organized stations at the Stewards' disposal. A forest of evergreen trees bordered the field, allowing for the occasional tracking or hunting exercise. Mason spent every moment he could spare there, keeping active and sane.

Today, he was assigned to clean the weapons in preparation for the Stewards' training, but he would get a little exercise before then. He descended the hill, his sights set on the storage shed, where extra weapons were kept for sparring. Mason would have no one to spar with, but he would benefit from the exertion.

He stepped to the open doorway, halting at the broad form that appeared in front of him.

Captain Braylee drew up short but recovered swiftly.

Mason stiffened and stepped back. "Captain."

Braylee's wide jaw shifted. His bulk seemed to fill the space of the room. "Private," he returned in his deep voice.

Tension coated Mason's skin. He still could not feel at ease around the man, aware his sentiment was shared by the veteran captain. No surprise, since Braylee did try to kill him at Joshun.

"Did you need something?" Braylee asked.

"Just wanted to get a workout before I start cleaning."

"You're sparring alone?"

"I'm not about to give you a chance to finish the job." The challenge slipped out before he could stop it.

Braylee's dark gaze speared him, and Mason held it, fully aware of his defiance. But the big man was hard to read, and it unnerved Mason more than a reaction of anger would have. He was about to retreat when Braylee spoke.

"I'll leave you alone then." He stepped to the side so Mason could enter. "We'll talk later." The promise rang with authority before he took his leave.

Mason waited until the captain was out of earshot before letting out a low growl. "Great, Mason. That's a great way to start your day." Then he rolled his eyes. "And now you're talking to yourself."

The realization made him want to both laugh and groan. How many times had he teased Seria for muttering to herself? Seemed she had rubbed off on him in more ways than he realized.

He massaged his aching temples. Oh, how he needed her.

Much to his dismay, his morning workout was interrupted by other Stewards anxious to get an early start on their drills. A cool rain began to fall, adding to the early autumn chill and doing nothing for his sour mood.

If Mason thought the rain would end the drills, he was to be disappointed. Captain Dudley had his platoon out working all morning. For every blade Mason polished or sharpened, another replaced it. He knew the work well, having done it when he was a young boy, learning under Bruin's tutelage. But it smarted to be reduced to nothing more than an errand boy. He was back and forth from the shed to the field, replacing imperfect weapons with those he had repaired.

A constant stream of traffic continued in and out of the weapons shed throughout the morning, tracking in mud and filling the small space with too much conversation and too many bodies until he was ready to explode. "Did you even use the blazing gum sleeve?" he demanded of one young knight when he brought back a sword that looked as if he had used it to hack a tree down.

"Aye, sir," the boy responded with wide eyes.

Mason thrust another sword into his hands and waved him off.

The steady hum of rain was about to drive him mad. Beside the constant noise that irritated the faint headache always lingering, it reminded him too much of Seria. His early days in her cabin had been spent under a spring rain shower, shutting them up alone together. At the time, he had thought he would claw his eyes out, listening to her nonstop chatter. Now they were some of the sweetest memories he could claim. But they were too painful to dwell on for too long.

Dakim showed up at one point, looking for more arrows. As he reached for a new bundle, Mason noted the downcast face. "What's got you so low?"

"They're going to kick me out of the army."

Mason stopped what he was doing. "Why would they do that?"

"I can't hit a blasted target. I was the first one out in the duel. They're going to think I'm useless."

Mason bit back a smile. He remembered thinking the same thing when he was training. "You're too stiff."

"What?"

Handing him the quiver stocked with arrows, Mason said, "You're trying too hard to impress. It's got you overcorrecting."

Dakim's lips turned down in thought. "Maybe you're right."

"They may not put you on the front lines right away, but I don't think they'll kick you out." Mason smacked the young man's head as he passed. "So quit whining."

Dakim chuckled as he trotted back out into the rain.

For some reason, the interaction lifted Mason's spirits. As other young knights came and went, he offered advice that would improve their stroke or shot. Each one brightened at the suggestion, ready to try it out on their next round. It was a needed distraction from his previous doldrums. Maybe he did have something to contribute to the Stewards.

15

The Lambient takes that which is broken and makes it new.
-The Sacred Code

"What are you doing?" Lionel stopped in the doorway of the shed and scowled at the chatting pair.

Dakim jumped up, dropping his rag. "I—I was polishing."

"Ease up on him, will you?" Mason cut in. "He's just helping me clean up."

Lionel shot a glare his way. "You do not give orders around here, Grey, especially to me." He turned back to the cadet. "And if I catch you talking to him again, I'll see that you're suspended."

Dakim reddened, and he ducked his head as he picked the rag up and put the polish back in its place on the shelf. "Aye, sir." He hurried from the shed.

Lionel met Mason's hard look with one of his own before he started to leave.

"I can see why you have no friends around here," Mason said.

He spun around. "Because you helped kill them all!"

Mason blanched, his defiance cracking on his hard-set expression.

For some reason, that reaction enraged Lionel more, disintegrating what little control he had left. "You spent your life with no thought for anyone but yourself, and then you think you can waltz in here and be a hero because you did one good thing." He jabbed a finger at him. "But you're nothing but a tool for us to use to win this war, and that's it."

He stopped short, his own words ringing in his ears. What was he doing? He didn't even recognize himself anymore. Words of hate and venom spewed from him with the same rapid flow of a rushing river. But these waters were dirty and poisonous, tainting his soul.

Mason stood like a statue, his fists clenched, his spine ramrod straight. His eyes shot icy daggers, but he did not fight back.

Lionel sucked in a ragged breath. He couldn't take the words back, even if he wanted to. But a sick feeling spread through his middle, making it hard to breathe. This wasn't his fault. Mason didn't belong here. Maybe a Steward shouldn't say the things he had, but that didn't make them false. It was time Mason knew the truth, even if it was harsh.

But the way Mason stared back at him, silent and resigned, poked at his rationale. The Reader did not look surprised at the words that hung between them. Angry, but almost defeated. Lionel ground his teeth and left, his own words pounding at his conscience. They were true. A Darkman—a *Shadowman*—could never be a true Steward.

With Lambient, nothing is impossible.

He shook his head and stormed to at stop at the top of the hill where the shed was located. His heart beat erratically in his chest as he stared down at the trainees, trying to pretend all was normal.

Someone coughed. Lionel started and turned to see Dudley nearby, rolling a broken arrow between his fingers. "You all right, Lieutenant?"

Lionel's heart jumped. Had he heard Lionel's outburst? A Steward would never be condoned for reacting the way he had, no matter how right he was. He coughed. "Fine. Just had to deal with a situation with Grey."

Dudley glanced back at the shed, where Mason could be seen with his back to the large window, bent over the table, his shoulders tight and hunched. Lionel turned his back to the shed and faced the captain, but the older man was staring down at the broken arrow.

Dudley held it up. "Lost another arrow today. This one held up for a while, but someone forgot to treat it, and it broke under the pressure." He raised his sharp gaze to Lionel. "I'll see you around, son."

Lionel's eyes slid shut as the captain left. He wasn't sure if Dudley was talking about the arrow or him.

Stay calm. Don't lose control.

The words did not stem the raging inferno that Lionel's words had stoked.

Mason braced himself against the table, his body trembling with the effort to keep his anger from taking over. Lionel's opinion didn't matter to him. He had made his feelings clear from the beginning. All he had done now was voice them. He was nothing more than an arrogant knight who expected those beneath him to toe the line.

Mason gritted his teeth, spasms running through his jaw. A dull drum beat in his head, and he squeezed his eyes shut against the pain. *Lambient...*

His prayer drifted away to silence. What was the point? Lionel may be impossible, but his words about Mason were true.

The drumming turned into a pounding, and a sharp pain pierced him right between the eyes. He pounded the table and swiped everything in front of him to the floor. The clatter of wood and metal shook him from his rage, and he pinched the bridge of his nose as the ache in his head receded. Then he put the equipment back in place. He moved to hang a wooden training sword up as Captain Dudley stepped through the doorway.

"Did you need something, Captain?" he asked, his tone dull. There was no point in trying to cover his actions. Dudley knew what he was. Probably shared Lionel's sentiments. Everyone else did.

"Nay, I'm done for the day. Just came to store this." He held up an arrow with a splintered shaft.

"Toss it. It's useless."

"I used to think so. Disposed of a lot of broken arrows over the years."

Mason did not bother replying and resumed his task. He may be an outsider, but they would not find any fault in his work.

Dudley crossed further into the room, rotating the wood in his hands. "Then I realized I was wasting a perfectly good piece of work."

"You can't shoot a broken arrow."

"You're right. Not well, anyway. And it would be dangerous to use it in battle. It wouldn't hold up. Could crumble just when you need it."

Would this old man ever stop rambling? "If you can't shoot it, I don't know what good it is."

Dudley cocked his head. "Just because it's not the same, doesn't mean it can't still be used." He held it up. "This could be a stake in a garden. A man can use this as a model for crafting new arrows or for practicing fletching. I've even seen creative sorts turn them into writing tools."

Despite himself, Mason caught himself listening. "It's still not the same."

"Can't argue with you there. But that doesn't mean it can't have a new purpose." He fell silent for a moment, his brow creased. "When you think about it, broken arrows are a lot like broken men."

Mason shot him a quick look. Was he about to hear a lecture about how broken he was?

"A man who's broken is never the same. He might forget himself for a while and struggle to find his way, but given time and patience, he can still be a good man."

Understanding dawned, and it irritated him. "Sir, is this your subtle way of saying I need to be nice to Lionel?"

Dudley squinted at him. "*Lieutenant* Lionel. And he's had a lot on his plate lately."

"That's not my problem." Mason wasn't sure if he was verging on disrespect. Of course, Dudley would defend Lionel. All the Stewards stuck together, but he was done with dealing with Lionel's bad attitude.

"Ollen Knavis was his closest friend."

If Dudley had hoped to catch his attention, he had succeeded. Mason's movements slowed, his grip tightening on a bow before he hung it up. Again, he saw the young Steward on the ground, attempting to point Mason to the light with his last breath. If the death of a near stranger had impacted Mason so much, how much more would it mark a close friend?

He swallowed. "Does that make his attitude right?" he asked, but the question lacked conviction.

"Nay, but I expect you would know how grief can change a man."

Blazes, the captain had a way of making him feel like a young boy, caught in his bad behavior.

A twinkle lit Dudley's sharp blue eyes. "I'd wager there's not a man in the Stewardship who's not guilty of acting outside of what is good and right at some point or another. It's fortunate the Lambient is as patient as He is, or we'd all be without hope." He moved to a small cupboard in the corner of the shed, opened the door, and placed the broken arrow inside. Once the door was shut, he gave it a tap, then left without another word.

Speechless, Mason stared at the cupboard, wondering how he had missed it before. The door was made entirely of broken arrow pieces.

16

"I get the impression you don't care very much for me, Miss Seria."

Dismay filled her that she had let her feelings be so transparent. "Nay, of course not!" She caught herself. "I mean, of course, you're the king. I mean, you're Er—Prince Eric's father." Her agitation spouted out of her in nonsense.

He crossed his arms, his thumb tapping against his elbow. "You must have been upset at the sentence I gave you."

She straightened. "My actions deserved punishment. I could not fault you in seeing justice."

"Did you not think me unfair, separating you from your young man?"

"He's not my young man," she said, even as her heart pricked. When Aden's blue eyes narrowed, she stammered, "I mean, not anymore. We were both wrong to...be together."

"You did not feel your sentencing to be too harsh?"

"Nay," she said firmly.

Aden squinted up at her, skepticism clear on his face. "Why not?"

"Why not?" She put her hands on her hips. "King Aden, I know I was wrong. That's why I confessed it at the trial."

"Did you confess it to the Lambient, ask for forgiveness?"

"Of course I did." Frustration sharpened her tone, and she took a deep breath. What was he trying to get at?

"So, you don't feel I was excessive to sentence you anyway?"

"Of course not."

"Why not?"

"Because I had to prove to Him and everyone else that I was sorry."

"You mean you had to earn your forgiveness."

"Aye," she blurted, then stopped short. "Oh." Was she trying to earn Lambient's forgiveness?

The king arched a silvery brow at her, and she reminded herself it was not proper to scowl at royalty.

The lines around his mouth softened. "The Lambient does not expect anyone to earn His grace through good works. If that were so, we'd all be without hope."

She sank into the chair beside the bed, her thoughts whirling. "But...there must be consequences."

"Aye." He gave a resolute nod. "I am a firm believer in that. I think we've fallen into the belief that forgiveness means no restitution. And that's simply not true. If I steal from someone, and then truly repent, I am still responsible for restoring what I've stolen."

Seria shrugged. "I thought that was what I was doing."

"Maybe in part and maybe in the beginning." He grew thoughtful. "But it's easy to turn that sincere intention into a drive for His approval, to try to cover our mistakes with good deeds. My son and I have both done so." He shifted and looked at her again. "I want you to understand that in bringing you here, I was not attempting to play the role of judge and executor. That belongs to Lambient. But I felt you and your young man both needed time to deal with your mistakes apart from one another, to learn what Lambient wants you to learn."

Relief filled her. "I thought you were angry at me," she admitted.

He angled his head, regarding her. "I was troubled, to be sure, at the risk you had taken. But in truth, I was impressed that both of you young ladies had the courage and integrity to admit your wrongdoings to everyone."

"I figured I had wronged everyone there, so they had a right to know."

He pursed his lips. "I admit, I was taken aback at Mason's defense of you and Miss Lena, yet he had none for himself. That said a lot to me, especially when that Beacon lit up."

She remembered that moment at the trial and the way her heart ached at the stricken look he gave her.

"Your Mason has a lot more to live down," Aden continued, "even with his change of heart. The people of the fort, Stewards included, need more reason to accept and trust him."

Which explained why the king left him there to spend his days in service. Seria only hoped Mason would see that in time and use the chance given him to make a place for himself.

"I must ask you a question, though," she said, watching him. When he offered her a nod to continue, she did so. "Why did you feel the need to punish Lena so?"

"Was she not wrong in helping you deceive everyone?"

"I mean, maybe," Seria admitted, "but she did it with the best of intentions. And she still did not go to the lengths of deceit that I did."

He studied her for a moment. "That may be so," he finally said. "But in considering the future of Paladin, I felt it wise to keep the object of the prince's affections safe during this war."

She gaped at him. *"What?"*

He beamed at her. "It seems my son and your friend have forged a tentative connection, though I'm sure he is the one who is holding back."

Dumbfounded, Seria thought back to all the times she and Lena had talked about or crossed paths with Eric. It all made sense now. Lena's quiet contemplations every time Eric was mentioned. Eric's boyish awkwardness when Lena was around. "How did I miss this when you figured it out all the way back here?"

"The Lambient sees fit to bless an old man with an even sharper sense of perception in his later years." He paused. "It also helps to have a couple of captains there reporting their suspicions."

"Why, King Aden, you rascal!" She bit her lip at her outburst, then relaxed when he only winked.

Then he pointed a finger at her. "Now, don't you be troubling waters that aren't yet ready to be stirred up, young lady."

She put her hand on her chest. "Who, me?"

For the first time since she had met him, King Aden laughed, the action making him look much younger and more lighthearted. And also for the first time, Seria was glad she had taken this job.

17

When my heart falters, the Lambient will be my strength forever.
-The Sacred Code

"Loosen your grip." Mason watched as Crue readjusted his hold on the sword, his face a mask of concentration.

They were in a corner of the inner bailey, behind civilian houses and surrounded by a few trees. It was almost sundown, so they did not have much time, but they were hidden from view here. This was their fifth session, and so far, each one had gone smoothly and, more importantly, unnoticed.

"That's good, but you're still holding the hilt too tight. It's making your movements stiff." Crue made another attempt. "There you go." The teen's pleasure made his heart throb a bit. Teaching Crue brought to mind the lessons he used to give Seria. It seemed like a faraway dream now. Did she get a chance to practice anymore? Would she be able to defend herself if she ended up in danger again?

Wherever she's at, she is safer there than here with me. The reminder was a harsh comfort, for it did not take away his longing to see her again and know how she was doing.

He pulled his focus back. He shouldn't be thinking of her at all. The king had declared that their association was to be severed. And Seria herself had made it clear that she was stepping out of his life, as she should. He hoped for nothing but the best for her. Even if it cut him to the core that he was not it.

"Master Mason?"

Mason shook his head. "I'm not your master anymore. You can call me Mason."

There was a mix of hesitation and delight at the permission.

"Okay, now I want you to watch me." He stood before Crue with his own sword in both hands. "This is an easy defense move."

Crue studied every motion, his hands already curling over the hilt of his short sword to mimic Mason's hold. As Mason raised the weapon, Crue's eyes followed, then widened at something behind Mason.

Before Mason could pivot, he was pummeled to the ground. A heavy weight settled on his back, pinning him down and taking his breath away. Rough hands seized his arms and held them out to the sides. A rag was stuffed in his mouth.

"Stop it!" Crue's shout rang out. "What are you doing? Let him go!" There was a shuffle and a grunt as Crue tried to intervene.

That the boy saw him in this helpless position tore at his pride, but anger pulsed louder. Who had attacked him? His mind shot to the Shadowmen in the dungeon, and fear for his student replaced some of the anger.

Voices drifted around him. At least three men were holding him, maybe more. He stiffened and resisted as they forced his arms back to tie his wrists, but he could not fight against three men, especially flat on the ground.

"Leave him alone!" Crue stepped into his view as he awkwardly brandished his sword. A man evaded his swing and promptly unarmed him.

"Now, boy, we don't blame you." Mason did not recognize the speaker. "We know he was controlling you."

"Nay! He was helping me!"

Mason was yanked to his feet, his hands bound tightly behind him and another rag tied to keep the gag in place. He glowered into the haughty mug of Hiram.

"I knew I'd catch you endangering our civilians," he said. "What's Lt. Lionel going to say when he hears you were threatening a young boy?"

Heat flooded Mason's veins and burned his eyes, but without his voice, he could not stop them.

Crue jerked at Hiram's arm. "He was helping me!"

Hiram shoved his hold off. "He's making you think that, boy. But you'll find out later that he was using you."

Two other men held Mason's arms in ironclad grips, their nails digging into his skin. Another man stood by with an ax handle, ready to act if needed. Mason tried to catch Crue's eye, tried to send silent cues for the boy to back off. He didn't need Crue getting himself into trouble on his account.

Frustration pounded into guilt. He had known better than to work with Crue. It was a direct violation of his probation. Lionel wouldn't let this one slide. And Eric would not step in for him when Mason was clearly in the wrong.

Hiram stepped closer, blowing ale-laced breath into Mason's face. "I always knew you were no good. Now, I'll make sure you don't cause any more trouble around here."

"He wasn't controlling me." Crue tried to push his way between them.

Hiram thrust him aside, and Mason acted on instinct, bringing his knee up to Hiram's groin. The bigger man doubled over, hissing through his teeth. Mason swung his foot up and knocked him flat on his back. The fourth man cracked the ax handle across Mason's jaw, stunning him to immobility.

"Stop!" Crue cried out.

Hiram climbed to his feet, snarling. "Think that was funny, huh?" He slammed a meaty fist into Mason's jaw, then caught his cheekbone with another hard hit. "How about that?"

"Hey, we better not rough him up too much," one man said, "or they won't believe us."

"We'll tell 'em he resisted arrest."

Crue jumped on Hiram's back, pounding on his head. Hiram grabbed his arm and pulled him off, dropping him on the ground.

Mason growled and pulled against the men.

Hiram grabbed Crue's shirt and pulled him to his feet. "Now listen, kid. We're doing this for you."

"You're not!" Crue's eyes blazed. "You're big, stupid oafs who don't know your head from a lump of meat!"

"Let's take them both to the lieutenant," one of his captors said. "He'll take care of 'em."

Apprehension made Mason stiffen and dig his heels in, but he didn't know why he bothered. Even a master swordsman couldn't fight multiple men off with no weapon and bound hands. His dismay grew with every footstep that they dragged him along. The four walls of the dungeon cell seemed to close around him.

"What's happening here?"

They halted as Eric approached, scanning the situation with a hard look. Braylee followed, his dark brows bunched.

Hiram straightened. "We were taking the Reader into custody, Sire."

"What is his crime?" Eric asked, his eyes narrowing.

"Breaking the terms of his probation, Sire." Hiram released Crue. "We caught him congregating with the boy."

Eric and Braylee exchanged glances.

"That's not what happened!" Crue cried. "He was helping me."

Hiram shook his head. "He controlled the poor boy so he's all worked up."

"We gagged him so he couldn't control anyone else," another man said. "But he still put up a fight."

"He didn't control me," Crue growled.

"You don't think he would?" another man taunted.

"Nay." Crue shook his head. "He wouldn't control me."

"Hasn't he controlled you before?"

"That was different!"

"Enough." Eric's command whipped through them.

Every person there fell silent, Crue looking ready to cry. Eric's face was impassive, his thoughts blocked from Mason's. A few other spectators had gathered around the perimeter, all talking and pointing at the spectacle. Mason clenched his teeth, trying not to gag over the soaked rag. Everything in him burned to scream and lash out. Fire raced through his head, piercing his skull. The voices began to scream, and his arms shook.

Lambient, get me out of here.

"Release him."

"But, sir," Hiram dared to protest.

"I said release him!" the prince snapped.

While the two men worked to loosen the tight knot, Hiram tried again. "Sire, we caught him directly disregarding his probation terms—"

Eric cut him off again. "I don't see that being a reason to bind and gag a man."

"But he was—"

"Silence!"

Mason's muscles knotted as the rope around his hands fell away. He ripped the gag out and spun on Hiram, ready to unleash the fire raging within him. The Reservist's red-rimmed eyes widened.

"Stand down, Mason."

He did with great effort, gritting his teeth until he thought they would break.

Eric gave a slight tip of his head. "Go to your quarters."

The dismissal irked. Mason saw it for the chance of escape it was, but he burned to defend himself, to smash Hiram into the ground. But the eyes of the spectators pierced him like needles. Lena's mother, Ayna Carwright, gaping with her mouth open. The idiot Marcus, looking as if he had no idea what was going on. Barry, the blacksmith, standing by with his hands on his hips.

Humiliation sunk its talons in deep. They had all seen his weakness, heard of his wrong. They already thought he was responsible for the Shadowman's breakout.

His vision blurred, and he fisted his hands. With one more piercing glare at the men around him, he pushed himself through the circle, then through the crowd of spectators. His boots pounded the dirt, sending shockwaves up his legs and a reminder drumming through his mind with every step. *You don't belong. You don't belong.*

The barracks were in sight when someone stepped out in front of him. Mason ran right into the man. "Watch where you're going!" He pushed the clumsy oaf back. Ira Dankton's eyes widened at the sight of him.

"You," Mason snarled, stepping back into the other man's space. Angry as he was, he was ready to pound the dumpy man into the ground for all the trouble he put Seria through. It might be a good outlet for his fury.

But Ira dropped his head without a fight. "I know."

The gesture drew Mason up short. For the brief moment he had held Ira's gaze, he had seen his shame for his previous actions.

Ira took a deep breath and risked looking up again. "You have every right to hit me after the way I treated your young lady friend. My actions were despicable."

He was genuine in his admission, and Mason fought to hold on to his resentment. He had been no better to Seria in the beginning. "I'm glad you finally see it that way," he bit out, not ready to make nice to the drunk.

"It took spending some time in the brig for me to see where I'd let my life sink to." Ira shook his head. "I might still be in there if it wasn't for a young Steward befriending me, getting me the help I needed." He stood tall. "He got me a job, and I have not touched a strong drink in months."

Mason was stunned at the difference. Ira's gaze was clear and direct, and his expression held more thoughtfulness than he had ever witnessed before. "That's...good."

Ira sighed. "Sgt. Ollen was the first and only friend I've had in a long time. I was saddened to hear of his death."

At that, Mason's anger drained completely. Somehow, he was not surprised to hear that Ollen had a hand in Ira's change.

"My life is still nothing to envy," Ira continued, "but I'm trying to take what he did for me and do for others."

Mason huffed. "You're making it hard for me to want to hit you."

Ira chuckled, the action making him look like a completely different person. "I do owe you an apology, though, for how I acted."

Mason waved it off. "Believe me. It doesn't matter now."

Ira studied him for a moment, and Mason caught a glimpse of the man he must have been at one time. Perceptive and intelligent. "I'm glad I ran into you. Literally," he added with another chortle. "I've wanted to make amends for a while."

At a loss for words, Mason gave him a nod, and they parted ways. His mind spun with the exchange, almost distracting him from the incident with Hiram. Almost, but not quite.

Disbelief warred with consternation in Braylee's chest as the prince tried to get to the bottom of what had happened.

"All right, Hiram. You have the floor," Eric said, his voice stiff.

Hiram drew himself to his full height. "I came across the Reader—"

"He has a name."

The man blinked. "What?"

"If you're going to accuse a man of wrongdoing, give his name."

"All right." Hiram blinked a couple of times as he regrouped. "I came across...Mason with this here lad. He had a sword to him, threatening him. I knew he wasn't supposed to be around kids, so we put him under arrest."

"Was he too much for you?"

Hiram swelled. "Not for us, Sire."

"Then why was he bound and gagged?"

"Oh, because he's dangerous."

"Did he threaten you at all? Make you feel that you had to restrain him?"

Hiram looked at his accomplices. "Well, he can put people under a spell, so we removed that threat."

"What about the bruises he sported?" Braylee asked.

"He resisted arrest."

"One more question." Eric stepped closer. "Who directed you to put Mason into custody?"

"Lt. Lionel, sir." Hiram puffed his chest out.

A muscle jumped in Eric's jaw. "He gave you the authority to arrest one of my Stewards?"

The men all faltered, but Hiram paled, then reddened. "W-we know the lieutenant don't trust him, so I told him we would watch and make sure he didn't break his probation."

"Which in this case was...?"

"Associating with adolescents and threatening civilians."

"I see."

Braylee crossed his arms, working to keep his thoughts off his face, but the whole incident was so strange and troubling.

Eric looked to Crue. "Can you tell me what happened?" he asked, softening his tone.

Crue took a shuddering breath. "He wasn't threatening me. He was showing me a defense move, and then all of a sudden, these guys jumped him from behind."

"From behind?" Braylee repeated. None of them were in his company, but he was familiar with Hiram, with his bolster and swagger. All the men reeked of ale.

Hiram pulled at his collar even as he jutted his chin out.

"They tied him up before he could even defend himself."

"Did he fight them?"

Hiram spoke up. "He kicked me!"

"Only because you pushed me," Crue returned, his fists clenched.

"So, you manhandled the boy, as well?" Eric asked. None of them were willing to respond to that.

"Why was he showing you a defense move?" Braylee asked the boy.

"I asked him to." Crue wilted and ducked his head. "H-he was helping me train to...become a Steward someday."

Braylee smiled. "A worthy cause."

Bolstered by the confirmation, Crue brightened. "I've been around a lot of Darkmen. They can be mean. But I know Stewards treat people with respect." He cast a disgusted look toward Hiram and his friends.

"I wish that were always the case, but Stewards are but human."

Hiram tried one more time. "He still was in direct violation of his probation, sir."

"Thank you, Crue," Eric said. "You've been a big help. You're free to go."

Crue looked as if he wanted to say more, but his chin lowered in deference. "Thank you, Your Highness."

Braylee slapped his back as he passed him. He would be sure to talk to him again later after everything had calmed down.

Eric turned a hard look on the militiamen. "You all will come with me to the Council Hall for an official report."

"What?" Hiram bristled. "Why are we being reported?"

"You are questioning the prince, Hiram," Braylee said. "That's never going to bode well for your defense. Especially since you know drinking is prohibited."

Hiram grimaced and led his three comrades to the hall.

Eric looked to Braylee. "I think you better find Lionel."

"I will."

Most of the crowd had dissipated by the time they moved to their separate tasks. Braylee headed to the back wall, where Lionel had his men on duty. It didn't take long to spot his tall form at the top. As he climbed the steps, he could hear Lionel scolding a young private and did not hesitate to interrupt. "I wonder if I could have a moment of your time, Lieutenant?"

Lionel signaled the boy off. "Don't be late again, private, or you will be disciplined."

"Trouble with the men?" Braylee asked.

"Only when they are not where they're supposed to be," Lionel replied.

Braylee studied him for a moment. Lionel was tense and short-tempered, his back straight, nothing like what he used to be.

"Is something wrong, Captain?"

"I'm afraid there might be." Braylee crossed his arms and leaned back against the wall. "Hiram and a few of his companions attempted to arrest a Steward."

"Why on earth would they do such a stupid thing?"

"He said you would approve."

Lionel frowned. "That's preposterous. I would never give an order like that to a militiaman, especially one as reckless as Hiram."

"Would you not?"

"Nay, of course not."

"Even if it was Mason Grey?"

Lionel froze. After a long moment, he asked, "What happened?"

"Hiram and his friends overpowered Mason and roughed him up for breaking the terms of his probation. Said they were bringing him to you."

"I never requested such a thing."

"That's good to hear." Braylee pushed away from the wall. "We'll need you to report that to the Council. Eric has them in discipline now for their actions as well as excessive drinking. There's one thing I can't figure out, however."

"Aye, sir?"

"Hiram swore Mason was breaking his probation for congregating with an underaged citizen." He rubbed his jaw. "But as far as I know, that's not one of the terms of his probation. So, where did he get that idea?"

There was no change on Lionel's stone face, but his cheeks paled. Braylee left him to ponder the question.

18

It is He who will avenge the wrong done against me. He will bring the offenders to justice.
-The Sacred Code

The kitchen was bustling when Seria stepped through the door before the evening meal. The king seemed more uncomfortable today, so she needed a fresh batch of tea to help him rest.

Lena greeted her with a wave from across the room. Seria waved and stopped by the hearth to put her tea on to steep. Then she made her way to the table where Lena worked.

"Are you rolling out some tarts?" she asked.

"I am." Lena cut a square of thin dough and placed it on a tray. "Captain Aladee requested that I make the Steward officers a treat for an upcoming anniversary." She arched a brow Seria's way. "I can't imagine how she heard about my pastries."

Seria gave an exaggerated shrug. "I can't imagine."

Lena chuckled as she set the last bit of the dough on the pan. "Well, thank you. It's a nice break from the usual kitchen duties, though I don't want to complain."

"You never do. What are you making? Honey tarts?"

A soft smile teased Lena's lips. "Nay. I save those for special occasions." She pointed to a bowl filled with red berries. "She asked for berry pastries."

"One of your best dishes," Seria said, taking an appreciative sniff of the aroma drifting from the sweet mixture.

Lena lifted the wide tray. "Let's hope they turn out better than the last attempt."

Seria stepped out of Lena's way. "They will, I'm sure." She moved back to the fireplace to check on her tea. It wasn't hot enough yet, so she stirred it and glanced in time to see Lena carrying a tray of perfectly baked tarts. But before she could set them on the table, someone stepped in her path, and they collided. Lena's tarts fell to the floor in squashed clumps.

"Oh, I'm so sorry!" Lena exclaimed.

"You big ox!" Naomi blared. "Look at this mess!"

Heat poured down Seria's spine, and she hurried to her friend's side. "That wasn't her fault!"

"It's all right, Seria," Lena said, her hand on Seria's arm.

"Nay, it's not. She walked right into you."

Naomi gave her a dark look. "You best mind your business, missy. You both been nothing but trouble since the day you stepped foot here."

Seria ground her teeth together. "Lena hasn't done anything to warrant the way you treat her."

"*I* am in charge here," Naomi repeated. "Not you. I will do what I like."

Lena stepped between them. "I think we all need to calm down." She said it with such calm authority, that even Naomi faltered. Then she bristled.

"You don't give orders around here. From here on out, you're on floor duty. And you," she turned on Seria, "are banned from my kitchen."

"You can't do that," Seria protested.

"This is my kitchen, and I certainly will not put up with a good-for-nothing Darkman loyalist causing disorder."

Seria curled her fingers into fists, trying not to succumb to the temptation to slap the other woman. She started to lash out again when the women around her shifted away, their attention riveted on someone else. She turned to see Aladee approach, her dark face serious. Swallowing back the angry words on the tip of her tongue, Seria took a step back. It was time to let someone else take over.

"What's going on, Naomi?" Aladee asked, sweeping the three of them with sharp eyes.

Naomi pointed at Seria, shooting visual daggers. "Every time this girl comes here, she slows the workers down, yacking with her friend." She gestured toward Lena. "And that one keeps wasting her time and our staples trying to get out of her usual work."

"She—" Aladee held her hand up, and Seria fell silent. Frustration rose within her like volcanic ash, ready to spew from her mouth. Confidence lifted Naomi's head high.

"All right, ladies," the Stewardess addressed the crowd. "The knights will be expecting their midday meal soon."

The women dispersed, their murmurs rising and falling as they resumed their work. Aladee crossed her arms. "How is it you know about the Darkman, Naomi?"

Naomi waved a wild hand. "Why, it's common knowledge. I have to watch them both, the way they talk between themselves. I don't trust her."

Humiliation washed over Seria. How many knew of her history with Mason? Did everyone know that she had been sent here as penance? That she had dragged Lena's good name into the dirt as well smarted like a razor cut.

"Hmm." Aladee narrowed her eyes in thought. "Did Charlin inform you that I made a request for berry tarts from Lena?"

"Oh." Naomi blinked, her mouth opening and shutting. If she was not so angry, Seria would laugh at Naomi's discomfort.

"S-she did mention it, now that I think about it," Naomi said, her tone much more subdued. "But I don't know if that's such a good idea, Captain. The last time she tried to bake something she ruined a whole batch of tarts."

"But you are not authorized to override my directions. Because, regardless of what I heard you say, it's not *your* kitchen. No more than it is mine."

Naomi wilted. "Of course, Captain."

Aladee released a long sigh. "Naomi, I am relieving you from your position as head kitchen supervisor."

"What?" Naomi gawked. "B-but I'm not the one—"

"I want you to go to your quarters and remain there until I speak to you again."

Her cheeks mottled in her offense. She balled her fists and flounced away, her nose high in the air.

Seria drew in a shuddering breath, expecting Aladee to scold her next. "I apologize for causing such a scene, Captain Aladee. I overreacted, I'm sure. But I couldn't stand back and say nothing."

"I understand. This is not the first time she's overstepped. She holds this position with too much self-gratification. You must have threatened her pride. I had hoped she would settle down and remember how it was that she got here in the first place." She bit her lip. "But I won't get into that."

Catching the looks she was getting from the other women in the kitchen, Seria sighed. "Maybe I shouldn't be treating the king right now." When Aladee gave her a quick look, she added, "I don't want to stir up any more gossip than I've already done." Even as she said it, she was aware of how much she would miss the work. Not only did she have the chance to use her healing skills again, but she was starting to enjoy spending time with the king.

"King Aden is quite accustomed to stirring things up with his choice of staff." Aladee chuckled. "Including the time he hired a thieving young girl to work with his bookkeeper."

Seria exchanged confused looks with Lena. "Who?"

Pressing a finger to her chest, Aladee answered. "Me."

"You?" Seria squeaked.

"You'd be surprised how many people working on these grounds came from less than stellar backgrounds, Seria. Thieves like me. Drunkards. Women of dishonor. From his early days, the king took it upon himself to take in people whom he felt needed a new lease on life. Some place to find themselves."

Wonder erased the embarrassment that had clouded her spirit. "I never would've guessed," she murmured.

A young girl brought her a tray laden with the tea that she had forgotten. "I caught this before it spilled over."

Remembering what Aladee had said about Aden's workers, Seria looked her in the eye as she took the tray. "Thank you so much."

The girl ducked her head shyly and moved away.

Her respect mounting for the man she had been tending to, Seria straightened her shoulders. "I best get back to King Aden. He'll be needing this tea to rest." She gave both ladies a nod and headed for the hall, thankful that she had the chance to aid him during this difficult season of his life.

19

As the sun rises every morning, so the Lambient's mercy shines new.
-The Sacred Code

Eric quietly removed the dagger within Mason's reach from the table before he smacked the sleeping man's foot. Just as he suspected, Mason jolted awake and blindly grabbed for his knife. "Time to get up, sunshine," Eric greeted.

He received a dark glare in return. "Are you wanting me to cut your hand off?" Mason asked, his hair standing up on end.

"Not at all." Eric held the weapon up and winked. "Now you get dressed. We've got work to do."

"What's so important you have to get me up at the crack of dawn?" Mason groused as he sat up. He looked ready to bite Eric's head off, but after facing Braylee's moods in the morning, Mason didn't rattle him a bit.

"After yesterday's fiasco, I decided you needed to get out, so we're going on a scouting assignment." He dropped the dagger on the cot. "Be ready in ten minutes."

"And if I'm not?"

Eric paused and fixed a hard look on him.

Mason raised his hands. "All right, all right. My apologies." The apology was barely heard in his grumbles, but Eric accepted it.

"You don't give me much time to eat," Mason said, pulling his shirt on.

"Then you better hurry. Barry already has our horses saddled. I'll see you at the outer gates. Ten minutes."

Eric left him there to stew and went to get Oakley. Mason's roan watched with ears perked as Eric mounted the big gray.

"Don't worry, he's coming," Eric assured the gelding before urging Oakley to the outer bailey.

Mason's pride alone would not allow him to be late, especially after what had happened last night. He would be on time, even if he had to skip breakfast.

Sure enough, the roan was soon trotting down the well-worn trail to meet Eric at the meeting spot. Mason's face was shuttered, his eyes daring Eric to say anything.

Eric tossed a small cloth bag. "Here. A couple of Nola's biscuits and some bacon so you won't faint."

The hard mask slipped, and Mason blinked at him. "Uh...thanks."

"Let's go."

Their ride through Cadence was a quiet one, the air broken by bird-song and hoofbeats.

"So, what's so pressing we had to leave before the day began?" Mason asked around a biscuit.

"I've been keeping tabs on the areas around the fort," Eric said. "Lionel's taking his squad down south to Cuthrel. We'll go north."

"I didn't think I was allowed to leave the boundaries of the fort."

Eric grinned. "Something tells me you've never been a stickler for rules. Besides, you're with me. No one can say anything when I give the orders."

"Since when did you get so snarky?"

"Hm. Don't know." Eric studied the sky. "Must be the company I'm keeping."

Mason rolled his eyes. "So where are we going?"

"Rackson." He could feel Mason's stare.

"Why Rackson?"

"I've had a few men stationed there since it was attacked, and I want to look in on things." He aimed Oakley northwest to skirt the bluffs that gathered around the Gateway.

"We could save some time going through the bluffs."

Eric glanced over at the other man. "Through them?"

Mason gestured at a long incline. "There's a tunnel up there. Cuts right through the bluffs."

That got Eric's attention. "A tunnel?"

"Aye. I used it when I...came to see Seria."

"Where does it lead?"

Mason shrugged. "The other side."

His curiosity piqued, Eric motioned for Mason to lead. "Then let's see it."

The horses clopped up the rocky ramp that looked like it stopped in the face of the rock. To Eric's amazement, however, there was a crevice that remained hidden from a casual view. Once at the top, Mason dismounted and led his roan in on foot. Eric pulled his Beacon from his belt and lit the way as they proceeded. The passage was narrow and completely cut off from any daylight, due to the sharp angle. Oakley snorted his displeasure at the closed setting, but he followed Eric without hesitation.

After a while, Mason paused before a fork. Eric shone the light ahead. "Which way?" he asked.

"This way." Mason pointed to the left with a limp hand, a strange look on his face as he studied the right-side path.

"What's down this way?" Eric stepped around him to peer down the other way.

"I don't know. It's too narrow." He gave Eric an unreadable look, a thin sheen of sweat on his forehead.

"Something wrong?"

He shook his head and looked away. Eric moved closer to the passage and lifted his Beacon. The passage was indeed too narrow for a full-sized man to go through. "It probably leads to a dead end somewhere in the Slates."

Mason moved forward, though he seemed hesitant.

They didn't go far before coming to another sharp turn, and then they broke through the end of the tunnel and back into the light of the sun. Eric blinked to take in the view. "That shortcut saves miles around the bluffs."

"Too bad it's so narrow. It would be hard to get an army through it."

"I can't believe no one else knows this is here." Eric holstered his Beacon, and they mounted their horses again. "How'd you find it?"

"Seria found it."

"That so?"

Mason nodded as they set a comfortable pace. "Said she stumbled across it one night on her way fishing."

"Try as I might, I can't picture her fishing."

"She's pretty adept at it." A slight smile lifted Mason's voice. Then he sobered.

"You're missing her, aren't you?"

Mason scowled, looking more like his disgruntled self. "She's better off without me."

"Maybe." Given the past few months, Eric could not deny it. "But you're not the only one who misses her."

"You're right. Her donkey is quite unhappy."

Eric laughed. "So is Nola." He sighed, thinking of Seria's sunny personality. "Nay, there are quite a few who miss her." Without permission, his mind drifted to her friend. "Both of them."

Silence stretched between them until Mason broke it. "You and Lena, huh?"

Eric started and blinked at him. "What? Are you reading my mind?"

Mason's brows rose as he pointed to the Beacon. "Not with you wearing that thing."

Eric groaned and dropped his head back at giving himself away. "I meant only that the soldiers miss her tarts." His denial sounded juvenile.

"Mmhmm. Does she know?"

His neck heated, and he scowled. "No one is supposed to know." He shifted his position. "Besides, it's a little hard to communicate when I don't even know where she is anymore."

Mason fell silent, but Eric caught a hint of regret. "It's not the right time, anyway," he added. "I've got a war to fight. It wouldn't be fair to make any kind of declaration. And that's if she would even be interested."

Stretching his neck, Mason asked, "Want me to see if she likes you if I see her again?"

The idea took root in his mind before he realized what he was doing. "What? Mason, nay! That's not appropriate."

Mason gave a snort that sounded almost like a laugh and held his hands up. "You were the one thinking about it."

"Not seriously." Eric scowled at him, not sure if he was glad or annoyed to see Mason's mood lighten. He had not expected to become the object of his teasing.

Conversation fell away as they turned west. The trip to Rackson was made with little difficulty. Eric spoke at length to the Stewards based there. Most of the buildings had been burned during the attack, but a few were solid enough to house the knights. Mason, he noticed, was quieter than usual as they moved about the town. Eric suspected his thoughts were taken up with the last time he had been in Rackson, when he was wounded and taken in by Seria.

There were no reports of difficulty anywhere near the area, to Eric's relief, so he did not stay long. He spent the rest of the afternoon touching base with a couple of other small villages not far from Rackson. The Stewards at Rackson kept an eye on them as well, but he wanted to see for himself that all was well. He talked with the leaders, offered what encouragement and council he could, and urged them to come to the Gateway, but most insisted that Jader had no interest in them anymore. Not since his attention had been turned to the fort.

Eric could only hope they were right. The courage and determination of the people bolstered him. Their faith in the Lambient was strong.

The sun had begun its downward arc by the time they turned for home again. Trees sprang up on one side, fed by the creek that flowed nearby. On the other side was the base of the mountains. The setting was peaceful and soothing.

"What did he mean about why he came here?"

Eric rested his hand on his thigh, Oakley's steady rhythm relaxing. "Who?"

"That councilman." Mason fidgeted. "He said something about the Lambient coming to earth."

Pulling his gaze from the woods, Eric stared at Mason. "Have you never heard the story?" When Mason did not answer, he winced. "I'm sorry. I forget you've not been exposed to the teachings. There's a written record of Lambient taking the form of a man to fight against Shreil's attack on humankind." Wonder always filled him when he contemplated the story. "The story says He stood side by side with my ancestors against Shreil's darkness. Even gave His life to save the people."

Mason's head swiveled his way. "He died?"

Eric's mouth flicked up. "And then came back to life."

"How could He do that?"

"He's the Creator of all life. Death could not hold him. But that's why we can be victorious against all of Shreil's attacks. Because He's already won the victory."

A thoughtful look crossed Mason's face. "I've never heard that."

"I can believe that. Jader would hate the story, and many people deny it."

"It sounds too easy."

"It does," Eric agreed. "But that's because we're incapable of understanding the depth of His power and His love for us."

Mason still looked skeptical.

"Can I be honest with you?" Eric waited for Mason's hesitant nod. "I think you're trying too hard to prove yourself." When Mason stiffened, Eric put his hand up. "Hear me out."

Mason did not look at him, but when he did not argue, Eric went on.

"You know that what you experienced with the Lambient is real. Even if you don't understand it, you know in your heart He has forgiven you. But you also knew that your presence was not going to be easily accepted. So, you came in determined that you had to prove yourself. And in doing so, put up some walls that keep others from getting too close."

Mason had nothing to say, and Eric did not press him. The fact that he didn't get defensive was enough to let Eric know he was at least considering what he had said.

They were still more than a mile from the tunnel when Mason pulled to a stop. "I hear voices," he murmured.

"Where?" All Eric could hear was the rustle of a breeze through the limbs.

Mason pointed straight ahead. He tilted his head, listening. "Sounds like someone making camp."

Understanding came quickly then. Mason must be hearing the muffled sounds of Shadowmen.

Eric's pulse quickened. Why would Shadowmen be setting up camp out here? "How many?"

"I only hear two."

They could bypass them and skip the tunnel, but that would take them miles from their path. And that didn't mean there were not more out there. "Let's circle around them," he said. "Catch them in the middle." It was not a coincidence that these Shadowmen were out here. If they could catch them before they carried out whatever their intentions were, that would save a lot of trouble.

"I can hide in the dark. What are you going to do if they spot you?"

Eric pulled his Beacon. "Put a little light on them."

Mason's apprehension was thick, but he dismounted the roan and tethered it to a limb. Then he disappeared into the trees.

Eric tied Oakley nearby and headed for the spot Mason had pointed out. A thin tendril of smoke wafted up through the trees. He ducked into the brush and pressed ahead. Now he could hear the voices as he neared the site. Then finally, Eric could see movement. Sure enough, two men sat in front of the campfire, facing his direction. From where he crouched, he could see their stones hanging around their necks. Why were two men out here by themselves?

Eric's skin prickled, and a sense of dread dropped on him. He spun around on his heels and snapped his Beacon up.

Half a dozen more Shadowmen came bearing down on him.

20

He has led me into darkness; where is the light?
-The Sacred Code

The closer Mason got to the campsite, the more ill at ease he felt. He crept through the trees, keeping his eye on the open space up ahead where the men sat and chatted, as if unconcerned about being heard or seen.

Why would two Shadowmen camp out here by themselves? He slowed to a complete stop, trying to understand his former mentor's reasoning. What purpose would Jader have for them being way out here? There was no town within miles.

This was no coincidence. They were here for a reason, to carry out a specific task that brought them to this location at this particular moment. They weren't here when he and Eric had passed over that morning. So why now?

The hair on the back of his neck stood up. *Blades.* They had walked into a trap.

He started to backtrack, but when yelling erupted on the other side of the site, he tensed. Eric was over there. The two Shadowmen before the fire jumped to their feet, but instead of running to where the commotion was, they turned and headed for *him.*

Mason pulled his sword and met them head-on. He had no Beacon to fight with, but he pulled his dagger as the first one reached him with his sword high. Mason ducked it and stepped close enough to slash the knife across the man's throat. As he fell, the second one attacked.

They traded several blows, Mason staying light on his feet and back-stepping to trick his opponent into overconfidence. Sure enough, the Shadowman grew cocky and careless, leaving himself open after Mason feigned a stumble. Taking advantage of the moment, Mason disarmed the man and smashed the hilt across his face.

His blood pounded in his ears as he ran in the direction Eric should be. Already the noise had died down, and he did not want to imagine why.

A twig broke behind him, and he spun around, holding his sword up. A shadow took shape, drawing closer to him. He backed further into the shelter of the trees, unsure if he could be seen.

The shape shifted until he could make out a woman. Dreeya appeared, her eyes pinned to him. He froze as she stopped in front of him, her long hair hung in a low ponytail. "What are you doing out here, Dreeya?"

"You seem a little lost. I thought you might need some help finding your way back."

Keeping his blade between them, Mason tried to reach her thoughts, but they were closed off to him. "I can manage."

She raised her head with a sneer. "I wasn't asking."

Mason backed away, his grip tightening on his sword. "Stay where you are."

She gave a small laugh. "Please, Mason. Don't think you can control me like some dim-witted fool." She reached for a chain around her neck, yanking the purple stone at the end from beneath her clothes. "I don't take orders from you." She let out a screech and lunged for him.

Mason jumped out of reach of the sword that appeared in her hand. He sidestepped and blocked her wild blows, waiting for his moment. She had always been fast, but also impatient, which always worked in his favor when they sparred in their early days. Sure enough, she grew tired of his evasion and moved a little too quickly, leaving herself unbalanced. He took advantage of the moment to knock her flat on her back with the tip of his sword against her neck.

"You gonna kill me? Or are you too good for that now?"

"I'm not going to kill you, Dreeya. But I am going to give you another chance to think things through." He reached down to yank the chain off her neck and drilled his eyes into hers as he tossed her stone. "Get away from here. Don't come back."

A leer spread across her lips. "Nice try."

Mason looked up, his heart dropping at the shadowy forms that encircled him, their swords drawn. His mind flew through his options, but they were few. He couldn't even use Dreeya as leverage. The Shadowmen would not spare her to get at him.

"Drop your sword," one man ordered.

Not ready to concede, Mason straightened and gripped it with both hands. "You don't want to do this."

A blast of cold air hit him, taking his breath away and sending chills up and down his skin.

Another man stepped out of the woods, his tall silhouette more than recognizable. Bruin emerged into view and faced him, as cold as ice.

Something cracked across the back of Mason's head, and he fell to his hands and knees, gasping at the lights that exploded in his skull. A cold awareness filled him. He would not be meeting up with Eric again. He may very well be dead by the time the prince made it back to the fort. *If* Eric made it back.

He raised his heavy head as Bruin's footsteps drew nearer, clamping his mouth shut against any weakness they hoped to see from him.

"Hold him," Bruin growled, his eyes almost white.

Two men grabbed Mason from where he knelt on the ground and jerked him up by the arms. He gave another quick look around, searching for access into someone's will. But all their minds were blocked. Bruin produced a coil from his belt, and Mason's heart dropped to the ground at the thought of his hanging. But it was not a noose Bruin unwound, but a whip.

There was no way to fight his way from this, so he would not give Bruin the satisfaction of seeing him struggle in vain. His skin already recoiled at the coming pain, but he glared back at Bruin with a clenched jaw.

Bruin flexed his fingers and slid them along the whip. "You think you're ready for this, don't you?" His whiskers shifted around his cruel grin. "Think because you've been with the Stewards for so long that you can handle the agony I'm about to put you through?"

The men holding him dragged him to a tree and pulled his shirt off him, opening it up for the stripes of the whip. Then they wrapped his arms around the trunk of the tree, lashing his wrists together. Briefly, he wished Seria had taught him how to escape his bonds, but that would not help him in this situation. There were too many of them. He said nothing, though his muscles clenched at the sound of Bruin's approach.

Then there was a crack, and the whip tore into his skin. He gritted his teeth, digging his fingertips into the bark of the tree. Before he could draw another breath, another lash struck him, sending fire through his back. Then another. A grunt slipped out through his clenched jaw.

There was a pause and then footsteps. Bruin rounded the tree, dragging the whip behind him. "If I had my way, I'd string you up from the nearest tree. You remember that's what we do with traitors, right?"

Shon's lifeless body wavered through Mason's pain-fogged mind. He unclenched his teeth so he could speak. "You mean that's how you kill anyone who doesn't agree with you."

Bruin leaned closer. "You're fortunate Jader wants you alive and alert. Or I'd make a mess of you right now." Then he walked out of sight.

Mason did not move, every muscle quivering in anticipation of the strike of the whip. Whispers sounded behind him, then muffled footsteps moving away. He leaned against the tree, dragging in a ragged breath, and waited for the men to release him and drag him wherever Bruin wanted him.

Another snap split the air, hitting him across open wounds. Caught by surprise, he could not stop the cry that burst from him. Pain like nothing he'd ever felt consumed him, lighting his already torn skin with red-hot agony. The whip struck again.

CRACK!

Eric yanked his Beacon back, pulling the coil of light back into the rod. His lungs seized for air, and his muscles spasmed.

Three Shadowmen fell dead from the light whip. The rest flinched and shielded their eyes, giving Eric enough time to use his Gift to pull their weapons from their grip. But more burst through the foliage around him. Across the campsite, he heard more yelling, and his heart sank. He could not hold them off for long.

Stretching his hand for a fallen log nearby, he lifted it in the air and threw it against the newcomers. Then he shot another blast of light from his Beacon and bolted for where the horses were tied.

Oakley and Mason's roan were still where they had left them, to his relief. But the roan's empty saddle ramped his concern up again. Where was Mason? He paused at Oakley's side, his mind spinning. His heart knocked around in his chest like a dislodged stone on a hillside. The Shadowmen would pursue him, may already be closing in on him, but he would not hear them come up behind him.

"Mason!" he risked calling out, but all he heard was the distant shouting turn into jeering.

Not good.

The thought of leaving Mason behind went against everything in him, but something told him there was nothing he could do now. He could not fight against a company of Shadowmen on his own. And it would be dark soon.

He's in My hands.

The silent whisper both comforted and wrecked at him. Self-loathing gutted him as he ripped the ties loose of both horses and jumped on Oakley's back. He would have to ride hard to get back here before the sun went down with reinforcements to help Mason.

If it was not too late by then.

Bruin stepped back as the Reader slumped against the tree, blood pouring from the deep cuts on his back. At his signal, two Shadowmen untied Mason's hands and let him fall. He slid down to the ground and landed on his side with a groan. Blood coated his back. For a long moment, he didn't move, and Bruin almost hoped he would die where he lay. Jader wouldn't be happy, but Bruin felt no remorse.

But with slow, clumsy movements, Mason rolled over and pushed himself up on his hands and knees. He raised his head, blinking heavily, and stared up at Bruin, challenging him still yet.

Amusement cut through Bruin's indignation, and he leered at the broken man before him. Mason had no idea what he was about to go through.

"Cover the wounds so he doesn't bleed to death," he ordered. "And then get him mounted. Jader will want to see him."

21

I am the Light of this world. Follow Me and you will not stumble through the dark. The path before you will be flooded with the light of life.
-The Sacred Code

Lionel had just released his men and dismounted when Prince Eric thundered into the inner courtyard on his big gray, leading the red roan that belonged to Mason.

"What happened?" Braylee exclaimed, catching the roan's reins.

"Shadowmen!" Eric spun Oakley to a stop. "We were ambushed. They captured Mason."

Lionel's feet rooted to the ground as murmurs rose around him.

Dudley arrived on the scene. "Where?"

"On the other side of the bluffs." Eric addressed Dudley. "Captain, I may have need of your long sight."

"Of course."

Eric looked up at the purple sky. "We don't have much time."

Braylee called out. "Let's get a search party together. Be mounted and ready to ride in five minutes!"

People scattered then, with some knights hurrying to the barn to get their horses. Civilians drifted off, eager to spread the word.

Lionel walked away, a sickening dread dragging his steps. On the way, he spotted the shocked, anxious faces of Mason's supporters. Dakim, his biggest fan in the cadets. Crue, the boy who had been controlled into bringing Ollen's body back.

This is my fault. Lionel was no fool. He knew the only reason Eric had taken Mason out on a scouting assignment was because of the incident last night. An incident Lionel was responsible for.

He had spoken the truth to Braylee in that he had never told Hiram to turn Mason in. But he had not discouraged his actions either. Hiram had known of Lionel's animosity toward Mason, had shared in it. When he assured Lionel that he was watching the former Shadowman, Lionel had let the statement slide. In the back of his mind, he had even hoped the impulsive militiaman would be useful. But now things had gone too far, and Mason would pay the price for it.

The interrogation the night before had ended with Hiram and his companions placed under disciplinary action for their intoxication and harassment. They would take on extra duties and spend some time in isolation. Lionel had caught Mason's bewilderment when he was not reprimanded for working with a juvenile. Hiram had become so sullen that he said nothing about it, allowing Lionel to keep his silence.

But his conscience had grated at him all night long.

The rumble of hooves turned his head. A company of at least twenty men rode out the gates, led by Eric and Dudley. Braylee stood by and watched them go, his arms crossed.

Lionel had not volunteered to join the search party for the same reason he was sure no one asked him to. More than likely, it was the same reason no one spoke to him as they milled about. He doubted anyone blamed him for the abduction. They would not know the subtle part he had played. But he had made no secret of his resentment of the man. He caught a few curious glances as he made his way to the mess hall. People watched him, waiting to see how he would react to the news that his antagonist had been captured by Shadowmen.

Lionel had never been a favorite around here. Even after Ollen had died, he couldn't fill that role. So, he had quit caring what people thought of him. But in doing so, he had forgotten some of the other traits that made him a Steward. Grace. Patience. Forgiveness.

Bypassing the door into the mess hall, Lionel rounded the corner until he was in the back, away from nosy eyes. He leaned back against the wall and ran a trembling hand over his face. "Dear Lambient, what have I done?"

Unknown location in The Gateway

Breathing hurt, and blood coated his throat, choking him. Weakness made his limbs heavy, and pain racked his back. The rag wrapped tightly around his eyes made his head ache.

Mason tried not to dwell on the agony that rolled over him with every step the horse beneath him made. Tried not to imagine what Jader and Bruin had planned for him. Instead, he thought of Seria. For the first time in months, he permitted himself to fill his mind with the memory of her bright smile, sunshine hair, and sparkling spirit.

Before, it was too hard to think of her, to be reminded of her when he doubted he would ever see her again. But it didn't matter so much now, because he was pretty sure he was about to die. Remembering her took his mind off what was happening. He talked to her in his mind, told her how much he loved her.

She couldn't save him, but he did not expect a rescue. Maybe Lionel was right. Maybe Lambient had only seen fit to use him for the Stewards' benefit for as long as he was useful. Maybe that was why he had been captured now, to pay for his crimes. His usefulness had worn off.

Everyone would be better off once he was gone, himself especially. Seria would mourn him, but she would get over it, and maybe even find it easier to build a new life without him in the background of her mind. Eric would feel some guilt, but it wasn't his fault.

Just let me die well. He ground his teeth together as he tried not to fall off the horse. From what he could hear, riders were positioned on either side of him, and front and back.

To his relief, Eric had not been caught, so the prince would still be able to lead his army against Jader's onslaught. That brought him some satisfaction.

The hoofbeats below took on a new sound, hard and dull. The scent changed as well, losing its green, grassy smell and becoming dry and dusty. It seemed they had left the woods behind and shifted closer to the mountains. So, if they weren't heading back to Ignadon for his public execution, where were they taking him?

The air cooled, and the darkness became deeper. His heart sank, though he did not know what difference it made if night fell or not. He was on his own, surrounded by dark soldiers who hated him.

His horse halted, and the sound of leather creaking and footfalls filled the space before someone jerked him sideways. With his hands bound, he had no leverage to catch himself and fell hard on his shoulder and hip. There were a few chuckles, then rough hands pulled him back to his feet.

They went on, pushing him through thick, thorny foliage and into what felt like a narrow tunnel in a rock wall. For a moment, he wondered if they had found Seria's shortcut.

But it went on too long and turned too many times. Then he was shoved into a wider space. An echo surrounded him, and his brows bunched, though even that slight movement hurt. The ground was smooth and packed, and the voices of his captors bounced off of some kind of barrier all around them. A cave?

A familiar blast of heat hit him, drying his lungs. A strange pull drew him forward, stirring up the same reaction he had experienced in Seria's tunnel at the fork. Eric had not seemed to notice the eerie atmosphere when they crossed through.

"Stop here," Bruin ordered from somewhere ahead. "Emperor Jader will be here soon."

Someone pulled the blindfold off, and he blinked at the tall, fuzzy form until Bruin took shape, stone-cold and sharp.

"Welcome home," the commander said and stepped aside.

Mason examined his surroundings. Though the area was expansive, rocky walls enclosed him on all sides, making him feel closed in. Large stalactites hung from the high roof like gaping teeth. The air in the cave was hot and thick, and everything was cast in a red sheen.

Bruin clamped a hard hand on Mason's shirt and heaved him in further. Mason's heart jumped at the canyon that appeared at his feet. He jolted back, but Bruin's firm hold prevented him from moving a safe distance away. The hole was wide and deep, the lava-streaked sides capturing Mason's awareness. Within the red walls were cracks of deep purple, strains of another source of stone shining through the fiery rocks.

His breath returned in rapid gasps as his chest heated right where the Shadowstone used to hang. Something within him reached for the pit before him, but he leaned back as far as Bruin would allow him as it became very clear where they had taken him.

The Shadowpit.

Bruin swiveled him back around. Dizziness made his head swim, and he swayed on his feet. "Better make yourself comfortable," Bruin said, gripping Mason's shirt in his clenched fingers. "You're going to be here for a while."

Mason stared back at him but could not repress the shudder that went over him. Already sweat poured from every pore of his body, and everything in him ached for the feel of the Shadowstone.

Bruin turned him over to a Shadowman named Naman. Mason had worked with him several times over the years, but Naman was closed off to any familiarity.

Naman and another man dragged him to a hollow in the wall that was too close to the pit for Mason's comfort. His hands were stretched out and padlocked to chains that hung from the ceiling. Then his feet were spread out and chained to shackles on the floor. It was awkward standing spread-eagle, with no place to rest his head or sit. His muscles were tight and sore, the skin on his back stinging.

Of all the scenarios Mason had imagined, this was not one of them. What did they plan to do with him?

A black cloud swirled in front of him, and he wondered if he was losing consciousness. But the fog dissipated, leaving Jader in its place. Very real terror robbed Mason of what little air he had left. If Jader could appear out of thin air, then he was much more formidable than Mason had ever realized.

The emperor walked to stand before Mason, his robes sweeping the ground at his feet. His demeanor was calm, but his eyes were cold. The lighting made his russet hair look black, making him appear even more ominous.

Nothing was said for a long moment. Mason gritted his teeth, refusing to beg for mercy or forgiveness from the man who had deceived him.

Blood poured from a gash on his cheekbone where the end of the whip had caught it. His vision was blurry, his head pounding. His back screamed at him, and air seemed to leak from his lungs. But strength seeped into his resolve, bolstering him. He pushed himself up as tall as he could manage, every move torture. Then he raised his chin to look Jader square in the eye.

"I will not be used by you anymore, Jader."

Instead of growing angry, Jader's thin lips curled up. "We shall see." He turned to the pit and peered within, as if mesmerized. "It is lovely, is it not?" he murmured. "So powerful and brimming with energy."

Mason shut his eyes against the sight, wishing he could plug his ears from the almost soothing sound of Jader's voice that he had fallen prey to so many times before.

"This is the very seat of Shreil's power, and it holds a part of each one of us who has pledged ourselves to him."

"I don't serve him anymore," Mason croaked.

A soft sigh sounded. "After all I have done for you, Mason, all that Shreil has done for us, I am disappointed in the way you have turned from me."

Mason's eyes flew open, and heat surged through him. "You had my brother killed."

"It was a Steward's sword that drained your brother's blood." He stepped closer, his good eye piercing him. "Or have you so easily forgotten?"

"You arranged it."

Eric had shared his suspicion, and Mason had almost gotten a glimpse into Jader's thoughts once. He knew it to be true. Jader was responsible for Liam's death.

Jader folded his hands before his chest, his one seeing eye locked on Mason. A cold feeling of fear and despair wrapped its tentacles around Mason, sucking the oxygen from him. He clenched his jaw to keep his teeth from rattling, fighting to keep his body still. But doubts assailed him.

He would never get out of this cave alive.

No one would come looking for him.

He was alone.

Then Jader lifted his hand, and a chain dangled from his fingers. Mason's eyes riveted on the Shadowstone. His breathing shallowed at the promise of relief it screamed at him. Just the feel of it against his chest would erase the agonizing chill that clung to his spine and froze his fingers. It would fill him with purpose again.

But he forced his gaze away and licked his cracked lips, his tongue thick and dry. "I don't want it."

"By the time we are finished here, you will beg me for it."

He shook his head, but the movement made his head spin. His heart rate accelerated, and spots danced at the edge of his vision. The loss of blood had weakened him, and his body sagged against the padlocks that held him up. Before he was lost to the abyss, Mason foggily wished he could see Seria one last time.

22

The Lambient has risen like the sun in a morning without clouds, and He lives, the rock of our salvation.
-The Sacred Code

When Seria began her job as the king's caretaker, she was given a room off the royal suite to sleep in. It was small and functional, nothing more, but it held a comfortable cot and even a sitting chair. It made sense for her to stay close, in case her patient needed her.

Tonight, sleep was evasive as she stared up at the ceiling, reliving the scene in the kitchen over and over. Anger simmered until she found herself more awake.

"All right, Seria," she said aloud. "You've got to get to sleep." She would be no good to her patient if she had to drag herself about the castle tomorrow.

She wrapped herself in her blanket and rolled over on her side. Pushing the events of the day out of her mind, she relaxed her body into the softness of the bed and felt herself drifting.

I love you, Seria.

Her eyes popped open. Mason's voice had sounded so clear in her head. Had she dreamed it?

I will always love you.

She sat up straight with a gasp. Holding her breath, she waited, but it did not happen again.

What was that all about? She wrapped her arms around her middle, her chest aching. Most of the time, she could stay busy enough to keep from thinking of him too much. Though she still missed him at times, she was at peace with her decision. They were both where they needed to be. But sometimes, she still longed to see him.

Maybe this was one of those times, and her imagination had contrived his voice and those achingly beautiful words.

"Be with him, Lambient," she prayed as she always did when he came to her mind. "Keep him safe, and help him be strong."

She lay down again, but the sound of creaking in the big room next door drifted to her in the dark. It sounded like the king was having trouble resting as well. After a few minutes of listening to him toss and turn, she rose and lit a candle.

"King Aden, are you all right?" she asked as she entered his suite.

He frowned up at her from his bed, his eyes distant. "I need to speak to Eric."

Seria cocked her head at him. "He's at the fort."

"I know." He shifted to a sitting position. "It can't wait."

Wondering if a fever was making him confused, Seria lay a hand on his forehead, but his skin was cool.

Aden reached for something on the table by the bed. "I must speak to him now." He held up a Beacon.

"Oh." Seria bit her lip. "Should I call someone?"

He shook his head and motioned to a small stone basin on a table in the corner of his room. "Just get me over there."

Seeing he would not be swayed, Seria dragged a chair to the low table and padded it with pillows. Then she helped Aden cross the room to the table. He moved slowly and stiffly, leaning on her heavily. He sat on the chair and lowered the light rod into the water.

"Would you like me to step outside?" she asked as the water swirled.

Aden shook his head, not looking away from the basin. Seria moved out of the line of sight but stayed nearby, ready if he needed her. She busied herself with fluffing up the pillows on the four-poster bed, trying not to listen.

A light rose from the water, and Eric's worried voice sounded. "Father, what's wrong?"

"Nothing here," Aden assured, bracing his hands on the basin.

"Then what are you doing up at this hour?"

"Something has happened, hasn't it?"

Eric's sigh preceded his next words. "I'm afraid so."

Despite her good intentions, Seria strained to hear him.

"Mason Grey was taken captive by Shadowmen."

Her heart crashed, and she spun around with a soft cry. "Oh, no, please." Thick strands of fear held her, as cold as her fingers gripping her nightdress.

To his credit, Aden did not look her way. "How did it happen?"

"We were coming back from Rackson." Eric sounded weary. "We were ambushed by Shadowmen and separated. I managed to get away, but he was gone."

Seria slumped against the bed and slid to her knees on the floor.

Shadowmen, the very men he had betrayed. She drew in a shuddering breath. What would they do to a traitor? What would Jader do if he got his hands on him again? Tears blinded her, and her imagination ran away with her, flooding her mind with images of Mason being beaten and tortured. Or even executed.

Eric's voice drifted to her through the fog of fear. "We went back out to search for him, but night fell too fast. I fear they will be long gone by morning, but we won't stop looking."

"Jader lost him once. He'll not easily give him up a second time."

Seria stifled a sob as she pictured that teasing glint in Mason's amber eyes. That shock of hair that swept across his forehead. The way he clung to her the last time they spoke. *Oh, Lambient, please.*

The bed creaked beside her, and she started. King Aden was sitting on the side of the bed, his blue eyes dark with compassion.

Swiping at her wet cheeks with a trembling hand, she forced herself to her feet. "I'm sorry, Your Majesty." She clenched her jaw and tried to still her chin from quivering. "I didn't mean to leave you on your own."

"Miss Seria."

She shook her head against the emotion threatening to drown her. "I'm fine."

"Little one, you don't have to hide your concern from me." At his gentleness, she broke, and a sob escaped. She tried to turn away, but

Aden's worn, soft hands took hold of both hers. "I mean it. You have every right to be concerned for him. I know what he means to you."

"What's going to happen to him?" she asked.

"I don't know. The emperor is a ruthless leader. But don't lose heart now. From what I have witnessed, Mason has a strong constitution." He squeezed her hands. "He needs you to be strong for him."

How could she be strong when everything in her shook, ready to collapse like a house of cards?

He gave her a smile, as if he knew what she was thinking. "You pray for him tonight, Miss Seria, with all the faith you have." His eyes clouded over. "Pray for him and everyone who will risk themselves to find him. Because I think we both know that Lambient is the only one who can rescue him."

Aden tried to get Seria to take the next day off, but she refused. She knew it was audacious of her to refuse the king's direction, but he did not know how she needed to stay busy. If she sat in her room with nothing to do but wonder what Mason was going through, she'd fall apart.

She talked briefly with Lena that morning and told her what she learned. Lena promised to keep the news to herself and offered Seria the encouragement she needed to get through the day. Seria tried not to dwell on what was happening and focus on her duties, but every time her mind drifted in that direction, she sent a prayer upward.

Aden did not eat much and was quiet and pensive as the morning passed. Seria checked on him multiple times, but he insisted he felt well enough, and his breathing was not labored. His mind was clearly at the fort with his son and Stewards. She caught him staring up at a sword hanging on a simple bracket on the wall beside his bed. At his grimace, she asked, "Are you all right?"

He blinked and stirred. "Just thinking. In my younger days, I would've been right there with the Stewards."

"Is that your sword?"

"Aye." Then he shook his head. "Well, Lavrynth was the last sword I carried. It's the family sword, passed down from generation to generation."

"Eric showed it to me once." Seria perched on the edge of his bed, glad to have something to talk about. "It's beautiful."

"It holds more than beauty. It carries the blood of my ancestors and the Lambient."

"Your son mentioned something about that, but I'm afraid I didn't understand what he meant."

Aden brightened. "Lambient Himself stepped down to this earth to fight alongside my ancestors against the power of Shreil. Even sacrificed His life to save the people from darkness."

"I've heard this, but I never quite grasped what it really meant. It's too awful to think about."

"It would be, save for the fact that He defeated death and then returned to defeat Shreil. Sent him to the pit of the earth where he belongs. Unfortunately, mankind is still tempted by his dark powers, so he lives on, always trying to usurp Lambient's authority."

Awe stirred within her. "Put that way, what a wonderful story. It's too bad so few know it."

"Sadly, many have tried to cover the Lambient's existence. It's too uncomfortable. It means that they have someone to answer to. History is told, and truth is sometimes left out. But it's in the Sacred Code."

"Do the Stewards all know this?"

"By the time they take on their Beacon, they do. Every man and woman comes to the Stewardship with varying levels of knowledge, though their commitment is sincere."

"My father didn't talk about it much. I wonder why." Seria cocked her head. "But then again, my parents probably could not trust me to keep my mouth shut when it came to secrets."

Aden pointed to the sword. "That was my first sword, given to me by my father before Lavrynth was passed down to me."

Seria stood to get a better look at it.

"Go ahead and take it down."

She was hesitant to touch it, lest she send it crashing to the floor. But she reached out and took it in her hands. The weight of it reminded her of her lessons with Mason, and her throat constricted.

"It's very basic," Aden said. "But it does the job. That's the sword Eric carried when he first took the command of the Stewards."

That would have been when the young prince made the devastating order that led to the Handan massacre.

"He was quite against taking Lavrynth when he returned to The Gateway, but I knew it was time. He will need it to defeat the power that Jader wields."

At the mention of Jader, Seria swallowed. "Maybe someday, Eric's son will use this one before he is given Lavrynth."

"That is my hope."

Seria positioned the sword back in its place. "Thank you for sharing with me. I find it all very fascinating. Especially about the Lambient."

"You are very welcome." He rested his head back against the pillow. "It's a good reminder for me, as well. It's easy to get so caught up in the work that we forget Who it is we're doing the work for."

Seria was caught by the statement, thinking of all the times she fretted about the kind of work she was required to do. Maybe she was guilty of the same thing. Maybe she needed to focus more on the One she was working for.

23

Woe to those who sit in darkness and the shadow of death, bound with affliction and iron.
-The Sacred Code

The Shadowpit

Thirst was a constant itch, drying his mouth and thickening his tongue. His bones ached from the awkward stance, and he longed for something to rest his head against. Even a rock behind him would offer some relief.

Mason tried to swallow, but it was like trying to force a mouthful of gravel down. He blinked from his half-asleep stupor and looked around. Alone again. That was a bit of a relief in itself, but he knew it would not last. Every time he managed to slip into some form of sleep, someone always dragged him back to wakefulness, usually with a sharp open-handed slap. Bruin did not leave him for long, and if he wasn't there, one of his men was.

The cave was hot and sticky. And dark, though Mason did not have any trouble making out the red-tinted walls around him. Sweat poured from his pores, and his limp hair hung in his eyes.

Echoing footsteps. He raised his head and braced himself against Bruin's return. But it was Jader who appeared in the arched entrance. Something that looked a lot like regret twisted his features.

Mason stiffened as he approached, already dreading the appearance of the Shadowstone that was sure to come. But Jader stopped at the

Shadowpit and gazed into its depths. Nothing was said for so long that Mason grew more and more uncomfortable. Was this another tactic to put him off his guard?

"Have you ever heard of Moverik the Great?"

The question was so random Mason almost laughed.

Jader did not wait for an answer. "He was a master Shadowman almost two hundred years ago. Records tell of the great power he wielded and the connection he shared with Shreil."

Already bored, Mason looked up at the ceiling, counting stalactites to distract himself.

Jader droned on. "Moverik was the first man to discover this very place. And he was also a Reader."

Despite his resolve, Mason's eyes flitted to Jader's pleased smirk.

"Moverik's Gift grew unstoppable, and he became a great tool in the hand of Shreil. Together, they destroyed those who stood against them." Jader folded his hands. "I have always been fascinated by the power Moverik carried. To possess the ability to control the wills of others for a greater purpose."

"I don't think that was Lambient's purpose," Mason ground out.

The emperor stiffened at the mention of the Lambient. "You were on the path to greatness. Your Gift had you poised to rule this land."

Mason scoffed. "With you at the helm, right?"

"I am merely a willing captain for Shreil's service."

"And if I had the choice, I'd be rid of it for that very reason."

Jader sighed. "I wish you would not fight me so much, my boy."

"I'm not your boy."

"After all I have done for you? I took you in and raised you. I cared about you as if you were my own son. Still do."

Mason let out a short laugh. "Is that why you're torturing me?"

"I am not torturing you, Mason." His eyes widened in his fervor. "I am trying to *save* you."

"Too late. Someone else already did."

"And yet here you are, left alone to suffer. Where is your savior now?" Jader stepped closer. "Tell me, Mason. How did the Stewards accept you when you claimed to be one of them?"

Mason pressed his split lips together and stared at the wall behind Jader. He would not allow the emperor to get into his head.

"What did you think would happen? Did you think they would welcome you with open arms?"

"They had reason not to." How could he expect anyone to see him as a friend when he had acted as an enemy? Eric was right. Mason's pride had put a barrier between him and the Stewards.

"They rejected you?"

Don't answer. Jader would only twist his words.

"Of course they rejected you." Jader pressed a hand on Mason's chest. "Because of the power you hold here."

Cold and heat drilled into him, sucking the air from him and shooting razor-sharp streaks through his limbs. He clenched his jaw against the agony trying to escape his lips, his back arching and his body shaking.

Jader withdrew his hand, and the sensation stopped. "The power that you accepted and bound yourself to."

Mason coughed. "I changed my mind. It's called a choice, Jader. The very thing you advocate for in your Realm."

"That is not an option." Jader's voice chilled. "Once you take the Shadow Pledge, there is no turning back."

Lifting his heavy head, Mason met Jader's one-eyed gaze. "You do not control my heart and will, Jader."

Jader released a thin smile, sending an uneasy shiver down Mason's spine. "That is what you think, my boy." He left without another word, leaving Mason to wonder what he meant.

Eric leaned against the stone wall of the fort as the last of the search party rode through the gates of the outer wall below. Without Mason.

He bowed his head in defeat. The second night since Mason's disappearance approached, and there was still no sign of him or the Shadowmen who had taken him.

For the hundredth time, Eric beseeched a higher power. "Why?" he whispered into the still air. How had Eric not sensed the danger before they separated? Why had Lambient allowed Eric to escape, leaving Mason on his own?

But there was no answer. His intuition did not make him omniscient, and Eric could not guess Lambient's reasoning.

Eric's stomach tightened with every minute Mason was in their possession. The Reader was vulnerable right now. What if his recent struggles made it hard for him to stand his ground? And what would they do to him if he did?

Not only did he worry for the man on a personal level, but as the leader of an army facing war, he was fully aware of how dangerous Mason would be if Jader once again had him under his influence.

Braylee joined him on the wall, his presence solid and reassuring. "Despite everything you're telling yourself, Eric, there was nothing you could do at the time."

"I never should've left him." Maybe he had misunderstood the direction to leave him.

"You both might've been captured then."

Eric could not deny the possibility.

"Have you heard the rumors?"

"What rumors?"

Braylee rested his elbows on the wall. "Some of the militiamen are saying Mason gave you the slip to go back."

Eric gave a huff. "It doesn't matter. They're going to believe what they want."

Braylee scratched his whiskered jaw. "I suspect Hiram started it to deflect the pressure off of his actions."

"Well, it won't work. He will still answer for what he did."

"I think Lionel is a little shaken up," Braylee said. "Mason's capture is a weight he has to carry, even if he doesn't like him."

A heavy breath left Eric's chest. "Two days, Braylee. What is he going through?"

The other man didn't respond for a long moment. "We can't dwell on that. Mason accepted the Lambient's hand on his life, even if he struggles with forgiving himself. The Lambient is in him and with him. He can do more for him than we ever can."

They stood side by side for a few minutes longer, quiet in their thoughts. Then Braylee straightened and clapped Eric's back. "I'll get the report from this last party so we can decide what to do next."

It was hard not to go back to the same worries that had gripped him before Braylee had joined him. Eric closed his eyes and breathed deeply, trying to release his cares back to the Lambient. Mason was in His hands now.

He turned to leave the wall.

The Shadowpit.

He froze, his skin prickling as Mason's voice reverberated in his head. It had happened once before in the Gateway. His heart pounded as he looked back out at the sunlit valley. "Mason?" he whispered. Was the Reader trying to reach him again?

I'm in the Shadowpit.

Eric sucked in a breath. Was it possible? Had they taken him to the very source of their power, the source Eric had sought for so many years? Could Mason lead them there?

Where, Mason?

He waited, but heard nothing.

24

My days are like a declining shadow; I am withered like dying grass.
-The Sacred Code

Mason lost all track of time. How long had he been chained by the Shadowpit? Days? A week? Longer?

Hunger gnawed at his hollow stomach, aching for the next bite of gruel that would be offered to him. He would take whatever they gave him so he would have the strength to get out of this. If he ever did.

The quiet was enough to drive him mad, suffocating him like a thick, woolen cloak on a hot summer's day. It pierced his mind, turning his thoughts more and more to the relief the pit offered. The source of the Shadowstone.

Whenever that happened, he would force his mind away, thinking of anything that would distract him from the Shadowstone calling to him. Teaching Crue to use a sword. Training with the cadets. Stealing carrots from the kitchen for Sanjo. He mostly thought of Seria. The memory of the radiance of her smile, the light in her green eyes, the glow of her innocence—it kept him from drowning in darkness.

But it was getting harder. He could handle the pain from Bruin's blows. Even the thirst and hunger could be ignored. He was a soldier. It was the pull of the Shadowpit that scared him. He couldn't shake it. And Jader's frequent visits made him weaker against his words. What if he couldn't hold up?

He tried to pray, but his prayers were fragmented pleas that made little sense. Maybe the Lambient was done with him.

In desperation, he attempted to reach out with his mind to Eric. It had worked once in the Gateway when he warned Eric against walking into a trap. So, he called out again and again, calling out the name of the place. But he had nothing more to share about the location. He had been blindfolded for the whole journey, though it had not taken long to get here. Maybe Eric could track it down.

But it was more likely no one was looking for him. Why would they? Mason had been nothing but a trial since granted the chance to join their ranks. He walked around with a chip on his shoulder, holding himself apart from them as if he were the one with reason to hold a grudge.

Dreeya arrived with his gruel. She walked with purposeful steps and held the spoon of the grainy substance to his lips. He sucked it in greedily, licking every remnant he could off the spoon before she withdrew. She stared at him for a long moment, her eyes hooded. "You look pathetic."

He forced the mush down his parched throat. "What makes you say that?" He forced a tone of lightness into his hoarse voice.

"You're doing this to yourself, you know." She set the spoon aside on a rock and put her hands on her shapely hips. "All you have to do is admit you were wrong. The emperor is willing to forgive everything."

"Nay. He wants to use me. That's not forgiveness."

"That's funny coming from someone whose Gift involves using other people."

"You're right." He shook his hair from his eyes. "I have no more right forcing my will on someone than Jader has."

"Don't you miss what you had?" A hint of vulnerability crossed her stony features. "When it was you and me? And Shon?"

The mention of his friend cut like a razor blade. He drew a shallow breath into his thin lungs. "I do miss him."

"Then why would you run to the very thing that got him killed?"

He shook his head. "Nay, Dreeya. The truth didn't get him killed. Jader's hatred for the truth is why Shon was executed."

She narrowed her eyes at him. "I used to admire you, you know. You had a purpose, and nothing was going to shake you from it. You were strong."

"I was weak."

"How can you say that? You worked for everything you earned. You were the most respected soldier in Bruin's command."

"I was weak," Mason repeated. "It was easy to succumb to the anger and let it turn into hatred. Vengeance is not strength. It's weakness."

She gaped at him. "You sound as deluded as those Stewards, Mason."

"Do *you* ever wish things were different?" he asked before she left.

"What things?"

He stretched his sore back, hissing as the stripes pulled. "Your life. What it could've been. Aren't you ever angry at what it took from you?"

"What has it taken from me?"

"Your family. Your home." Mason watched Dreeya's expression flicker from annoyance to something he couldn't define. "Jader robbed you of a childhood."

"Oh, please." Dreeya scoffed. "My family had nothing. Poor, pitiful wasted members of society who were more interested in gaining what their offering could bring them. In the end, they chose to keep their son and turned me over."

"I'm sorry."

"Don't be. I'm better off without them."

Mason doubted she believed that as much as she thought she did. "You ever wish you could go back?"

A cold mask slipped over her face. "There isn't anything to go back to," she said. "Or anyone. I made sure of it."

Horror chilled the constant burning within him. "Oh, Dreeya, you didn't."

"Don't you 'Oh, Dreeya' me." She laughed. "How do you think I earned this stone?" She held it up for Mason to see, and he flinched. "This is worth everything I've been through."

"I used to think so." He refused to look at it, his heart sinking at the length she went to get it. "But I was wrong. There are some things more important than power."

"Like?"

"Peace."

She narrowed her eyes at him. "Peace comes when our enemies are dead at our feet."

"And what about when the next enemy rises after that? Or the next one?"

"What are you trying to say, Mason?" She was growing impatient.

"There's no peace in the life you've chosen. Jader is using you like he used me."

As if he heard his name, Jader appeared in a cloud of black smoke.

Dreeya sneered. "I will gladly be used in Emperor Jader's service until the day I die."

Jader did not appear to hold any of the forced compassion he had shown earlier. Mason tightened his lips and studied the rocky ceiling, clenching his fists and trying to close his mind off to whatever Jader would say to him.

"You may go, Sgt. Dreeya. I appreciate your efforts."

Casting Mason one more scornful look, Dreeya bowed and departed, leaving Mason alone with Jader.

"I am disappointed in you, Mason."

"That's nothing new." Gripping the chains that bound his wrists, Mason centered his thoughts again on Seria. A small spot of beauty in the ugliness around him.

"I never expected you, of all people, to fall to the lies of the Passions and their Stewards. You, who thrives in the darkness, want to believe that their paltry lights will hold up to the power of Shreil?" Mason did not respond, his heart rate speeding up as Jader drew closer. "Do you realize what I can do to you? You swore yourself to me, and no shining light can erase the shadow that is in your very soul. You may as well stop fighting it."

Then it began, the sharp, invisible knife that cut through his chest and into his very marrow. Mason gritted his teeth against the scream that tried to break through, fought against the darkness clawing at his mind. Seria's face was lost to him.

Jader's good eye pierced him. "Do not resist, son."

He shook his head, his jaws throbbing with the effort to bite back the agony. *Fight it!* But there was only an emptiness that was quickly being filled with darkness.

"I can make it stop. All you have to do is ask."

Mason tried to shake his head, but another wave hit him, even harder than the last one. A deep groan escaped his lips.

Through it all, Jader stood immobile and impassive. "You accepted the pledge, Mason Grey. It cannot be reversed."

Arching his back against the currents shooting through his spine, Mason tried to shut the words out, but they pounded in his head.

"Darkness begets submission. Submission begets power. Power begets victory."

With the last word, the pain became excruciating, and Mason released a guttural yell, the cry echoing in the cave and reverberating in his ears, in his very being.

"I can make it go away." Jader's voice was calm, soothing, a balm to the pain. He held up a chain, the purple-black stone swinging from the end. "All you have to do is ask."

Everything in him screamed for him to take the offer, to end the torment. The small part that resisted grew weaker until it withered and died. Mason heaved in a jagged breath through splintered ribs and nodded. Just once. Anything to make it stop.

Jader's thin lips curved up as he lifted the stone over Mason's head. The stone settled over that familiar place on Mason's chest as if it had never been missed. And relief swept over him like a cool breeze.

His legs gave out, and he gasped in loud huffs as the pain faded. But his heart squeezed at his failure. When persecution hit, he had caved like a coward.

Jader's hand landed on his shoulder. "It will take some time, but I look forward to having you with us again, son."

Mason shook his head, his attempt feeble now with the Shadowstone hanging on his neck. "Nay."

"There is no use defying me now, Mason."

The truth sank in, rooting itself into his subconscious. He had already relented, allowed Jader to beat him down. What point was there in opposing?

Jader squeezed his shoulder and then stepped back. The black smoke rose and engulfed him, then drifted away. Jader was gone.

The calm did not bring with it the peace he craved. Mason was alone.

Even the Lambient would not help him now after his failure.

Without warning, Ollen's death rushed back to the forefront of his mind. The young Steward had not feared death, had stood his ground with his dying breath. Whereas Mason had failed.

He pushed himself up on his feet again, the weight of the stone heavy on his neck. Regret pulsed through him. The Stewards were right to doubt him. When it came down to it, Mason let his flesh dictate his decisions, even knowing he was wrong.

"I'm sorry." He pushed the words past stiff lips. "I didn't mean it."

He wished he could tear the stone off and throw it as far as he could. But his hands were still bound. Despite his victory, Jader still didn't trust him. The fact brought a little hope to his exhausted spirit. Maybe Jader knew his acceptance of the Shadowstone was not a complete recantation.

But how could he walk away from this, knowing how he had failed? How could he look anyone in the eye with the knowledge that he had succumbed to Jader's empty promises?

Despair pressed on him. The Stewards would never accept him. Especially now. And he didn't blame them. Eric would not trust him to stand strong when he needed him. The captain would know Mason was every bit as useless as he had believed from the beginning. Seria would be so disappointed.

And the Lambient...

Mason squeezed his eyes shut against the stinging that blurred his vision. A fragmented memory of one of the chapel services he had sat through teased at him. The thick voice of the Head Councilman, Gaynor. "Lambient's grace never fails. Even if we do."

He clung to the fragile thread of hope that he had another chance. *Please don't forget me.* He slumped to the ground as low as the chains would allow him, his head bowed low.

I am here.

The whispered words were but a breath against a hurricane bent on destroying him, but he grabbed hold of them with the desperation of a drowning man. He wasn't sure if the Lambient had spoken to him or he was losing his mind, but the promise brought more reassurance than the

Shadowstone ever had. And for now, that was all he had.

Bruin strode into the pit and fixed his hard glare on Mason. The younger man was a mess. Welts and bruises covered his face and arms. Dark circles hung under his eyes, his hair limp and flat. Gone was the cocky sergeant who thought he could do what he wanted. But he had held out longer than expected, Bruin would give him that.

Mason's head lolled, his eyelids pressed together in a feeble attempt to sleep. Bruin stepped in front of him and backhanded him. Mason started and jerked upright, clenching his jaw. "That time of day again?" he croaked.

"Don't give me any lip, boy." Bruin leaned inches from Mason's nose. "You're lucky you're even alive."

"That's what you call this?" Mason drew in a faint breath and winced. "Why don't you kill me and get it over with? That's what you want, isn't it?"

It was, but Jader had a different plan. "It's not time for that. Soon, though, and when it is, I'll make sure I'm the one to do it."

"Didn't know you felt that way about me, Bruin."

Ignoring the jab, Bruin waved some men over. "In the meantime, you're getting a new room."

Apprehension darkened Mason's countenance. "Where're you taking me?"

"You'll see."

Three other Shadowmen took their places on either side of Mason and released the shackles from his ankles and wrists. Unable to hold himself up, he fell to the ground in a heap. Bruin hauled him up on his feet, digging his fingers into Mason's arm.

"No time to rest. Jader has a job for you."

"I'm not doing anything for him," Mason spat, intensity still burning in his eyes.

Bruin snorted. "You have no choice."

One of the men covered Mason's eyes again and another one gagged him, silencing the cocky jabs, as well as any chance for him to control anyone. Bruin turned him over to the others and led the way from the pit, into the narrow tunnel. He rounded a couple sharp corners before emerging back outside into the still of the night. Mason was hauled up onto the back of a horse, his hands tied to the saddle horn. He swayed wildly, but he managed to keep himself upright.

Bruin mounted his horse. "Let's go."

25

I will keep my mind fixed on You and know perfect peace because I trust in You.
-The Sacred Code

Machlin, The Gateway

Mason had no idea how much time had passed by the time Bruin called for a halt. The coolness of the air told him it was after dark, which was no surprise, but that was the only hint he had about the setting around him. Spasms went through the aching muscles of his arms and legs. Hunger and thirst were so constant that he was growing used to it. Maybe he would get another bite of gruel when they got to wherever they were heading.

Someone untied Mason's hands and roughly pulled him down. He had barely found his feet when the blindfold was ripped off. He blinked into the moonlight, savoring the feel of the cool air.

The town was small, more like a village, but Mason had no idea which one it was. Jader's army had been busy recently, doing their best to beat down the towns that cowered under his rule. Had this one succumbed as Mason had?

No one was out at this time of night, though a few windows blinked with lantern light from within. Bruin led the way to the largest building. It looked like the town hall, with wooden posts framing the front. Two men kept a firm grip on his elbows, but he was in no shape to run. Not yet. Not until he got his bearings.

They crossed the portal into the building and entered a large foyer. Mason was taken to a small, dark room off one side. The Shadowmen pressed him to a corner and tied his hands to a large hook in the ceiling, leading Mason to wonder how many prisoners had been tethered to it. His ankles were tied together with tight cords, but this time, he had a wall to lean back on.

Once they were done, the Shadowmen left him alone with his thoughts. He sank back into the corner with a grateful sigh. It was by no means comfortable, but his body had been forced to stay upright with no support, save the chains holding him up, for far too long. Exhaustion weighed him down, slowed his movements, dulled his thinking.

The Shadowstone hummed against his chest, warm and comfortable. But he resisted it, tried to pretend it wasn't there. It had served to stop Jader's torment, but he loathed the feel of it against his skin.

He looked around the room. A large table stood in the middle, lined by tall, straight-backed chairs. There was not much else in the room, save a smaller table where a pail and dipper sat. The very sight of it dried his tongue.

Again, time seemed to pass him by. Tucked away in the middle of the hall as he was, he had no idea if it was morning yet. He dozed for a while, his back pressed against the corner, but the sleep was not restful. It teased him into a sense of floating, then yanked away, leaving him blinking into the shadows.

At least he was not hanging by the pit anymore. The constant call had sunk beneath his skin, luring him back to the shadows. Maybe that was why he had fallen to the temptation of the stone. The strange pull had weakened him. Not that it mattered. It was still wrong, and as soon as he was able, he would chuck this one as far as he could throw it.

He tried to picture Seria again, but she was blurry in his mind, lost in the haze of his weariness. Even her memory could not help him anymore. Only Lambient could.

So, Mason talked to Him in his head, pouring everything out to Him. His shortcomings and his fears. His longing for Seria. His struggle to find his place at the fort. And he begged for forgiveness.

The door opened, cutting off his one-sided monologue. An unfamiliar soldier entered the room, his long, dark hair pulled back in a low ponytail. His eyebrow was arched, and one corner of his mouth turned up, as if he was amused. He carried a small mug with a spoon. Mason's daily gruel. "So, you're the famous Reader."

Mason gave a one-shoulder shrug.

"I'm supposed to make sure you're still alive."

Another shrug.

The man pulled his gag off. "Don't try anything stupid."

"Would it do any good?"

A spoonful of gruel was the only answer he received. As Mason worked the dry mass down, the man stepped back and regarded him. "You done?" he asked.

Mason tried to swallow. "I don't suppose I could talk you into giving me a drink, could I?" He jutted his chin to the pail.

"Nay."

"That's what I thought." Mason exhaled, sore from the upright position of his arms. All he did these days was hurt.

The man headed back to the door. He slowed down as he passed the bucket of water and cast a look back at Mason. Rolling his eyes, he picked the dipper up and carried it back. "I'll get nailed if you end up dying on my watch," he muttered and raised the dipper.

Mason gulped the few sips down. The water was tepid and tasted of wood, but it was like a spring of mountain rain, running down his throat and cooling the heat burning within him. Too soon, the man pulled the dipper back.

"Thanks," Mason said, licking his lips.

"Don't mention it." He frowned back at Mason. "And I mean it." He dropped the dipper back, letting it splash.

Something registered in Mason's foggy mind as the man headed out the door. "Hey, wait, are you a Shadowman?"

The man waved a hand over his head and disappeared through the portal. "Not yet."

"Wait, come back!"

But he was gone, and so was Mason's chance. He dropped his head back with a groan. The one unguarded moment offered to him, and he missed it. Though why Bruin risked sending in anyone without a Shadowstone was beyond him. Maybe he was a foolish Darkman sneaking in for a glimpse at the famous Reader, but it didn't matter. Mason would not get another opportunity like that.

Sure enough, Bruin entered the room, his face a thundercloud, and yanked the rag from Mason's neck, the coarse fabric burning his skin as the knot undid itself. "Don't try it again, Mason," Bruin growled as he pushed the rag between Mason's teeth and secured it tightly at the back of his head. "Karsch may be stupid coming in here unguarded, but he won't betray me as you did." He gave the gag another yank. "Emperor Jader will be here soon. You best rest up until then."

Mason held his gaze until the commander turned away to exit. He worked the rag with his tongue, but it held fast, biting at the corners of his mouth.

Resignation caused him to do as Bruin suggested. He rested against the wall again. The gruel settled in his tense stomach like a rock, the quick drink he had been allotted forgotten. He had no idea what Jader planned, but it didn't matter. With or without the Shadowstone, Mason would no longer obey his commands.

"Three days, Lena. Where is he?" Seria fingered the mug of cider before her, too uptight to eat her breakfast.

"You know Prince Eric is doing everything he can."

"Aye, but I also know how powerful Jader is. What is he doing to him?" She shut her eyes against the question. It was too awful to contemplate.

Lena laid her hand over Seria's knotted fingers. "We have to trust him to Lambient's care."

She was doing her best, but every so often, her worries would take over. When that happened, she would take refuge in the chapel. Especially when she heard Mason's voice in her head. It didn't happen very often, but when it did, he sounded weaker, more resigned. It scared her. She wasn't even sure if it was him calling out to her, or her imagination running out of control.

After sending another prayer heavenward, she forced herself to take a bite of her toast. She would need to return to the king's room soon. Aden was slowly regaining his strength and still needed help getting in and out of bed.

She had swallowed the last bite when Aladee's call sounded in the room, stopping all activity. "Seria, we need you!"

Jumping to her feet, Seria hurried across the room and met Aladee at the door. The Stewardess headed up the hall, her steps urgent.

"What's wrong, Captain?"

"It's King Aden. I think he's had another attack."

"Oh, no." Seria gathered her skirts in her hand and quickened her steps, fairly running through the halls ahead of Aladee.

The doors of Aden's room were already open, so she flew inside and stopped by his bed.

The king was deathly pale, and he lay so still that she checked his breathing. It was shallow but accelerated.

"When did this happen?" she asked Daslyn, who had been tending to Aden while Seria ate.

"Just a few minutes ago," Daslyn said shakily. "I was getting his day clothes when he gave a gasp and fell back into the bed, holding his chest."

Seria shook her head as she loosened his clothes. "He's been uneasy ever since..." She bit her words back, chastising herself. In all her worrying and fretting, she had overlooked Aden's health. And now, still weakened from his last illness, he had suffered a setback. Would he recover from this one?

"Seria, what do you need?" Aladee asked.

"Some all-flower seed broth," she answered. "He won't be able to eat anything, but I need to get some of the seed in him."

"I'll get it." Daslyn hurried out the door, almost running into Jervis.

"How is he?" Aladee asked Seria when they were alone.

"In distress."

A strained silence fell as Seria worked until Daslyn returned with the broth. The maid held the old man's head up as Seria dripped a few drops at a time into his mouth. Everyone seemed to hold their breath as time ticked by. At long last, the king stirred and blinked up at her. "Miss Seria?" he croaked.

Tears of relief nearly blinded her. "It's about time you woke up."

He took a slight breath. "I'm sorry if I troubled you."

She brushed a strand of silver hair off his face. "That's what I'm here for. How are you feeling?"

He frowned in thought. "My chest doesn't hurt so much."

"Good." That was a good sign. "You gave us all a scare."

Aden looked from Seria to Aladee to Jervis. "I think I scared myself."

"You're doing better," Seria assured. "Now, you need some real rest. I'll have some more broth for you to take, and then some chamomile tea so you can sleep."

"Sleep sounds lovely." His eyes drifted closed, and Seria wondered if he would even need the tea.

Moving over to where the Planks waited, she took a deep breath. "I think he's over the worst."

Aladee released a breath. "For a minute there..." Jervis took her hand, and she held tight. "Thank you, Seria."

"I'll stay with him now. I'll let you know if I need anything."

"I'll be back to check on you after morning rounds," Aladee said.

As soon as Seria was alone, she took her chair beside the bed to wait for the broth and stared at the king's wrinkled face, relaxed in sleep. His cheeks were ruddier now, rather than stark white as they had been earlier. She breathed a prayer of thanks as she leaned back in her seat.

"Thank you, Lambient, for sparing him." She rested her head on the chair. "I know I've been fretting over Mason too much, and I'm sorry I let it consume me. I know that...there's no future for us. And I've accepted that. But I still care about him, and I want to know he's safe."

Tears gathered, making it hard for her to continue. "But I can't do anything for him. Only You can bring him out of this, just as You brought King Aden from this attack." She watched the old man sleep, peaceful now, and managed to speak one more time. "He's in Your hands now."

26

The Reader, Moverik, managed to use his link to the Shadowpit to wield control over all those who submitted to Shreil.
-The Lost Record of the Gifts

Eric tossed his belt with his sword and Beacon on the bed and paced the confines of his room, wearing a trail from the window to the door. The search parties had all come up empty, and he had no idea what more he could do. It was as if the Reader had disappeared into thin air.

He tried mentally calling out to Mason, but it was like talking to the walls. It was foolish to try, but he was running out of ideas. To make matters worse, word of his father's setback had reached him that day. Jervis had assured him the king was stable, but it did not erase Eric's growing concern. So, he turned to prayer. Again.

Stopping by the window, he looked out over the street below him. This was the same window from where he had first laid eyes on Mason when he had managed to sneak into the fort. That was when Eric had realized that Jader had a Reader in his army.

How much had changed since then.

Someone pounded on the door, and he called an immediate entry. Dakim entered, panting. "Prince Eric. Captain Braylee told me to fetch you."

Eric's breath quickened. "What is it?"

The boy shook his head. "He didn't say, only that it was urgent."

"Where is he?"

"The Council Hall, sir."

It didn't take long for Eric to descend the stairs and enter the large room on the first floor of the Great Hall. Braylee talked with Dudley in low tones beside the long table. Both looked sober but not troubled.

"What is it, Captain?"

Braylee faced him. "I received a message from Kullen. He said he tried to reach out to you but got no reply."

Eric patted his holster and let out a sigh. "I dropped everything on my bed to walk the floors. What did he have to say?"

"He knows where the Reader is."

Optimism mushroomed within him, quickly followed by caution. "How does he know?"

"I spoke with him myself in the pool, Sire," Braylee said. "I saw no reason to doubt his word. As to how he knows, he did not give out that information, but we know how careful he needs to be."

Eric rested his hands on the back of a chair. "Where is he?"

"In the town of Machlin. Says he was brought there last night under heavy guard and the cloak of darkness."

Dudley spoke up. "I wonder where he's been before this?"

"Did he say anything about his current state?"

Braylee shook his head. "Only that Jader is planning something today."

Eric clasped his hands together at the top of the chair, contemplating his next move. "Machlin is not that far."

"We could be there in a few hours," Braylee said.

They could not risk losing a war for one man, but neither could Eric leave one man in the clutches of Jader. And this man, in particular, could prove to be more dangerous if Jader somehow managed to use his Gift. "Let's get some men together."

A little while later, a platoon had been organized. To Eric's surprise, Lionel was the lieutenant on hand, though he did not ask how that came to be. Frakes was also in attendance.

"I don't know what to expect out there," Eric said once he was mounted on Oakley's back. "From what our source says, there are about fifty or so Darkmen and Shadowmen there. We're going to get him out as quickly as possible."

Zakkias spoke up from his place by his mare. "I'm with you, Sire." He looked startled when everyone looked at him. "Mason Grey is the reason my squad was brought back home. It's the least I can do for him."

Eric caught the looks of respect the younger man got, and Frakes nodded in agreement. There was not a trace of reluctance or resentment on any of the faces before him. Despite the strain between them and Mason, he was one of them. A Steward. And they were ready to risk life and limb to bring one of their own back.

"Very well." Pride in his men swelled in Eric's chest. "Let's bring him home."

At the sound of the door opening again, Mason raised his head, half expecting his usual dose of gruel. But it was Jader who entered this time, with Bruin following. "It is time, my boy."

Bruin loosened the gag, his face set like flint.

"I told you not to call me that" was the first thing out of Mason's mouth.

"I cannot help it. I took you in as a boy, and I will always see you as family."

Mason grunted as Bruin loosened the strap around his feet. He was tempted to give the tall man a good kick across the jaw but didn't have enough strength in his legs to do so. "You took away the only family I had."

"I was not the one who killed your brother. Surely you have not forgotten. The Stewards attacked those boys and struck them down one by one. And they would have killed you had I not intervened."

"Are we both going to pretend that you didn't orchestrate that attack, Jader?" Mason bit back a groan as his arms were lowered. White-hot streaks shot through his shoulders. "You're the reason Liam died, along with every other boy there, and Baris, too."

"That idiot almost got you killed."

Mason stilled, rubbing at his stinging wrists. "What are you talking about?"

Bruin answered. "Baris was supposed to keep you out of harm's way. Instead, you almost died with all the rest of them."

"Are you saying..." A sick feeling washed over him. "Baris knew?"

"Of course, he did," Bruin answered. "But he botched the one job we gave him."

"So, you let the Stewards kill him?" Mason was still reeling from the fact that the one person he had thought a friend so long ago had been sent there only to watch him.

"Nay." Jader straightened his cloak. "He got himself killed."

Mason shook his head slowly. "You really are a monster, Jader. Both of you," he added when Bruin opened his mouth to protest.

"Do you not see?" Jader narrowed his good eye. "No one has ever cared for you. You were too dangerous. No one understood you as I did. We both share a rare and powerful gift."

"Nay," Mason ground the word out, memories stinging him like bees. "I have a Gift. You chose to live in darkness."

Jader looked amused. "So did you, my boy." He turned to leave.

Bruin grabbed Mason's arm and dragged him after the emperor. "You have a lot of gall talking big, boy," he said lowly, "when we could kill you where you stand."

"Do it first, then brag."

The tall man grabbed him by the neck with his free hand, cutting off his airflow with a viselike grip. "Don't tempt me."

"That is enough, Commander," Jader said without even turning around.

Bruin released him, and Mason coughed to catch his breath before speaking again. "I'm not doing anything for you, Jader."

They went up a flight of steps by the door onto a balcony that led outside.

"As I said before, Mason. You have no choice." Jader pushed the drapes aside and stepped out onto the landing. Bruin shoved Mason to stand beside him. Mason caught himself against the railing and looked down at the crowd that had gathered below. His heart sank.

A group of twenty or thirty men looked up at him, all wearing civilian clothes and looking worn down by the cares of life. All around them, Shadowmen guarded. A few Darkmen lined up across the street.

"Men of Machlin, I thank you for coming on such short notice." Jader looked down at the civilians. "I understand that you have some concerns about my rule."

A few of the men scowled up at him in defiance. Many others shrank back in fear.

"To convince you that I have your best interests at heart, I will enlist the help of my accomplice, Mason Grey."

Mason ground his teeth. He refused to say anything that would cause these men to succumb to Jader.

The emperor looked to Mason, his dark eye glittering. "Tell them to strike each other down dead."

"I will not."

Jader almost looked glad he refused. Instead of growing angry, He reached out to lay his hand over the Shadowstone Mason wore. "Tell them."

A gray fog fell over his mind, even as pressure built against his chest. Mason blinked once, twice. What was it Jader had asked him to do?

"Tell them to strike each other down." Jader's voice pierced the fog, settling deep into his will. "All of them."

Of course.

Feeling as if he were underwater, Mason looked down at the men staring at him from the ground. Something told him to stay quiet, to fight the command, but he couldn't. His mouth opened of its own accord. "I want you to kill one another."

And they did.

27

Do not rejoice against me when I fall, for I shall arise again. When I sit in darkness, the Lambient shall be my light.
-The Sacred Code

Mason blinked to wakefulness, still chained to the ceiling in the dark room of the town hall. The last thing he recalled was Jader and Bruin taking him to the balcony. How had he gotten back here?

He struggled to clear the cloudiness, but nothing came to him. It was as if he had a black hole in his memory. The more he tried to remember, the less he could. The Shadowpit was still clear in his mind, as well as the pain inflicted on him. Almost everything else was lost in shadows.

Something moved in the corner, and he stiffened. He was not alone as he had assumed. Areem stepped into his line of vision, his face shuttered, but his mind was free for Mason's perusal. Confusion and anger colored Areem's thoughts. And regret, to Mason's astonishment. Regret about his roles in the kidnappings of Joshun and Shon's death.

The gag wrapped around Mason's mouth like a chain, holding back what he wanted—*needed*—to say to this misled young man.

But Areem's chin jutted out, as if he knew what Mason was doing. "You were my mentor. You taught me everything I know, got me to where I am now. And now look at you."

His chest caved in at the regret. Areem was right. Mason was responsible for shaping him into the soldier he had become. He shook his head, drilling his gaze into Areem's, wishing he could speak, tell him how wrong he had been.

"How can someone change their mind so fast?" Areem asked, his voice harsh. "It doesn't make any sense. You were a Shadowman. Still are." He motioned to the stone around Mason's neck, prompting Mason to shake his head harder.

Areem only scowled. "You told me there was no going back once you became a Darkman, and even more so if you took the Shadowstone."

Mason exhaled and dropped his head. If only he could go back in time and repair the damage he had caused. But there was nothing he could do or say now, especially with the gag in. He looked up again. *I was wrong.*

Areem blanched and took a step back. "What are you doing?"

Hope sprang up. Had his words spoken to Areem? Mason straightened and tried again. *Areem, get out while you can. Jader will destroy you to get what he wants.*

"Stop it!" The boy shook his head and retreated further, his thoughts a chaotic mess. "You've gone mad. And you're trying to take others down with you."

There was nothing Mason could do to stop Areem from leaving. He pulled against the chains as Areem cast one more disdainful look back. But Mason caught the note of uncertainty in Areem's mind before he slammed the door behind him.

Lambient, please get him out of this before it's too late. Mason had once been Areem—young, brash, and bold, ready to pledge his life to Jader's cause. And so foolish.

But just as Jader had led Mason to a path of darkness and hatred, Mason had done the same for Areem.

The door opened again, and a spark of hope lit, immediately extinguished when Jader and Bruin walked in. Dread made his limbs go limp, and he locked his knees straight, hating himself for his weakness. He was supposed to be stronger than this.

Jader stopped before him, and Bruin yanked the gag out. "I want to thank you, Mason," Jader said. "You have been a great help."

Mason frowned. "I told you I'm not helping you anymore, Jader."

"Ah, but you already have, my boy. Machlin has never been more compliant."

He was lying. There was no other answer to it. From the beginning,

Mason had refused to succumb to Jader's authority again.

Like you refused the Shadowstone?

His heart froze in his chest as he searched his mind for something he may have said or done that would warrant Jader's satisfaction. But a heavy gray fog hung over his mind where the memories of the last few hours should be.

Shouting rose outside. Jader gave Bruin a slight nod. "I will meet you outside," he said as calm as ever. But Mason caught the slight narrowing of his eyes.

Jader looked to Mason again. "It is time for me to take my exit, but I look forward to working with you again." He walked out of the room.

"I told you—"

"Save it." Bruin took the emperor's spot. "You're still sitting pretty high-minded for a man who's been broken and conquered."

Mason's stomach tightened. "You stand pretty tall for someone who's nothing but a lackey." He bit back a groan at his foolishness. When would he learn to keep quiet?

Bruin's jaw shifted. Footsteps ran up and down the outside hall, but he acted as if he did not notice. Then his fist lashed out, catching Mason square on the jaw. Mason's head jerked back, and stars flashed. But Bruin wasn't done. Blow after blow struck, sometimes catching him in the face, other times in the gut. The taste of blood filled his mouth, and fire raged through his wounds.

Finally, the beating stopped. Mason raised his chin and peered up at the tall man with bleary eyes. The stubborn side of him was ready to smart off again, but the weakened part of him wouldn't cooperate. It was probably for the best. He wasn't sure how much more abuse his body could go through before he lost consciousness.

Bruin moved closer, grabbing Mason's jaw in his iron grip. "The next time I see you, I will kill you." Ice coated his words. "I don't care what side you're fighting for." Then he swiveled on his heel and left the room.

Mason's legs gave out, and he hung limp from the shackles still chaining him to the ceiling.

Braylee rode Beast straight down the middle of Machlin, his sword swinging.

"Surround the town!" Eric shouted from the front, Lavrynth held high. Stewards veered on both sides to follow his order.

There were a few Darkmen positioned around the main street, firing at them with their crossbows, but not as many as Braylee would have expected. Others came out on horseback to meet them in the middle. Lionel rode at his side, stoic and silent. The rest of his men spread out, forcing the enemy into a quick retreat. Maybe this would be a swift victory.

But then a tall form caught his eye. Bruin Pralus stepped off the porch of the town hall, his focus zeroed in on the prince. Gritting his teeth, Braylee urged Beast between Eric and Bruin and met the dark commander's challenge head-on. Bruin's lips curled into a sneer, and he raised his hand to the sky, but Braylee pointed his Beacon, shooting a quick blast of light straight into the other man's chest.

Bruin stumbled back against a wooden post, then quickly regained his footing, rage filling his face. Knowing horseback was not the place to be if Bruin utilized his weather Gift, Braylee slid to the ground and confronted Bruin before the building. His pulse throbbed steadily in his ears, and adrenaline heated his veins. Their swords clashed again and again, the clang lost in the din of the battle around them.

The commander stood at least two inches taller than Braylee, his form as unyielding as an oak tree. Braylee spread his solid weight evenly on his feet, muscles coiled and tense. It took every ounce of concentration to keep up with the other man's movements, to keep him from having a spare moment to utilize his Gift.

He blocked a strike aimed at his head. Bruin spun and elbowed him in the back. Braylee stumbled a step, then swung around in time to sweep Bruin's blade away. They paused for a moment, both breathing heavily and eyeing the other warily. That's when Bruin reached for his stone.

Braylee felt the chill trying to close in on him, but his faith in the Lambient rose up in him, strong and swift. "I don't think so," he growled, raising the light and breaking the hold that Bruin tried to lay on him.

Bruin's hand snapped away as if he had been burned. A black cloud formed above them, twisting and writhing like a great viper. Braylee's lungs froze as fangs flashed through the blackness.

The cloud spread and lowered itself over the street where the Stewards still pushed the Darkmen back. Braylee backed away and lost sight of Bruin, keeping his weapon at the ready. Then the cloud dissipated, and Bruin was gone.

Typical.

Braylee bolted for the door of the town hall. Stewards and Darkmen still fought on behind him as he flung the door open. A dark foyer stretched before him. He raised his Beacon, casting light into every corner. Empty.

There were only two doors, both at the right of the foyer. He checked the first one, but it led to an unoccupied sitting room. He moved to the second. It was a meeting room of some kind, simply furnished and with no windows. But it was the slumped figure in the corner that arrested Braylee's attention. Mason hung by his hands from a chain bolted to the ceiling. His legs were crumpled beneath him, and his head hung limply.

"Mason?" Braylee holstered his Beacon and hurried to him, feeling for a heartbeat. His fingers grazed the hard lump of the Shadowstone. What did that mean?

A groan fell from Mason's lips, and he lifted his head. He blinked at Braylee, his brows furrowing. His face was a mess of abrasions and bruises. He was haggard and pale, nothing like the strong, cocky soldier Braylee had last seen.

"Braylee?" he uttered, his voice thin. He squinted at him, as if unsure of what he was seeing. "You came for me?"

The disbelief that marked his tone broke Braylee's heart. "We all did." He helped Mason stand to his feet and looked up at the chain. "Hold still so I can get you loose."

"Get it off me."

"I'm trying." Braylee aimed his blade for the rusty chain but stopped when Mason shook his head.

"Nay. The Shadowstone. Get it off me." Mason's eyes beseeched him. "Please."

Braylee eyed the rock, hesitating only a moment before he slipped it off Mason's neck. Then he pitched it across the room. "That better?"

"Much." Mason drooped as if a heavy weight had been shed. "I never wanted it back. I didn't mean to take it." Remorse darkened his pasty countenance. "But the pain—I couldn't take it."

"Don't talk about it now." Braylee raised his sword again and struck the chain, sparks flying as steel hit metal. After the fourth time, a link snapped, and Mason's arms dropped. His legs gave way, and he would have collapsed to the floor if Braylee did not have a firm hold on him. "Easy now."

Mason shook in his exertion. "I meant what I said. Look, I'll prove it." He grasped for Braylee's Beacon, staring at it with wide eyes. The fear and hope on his face as he waited for it to light tore at Braylee's compassion.

But the Beacon lit for Mason, just as Braylee knew it would. He closed his fingers around the rod above Mason's desperate grip. "I believed you before."

Mason stared back at him, his eyes wide and haunting. After a long moment, he gave a slight shake of his head. "I didn't think anyone would come."

"Then you don't know the Stewards." Braylee put Mason's arm around his neck and secured his own around Mason's torso. "They don't leave anyone behind if they can help it. And neither do I. Let's go."

Mason tried not to groan as Braylee half led, half carried him out of the room. His heart raced, and every movement hurt, but he pushed past his discomfort and tried not to slow the Steward down.

They reached the hall when the main door flung open. A Darkman rushed in and slid to a stop before them, his eyes wide. It was Karsch, the same man who had allowed Mason a drink.

Mason's breath hitched as Braylee tensed beside him, lifting his weapon. But Karsch scowled and backed off. "I'll not lose my life for the likes of you." He directed the words to Mason, then fled for the back door without another look back.

Mason huffed out a weak laugh.

"I guess not all of Jader's men are willing to die for him," Braylee said as they walked the rest of the way to the door.

Braylee positioned Mason against the wall by the door, and Mason spread his feet to keep himself from sliding to the floor. Opening the door a crack, Braylee looked out. "Think you can make it to my horse?"

Mason peered through the narrow opening to where the big bay waited, his feet dancing in agitation, across the street. He measured the distance, trying not to lose heart. His legs shook beneath him, and his abdomen throbbed from Bruin's earlier beating.

But he would crawl if it meant getting out. "I'll make it."

"Good. I'll cover you, but you may draw some notice." Braylee opened the door wider.

Mason sucked in a breath at the fighting still going on. Dozens of Stewards tangled with Darkmen in every direction. "So many," he breathed, peering out through the door. "So many Stewards."

"Aye, so make sure we don't waste our time coming for you, all right?"

Braylee's reminder brought him back to the moment, and he pushed off the wall and flexed his fingers. "I'm ready."

"Good. Let's go."

The glare of the sun nearly blinded him as soon as he stepped out, but he shielded his eyes with one hand and tracked Braylee's steps. The big man moved boldly through the throng, his steps sure. Mason blinked hard, trying to shake the sunspots from his eyes. Stewards circled the two of them, and at least a dozen Darkmen darted about, shooting from the shadows. There were no Shadowmen.

Gathering all his strength, Mason shouted out hoarsely, "Stop!" Then dizziness struck him, and he stumbled to his knees before he could tell if his Gift had worked.

Braylee grabbed Mason's arm and lifted him from the ground. They made it the rest of the way to Beast, and Braylee mounted, then reached for Mason. His head and heart pounding in unison, Mason gripped his hand and scrambled up behind him, relying on Braylee's strength more than his own. As soon as he landed, he swayed, in danger of toppling off the other side.

But Lionel appeared, steadying him with a hand on his shoulder. Mason did not have time to wonder about it before Braylee tapped the horse's flanks, and they jumped to a gallop. With no choice but to hang on for dear life, Mason shut his eyes against the fleeing landscape and concentrated on staying upright.

He was afraid to hope and, with every stride of the animal beneath him, expected to feel the sting of an arrow or the grip of a Shadowstone. But the sounds of the fighting faded, and only the wind filled his ears. Even then, he could not relax, though he chanced a look behind them. Machlin shrank in the distance, and a cloud of dust rose to shroud it from sight. Anxiety spiked at first, until he realized it was the Stewards raising the dust as they all followed Braylee. Then it began to sink in.

Lambient had not forgotten him, as he had feared. The Stewards had come for him.

Dust stung his eyes, making them water. Overwhelmed with relief, he bowed his head and tried to swallow the rock-sized lump in his throat. He was free.

28

Light rises from the darkness for those who live justly.
-The Sacred Code

The news hit the castle during the midday meal. Seria had stayed close to Aden's side all day, watching him carefully for signs of exertion. He had rallied from his earlier attack with a speed that amazed her. Already he was sitting up in a stuffed chair, eating soup at the small round table.

Jervis stepped into the room and gave a quick bow. "I received word from Captain Dudley, Sire. The Reader has been recovered."

Seria rose from her seat. "They found him?" she gasped.

The captain's eyes twinkled back at her. "He's safe, Miss Seria."

Clasping her hands beneath her chin, Seria tried to hold back the tears. "Thank the Lambient."

"Is everyone well?" Aden asked.

Shamed that she had not thought of anyone else, her heart stalled as she waited for the answer.

"No lives were lost on our side," Jervis said. "A few minor injuries. The Darkmen were unprepared."

"Good." Relief colored the single word. "And what of the Reader?"

"He's a bit roughed up and weakened, but Luron seems to think it's nothing that rest and good food won't cure."

Weakness invaded Seria's limbs, and she sank back down. "I'm so glad," she breathed. "It could've been so much worse."

Jervis agreed with a nod. "Captain Dudley said the prince will probably contact you soon with a more detailed report, but he knew you would want to know right away."

Aden thanked Jervis, and the captain bowed before departing. "What did I tell you, Miss Seria?" he asked with a wide smile. "The Lambient cares for His own."

She released a pent-up laugh, wiping the dampness from her eyes. Her spirit felt light for the first time in days. Mason was safe. Her healer's heart longed to see him for herself, to tend to his wounds like she had done before. But she knew Luron would treat him well.

They sat in quiet contentment for a while, mulling over the good news. Suddenly tired, Seria longed for her bed and a good cry.

"Do you miss him?"

Her eyes flew to Aden's. Words fled her as she contemplated how to answer the question.

"You can be honest with me."

Seria took a breath. "I do, but more like it was in the beginning. Before I knew what he was. What he used to be. Things were simpler then. But..." She tugged at the ties on her tunic. "I was wrong to continue the relationship and lie to Eric, no matter what I felt for him."

"And what about now?"

Not sure what he was getting at, she cocked her head. "I don't know. I've not had a chance to get to know this Mason. I have no idea how much he's changed."

If Aden knew anything about Mason's time in the fort, he was not sharing. Seria offered him a cup of the tea that sat forgotten on the table then took some for herself, hoping it would soothe her buzzing nerves.

"You remind me very much of my wife."

Seria nearly choked on her tea. "I beg your pardon?"

Aden smiled at her surprise. "She had long blonde hair and a charming personality, just like you."

A splash of tea fell on her gown, and she set the cup down before she spilled more. "I'm sure she had more polished manners," she said as she wiped excess moisture from her clothes. That was the second tunic she had stained that week.

"Not in her first years." He chuckled. "She had a tendency to speak her mind, no matter how improper the situation was. And she would tolerate no one speaking ill of her husband, even if it was the head Councilman himself."

"A loyal, royal lady, huh?"

"Not so much royal, especially when I first met her." He set his cup down and folded his hands across his chest, his gaze distant. "She was a civilian then. A tanner's daughter."

She gaped at him. "The queen was a peasant?" She drew back. "I'm sorry. That sounded rude."

But he only laughed. "Aye, she was a peasant. One of great moral character and integrity. When I met her, she showed me respect, but no more than she showed my flag bearer. That was the first thing I noticed."

"Er—Prince Eric does not speak of her much."

"You might as well drop any pretense of formality around me, Miss Seria," Aden said. "You see Eric more as a friend than a prince."

She bit her lip. "I always forget."

"His mother was much the same way."

"She sounds like a wonderful lady."

"She was. And a good mother." His eyes darkened. "Unfortunately, the queen died when Eric was very young, so he does not have many memories."

"I'm sorry."

"I was too." He exhaled. "We waited for years for a child, but the Passion bloodline is known to be very narrow. Most of my predecessors had no siblings. We were thrilled when Eric was born, my wife ecstatic to have borne me an heir. But the pregnancy was hard on her body, and she never fully recovered."

"My father met my mother in his later years as well."

Aden raised his head. "That so?"

"She was quite a bit younger than he was, but they were perfectly suited for one another." Seria could still picture them, sitting side by side in their wooden chairs before the fire. "He never let a day go by without thanking the Lambient for the wife and children he'd been blessed with."

The king reached for his cup, his lips twitching as if he were trying not to laugh. He took another sip and sat back in his chair again. "Your father was a prankster."

"What?" Her jaw dropped. "Not Papa."

"Aye, your papa." He chuckled. "Shasta Gayle loved to make people laugh. He never went so far as to embarrass or upset anyone, but many a fellow soldier fell prey to his tricks."

She stared at him, trying to comprehend that the king had known her father. "He did enjoy games."

"Made up quite a few, from what I hear. Shasta felt that laughter would bring people together much better than common interests."

Her eyes smarted, and she sniffed.

Aden looked startled. "I didn't mean to upset you."

She shook her head. "Nay, you didn't. It's just..." She hunched her shoulders. "I've felt so cut off from my family. No one in Cadence knew them, so there was no one I could talk to about them. It was a lonely feeling."

Aden reached over and rested his soft, worn hand over hers. "I'm happy to talk with you about him any time you like."

"Hearing about his young soldiering days makes him seem alive again."

"He was a good knight. A good man. Always willing to do the hard job." He sobered, looking down at the table. "I was sorry to see him leave the army after Calla's War. Even sorrier to hear of his death."

She ducked her head, gulping back tears. "He didn't speak of you much, but I realize now that was probably to protect us." She let out a wet laugh. "But he was very clear in his support for you. All the way to the end."

Now it was Aden who swallowed. "I consider that to be the highest of compliments. And I am delighted to have gotten to know his daughter. He would be mighty proud of you; I have no doubt."

"All right, you're going to have to stop for now, or I'm going to be blubbering all over my tea."

He chuckled. "I'm thinking I'm ready for a nap now anyway."

"Of course."

She helped him to the bed, pleased that he did not need to lean so much on her. "You really are improving."

"Good." He lowered himself to the bed. "I hope to be back on my feet soon. My son should not be worrying about a sick father on top of everything else."

"He will be glad to know you are well."

Aden nestled back against the pillows, looking quite content. "I'm feeling better. So much so that I think you need a day off."

"I'm fine," she said as she tucked the covers around him. "All I need is a good night's sleep now that I know everyone is back at the fort where they belong."

"I said you need a day off, and you'll get a day off." He pointed up at her. "You need to learn to stop arguing with the king."

She laughed. "I always did have a problem questioning authority."

"Well, I'm serious." He covered a yawn. "As soon as I can arrange it, you'll get your day."

She patted his arm. "As you wish, Your Majesty."

It did not take him long to nod off. The excitement of the good news had tired him, but he did not look worn out. Indeed, he looked much improved from when she had first taken over his care.

Retreating to her room, she curled up on her cot. Her thoughts drifted to Mason again and all the Stewards at the fort. Gratitude swelled up within her. She was wise enough to know this was not the end of it. Jader would not give up after losing his prized soldier again. If anything, it would spur him to act, to speed the advance of the war. The thought made her shudder.

But knowing that Mason was out of enemy hands and surrounded by friends again comforted her to no end. She had no idea how he had fared the last few months, and knowing him as she did, she feared that he had not made it easy on himself. But in the end, it didn't matter. Even if he never accepted his place within the Steward ranks, the Gateway Stronghold was still a better place to be than any camp of the Dark Army.

Emotion rose within her, and she was tempted to sob in her pillow. She could not even define all the emotions that swept over her. She must be as tired as the king. Or maybe he was right. Maybe she did need a day off.

29

By Your hand, I have overcome the enemy. I have escaped their grasp and broken my chains.
-The Sacred Code

The pounding in his head was not as hard now, though a dull ache still hung over him. His arms and legs felt weighed down, and it hurt to breathe. But the discomfort was a welcome reminder that he was still alive.

Mason fought to open his eyes and blinked up at the blurry space above him. It was quiet, but it was not a heavy silence that pressed in on him. This was a peaceful stillness, one that breathed reassurance into his soul. He was safe, free from the clutches of Jader and Bruin.

It was too good to believe, but the proof was all around him. He did not hang from chains but rested on a soft mattress, covered with a warm blanket. The darkness of the pit and the town hall was gone, replaced by the soft sunlight seeping in from the row of windows above him. And there were no Shadowmen. No Darkmen.

Movement to his right startled him, and he flinched as a gray-headed man appeared. "Easy, son," he said, standing over the bed. "I didn't mean to startle you. I didn't expect you to be awake."

The man looked familiar, but Mason could not place him. "Where am I?" The last thing he remembered was riding out of Machlin on the back of Braylee's horse.

"You are back at The Gateway Stronghold. I don't think we've had the pleasure to meet." He stretched a hand out. "I'm Luron Fervor. This is my infirmary."

Mason hesitantly took his hand, not liking being flat on his back.

"Here, you look ready to sit up now." Luron grabbed a pair of pillows from another cot and helped Mason push himself up, setting the pillows at his back. "How's that feel?"

"Fine." Mason sucked in a breath at the sharp streak shooting through his ribs. "How long have I been asleep?"

"You've been out for two days."

Mason gawked at him. "Two days?"

The physician perched on the cot beside him. "You weren't in too bad shape when they dragged you in here. A few cracked ribs and a lot of deep bruises. Had a couple of knots on your head, and I had to stitch up some of those stripes on your back. But you were mostly exhausted and half starved." He squinted at him. "Think you can keep something down?"

His stomach rumbled in reply, and Luron chuckled. "I'll have some stew brought in."

The mention of stew brought memories rushing in on him, and he barely acknowledged Luron as he left. How many times had he complained about the mushy stew Seria served him day after day in those first days he was stuck in her cabin? Longing writhed within him like a hungry beast. How he missed her. Maybe it was his weakened state that made him want to cry like a lost boy. But she was far away, and he didn't want her to see him in this state. Did not want her to know how much he had messed up in the last few weeks. For the first time, he was glad she had been sent away.

He rested his head back against the pillows, feeling weaker than he had ever felt. Even when he was laid up in Seria's cot, he still had his fighting spirit. Now the very idea of moving from this bed made him want to hide beneath the covers.

But then he remembered what Jader and Bruin had put him through, the doubts and fears they had stirred up. And he knew he could not hide forever.

Marcus delivered the stew and managed to hand it to Mason without spilling it. "It's good to see you again, sir," he said shyly.

"Thank you." Mason gave a nod, not sure what else to say. Fortunately,

Marcus was as awkward as he was and left without another word.

"Now, take it slow with that," Luron warned. "I don't know how much your stomach can take."

Mason tried to heed his advice, but as soon as the gravy hit his tongue, his appetite roared to life. He barely chewed the bits of meat before he scooped up more.

Luron scowled down at him. "Don't make me take that from you."

Mason met the man's challenge head-on. "You don't want to try."

Laughing, Luron held his hands up. "Well, it's clear you still have a stubborn streak, so I'll leave you to figure out your limits on your own."

Mason let him go, glad to be left alone to eat in peace. He had just scraped the last remnants of the thick broth from the bowl when the door opened, and Eric entered. "Look at you. You ready to clean the stalls tonight?"

Tempted to chuck the bowl at him, Mason set it aside and crossed his arms. "Funny."

"Sorry." Eric took the seat Luron had claimed earlier. "I'm glad to see you looking so good."

Mason grunted. He knew a lot could be said about his appearance, but good was not one of him. Bandages covered a good portion of his skin, and he could not count the number of bruises covering the rest of it. "You mean alive?"

"That too." Eric rested his elbows on his knees and clasped his hands. "How are you?" The question was genuine.

Mason sighed. "I'm not sure yet." Physically, he knew he would survive. But how much had Jader gotten into his head? His conscious pricked at him, not allowing him to forget that he had conceded and allowed Jader to put the Shadowstone on him again. "I slipped."

"What do you mean?"

"I couldn't take the pain. I let him give me the Shadowstone."

Eric gave him a stern look. "Did you make the pledge again?"

"Nay." Mason gave a quick shake of his head, then winced and pressed his fingers to his temples. "I didn't. All I wanted was for him to stop." What kind of soldier was he that he couldn't take a little pain?

"Mason, you're human. We're all vulnerable at times."

"I should've been able to fight it."

"Did you ask His forgiveness?" When Mason frowned and looked away, Eric pressed him. "When you realized what you had done, did you tell Him?"

"Aye, but the Shadowstone—"

"Is only a piece of rock." Eric's voice hardened. "It holds power, aye. And in your weakness, you wanted it to relieve your pain. It was wrong, sure, but you've acknowledged that. The Lambient does not forsake us for being fallible."

The reassurance still felt flimsy, but for now, Mason would take it. "How long was I gone?"

"Four days."

The answer stunned him. "That's all?"

"I'm sure it felt like much longer."

It had felt like an eternity. Mason was sure he had been held for at least a week.

Eric stood. "I can see you're tired, so I'll leave you. We can talk more later."

Before Eric could leave, Mason spoke again. "Wait."

The prince turned. "Aye?"

Biting back the pride and humiliation that reared their ugly heads, he met Eric's gaze. "Thank you." The words were pitiful in light of all he owed him, but at the moment, they were all he could manage.

But Eric seemed to understand. "You're welcome, Mason."

30

The only way to stop a Reader's power once it has reached its fullness is by death.
-The Lost Record of the Gifts

Mason spent a lot of time thinking over the course of his recovery. Luron insisted on keeping him in the infirmary for several days, until his strength returned, which happened rapidly with regular meals and rest. Despite the trauma his body had gone through, none of his injuries were long-lasting. He could not say the same for his state of mind.

Eric came by again, but he was not his only visitor. Crue stopped by more than once to check on him. Mason had to reassure him multiple times that he did not hold Crue responsible for what had happened to him. "My actions were my own," he told the boy. "And that means the consequences were my own as well."

He wasn't sure Crue was convinced, but he did stop apologizing after a while.

Marcus continued to deliver his meals from the mess hall. Though they didn't share much in the way of conversation, Mason caught him studying him at times, as if trying to figure him out. It discomfited Mason at times, but he tried not to show his annoyance.

His most unexpected visitor, however, was Frakes. The Steward came to see him on the second morning, his expression piercing, but not cold. Mason had to refrain from bunching the blanket in his fist as he returned Frakes's direct look and held his tongue. Frakes would make his reason for being here known soon enough.

"I wanted to stop by and tell you I'm glad you made it back."

It was the last thing Mason expected him to say, and he blinked up at him before he could respond. "Uh...thanks."

The lines around Frakes's eyes deepened. "Regardless of what you may have believed all this time, Mason, I don't hate you. Neither do any of the Stewards that I know."

Mason fidgeted, staring at the wall on the opposite side of the room.

"We hated what you used to be. What you did to us," Frakes continued. "Which should come as no shock, as I suspect you must feel the same way."

When silence indicated Frakes was waiting for an answer, Mason stirred. "Aye."

"Good. Then we agree on that. I admit, we were a little standoffish, especially in the beginning, because it was difficult for us to see one of our former enemies among us. After a while, we were willing, with Lambient's help, to make you one of our own. But it didn't seem as if you wanted that."

The hard-hitting words battered at what was left of Mason's pride. But he could not deny them. He had come to that conclusion hanging in the Shadowpit.

"After what...you went through, I hoped to clear the air. What's done is done, and I'm willing to put it behind us if you are."

Mason forced his gaze up to the Steward's. Even without reading his thoughts, he could see the honesty staring back at him. Any desire to hold on to the resentment that had driven the wedge between him and the Stewards drained from him. "I'm willing."

"Good." Frakes offered his hand. Mason stared at it for a short moment before gripping it with his own. Frakes gave it a solid shake, offered a hint of a smile, and then left.

Mason woke early on the day Luron was to release him.

"Try not to overdo it now," Luron cautioned. "Give yourself time to build your strength."

"Sure, of course," Mason agreed, inching his way to the door.

Luron waved him off. "I can see you're not paying any attention, so get on out of here. Just see you don't end up back here."

"I don't plan to," Mason said.

He took a deep breath of the sunshine and headed straight for the stable. There, his roan, Oakley, and even Beast nickered upon seeing him.

"Good to see you again too." Then he went to the donkey corner, where Sanjo waited patiently for him. "You're looking as old as ever," he said, rubbing the animal's ears. Footsteps preceded Eric's appearance.

"How's everyone here?" Eric asked, giving Oakley a pat.

"Fat and lazy," Mason said, gesturing to the donkey in the corner. "It's too bad we can't ship that bag of bones back to Seria."

Eric smiled. "I'm sure he'll be fine."

As they talked, a strange black cloud fell over Mason's mind, muffling his thoughts. Before he could shout a warning, Jader appeared beside him. "Kill the prince."

Mason's hand moved without permission, pulling the sword from the sheath. At the swish, Eric turned, his eyes widening. "Mason, nay!"

"I have to." Mason advanced toward him, his movements automatic.

"Don't do it, Mason." Eric held his hands up, his tone beseeching. "You're a Steward now."

A weight settled over his chest, and he looked down at the purple stone hanging there.

Jader spoke again. "You're a Shadowman. You'll always be a Shadowman."

"I'm a Shadowman."

Eric shook his head, retreating a step. "I won't fight you."

Gritting his teeth, Mason raised his sword. "Then you'll die."

"*No!*" Mason struck, and the prince slumped to the floor, lifeless.

Running steps drew him around. Dudley gaped at him. Jader's voice pierced his skull, and Mason killed him too. Then Braylee, who appeared out of nowhere. Frakes, Lionel, even Ollen. All of them fell before his sword. Revulsion turned his stomach with every blow, but he could not stop himself. A dozen bodies lay before him, their blood mingling on the ground.

"Mason?"

The tentative petition struck terror in his heart, but he could not stop himself from facing the girl behind him. "You shouldn't be here." He tightened his grip on the sword, struggling to keep his hand down.

Her green eyes glimmered with tears. "What have you done?"

"I didn't mean to. I can't fight it."

Jader stood behind her. "Get rid of her."

"I thought you were a Steward." Her face beseeched him.

"I'm too dark." He shook his head, trembling as he lifted his weapon. "Seria, run."

But she remained there, the sadness streaming down her cheeks in a river of tears.

"Run!" The order burst from his lips even as his feet drew him nearer. But it was not enough. She remained motionless, even as he raised his sword and swung it.

Mason sat up with a cry. He shot a wild look around him in confusion. Rows of cots. Small square windows letting in the pale dawn. He was still in the infirmary.

Relief poured over him like the sweat that ran down his face. Swinging his feet to the floor, he cradled his head in his hands. Another lousy dream. But it had felt so real, from the smell of the horse hide and hay to the sound of Jader's voice. The details faded into the recesses of his subconsciousness. But the horror had followed him here. He could see the prince falling before him. Every Steward who appeared. Until the end, when his worst fear unfurled, and he could not stop himself from hurting Seria.

A sickening awareness chilled his damp skin. Jader would never stop trying to pull him back into his clutches. He would always see Mason as a weapon. The doubts in his dream whispered to him.

"I'm a Shadowman."

"I can't fight it."

"I'm too dark."

What if they were true? Perhaps the Lambient had accepted him, but Mason still held on to his own darkness. Maybe Jader could sense he had never surrendered completely, and that was why he refused to let him go. Maybe it was too late.

Running his hands over his head, he clasped them at the back of his neck, elbows planted on his knees. He spotted a small knife Luron had left on the table when cutting through his bandages. Taking the small blade, he turned it in his hands, the cool metal comforting against his skin.

Something twisted within him as he stared at the sharp edge. After all Eric and the Stewards had done for him, he could not bring more harm to them. Or to the few civilians who did not carry the protection of the Lambient. Or Seria.

He would die before he let that happen.

"Mason!"

He dropped the knife and jumped to his feet. Lionel stood in the middle of the room. "What are you doing?"

Great. Mason threw him a scowl and said the first thing that came to his mind. "I figured you'd be glad to have me out of your way."

Lionel shook his head. "That's really how you want to thank the Stewards for going after you? And the Lambient?"

Abashed at the temptation, Mason dropped down on the cot. "I wasn't going to." Not really. He was just too tired to fight anymore. He stared out the small window on the other side of the room, wishing he could redo the last few minutes. Lionel could have him removed from the Stewardship. What army wanted a soldier who tried to escape through death?

Lionel lowered himself on the cot across from him, and Mason prepared himself for more self-righteous scolding. "If anyone gets the pleasure of killing you, it should be me."

Surprise jerked Mason's gaze to Lionel, where a teasing glint lightened the words. He let out a short bark of laughter. "Of course."

Lionel shrugged. "It seems only fair after all the trouble you caused me."

A heavy sigh drew him down. "That seems to be all I'm good for."

"I hear you clean a good stall."

When Mason didn't laugh, Lionel exhaled. "Look. I don't know what's going on in your head, but surely it's not that bad."

"Says the man with not so much as a scratch on his reputation." He waited for Lionel to wave him off and leave him alone. That he had bothered to be civil at all told him how pitiful he must look.

Lionel roughed his hair. "I wish I could say I've done it all with the best of intentions, but I can't." He leaned forward, planting his elbows on his knees. "I can't seem to do anything right these days. Especially since Ollen's death."

Mason was taken back to Ollen's last moments, when the course of Mason's future was altered forever.

"What was he like?" he asked.

Lionel looked up. "Who? Ollen?" At Mason's nod, he blew out a breath. For a moment, he sat there, lost in thought. "He was good. In character and everything he did. Always a step ahead of me. Got better marks all through our training and the first promotion."

Mason swallowed and looked at the floor, as scuffed and scarred up as he felt.

"He was not easily ruffled." Lionel chuckled. "I was the only thing that could get under his skin. That's why I couldn't believe he was so resistant against Prince Eric taking the command. In fact, I thought that was my chance to raise myself in my superior's eyes. I was devoted to the Stewardship and the new Grand Marshal. Instead, he gets promoted to lieutenant, and I was left behind in Shales while he was killed."

The last statement drew Mason's head up. He caught the pain behind Lionel's usual swagger. "That wasn't your fault."

"Maybe not. But he's dead, and I'm wandering around like I don't know what I'm doing. There are times I wonder if he's not the reason I got into the Stewardship in the first place."

"I don't think that's how the Beacons work." As soon as he said it, Mason held his breath, sure Lionel would get offended that a Shadow-man would try to counsel him on the Beacons.

But Lionel only nodded. "I know. But I never realized how much I tried to match his life until he was gone."

An awkward moment passed before Mason gathered the nerve to speak again. "He thought about you. Before he died." He met Lionel's gaze. "He respected you."

The other man looked away, his Adam's apple bobbing. He didn't speak for a long moment. "Thanks," he managed.

Mason picked the knife up, setting it back in its place on the table. "Friendships like that don't happen in the Dark Army. We were all too busy looking out for ourselves." His mind drifted back to his time with Shon. "I had one for a while. He was a scout, like me. We always competed, pretended we could best each other in a fight. But I never could outwit him." He huffed. "He could be as loud as that red hair of his." His words trailed off, remembering Shon's last few days.

"What happened to him?" Lionel asked after a moment.

Mason stirred. All he had gone through the last few days must have left him contemplative because he was more talkative than he had ever been with anyone besides Seria. It wasn't clear to Mason if Lionel's interest was genuine or born out of obligated politeness.

"He was executed by his own people. Hanged for giving a Steward a drink of water." All the emotions of that day hit him like it had just happened. The jeering crowd. The taut rope. And Jader's casual dismissal of a man's life. His fingers curled into fists. "He was sharp. Figured out something wasn't right with all Jader's claims before I did. He dared to offer his canteen to a Steward in Shales."

"And for that, he was hung?"

At the terse question, Mason gave Lionel a sharp look. The Steward's face had washed out, his posture stiff. "That's right."

Lionel groaned and stood, massaging the back of his neck.

Mason frowned at his back. "What's wrong with you?"

He faced him. "I have to tell you something, Mason, and you're probably going to hate me even more."

Rising to his feet, Mason stared, a strange dread rolling in his stomach.

"I'm the Steward."

"What Steward?"

Lionel let out a long breath. "The Steward in Shales."

The world spun to a slow stop. "You mean..." The shock of the truth rocked him, and he ran a hand over his jaw, averting his gaze to the window.

Lionel continued, his voice heavy with regret. "He showed up out of nowhere, wouldn't give his name. But he seemed nervous and left in a hurry."

Mason's eyes slid closed. Shon would be nervous. He knew what he had done would mean his death if anyone saw him. Unfortunately, someone did. Areem, one of the cadets Mason had trained to be loyal to the Dark Army. Tension stretched between them, tight and waiting. But Mason discovered that he wasn't angry. At least, not at Lionel or even Areem. He took a deep breath and rubbed at his wrist. "You're not the reason Shon was killed. Jader's responsible for the hate he bred through his policies."

Lionel studied him. "You don't even want to hit me?"

"If I was going to hit you, I have a whole list of other reasons to do so."

Putting his hands on his hips, Lionel dropped his head. "Probably more than you realize." He rubbed his temples, and another pause lingered as Lionel looked everywhere but at Mason.

"You know I can't read your thoughts, right?"

"I think this would be easier if you could." He cleared his throat. "I, um, I know I gave you a hard time."

Mason waved it off. "It's no more than I deserved, and I would've been worse had the tables been turned."

"Regardless, I let my stinking attitude get in the way. For a while, I was afraid I'd gone too far."

"And now?"

Lionel tugged on an earlobe. "Your capture made me realize"—he squeezed his eyes shut—"nay, that's not true. It was before that."

Mason crossed his arms and waited.

"My poor leadership led to the situation with Hiram, and for that, I do owe you an apology." Lionel still did not look at him.

"Hiram's an idiot, but I shouldn't have been working with Crue."

"That's not exactly accurate." Lionel finally met his eyes. "The stipulation against socializing with juveniles did not come from the Council."

"It didn't?" Mason tried to understand.

"Nay." Lionel sighed. "It was never official. Just my own attempt to keep you under my thumb."

A hiss of anger stirred now. Shon's death had come about through Jader's cruel policies. But this was something Lionel had done with the full awareness of what he had done. An intentional act to make Mason's transition to the Stewardship difficult. "Why?"

The other man didn't answer right away. "I have no excuse, really. I hated you being here when Ollen wasn't." He rubbed his hands together. "I felt like a failure, and then all those boys just...I never had that kind of influence."

For the first time, Mason considered how his arrival had upended Lionel's life. All he had seen before was the arrogance and animosity displayed at him. So, of course, he had dug in his heels and made Lionel's job as challenging as he could. When in reality, Mason was a poor replacement for the man Lionel had called his friend.

His anger drained from him, and he sat down again. "Well, for all I knew, it was part of my probation, which I was still wrong to disregard. So, let's just forget it."

There was no missing Lionel's astonishment. "That's it? I really thought you'd hit me for that one."

"Don't tempt me." Mason braced his hands on the frame of the cot on either side of him. "I can't hold a grudge after Machlin. I was in a mess, and I couldn't get out of it by myself."

"You weren't a pretty sight."

He snorted. "Thanks."

There was an awkward pause, and neither of them seemed to know how to end the conversation. Mason finally shook his head and waved his hand. "You better get out of here before this heart-to-heart makes me like you."

"Well, we can't have that," Lionel replied, and the tension eased. Then he hesitated and took the knife. "But I'll take this before you do anything stupid with it."

31

*You are chosen, loved, and set apart as My people. Praise the One who has
called you out of darkness and into His light.*
-The Sacred Code

King Aden insisted Seria was to have a whole day off, but she managed
to put him off until he could cross his room without assistance. She had
no doubt Daslyn would keep a good eye on him, but she wanted to be
sure he would not need extra care, at least for the day. She would have felt
better if Aladee was going to be close by, but the Stewardess had other
business that day.

"Now, you go and have yourself a good time," Aden said, looking
ready to push her out the door as she fluttered about the room, checking
that Daslyn had everything she needed. He sat at his table, looking robust
and in good spirits.

"We'll be fine, miss," Daslyn said. "You better go before he gets himself
all worked up."

Seria laughed at Aden's put-out expression. "All right, all right, I'm
going." She shook her finger at him. "Now, see you give Daslyn no
trouble."

He huffed. "I'm old enough to cause as much trouble as I want."

The women exchanged looks and laughed. Aden tried his best *not* to
make more work for his caretakers.

Grabbing her lightweight cloak on her way to the door, Seria said, "I'll
see you tonight."

"Nay, you won't," Aden called after her. "You're to sleep in your own room tonight and not return until morning."

"We'll see!" The door closed off any parting remarks he might have had, and she chuckled as she turned for the stairwell. What a long way she had come from her initial discomfort with the king. Now, she talked to him with as much freedom as she did his son.

Which is not really proper. The reminder gave her pause, but she shook it off. Neither man had ever given her reason to believe they thought her disrespectful. She preferred treating people as friends rather than royalty.

But none of that mattered now. She had a whole day to herself, though she didn't know what she would do with it. It wasn't like she had anywhere special to go, but she planned to spend a good portion of the day outdoors. The idea of walking under a blue sky beckoned her. If only she could find a good fishing spot.

She was on the last step when she noticed both Lena and Aladee waiting at the landing. "I wondered how long it would take you to tear yourself away," Lena said with a chuckle.

"What are you two doing here?"

Aladee answered. "We heard you had the day off. So, I thought I'd show you ladies around town if you want."

Seria looked to Lena. "Are you free too?"

"Someone who shall not be named made sure that we could spend the day together."

Seria's gaze swung back to Aladee. "I thought you had other obligations?"

"I do." She swept her arm toward the door. "Shall we go?"

Delighted with the company, Seria linked arms with Lena. "How perfect! Ever since I learned my father lived here for a time, I've been dying to see Calla up close."

"Well, then, let's not keep the lovely capital city of Paladin waiting." Aladee led the way to the courtyard. A small, simple carriage awaited them, along with two smart ponies, stomping their feet.

"Oh, how cute are they," Seria said as she climbed into the back seat. "They're no bigger than Sanjo."

"But quite a bit more spirited, I'd say," Lena said.

Aladee settled in the seat across from them. "Our driver can handle them."

An older man waved at them from the front and clucked to the ponies. The carriage took off rolling at an easy clip.

"What a lovely day." Seria breathed in the autumn air, soaking in the scenery.

The trees surrounding the palace were beginning to turn for autumn. Yellow, orange, red, and even purple flickered within the green leaves of the trees. Puffy white clouds dotted the sky, and golden morning light splashed across the ground.

"You needed a day off," Aladee said. "You've both been working hard."

"No harder than anyone else in the castle, really," Seria said.

"Maybe. But no one has been under as much scrutiny as you two. That can be as exhausting as the work itself."

"I think that's starting to improve," Lena said. "Especially now."

Seria guessed things were better for Lena now that Naomi was no longer in charge.

"In any case, you are not to worry about chores or sick beds or nosy coworkers. Today is a day to be enjoyed."

And Seria did. Aladee directed the driver to take them through the main street, where she described parades and ceremonies of past years. She took them to a small cafe where they consumed fine teas and the daintiest of pastries, though Seria insisted Lena's baking was far superior. Then they watched a minstrel show in the town square and laughed at a mime's act until their sides hurt.

She couldn't remember the last time she had experienced such freedom to simply enjoy a day.

"Thank you so much for taking us out." Feeling spontaneous, she threw her arms around the taller woman. "I didn't realize how much I needed that."

Lena agreed. "It was lovely to see beyond the four walls of the kitchen."

"I'm glad you enjoyed it, but we're not done yet."

Aladee would not give a hint as to what else she had planned, just gave them a mysterious smile as the carriage made its way back to the castle grounds. Instead of driving them up to the door, it followed a less-worn path that circled the estate.

"Where are we going?" Seria asked.

"A little birdie told me that the king's caretaker liked to fish."

Seria clasped her hands under her chin. "Oh, are we going fishing?"

Lena answered. "I've been dying to try, and when I mentioned it to Aladee, she was all for it."

They exited the carriage and walked down the hill that Seria and Lena had sat on so many times, watching the Stewards and Stewardesses practice their swordplay and archery skills. Men and women moved about, each busy with their tasks, but they offered a nod or wave in greeting as the women passed.

To Seria's delight, a lovely little creek streamed past the training grounds, hidden by a little grove of trees. "How perfect!"

One lone woman awaited them, arranging an array of weapons on a wooden table. A single target was set up not far from the stream.

"I've got it all laid out for you, Captain," the woman said, brushing her long red hair back.

"Thank you, Rossi." Aladee made the introductions. "Seria and Lena, this is my lieutenant, Rossi Evans."

Rossi turned her bold appraisal on Seria. "So, you're the one in trouble for meeting with the Shadowman?"

Seria was too taken aback to do anything but nod.

"Oh, Rossi," Aladee drew out. "Really?"

"Sorry, Captain, but how do I know if I don't ask?" Rossi stood several inches shorter than Aladee, her form stout and solid. She eyed Lena. "What are you in for?"

Lena pursed her lips as Aladee slapped a hand over her face with a groan. "What are *you* in for?" Lena returned.

Rossi shrugged. "I helped my employer blackmail his clients. The king sentenced me to a year of work in his gardens to pay my debts."

"And now you're a Stewardess officer," Lena said.

"Although I don't know how she managed it with a mouth as big as hers," Aladee said with a frown, but there was no missing the fondness she had for the other woman.

Seria laughed out loud. "I think I might've met my rival for chatter."

Rossi grinned back at her. "We should talk sometime."

"But not now." Aladee gave Rossi a playful shove. "You're on guard duty."

"Right away, ma'am." Rossi winked at the two women. "Have fun."

"Sorry about that," Aladee said when she was gone.

"She's delightful," Seria said. "Her honesty is refreshing."

"Refreshing is not the word I'd use," Aladee grumbled. "Tiresome, maybe. But enough of that. Show us how to fish!"

The next hour was spent in laughter as Seria demonstrated the joys of fishing. She was the one to dig the worms up and attach them to the hooks. Aladee offered, but at the look of repulsion that flashed across her face, Seria took pity on her. Lena refused to touch them.

Once the hooks were dropped in the water, Aladee and Lena attempted to match Seria's catch, but Seria pulled out trout after trout before their hooks even bobbed.

"I don't know how you do it," Aladee said in wonder as Seria pulled her fourth fish.

"My father taught me. I guess I developed a knack for it."

It felt good, being outside and fishing again. It breathed peace back into her soul. She gulped in the fresh air. The creek gurgled joyfully, and birds sang their hearts out.

She observed the target. "What's that doing here?"

Aladee dusted her hands. "That same little birdie told me you like to watch the Stewards train."

Seria slanted an exasperated look at Lena. "Are you giving away all my secrets?"

"Not all of them." Lena's brown eyes sparkled with mischief.

"I thought you'd like to play around with some things." Aladee waved at the table. "Please, pick something out."

"I have to warn you, I'm not very good," Seria said as she surveyed the array of training weapons.

"You don't have to be," Aladee assured.

"Good." Seria fingered a smooth rope. "Because the only thing I ever excelled at were escape games."

"What's that?"

"A game my father made up for his children." She smiled as she remembered the hours of merriment. "At the time, I thought it was just for fun. But now, I realize he was preparing us for possible dangers."

"How'd you play?" Lena asked.

"Papa would tie our hands or feet, and we would see how fast we could escape. We tried it in all different scenarios. Tied to a chair. In a dark room. Outside against a tree. Even with chains." She tilted her chin. "I was quite good."

"Really?" Aladee put her hands on her hips. "Can we have a demonstration?"

Seria started to refuse, but the interest both women presented changed her mind. "Sure, why not? Let's see if I can get out of a Steward knot."

Aladee wrapped a rope around Seria's wrists. "This feels wrong," she said. "I don't usually tie my friends up."

"I won't hold it against you," Seria assured, keeping her fists and arms tight.

"All right." Aladee stood back. "That's the knot we use to restrain prisoners if we don't have shackles. Does it feel too tight?"

Seria was already wriggling her hands. "Not at all." She could feel the stares as she worked the rope. At first, her face heated with the thought that she would fail and make herself look foolish. But then her right thumb slid through. A few tugs and twists later, she held the rope up for them to see.

"I'm amazed," Aladee said with wide eyes. "Think you can teach that to my ladies?"

Seria chuckled. "I'm happy to try, but I'm not the teacher my father was." She moved to the table and picked up a small bow set, running her fingers over the smooth wood. "My friend, Ollen, showed me how to shoot once. Before he died."

Aladee sobered. "Ollen Knavis, right?"

"Did you know him?"

"Nay, though I wish I'd had the honor. But Jervis knew him when he was a cadet in training, along with a few others in the squad. He was glad they were brought back home to be put to rest properly."

Seria hesitated to share who was responsible, but Lena did not hold the same restraint. "The Reader made sure they were all returned home."

"That so?" Aladee's dark eyes found Seria again.

Setting the bow down, Seria picked up a sword, remembering his patience while showing her how to hold a sword. "I think that was a big turning point for him."

Aladee fitted an arrow to a bow. "You must know him quite well."

"I did." Seria sighed. "It feels like such a long time ago now."

Lena studied her from across the table. "You seem more at peace here."

"Do I?" Seria took a moment to assess the notion. "I am. Being with Mason was wrong, despite how I felt about him. I don't have that constant guilt or fear of being discovered." She looked around at the fields around her, taking in the large, red-stoned castle rising in the distance. Her heart still longed for the simple life she had made for herself at the fort, but she knew this was where she was supposed to be. "It was hard to walk away from him, and I'm so glad he committed his life to the Lambient. But I know this was what I needed."

Aladee raised the bow to her shoulder. "The Lambient has a mysterious way of taking care of His children, but He always knows best." She released the arrow, and it hit the dead center.

Seria shook her head in wonder. "You weren't even standing in the shooting position."

"We train to shoot in every position from a variety of distances." Aladee took another arrow. "We can't guarantee that we'll have the perfect conditions in an actual battle."

"Captain Dudley likes to make his men train in the rain." Lena laughed. "How they would complain at that."

"He's right, though," Aladee said. "Bruin is capable of turning any kind of weather to Jader's advantage." She let another shot off, barely taking time to aim, and it buried itself right next to the other one.

"Do you ever miss?" Seria asked. "I've watched you ladies practice dozens of times, and it seems everyone makes it every time."

"It takes training and concentration, but we do have an advantage."

"What's that?"

Aladee rested the end of the bow on the ground. "It's almost a supernatural skill given to the Stewardesses once we've taken our Beacons."

Seria leaned against the table beside Lena. "How so?"

"The women of the army do not possess the same physical strength and stamina as the male Stewards. So, the Lambient granted us the ability to shoot with near-perfect precision. Even in times of great chaos and confusion, we can aim straight and true."

"I never knew that." Seria exchanged amazed looks with Lena. "That's fascinating."

"It's but one way the Lambient provides for us and allows us to serve Him and the king in a way that's different from the rest. We stay closer to the castle and the city, while the men go out to the front lines."

Seria tugged at the ties of her belt. "You ever feel your work isn't important enough?"

Aladee looked at her. "What we're doing is important. We're one of the last lines of defense for the kingdom, a backbone for the Stewards on the front lines."

"Aye, but it's the men who fight first, the ones everyone notices."

"But, Seria, my importance does not come from the work I do, no matter what it is. My being a Stewardess Captain does not make me any more or less worthy than Jervis. My value comes from being created and loved by the Lambient." Her words glowed with her passion. "If we were to fail to protect the kingdom, and Paladin falls because we are human and fallible, our value does not diminish in the Lambient's eyes."

Seria shook her head. "I always felt I had to get away from my title as washerwoman before I could ever be important. I let that desire drive every decision I made. Including my relationship with Mason." The admission slipped before she could stop herself.

A joyful light sent Aladee's eyes to dancing. "In truth, Lambient loved and cherished you every bit as much as a washerwoman as He does now that you are healer to the king of Paladin."

Seria sucked in a breath, her eyes stinging. "I've never considered it that way."

Lena wiped moisture from her own cheeks, and Seria laughed. "What are you crying for?"

Her friend gave a watery smile. "I needed to be reminded that working in someone else's kitchen does not negate my worth just as owning my own business does not make me any more worthy than anyone else."

Seria wondered if Lena was feeling inadequate as a possible romantic interest for Prince Eric. She leaned over and put her arm around Lena's slim shoulders. "You are truly a special and remarkable woman, Lena Carwright, and anyone who does not see that is a fool." Even if he was the prince of Paladin.

"That's enough, girls. Now you're making me all misty," Aladee spoke up.

They all laughed and moved on with their archery game. As Seria lifted the bow with her awkward grip and stiff pose, her heart felt lighter and freer than it had in a long time.

32

The day Luron cleared him to leave, Mason stood outside the infirmary for a long time, taking in the sight of the compound. He never expected to feel at home here, and he still wasn't settled. But during the nightmarish days in the Shadowpit, all he had wanted was to get back here.

Now that he was back, he wasn't sure what to do first. He felt in need of exercise to get his muscles working again. His hands itched to hold a sword again, to feel the security of the weapon after feeling so helpless.

But he was not ready to face the rest of the Stewards yet, so he turned to the mess hall. Maybe he could sweet-talk Nola into an early meal before the dinner hour started. Not that he had ever been good at sweet-talking anyone.

To his relief, the hall was almost empty. Two men sat in a corner and eyed him as he crossed the large room to the middle door, but neither said anything as he pushed through into the kitchen.

At his entrance, Nola turned from where she stirred something over the large hearth. "Mason!" she exclaimed, dropping the spoon. "You're back!"

Mason was forming a joke about being late for work when she threw her plump arms around him, hugging him close. "I worried about you," she said, close to tears.

Stunned at her response, Mason stood awkwardly in her embrace.

"I'm sorry." She sniffled and drew back. "I don't usually fall apart like that. When I heard you were missing..." She patted his cheek. "But here you are, just as handsome as ever."

He let out a strained chuckle. "And here I thought you were going to fire me."

She scoffed. "Fire you and keep Marcus and all his thumbs? Nay, thank you."

"I don't suppose I could get a bowl of soup before the dinner crowd comes in, could I?" he asked in an attempt to get things back on normal footing.

"Of course!" She pushed him into a chair and bustled to the pot. "I was making some rabbit stew. It should be ready by now."

Mason watched her hurry about to dish him up a bowl. Something about her genuine pleasure touched something deep within him. He had very few memories of his mother, though Liam had always spoken highly of her. What had her hugs felt like?

He shook his head and rubbed his face. Maybe he wasn't ready to leave the infirmary. One hug from the cook, and he was nothing but mush.

Seria would laugh and call me a softy.

Nola set the bowl in front of him before he could get lost in the memories again. "Eat up, my boy. You're far too thin."

Funny how different "my boy" sounded coming from her.

After draining two bowls, Mason promised to report to duty soon. Nola assured him she was fine and to worry about gaining his strength before he stepped foot back in her kitchen to work.

He headed for the barn next. While he had no doubt Crue had taken good care of his roan, Mason wanted to see the animal for himself, to feel the warm hide beneath his fingers.

"Sir Mason!" A Steward youth he didn't recognize trotted up to his side. "I'm glad I caught you," he said.

"Do I know you?" Was he one of the cadets who hung around with Dakim?

The young man shook his head. "I don't think we've crossed paths before. My name is Zakkias." He licked his lips and inhaled. "I was a part of Lt. Ollen's company."

Zakkias had Mason's attention now and he turned, bracing himself against what would come next.

"I should've come to you sooner," Zakkias said. "I stopped by the infirmary, but Luron said you were already gone." He shook his head. "I'm sorry. I'm rambling."

Hiding a confused frown, Mason nodded him on. What could this soldier want with him?

Zakkias took a halting breath. "I'm the one who led my squad to Joshun. And I'm the only one who walked away." Pain leaked into his words.

"I see." Mason reached for his wrist, where his bracer should be.

"I just wanted to thank you, sir."

Mason stared at him, sure he had heard him wrong. "Thank me?"

"For bringing my squad home. Sgt. Kleff and Lt. Ollen. And the rest. By the time I found Prince Eric..." He glanced away, his eyes reddened.

Rubbing his jaw, Mason tried to block the image of the bodies on the ground. Of Ollen's last breaths. "I got there too late. It was the least I could do."

"You did what I couldn't do. So, I wanted to let you know I appreciated it." He started to move away.

"Hey." Mason waited until Zakkias looked back at him. "It wasn't your fault, you know."

Scraping the toe of his boot against the dirt, Zakkias hooked his thumbs on his belt. "I left them there."

"You saved those kids."

"You were responsible for that."

Mason shook his head. "We all would've died if the Stewards hadn't come when they did. *You* saved those kids."

Zakkias shuffled his feet, fingers caressing the Beacon where it hung on his belt.

Running his hands over his hair, Mason walked a few steps closer. "I, um...I know what it's like being an only survivor." He chewed the inside of his cheek, not sure what more he wanted to say. But Zakkias's clear grief was too close to his own, and he could not let him leave without at least acknowledging that he knew what it was like.

"I heard about the Handan massacre," Zakkias spoke hesitantly, his look watchful.

"Aye." Mason dropped his hands to his sides. "Lost my brother and every other boy who had become like family." And Baris, who had never cared for Mason, but this wasn't the time to dwell on that. "It's not easy. Just don't lose yourself the way I did."

Zakkias regarded him with a maturity that marked him beyond his years. "I won't, sir."

"Good." Unsure how to end the conversation, Mason gave a little wave. "Now, go on and do your Steward stuff."

A small smile broke through the serious lines of the young man's smooth face. "Aye, sir."

The walk to the barn was taken with slower steps as he replayed the conversation. He never expected to relate so much to a Steward, but Zakkias's gratitude and guilt had resonated with him, softening a part of him that he had held rigid and hard for too long.

There were several horses out in the corral when he arrived. Most raised their heads at the sight of him, then resumed munching on the hay that had been tossed over the fence.

Mason's roan nickered and ambled over to see him.

"How are you, boy?" he asked, patting the rounded neck. "You look like you fared better than I did."

The gelding snorted and bumped his shoulder. Then he turned back to the hay. Mason chuckled low. "Glad to know you missed me."

Braylee's bay didn't bother to acknowledge him at all, too busy with his breakfast.

"Don't know how you manage to be a knight's horse, as fat as you are."

The horse did not so much as flick his tail at him.

Eric's stallion, Oakley, whinnied a greeting but didn't leave the company of the other horses. Mason looked around and headed inside. It wasn't until he saw the empty box stall that he began to worry. Where was Sanjo? His chest tightened. He had promised to take care of Seria's donkey. Had something happened to him while he was gone? *Please, let him be all right.*

Then a loud bray sounded from outside, piercing in its demand. Mason stepped outside, following the angry cries. A small shed with large windows was located at the edge of the barnyard. He caught a glimpse of large ears in one of the open windows before he threw the door open. Sanjo stood with his back to him, surrounded by hay and food, braying at the top of his lungs.

"Would you cut that out?"

The donkey's head swung around, quickly followed by the rest of his body as he clopped over to nearly collide with Mason.

"Blades, you crazy animal, take it easy." Mason held one arm against the bruises on his ribcage and tried to push Sanjo back, but he wouldn't budge, his head pressed against Mason's chest.

"It's about time you came back," Barry said from behind. "That beast about drove me crazy, bellowing at all hours of the night. I had to close him up in here just to keep him from scaring the rest of the animals."

Concern spiked. "What's wrong with him?"

"Blasted if I know." The blacksmith wiped his damp brow. "I was about ready to haul him off somewhere."

Sanjo gave a sigh and blinked up at Mason.

"That's the quietest he's been all week." Barry squinted at him. "Maybe he was missing you."

"More likely missing his former owner." Mason roughed the donkey's mane. "And he didn't have me around to throw the blame on."

"Maybe, but if he calms down, you can put him back in the box stall." He turned to leave, then spoke over his shoulder. "Glad to have you back."

Mason focused on the animal trying to nibble on his shirt. "Thanks."

There was no need to use a lead rope. Sanjo trotted after him like a puppy all the way back to the barn. Mason put him back into his regular stall and slipped him a bit of carrot. "I managed to swipe this from Nola's kitchen."

Sanjo barely noticed it and lipped at Mason's fingers instead.

"Don't you be biting me, or I won't visit you again." Even as he made the threat, he knew he would never follow through. Besides being his last link to Seria, the animal had become a source of comfort to him.

The memories of the Shadowpit swept over him, taking his breath away and making his heart pound. But Sanjo's warmth grounded him back to the present. That and his attempt to work the carrot from Mason's death grip.

"All right, all right, there you go." He cast a quick look around before wrapping his arms around the furry neck. "I missed you too."

"What can you tell me about the Shadowpit?" Eric looked at Mason from across the table in the Council Hall. Braylee sat quietly at the head, his arms folded. Eric had waited to hold this discussion until Mason was released from Luron's care, but he could not put it off any longer.

Mason's face tightened as he talked, his voice dull and flat. Eric's skin crawled as Mason described the purple veins within the red-hot pit.

"The source of the Shadowstone," he said, looking to Braylee. "Right here in the Gateway all this time. And yet we still have no idea where it is."

"Jader could be using some of his power to conceal it."

"Perhaps."

Mason's fists lay clenched in his lap, and a shadow hung over him, prompting Eric to ask, "What's wrong?"

He blinked. "I wish I was more help. But it's all a blur in my head."

"What do you remember?" Braylee asked quietly.

"Not much..." Mason shook his head. "I remember the pain. The constant thirst and hunger. Bruin was in and out. And Jader...trying to get me to take the Shadowstone." He scowled at the wall.

Braylee squinted. "You look like you have something on your mind."

"I can't figure out why they took me to Machlin. I was left chained in a room by myself most of the time. It doesn't make any sense."

Eric agreed. "The Darkmen fought back, but I didn't see one Shadowman, except for Bruin briefly."

"You think they wanted us to find you?" Braylee asked.

"It doesn't make sense," Mason said again. "But their defense was too weak."

The whole ordeal left Eric edgy, as if they were missing something obvious. But the conversation was taking an obvious toll on Mason. His eyes still held a haunted look, as if his spirit relived what his mind could not remember. There was nothing more they could ask of him, so Eric released him to get some rest and sat for a while after he had gone, his mind full.

Mason had come out of his ordeal different. He had less fight in him. Though he still seemed to prefer being alone, he did not carry the same hard edge of resentment. What emotional scars did he carry from his four days of captivity?

But under the worry, Eric still felt a strong sense of optimism. Mason was changed but not broken beyond repair. That fight would serve him well in his recovery.

The mood in the fort had shifted since the Stewards had brought Mason back. Many of them had seen the shape he was in, bloody and bruised, looking more dead than alive. And now, a heavy sense of anticipation draped over everyone. Retrieving the Reader had been a victory, but it was as if it stirred up all the foreboding of what was coming.

It bothered Eric. He wanted his Stewards ready, but he didn't want them to lose heart in the waiting.

"What do you think?" Braylee asked.

Eric had almost forgotten Braylee was in the room. "I think we need a sporting day." The decision was immediate.

"You think the practice is needed?"

"Nay, that's not what I mean, though it certainly won't hurt. The mood in the fort is heavy. We need a day to come together, in unity. A day to forget what's beyond those walls and rebuild connections here." The idea gained momentum as he talked. "A game day."

Braylee angled his head in thought. "Could be a good reprieve."

"I believe we need it."

"Then let's do it."

33

Anticipation buzzed over the entire fort for the upcoming sporting day. Even the civilians caught the fever and planned a community picnic to watch the games. The knights—Steward and Reservist alike—polished their swords and sharpened their arrowheads. The mood was jubilant and cheerful. Even Mason could feel it as he made his way to the mess hall early in the morning the day before to break the fast.

A group of men huddled about the door, talking amongst themselves. Mason paused and almost went on by, but he was hungry, so he swallowed his discomfort. He would never find a place here if he didn't put forth some kind of effort.

Gann broke off his conversation with Timothy as Mason approached. "You got your sword all polished?" he asked, his expression guarded but not unfriendly.

"I'm not sure how much I'll take part. But I'll watch."

Timothy cocked a brow. "So you can watch the rest of us lose?"

"The only surefire way to lose is to take on the prince," a beefy sergeant named Lux quipped.

"Or Captain Braylee. Speaking of whom..." Gann looked to Mason. "I don't suppose you'd do a favor for me?"

Reluctance made him slow to answer. "What's that?"

"We've been called to the training field to supervise the setup. The problem is, the captain has the only key to one of the weapons sheds we need to get into. Would you mind getting that from him? One of us would go, but Dudley's already waiting for us."

"And we do *not* want to leave him waiting long," Lux spoke up, earning a quick scowl from Gann.

Mason shrugged. "Sure. I'll go get it after I eat."

"I'd rather not wait. I'll have a cadet run back to grab it from you if that's all right." He waved his hand at the hall door, already edging away. "There's still plenty of time to eat."

Mason had a feeling Gann was taking advantage of his officer position to get the new man to do his bidding, but there didn't seem to be any animosity behind the request. "I suppose I can," he said slowly.

"Great. He's in the second room in the Great Hall. I thank you." Gann stepped off the shallow step, followed closely by the others. "Let's go, boys. We don't want to keep Captain Dudley waiting."

Timothy glanced back as they left. "See you on the training field."

Mason stood alone for a moment, trying to figure out if he should be annoyed. They were almost too friendly. But he shook it off and headed across the street to the Great Hall. He found room two easily and raised his fist to knock. When there was no answer, he pounded again. The door jerked open with the force of a cyclone, and Braylee glowered at him, his dark hair a mess. *"What?"* he barked, his eyes narrow slits of black.

Mason took a hasty step back. "Um, Gann said you had a key to...something."

"And?" he snapped.

"They need it?"

Braylee's face reddened. "Well, they can wait for it." He slammed the door.

Too shocked to get angry, Mason stared at the closed portal. After a moment, he felt someone watching him and turned to see Eric leaning against a wall, trying hard not to smile.

"What was"—Mason gestured at the door— "that?" He kept his voice down lest he stir the captain's wrath again.

Eric pushed himself off the wall and motioned for Mason to walk with him. "That was our mild-mannered Captain Braylee Wright in the morning." He let out a cough. "So, who hoodwinked you into waking him?"

"Gann." Mason scowled as they walked down the steps.

"I figured. After his first encounter with the grumpy bear, he's made it his business to make sure every new member gets the treatment." He smacked Mason's back. "You're officially a part of the team now."

Despite his annoyance, the statement sank deep into his mind. Was that what this was all about? Gann's sneaky way of showing his acceptance?

Mason caught the glimmer in Eric's eye. "Why don't you go ahead and laugh like you want to?"

Eric snorted, smothering a chortle. "Sorry. Believe me, even I've gotten bitten a number of times. Braylee sees no rank first thing in the morning. Don't take it personally. Give him time to wake up, and he'll be back to his normal self."

Once he had his meal, Mason arrived at the training field, ready to give a hand in setting up for the sporting events the next day. He spotted Gann with the others, overseeing the dueling field, and headed that way.

Gann met his gaze, laughter lurking behind his eyes. "Did you get that key?"

"You can get it yourself, thank you," Mason growled.

They all laughed, but surprisingly, he was not turned off, though he wasn't sure if he wanted to laugh with them or knock their heads together.

A little while later, Braylee arrived, aiming for where Eric and Dudley talked. He glanced over at Mason, then gave a slow nod. Mason returned it, recognizing that for the only apology he was going to get. He was not about to demand more.

Sporting Day dawned clear and bright, much to Eric's relief. He soaked in the sunlight on his way to the training field. "Bless this day, Lambient," he prayed. War could hit tomorrow, thus the future is not guaranteed for any of the men. He wanted to give his men this day to enjoy at least.

The shallow hills surrounding the fields were crowded with civilians sitting on blankets, chatting with friends, and passing a few predictions about their favorite competitors. The few children who still lived within the fort ran about, chasing one another and hiding. Laughter rang out like music, echoing through the open air.

The men gathered in large groups. The Stewards wore their green training suits, oiled to a gleaming finish. The militiamen wore brown leather pants and loose-fitting shirts. Dudley gathered his men on one side, while Braylee's met across the field. Those on guard duty would have their chance to join the festivities during the second round of contests.

"All right, we have a plan, so let's stick to it!" Dudley called out. "We don't want Captain Braylee's company making us look like fools."

Everyone laughed at his competitive nature, softened by the boyish twinkle in his blue eyes. The weathered captain loved a good contest.

Braylee was calmer, organizing his units into groups and giving a few instructions. Dudley teased him about being too fussy.

Eric stood on a small rise, able to see much of the crowd spread out before him. He crossed his arms, contentment swelling within him. Challenges were tossed out while they waited for him to give the official call to begin.

Amid the fun, his thoughts turned to Lena and Seria. They would have enjoyed a day like this. Seria would have joined in as much as she was allowed, teasing and encouraging the men by turn.

Lena would be quieter, standing back and taking it all in with her soft brown eyes, an amused smile on her sweet face.

Trying not to let the moment be dimmed, he closed his eyes briefly and prayed they were safe. He still had no idea where they were even at. His father had not shared, and Eric never asked, trusting him to do what was in the ladies' best interest.

But there was still a small part of him that held on to hope that he would see Lena again. That this upcoming war would soon be over, and he would be free to tell her how he felt.

"Prince Eric! Are you sleeping over there?"

Dudley's question pulled a laugh from him. Leave it to his first captain to bring him back to earth.

"Are you ready?" he called.

The answer was thunderous, rising from the hills where the civilians sat as well as from the soldiers.

Eric raised the white flag he held in his hand, holding it up long enough for silence to fall. "Then let the games begin!" He brought it down, and cheers filled the air.

34

The lack of a Gift does not demean a person, for Gifts are not given to the deserving. Often, men and women of the greatest character do not wield a Gift.
-The Record of Gifts

From the start, the competitions were tough but fair, highlighted by a lot of laughter and fun. Activities spilled out in all directions. Races were held on the paths that led in and out of the woods, some on foot and others on horseback. The hiss of flying arrows rose and fell over the thud of steel swords lined with gum sleeves. As the day wore on, more and more sat out, conceding defeat and content to watch. Those men were then surrounded by civilians, patting them on the back and offering them food and drink. No one was made to feel slighted because he could not win a round.

Dakim and his friends performed very well, considering their greenness. Every time he advanced to another round, Dakim cast a confident look at Mason, who waved him to keep going. Eric joined in the archery games, winning his round hands down. A few teased him about using his Gift, to which he laughed, remembering the first time he tried to show his skill off which resulted in embarrassment. In swordplay, Braylee outmatched all his opponents with a force that left his victims blinking and shaking their heads in amazement. His success came as no surprise to Eric. The big man's experience lent him a steady hand and a quick eye.

Soon, a chant rose. "Take the prince! Take the prince!"

A wide grin split Braylee's beard. "Shall we?"

Eric couldn't resist. "I've been waiting for the chance to finally beat you. Might as well do it with everyone watching so I'll have witnesses."

The challenge flashed in Braylee's dark eyes. "You sound pretty sure, Prince Eric."

"Let's just say it's time."

Other games came to a halt, and everyone called out their encouragement as the prince and captain moved out to the center of the dueling field.

"When you're ready, Sire." Braylee gave a bow, his sword at his side, patient and calm as ever, which never failed to unnerve Eric. So, as usual, he struck first.

The shouts and cheers faded in the background as he zeroed in on his opponent, recalling every trick and step Braylee had utilized before in their sparring. It served him well, as he kept up with every move and combated each offense. But Braylee did the same, and for a while, they moved like mirror images.

"Someone's got to win eventually!" Dudley called out, sparking laughter.

But Eric would not allow himself to be pulled from the moment. He never took his eyes off Braylee's steady gaze, waiting for the one unguarded moment. When it finally came, it was his, not Braylee's. The captain faked a step to the right, caught Eric's sword with his own, then gave a hard twist. Lavrynth sailed through the air.

Eric dropped his head back with a loud groan. "I declare that move will be the death of me."

Though never one to brag, Braylee twirled his sword over his head in victory.

"Sure, rub it in," Eric said, retrieving Lavrynth. Though frustration entwined with embarrassment, he couldn't get angry. "All right, all right." He bent at the waist. "I bow to your superiority, Captain Braylee."

"A man's got to have something to fall back on when he lacks a Gift." Braylee mopped his face, still smiling.

"Who needs a Gift when he can go through a half dozen men before breaking a sweat?"

The day had been far more enjoyable than Mason had expected. Though he chose not to join the games, he didn't feel the same distance as before. Several of the men had stopped by to talk during breaks in the activities. Crue and the cadets were never far from where he sat, though they were caught up watching the antics.

After his match with the prince, Braylee walked around the circle, as if scoping out his next prey. To Mason's dismay, the captain stopped before him. "How about you come out with me?"

Mason waved him off. "I'm only watching."

"You afraid?"

"I didn't say that," Mason answered shortly.

"I understand."

"Understand what?"

"You don't want to risk the chance of losing." Braylee drew closer and lowered his voice for Mason's ears only. "Might make you look weak."

Pride raised its head. Is that how they all saw him after his rescue? "I can still hold my own."

"Prove it."

The challenge hung in the air. To refuse would only prove Braylee's point. He reached for his sword. "Fine."

Cheers rose as Mason joined the captain on the field, but he was already kicking himself. Braylee had baited him, and Mason had walked right into his trap. But he wore his confidence like a mask as he replayed all the duels through his mind, picking out Braylee's style and technique so that he could use it against him. The older knight had size and experience on his side, but Mason had youth and speed. It would have to be enough.

"Don't go timid on me now," Braylee said. "Not with everyone watching."

"Not a chance." Mason readjusted his hold on his hilt. "Just planning out my victory speech." He resisted the urge to roll his eyes at himself.

Braylee beamed. Then he caught Mason off guard by swinging first. Mason parried the strike and returned with one of his own. It took a total of three moves for Mason to realize he was in over his head. Braylee didn't fight with the same intensity he had displayed against Eric, but Mason still felt the strength of every blow. He was going to lose this fight.

Determination quickened his steps, fueled his swings. Mason would not go down easily. If he couldn't beat an even-tempered Steward whose worst flaw was that he was grumpy in the mornings, how could he ever hope to bring Emperor Jader down?

He pulled back in time to miss the point of the gum-wrapped sword catching him in the chest, tension drawing his shoulders up tight. Distant voices echoed in his head, pulling him inward. Pounding his skull.

"Keep your focus," Braylee spoke, his deep timbre cutting through the noise. "Just you and me."

They traded a few more hits, and Mason's muscles tensed and coiled. Instinct kept him moving, staying out of reach of the blade. His former years of training rose within him, and he pulled out moves he had not used in far too long. His steps smoothed out, and his movements became sharper. Soon, he forgot who he was sparring with and enjoyed the rhythm of the swordwork. Maybe he would be able to beat the captain after all.

But he was growing tired, still not up to full strength. His lungs seized to gather a full breath, his arms ached, and his legs protested with every step. Sweat poured down his back. Stubbornness alone kept him on his feet. He had to fight, had to show what he was capable of. Even if he felt like he was about to die.

"Need a break?" Braylee asked in a brief pause, his tone normal now.

"Of course not." Mason swiped at him again, not about to admit he would not hold up much longer.

"All right then." The big man came in fast and hard, knocking the sword out of his hands and sweeping him off his feet. Mason fell hard on his back with a loud grunt.

As everyone cheered, Braylee crouched down beside him. "You did well, especially after all you've been through."

"Sure." Mason swiped his hands through his damp hair. "That's why

I'm on the ground."

"It's all right to admit you can't do it all, Mason." Braylee sobered. "No one expects you to."

Mason had no response, but when Braylee held his hand out, he took it, allowing himself to be pulled up from the ground.

"Thanks." He wished he could express how thankful he was to the captain, but, as usual, words failed him. This was the man who had risked his life to get Mason out of that town hall.

But Braylee gave a nod as if he knew he meant more than the duel. "Maybe we can do it again sometime."

"Don't do it, Mason," Eric warned from the sidelines. "Unless you like being thoroughly humbled."

Mason laughed along with the men, feeling for the first time that maybe he could be a part of them.

The merrymaking continued into the evening, but Lionel sat apart from it. For the first time in his knighthood, he did not participate in the fun and games, despite all the invites. He just didn't have it in him this time. Ollen's absence was too sharp. Sitting on a stool near the weapons shed, he watched it all, deflated. When Braylee called Mason up, he went to the shed.

After their last conversation, his resentment for the Reader had dissipated, snuffed by the humiliation of his own behavior. But it still rubbed at him to see Mason being accepted and included by his fellow Stewards after all that he had done. Maybe he was jealous. Or maybe it was something deeper he wasn't even aware of.

Whatever the cause of his feelings, it wasn't right, and he would have to deal with it sooner or later if he wanted to remain a Steward.

He meandered around the near-empty room. Most of the tools and weapons had been set up outside for the game day.

Someone knocked on the door. "Can I join you?" Dudley asked, his face reddened by the sun and exercise.

"I don't own it."

Dudley took one of the two chairs in the corner and motioned him to join him. "Come talk to me, my boy."

Reluctance dragged his steps, but Lionel could not refuse the veteran soldier. He plopped in the other seat, his eyes on the floor.

"Seems you've been carrying a weight around with you lately."

Lionel shrugged, then berated himself for acting like a schoolboy. "I've had some things on my mind."

"Anything you care to share?"

The temptation to unload on him was almost too much to resist.

Dudley crossed an ankle over one knee. "Everyone missed you out on the field today. You've always enjoyed these kinds of things."

"I don't know how to enjoy myself anymore." It wasn't the same with Ollen missing. Mason would never replace him. And Lionel had let his resentment damage his judgment.

"You know, I've wondered if you're not expecting too much of yourself," Dudley said. "As one of the youngest sergeants, and now lieutenants, maybe you hold yourself to too high a standard."

"I wanted to do a good job." When Dudley crossed his arms and regarded him, Lionel shrugged again. "Maybe I tried too hard."

"No one expects you to handle everything right every single time. The prince has made no secret of his mistakes. And I've certainly acted out in foolishness in my years as a Steward, especially in my younger days."

Lionel slouched in his chair. "I spent so much time trying to prove the Reader didn't belong. And in the end, I'm the one who fell short."

"Mason Grey is an interesting case," Dudley said, narrowing his eyes in thought. "The first of his kind, a Shadowman turned Steward. Never happened in history, as far as I know. Really shook up the faith of a lot of Stewards. I don't think anyone knew what to do with him."

"Especially when he constantly challenged everyone's authority."

"Everyone? Or just you?"

Lionel frowned. "I guess he resented me as much as I resented him."

"Of course he did." Dudley rested a hand on his knee. "You intimidated him."

"Intimidated?" Lionel snorted. "He thought he was better than me."

Dudley shook his head. "Nay. I don't think that's it."

"Captain, he challenged everything I said, disrespected me to my face."

"Aye." Dudley settled both feet on the floor and straightened in his seat. "Because everything you are represents what he could've been, had he chosen a different path. But he can't change what he used to be."

The idea was absurd, but something about it rang true. Lionel recalled the tense confrontations exchanged with Mason. Every time, Lionel had thrown his position around like a shield, while casting barbs about Mason's past.

"You can't change the mistakes you made either, Lionel," Dudley said as he stood. "But each day is a gift from the Lambient, a chance to start fresh. All you can do is learn from them and move on." Dudley crossed to the door and paused. "I miss him too, you know."

Lionel looked out the window to avoid the older man's pointed gaze.

"But you're here for a reason. You still have life." Dudley said. "Maybe it's time you start living it again."

35

The enemy persecutes my soul and makes me dwell in darkness. He waits for my death.
-The Sacred Code

Braylee stepped into the mess hall and spotted the prince sitting at their regular table. He took one look at Eric and asked, "What's wrong?"

Eric stirred from his contemplation. "I wish I knew."

Lowering himself in the seat across from him, Braylee folded his hands on the table. "What happened?"

"I woke up in the dead of night, sure that something had happened, but all was peaceful. I checked with the night guard and even contacted Jervis."

Marcus stepped to their table and asked for their order, but Eric waved him off. Braylee requested a cup of cider. "Why didn't you wake me?" he asked when Marcus left.

"Because there was nothing to report," Eric said. "Besides, I didn't want to get on your bad side." A hint of a smile lightened his features.

Braylee ignored the jab. "Your hunches aren't anything to take lightly."

Eric sobered. "I know, but I don't want to rely on intuition. It does not always guide me in the right direction."

"So, what do you want to do now?"

"I've been asking myself that all night. Sometimes, this intuition of mine is more than I can handle."

"But it's also saved a lot of lives, so you know better than to disregard it." Braylee took his mug of cider from Marcus and sipped. "Let's go over what we know." He waited until Eric looked his way again. "The Shadowpit is close, which is more than we knew before."

"I've had men out scouring the area since Mason's return." When he showed no more signs of distress, Braylee moved on.

"Scouts still see no sign that the Dark Army is moving this way. There's been no retribution for Mason's rescue."

"It's almost as if Jader has retreated," Eric mused.

"Or biding his time."

"For what?"

Braylee sat back and crossed his arms. "Hard to say, since Mason was unable to give us much information about the pit or Machlin."

"It was strange," Eric said. "I did not see a civilian in the time we were there."

"Nay, but we weren't there long. And most would've stayed out of our way."

"Maybe." Eric took a deep breath. "Everything has been going so well since the sporting day. The men are relaxed and at ease, and more united than they've been in a while."

"They're prepared and ready for when Jader makes his move."

"Things are tense here but quiet. The calm before the storm." Eric shifted forward and rubbed a circle on the table.

"But you still feel unsettled."

"Something is about to happen." He looked out the window, where the fort's occupants were starting to venture out for the day. "But I have no idea if it will be out there in the Gateway, here at the fort, or back at Calla." He went still.

"Eric?"

He turned back to Braylee. "Calla. We need to leave. Immediately."

Braylee gave a single nod. "I'll see it done."

And he was good at his word. Within the hour, a platoon was summoned to be ready to ride. Eric tried to remain calm as the men gathered at the back gates. It was a risk to leave the fort, but the urge to hurry would not be shaken.

Dudley was on hand when Braylee let Eric know they were ready. Before Eric could give the call to open the gate, Mason rode up on his roan and stopped before them. "I don't mean to interrupt, but I wondered if you would permit me to go along."

Eric cocked his head. "I think we've got all the men we need."

Mason did not look convinced. "I understand that."

"But?" Braylee spoke up.

"I, um..." Grimacing, Mason scratched his jaw and then looked Eric straight in the eye. "I'd like to go fight for the right side for once."

Eric studied him. "Do you feel up to it?" It had only been a few weeks since his ordeal at the Shadowpit.

Braylee answered for him. "He's fit enough."

After a long moment, Eric gave his assent. "All right, Mason. You'll come with us."

The king shifted in his bed again with a sigh, pressing Seria to ask, "King Aden, are you feeling unwell?"

He had not rested well the night before and was too restless to eat. But he shook his head. "No more than usual, miss." He sighed again. "Just wishing I could see my son."

The statement drew Seria up short. "You're getting stronger every day. Soon, you'll be up and running this castle like before."

His smile was too sad for her liking.

"Is there something you're not telling me?" she asked, scanning his features. His color was good, but the lines around his mouth were deeper than usual.

"Just an old man's intuition, that's all."

His blue eyes stared into the distance, and Seria's insides squirmed. This was Eric's father, with the same sense of perception. "What do you mean, sir?"

He reached for her hand and patted it. "I want to thank you, dear, for all you've done to care for me. I've never had a healer so compassionate in their work. No matter what happens, I want you to know that."

Her heart began to thump. "King Aden, you're making me nervous."

"I'm sorry, dear." He patted her hand again and released it. His silvery brows drew down over his eyes. "But I feel that something is about to change. And there's very little I can do to stop it."

"You need to rest." Seria fluffed his pillow and straightened his blankets, trying not to stress about his strange mood.

It was odd enough that Jervis had stopped by in the middle of the night, to check on the king, he had said. Seria had not told Aden about his visit, not wanting to add any more strain. But it added to the heavy feeling.

As the morning ticked by, Aden continued to be agitated. Seria listened to his heart, not liking the rapid rate with which it beat.

"I don't know what it is you're worrying about," she said at one point, loosening the blankets around his feet. "But you're going to have to relax before you have another setback."

Aden's clear blue eyes shadowed. "I don't think it matters much at this point."

Raised voices in the hall caught her attention just before the door slammed open behind her. She spun around, her skin prickling at the darkly clad man who burst into the room with sword in hand. It was Varon, Naomi's beau.

"What are you doing here?" she demanded.

Varon ignored her as two more men flanked him. His eyes fell on the king in the bed, and a slow, malicious grin slid across his face. "Captain Feegan," he called out. "I found him."

A gray-headed man with a captain's cape entered, a purple stone hanging from his chest. "Good morning, Your Majesty." His cold tone sent shivers down her spine.

When Varon moved to approach the bed, Seria rushed between them and slapped him as hard as she could. "Leave him alone!"

He cursed at her, but before he could make a move, Aden shoved Seria aside and rose up from the bed, his Beacon in his hand. A quick burst of light shot from the rod, knocking Varon flat on his back.

Feegan raised a crossbow and released a shot. A dart struck Aden's chest, slamming him back into the bed. Seria let out a strangled cry and bolted for his side, but the other two men grabbed her arms and yanked her back. She stiffened her limbs and fought them, desperation seizing her with icy fingers.

This couldn't be happening. Not right here in Daymont.

Varon scrambled to his feet, breathing heavily. "That's her, Captain."

Feegan swept her with a cold inspection. "Get her out of here."

She reacted like a wildcat, bucking and kicking as they dragged her away. Where were Aladee or Jervis?

"Go, Seria," Aden rasped from the bed, a red stain already spreading across his chest. "All will be well."

Feegan looked down at him, a dangerous gleam in his eye. "Oh, I wouldn't count on that, King Aden."

Seria screamed and dug her feet in, praying the Stewards would hear before it was too late. It took a third man, sticking the tip of his knife in the small of her back to force her from the room, and even then, she resisted as much as the pain would allow her. The last thing she saw before she was pulled down the hall was Feegan standing over Aden's helpless form.

36

Passing through solid walls is among the stranger of the Gifts, but one that can be very beneficial in times of need.
-The Sacred Code

Mason rode silently alongside Eric, Braylee on the other side. The prince's face was wracked with concern, though he tried to maintain a calm demeanor. Mason's chest thrummed with anxiety as the horses trotted closer and closer to Calla. He had no reason to doubt Eric's intuition, having already witnessed its strength multiple times.

They crested a small rise, the city of Calla in the distance, when pain and voices exploded in his head. He jerked at the reins, causing his horse to shy and nearly unseat him. For a moment, all went black, and he heard weeping. Screaming. Seria crying out. Lena whispering prayers. A raspy voice gasping in pain.

A band tightened around his throat. He had not experienced an episode like this for some time.

"Mason?" Eric cut through the fog, and he lifted his heavy head, heart thudding.

"Something's wrong," he whispered.

Eric's jaw clenched, and he looked behind him. "Let's ride!"

The air filled with the rush of hooves as the men urged their mounts to pick up speed. Mason gripped his horse's mane, resisting the urge to shout at the roan. He had no idea what he had just experienced, but the urgency would not be ignored.

Seria's voice cut through him, shooting fear into the cracks. Was she at the castle? Had she and Lena been there all this time?

Lambient! Help us get there!

They rode at a steady rate until Eric raised his hand to halt the army beside a small copse of trees. He motioned Braylee to follow him, and Mason took it upon himself to join them. They topped the final hill that allowed them to look down at the castle grounds. Eric reined Oakley in sharp and stared down at the courtyard, his face mottled with fear and anger.

Mason had never seen the home of the Passions before, but its splendor was lost on the sight before him. Soldiers in black milled about in the castle courtyard. Saddled horses lined one side of the open space, ready to go at a moment's notice. There was no sign of Stewards anywhere.

"Dear skies above," Eric breathed, gripping his saddle horn. "What's happened?"

"Steady," Braylee cautioned.

"What do we do?" Eric asked. "I have no idea how many are in the castle or..." He bit off the words.

Mason stared down at the men. A sickening feeling that they were there because of him filled his stomach. The Shadowmen he had helped get through the fort months ago were now building another Dark Army. Right on the doorstep of Calla's king.

His mind rolled nonstop as he adjusted his bracers. The other two men talked softly, going over options, Eric clearly working to control the emotions at seeing his home overswept with Darkmen. But his purpose kept him focused.

"What about sending a scout down?" Mason asked. "He can give you an idea of how many are down there and if there are any more reserves."

"That's not a bad idea," Braylee said.

"All right then." Eric gave Mason a direct look. "You go."

An hour later, Mason rode back up the hill to report his findings. "About a hundred men are guarding the courtyard, but they're scattered and distracted."

"We could split up," Braylee said, his dark eyes never leaving the ranks of soldiers. "Some could attack from the front, draw their attention. The rest could sweep around from the back."

"Catching them in the middle." Eric chewed his cheek, thinking. "It's risky. They could use my father as a bargaining chip."

Mason glanced at the prince. He said nothing about hearing the girls' voices, wondering now if Eric was unaware they could be in the castle as well. But impatience tightened his grip over the reins. What if there were Darkmen inside?

Eric gave a long sigh. "We have no choice." He looked up at the sky. "Fortunately, we have daylight on our side."

They turned back, and Eric divided the army into two. Braylee would lead the direct assault, and Eric would attack from the rear. Mason would go with Braylee.

He caught a long look from the prince and captain, words passing between them without being spoken. Then they shook hands and separated.

As he got into position in the ranks, Mason's breath seeped out through his teeth in little hisses. Braylee did not appear to carry any of the misgivings he wrestled with. The Steward positioned his bay in front and drew his sword. He swept a dark look over his men. "For the king."

They raised their swords in reply. "And the Lambient." Their voices rose in unison, carrying a sense of courage and determination. Mason drew in a full breath of air and rolled his shoulders.

Help us all, he prayed, wrapping his fingers around the hilt of the sword he had been given since his own was lost. A Steward sword.

Braylee aimed Beast forward. "Let's ride!"

They moved down the hill, straight for the throng of Darkmen.

Seria stumbled into the kitchen, her arms bruised and sore from the harsh grips and her heart bleeding as she pleaded with the men not to kill the king. The sight in the large room stalled her for a moment until the men shoved her once again. The kitchen staff was crowded into a corner, everyone on their knees with their wrists bound. Seria scanned the room for familiar faces, relief filling her at the sight of Lena unharmed.

"Make sure you keep an eye on this one," one of the men said, pushing her to the guard in the middle of the room. "We'll want to keep her."

Seria shuddered at the insinuation.

The guard motioned with his sword for her to join the other hostages, and she walked, trembling, to the huddled group. Before she could sit, the guard pulled out a rope and jerked her hands behind her. She gulped and positioned her wrists as he wrapped the rope around them. Then he pushed her to her knees behind the group. "Now sit down and don't move, unless you want to see someone else get hurt."

She looked over at Lena, who sat with her back against the wall, her gaze steady and pointed. Seria waited until the guard walked away and nodded once. Nobody moved for a long moment. The other two men had left again, leaving the guard with a dozen cooks and maids to watch over, all bound. Seria looked around, gauging the responsiveness of the guard and the emotional state of the staff. Someone coughed, and she shifted her position. The guard looked out the door, and she moved again, keeping her eye on the man.

The door opened again, and another group of castle workers were ushered in by sword point. Seria spotted Charlin and the other laundry workers, followed closely by Naomi. A few minutes later, Varon entered, his stride confident. "Got them all?" he asked.

Naomi's face drained of color. "Varon!"

"Aye," the kitchen guard answered. "All the staff is holed up here or in the barracks."

"And the Stewards?"

"We've got the women corralled in one of the storage rooms."

Varon stuck his chest out. "Nice work. Captain's got the king covered."

Naomi shuffled closer to him. "What are you doing?"

His expression soured. "Sit down and stay out of the way."

"But I thought—"

"That was the point, lady. Now sit down and shut up."

Naomi's posture wilted before him. She cast an apprehensive look all around before she took her spot with the other staff, allowing the kitchen guard to bind her wrists.

Varon smirked. "Feegan was right. Didn't take much at all to get my way inside." He glanced at the guard again. "Keep an eye on them. I'll go check the others."

Seria waited until he was gone before attempting another move. Little by little, she crept closer to Lena, who acted as if she didn't notice. Finally, after moving one painstaking inch at a time, Seria sat beside her friend, her feet underneath her. She stared at the guard, who looked around as if he was bored. She froze when his glance landed on her briefly, but then he looked away, uninterested.

Seria caught her breath and shifted so she could reach Lena with her bound hands. Lena curled her fingers around hers, still not looking at her. Seria felt Lena tap against her hand. Once. Twice. Three times.

Lena lunged backward, and Seria let herself fall with her as Lena used her Gift to pass them through the wall into the adjoining pantry. They landed on their backsides, then tossed a frantic look around the closet to make sure they were alone.

"Give me a minute," Seria whispered, shaking off her loosened rope. In a few seconds, she had Lena untied. "We've got to find Aladee or any of the Stewards. King Aden's in trouble. Can you get us there?"

"I can try, but we'll have to take it slow."

They paused to listen but heard nothing outside the room where they hid.

"The storage room is that way." Seria pointed to her left. "We can cut a couple of corners to get there."

Lena nodded again, pale but composed. Seria took her hand, and they crept through the wall into another room which was blessedly empty. They moved carefully from room to room, always cautious to listen and wait. At one point, they stumbled into the library and came face to face with a Darkman.

"Hey, how'd you get in here?" he questioned.

Lena pulled them both back through the wall, and they fled to the next room, but not before Seria spotted the large stash of swords and Beacons piled in the middle of the room. Finally, they reached the storage room, guarded by two men.

"We can get around it," Lena murmured, pointing to the adjoining room a few short feet from where they stood.

They passed through the room, darting into another closet when they heard footsteps, but not slowing down any more than they had to. Soon, they were peering into the back of the storage room, where a dozen bound Stewardesses sat on the floor, surrounded by crates and barrels. Aladee sat tied to a wooden chair, her hair disheveled and a bruise on her cheek. Her sword and Beacon were missing, but otherwise, she did not look wounded.

The guard leaned against the door and leered at the women. "If I'd known Aden was keeping himself a harem, I would've joined the Stewards a long time ago."

"You wouldn't make it past the entry level," Rossi retorted from another chair, not bothering to spare him a look.

"Oh, you think so?" He knelt in front of Aladee. "Want to see what I can do?"

Seria bit her lip, trying not to draw attention to the dark corner where she and Lena huddled behind a stack of crates.

Lena mouthed something and disappeared through the wall before Seria could protest. She looked back in time to see the man run a finger down Aladee's dark cheek. "You're awfully pretty to be kept for Aden's use." His eyes glinted. "Maybe I'll show you what freedom feels like."

Rossi scowled and wrestled against her bonds. "Leave her alone, dirtbag."

Aladee's nostrils flared, but she said nothing.

Then a racket sounded outside. Letting out a curse, the man stomped to the door and flung it open. "What's going on?"

"There's people in the next room," someone shouted, running in that direction.

The guard looked out.

Rossi jumped up and ran at him, taking the chair with her. Before he could turn to face her, she spun with a yell, slamming the chair into him and breaking it into pieces. Thrown to the wall, he sucked in a breath and slumped to the floor. Rossi rose from the ruins of the chair and swiped his sword. Seria hurried forward and pulled the door shut.

"Seria!" Aladee exclaimed as Rossi freed her from the chair. "How did you get here?"

"They have the king!" Seria worked on another Stewardess's binds. "He's already been shot, and I fear..." Her throat tightened around the words she did not want to voice. "Where's Jervis?"

Aladee helped with the restraints. "He took some men out this morning to check out a report of a riot."

Rossi rubbed at her chafed wrists. "Most likely, it was a setup to get them out so the infiltrators could take the castle."

"Then we'll take it back," Aladee said, her brown eyes flashing.

"They have the hall blocked," Seria said.

Lena reappeared through the closed door, pushing a strand of her disheveled hair behind her ear. "Not anymore. They somehow got themselves locked in the linen closet."

Weak laughter rippled, despite the seriousness of the situation.

"You'll find your weapons in the library," Seria informed them.

Aladee spoke to Rossi. "Get to the king's room as soon as you can."

Rossi handed the Darkman's sword to the captain, then raked a firm look over the rest of the women. "Let's go." The Stewardesses followed the lieutenant from the room, their fair faces hard.

Aladee gripped the hilt. "Let's get to the king."

A short while later, they crept through the walls into Seria's tiny sleeping quarters. Aladee opened her door a sliver, and Seria peeked out under her arm.

Feegan lounged in one of Aden's chairs, his ankles crossed and looking as if he had not a care in the world. Aden still lay on the bed, his eyes open in his stark-white face. Blood soaked through his clothes, and he struggled to draw a full breath. But he was alive.

Varon strolled around the room, knocking things over as he picked over items of interest. He picked up Aden's fallen Beacon. "What should we do with this?"

Feegan scowled at the rod. "It's nothing but a piece of useless glass like that. It's only in the hands of one of those bloody Stewards that it can be a weapon of great danger." He huffed. "As you found out."

"He took me by surprise," Varon objected. Then he snickered. "Still didn't do him much good, did it?"

"That's 'cause he's old." Feegan cast the king a look of contempt. "And weak."

"Hey, what if we take all the rods and toss them into Jader's Shadow-pit?" Varon asked. "Melt them all to nothing."

Jumping to his feet, Feegan glowered at the man. "Keep your mouth shut about things you don't know. And get that thing out of my sight." He grabbed the rod and flung it across the room. Seria flinched as it crashed into her door.

"I thought you said it was useless."

The statement seemed to irritate Feegan further. "Why don't you go walk your rounds?"

Looking morose now, Varon headed for the hall.

"And see you don't go throwing out any more of your harebrained ideas," Feegan called. "Our enemy does not need your help."

Once Varon had gone, Feegan approached the bed, his back to Seria's door. "You're not looking too good, King Aden," he said. "I thought you'd be happy to see me."

Aden did not bother to look at him, but his lips moved in silent prayer. A spasm passed over him, and his face twisted.

Aladee pushed Seria back and inched the door open until she could slide out.

"Don't you go dying on us yet," Feegan said, hooking his thumbs on his belt. "We want that son of yours to get a bad feeling about your safety."

Aden stirred, his weak voice sounding for the first time. "You have no power here."

The Shadowman let out a bark of laughter. Aladee took another step, bent, and retrieved the king's Beacon from the floor. She straightened, her jaw tight, and pointed the Beacon at the Shadowman. Feegan spun around as a burst of light shot across the room. He dove out of the way, his sword already in hand when he rolled back onto his feet. His hand streaked toward the Shadowstone around his neck, but Aladee did not give him a chance to use it. She sent out a shield of light so bright that Seria had to cover her eyes.

When the light faded, Feegan had fled. Aladee ran to the door and looked up and down the hall.

Seria burst from the room and hurried to Aden's bedside. "King Aden," she gasped, grabbing a cloth from her basket sitting on the floor. She examined the arrow sticking out of his chest. "We're here now. You're safe."

Aden turned his head slowly to peer up at her. "It is well, Miss Seria," he said with a soft sigh.

Aladee pushed the door shut and bolted it. "How is he?"

Seria pressed a rag around the dart, but blood soaked through the cloth. If she tried to pull it out now, he would bleed to death. She added another cloth over the wound. "You're going to be fine."

Aladee joined her at the bedside. "King Aden, I'm so sorry. They infiltrated the castle."

Aden gave a slight shake of his head, sweat beading his face. "It will be all right." Even as the bleeding slowed, his breathing shallowed.

"I hate to leave, but we have to secure the castle," Aladee said, low and sober. She looked at Lena. "I could use your help."

Lena picked up one of Aden's daggers and tucked it into the belt of her skirt. "Let's go."

Aladee pressed a hand to Seria's back. "Do what you can, Seria," she said. "Keep the door locked. I'll send guards as soon as I can." She left with Lena, melting through the walls into another room, rather than venturing out into the open hall.

Aden's eyes were closed now. He lay so still that she laid her hand over his chest, reassured at the subtle rise and fall. She kissed his brow, but her heart ached with an awareness that she fought against with every ounce of her willpower. King Aden was about to die. And there was nothing she could do to stop it.

37

Though you have been in darkness, you have known great light. Those who come to dwell in the land under the shadow of death will walk into great light.
-The Sacred Code

Worry and vindication whirled around in Eric's chest as he led his men around the back of his childhood home, staying under the cover of trees. There were a few men in black standing guard, but they were quickly overwhelmed by the Stewards. The rear of the castle was soon in their hands, and Eric assigned some men to keep watch, lest the enemy sneak in from behind. Then he went on around to the other side.

As he rounded the last corner, a great shout rose from the front, followed by bedlam. Braylee's men had reached their destination. That fact poured urgency into Eric's next steps.

"Go!" He spurred Oakley on, the stallion's long legs eating up the rest of the distance around Daymont's bulk. Eric was in front as they entered the courtyard. Already Braylee's Stewards were deep within the ranks of Darkmen, heavily engaged.

Eric's men did not hesitate to join the fight. On both sides, they streamed past him to aid their comrades, trapping the Darkmen in the middle. He caught sight of Braylee, both his sword and Beacon flashing. Mason was not far off, his movements swift and decisive.

Looking up at Daymont, Eric sent a desperate prayer heavenward. *Please keep him safe.*

A mounted Darkman cut across his path, slashing at Oakley's neck and slicing the reins instead. Dropping the useless straps, Eric gripped Oakley's sides with his legs as he battled the Darkman. He kept his knees tight, maintaining control of the trained horse, but the position made it hard for him to fight as freely as he needed to.

Then a volley of arrows whizzed all around him, and the Darkman hit the ground, along with a score of others. Eric looked up at the wall. A row of women raised their arrows again, firing with unnatural precision into the crowd of men. More Darkmen fell.

Triumph lightened the weight crushing him down, and he swung down to the ground, smacking Oakley to run for safety. If the Stewardesses were fighting back, maybe the situation within the castle was not as dire as he had feared.

He joined in the fighting around him on foot, working his way closer to the entrance. Braylee appeared out of nowhere, catching a blade that was headed for the back of Eric's head.

Horsemen rode in from another direction, and for a moment, Eric feared more Darkmen reserves were riding in. But it was Captain Jervis Planks leading his company of Stewards.

The small army posted before Daymont fell apart. It was clear they did not have the training of Jader's troops in the New Realm, and they could not hold up against the skilled Steward knights.

"Get to the castle." Braylee scoped the area around them. "We've got this."

Eric hastened to do that very thing. The obstacles lessened as he bolted through the doors of the ancient structure, every step sending panic through his veins. He ran through the main hall, so familiar with its polished trim and red banners. But the shouts and crashes that echoed off the walls gave it an eerie feel.

He took the steps two at a time to the landing on the second story. Bracing his hand on the railing, he rounded a corner, sliding to a stop before four men in dark clothing.

"It's the prince!"

Another arrow whipped past him, and the first man fell. As Eric took on the next man, the other two fell prey to arrows at the base of their neck. Eric turned and blinked at the two women who approached him.

"Prince Eric," Aladee greeted. "Your timing could not be better."

Eric stared at Lena, too stunned to move. "What are you doing here?"

Her face was pale and smudged with dirt, but her countenance shone with her usual quiet confidence. "Helping to clear your castle."

Something moved on the landing on the other side of the hall. A row of Darkmen had their arrows loaded and nocked, and aimed straight for the three of them.

"Look out!" He raised a hand to deflect the arrows from their course as he pulled Lena behind him.

Aladee's arrow was already in midair and met its mark. The rest ducked away.

"Captain, I need to get to my father," Eric said.

There was a slight hesitation. "His room is secured, but there are still Darkmen moving about in the halls."

"I can get him there," Lena said.

Aladee gave her a nod. "I'll try to clear the halls."

Eric started to speak, but Lena took his hand, her skin warm and real next to his. "Come with me, Your Highness."

Too dumbfounded to argue, Eric followed her as she ran to the end of the landing, straight for the wall. When she didn't stop, he threw his hand up against the incoming crash, then gaped as they passed straight through it.

His heart pounding and his thoughts scattering, Eric glanced at the woman beside him. "So that's how it works."

Hand in hand, they melted through the rooms and avoided the halls between him and his father's suite.

"How is he, Lena?" he asked, not sure she would even know.

Her response was a tightening of her fingers, which both calmed and frightened him. He held on to her like a lifeline as she took him through the last of the rooms.

All around them, fighting and yelling assaulted his ears. It felt like a nightmare, hearing the home of his family under siege. How had it happened? At what cost? But he held those questions back. There would be time to deal with those later.

Lena reached the foyer outside the king's quarters. Several of Aladee's

Stewardesses stood outside, which did much to ease Eric's mind. They all looked at him solemnly, opened the door, and stepped aside. Lena released his hand as soon as they were inside.

Please, Lambient. Eric stepped into the room and found Seria working frantically over the bed.

"Eric!" she called tearfully. "You're here."

Fear threatened to drown him until the man in the bed turned to look at him. "Father." He dropped to his knees beside the bed, gripping the old man's cold, worn hand.

Aden's face creased into a tired smile, despite the red stain in his upper left chest that drained him of air. "You came," he rasped. "I should've known Lambient would bring you here in time."

Seria still pressed on the wound, her chin quivering. "He's lost too much blood. His heart is too weak."

Through it all, the old man's regard was steady. "It is well, Eric."

Grief and awareness flooded through him, and he brought Aden's hand up to press a kiss to a wrinkled knuckle.

Seria's muffled sob brought his head up again. "Seria." He waited until she brought her tearstained gaze to his. "Thank you."

"I'm sorry, Eric," she cried.

"Don't be." He pressed his trembling lips together and looked back at a solemn Lena, who moved to put an arm around her friend.

"Come, Seria."

For a moment, it looked as if Seria would resist, ready to fight for the king's life until the end, but then her face crumpled, and she let Lena lead her from the room.

Eric rose and sat on the bed, leaning over his father. "I'm sorry I didn't get here sooner."

"You got here when you were supposed to," Aden said. Peace softened the signs of pain that lined his face. "It is time."

"I'm not ready," Eric choked.

Aden's eyes narrowed. "You are ready, son. You'll be a good king for Paladin."

"I mean, I'm not ready to lose you."

A deep breath expelled from Aden's chest, and he reached up to pat

Eric's cheek. "We will meet again in that High Light." His breathing grew faint.

"Father." Eric rested a hand on Aden's white hair. "Thank you for all you were to me." He blinked the tears back so he would not miss one moment. "I love you. So much."

"And I you, son." Aden lowered his hand. "I'm proud of you."

Sniffing, Eric reached down to unhitch the Beacon from his belt. He laid it on Aden's chest, adjusting his wrinkled hand over it. "May the Light of the Beacon guide your way, Father."

Aden's confidence was unwavering, even as his breath failed him. The Beacon cast a golden glow over him. "Go...with...Him."

"Always." Eric slid back to his knees on the floor and laid his hand over his father's.

Aden gave a slight nod, his eyes sliding closed. He flinched, and his breathing rattled. Then he was still.

Eric covered his face. Already he missed the light of his father's eyes. His low, raspy chuckle. Even the way he frowned at him when Eric overstepped. How was he ever to endure the years without him?

His shoulders convulsed with sobs that would not be held back. Putting his head on the bed, Eric wept.

Mason blocked everything out of his mind but what he was there to do. This was his first Steward mission, and he would not fail, not after what they had done to get him out of Machlin.

He stuck close to Braylee as they cut through the throng of Darkmen amassed at the castle gates, a squad of Stewards spreading out behind them. Riding out in the middle of them, Mason barked out an order. "Drop your weapons and surrender!"

More than a dozen released their swords and threw their hands up. It never ceased to startle Mason when his Gift allowed control over a group without eye contact. But even as the Stewards surrounded the unarmed men, something scratched at the back of his mind, like a memory working to unearth itself.

There was no time to dwell on it, however, as there were still others that his Gift had not reached. He moved around the courtyard, using his voice and sword wherever needed.

With the arrival of the third band of Stewards, led by the captain called Jervis, the troop of greenhorn soldiers was soon overwhelmed. Though the Darkmen displayed an eager willingness to fight the king's Stewards, they lacked the skill to push back against them.

But they kept on where they could. It seemed every time he thought they had gotten the upper hand, another bunch of reserves would appear. How had any Shadowman turned so many men against their king in such a short span of time?

The din of steel and voices seemed forever etched in his ears. He used his Gift as much as he could, ordering men to stand down, and soon, the tide shifted. More Darkmen were retreating, and the Stewards were on the offense more than defense.

Taking advantage of a brief respite, Mason dismounted. His roan snorted and shook his head, sweat droplets flying from his coat.

Braylee gave orders nearby. About twenty Darkmen were on their knees, their hands raised. The castle wall cast a long shadow over the ground as the sun began its descent in the western sky.

The captain looked up as Mason headed his way.

"How's it looking, Captain?" Mason asked, shaking sweat from his hair.

"I think we've taken it back," Braylee said. "But it would've taken a lot longer without your presence."

Mason shrugged, though the satisfaction at using his Gift for the right side could not be ignored.

As if he detected Mason's pleasure, Braylee smiled and sheathed his Beacon. "I'm glad you were here."

Something shifted in the distance behind Braylee, so slight that Mason almost missed it. Then it became clear. Hidden in the shadows across the yard, Feegan aimed a crossbow at the broad shoulders of the Steward.

"Look out!"

But the warning came too late. Braylee jerked and let out a throaty grunt, his back arching before he dropped to his knees.

"Braylee!" Mason darted to the big man's side as he pitched forward and caught himself with one hand. A dart protruded from high on the left side of his back, staining his tunic red. Mason grabbed him to keep him from falling face-first on the ground and glared into the darkness, but there was no more sign of Feegan.

The other Steward captain, Jervis, ran up to them and knelt on the ground. "What happened?"

"A Shadowman," Mason spat. "Shot him in the back."

Braylee reached for the arrow. "Get...it...out." The muscles in his jaw popped as he gritted his teeth.

"Nay, not here," Mason said.

"Let's get him inside," Jervis said. Together, the two of them lifted Braylee from the ground and helped the big man to the double doors of the castle.

Don't let him die. The request thrummed in his chest, pounding with every thump of his heart.

"Get the door!" Jervis shouted, and another Steward ran to comply. As soon as they were inside, two more men ran over to assist, lifting Braylee's feet so he didn't have to walk.

"I'm not crippled," Braylee mumbled.

His complaint did much to ease Mason's worry. "Nay, but you're heavy."

The halls were clear of enemy soldiers. A few Stewards stalked up and down the way, their stances alert. Women wearing the same garb of the Stewards mixed in with them. A tall lady with ebony skin carrying a bow crossed their paths.

"Aladee!" Jervis called.

She brightened at the sight of them. "Jervis!" The relief on her dirty face was short-lived as her regard fell to the wounded man. "Oh, gracious, Captain Braylee." She straightened and motioned for them. "Follow me."

She led them up a flight of stairs to a small room with a bed and a small table. The men laid Braylee on his side on the bed. Another moan slipped his tight lips. Aladee worked to remove his boots.

"Where's Seria?" Jervis asked, loosening Braylee's belt.

Mason's heart jumped at the mention of her name. So, she was here at the castle that had been overrun with Darkmen.

Aladee didn't look up. "She's tending another patient."

Relief lightened the weight pressing down on him. She was safe, still doing what she did best.

"Are you all right?" Jervis asked, his dark eyes fixed on Aladee's pinched face.

There was a slight hesitation. "I'm not hurt."

"And King Aden?"

Instead of answering, she rested her hand on Braylee's good shoulder. "We'll get you some help as soon as we can, Captain."

Braylee gave a short nod, his eyes shut. "I can wait."

Aladee made for the door then, Jervis on her heels. Mason hesitated, then glanced at the other Stewards still in the room. "Stay with him."

Jervis and Aladee stopped outside the door.

"What of the king, Aladee?" Jervis asked again.

A door opened. Mason turned, and the world slowed to a stop.

Seria stepped into the hall, leaning into Lena's arms. The sound of her sobs tore at Mason's heart, and his arms ached to hold her. But his feet seemed rooted to the floor. Aladee took a step forward, then stopped short and sucked in a shaky breath.

Lena was the one to speak. "The king..." She shook her head, her chin quivering.

Aladee covered her mouth with a trembling hand and reached for Jervis with the other one.

A shocked silence fell, broken only by Seria's cries, heavy with grief.

Mason took a step. "Seria."

Her head came up, and she stared at him. "Mason," she breathed, her voice wavering.

He walked before her, his eyes never leaving hers. "Seria, Braylee's been shot."

She seemed to wilt before him. "Oh, no. Not him too."

"He's alive," Mason hurried to assure her. He dared to reach out and squeeze her arm, hoping to lend her some of his strength. "But he needs you."

That snapped her back into the moment, and she straightened. "Where is he?"

"Over here." Jervis opened the door for her.

Seria gave him another quick look, heavy with unspoken questions, and followed Aladee and Jervis into the room. Mason looked to Lena, standing silently to the side, tears flowing down her face. His mind went to Eric, and he sighed deep within himself. They had stopped the siege on the castle, but not in time to save the king.

38

In times of distress or darkness, let the Lambient guide your way.
-The Sacred Code

Braylee knew he was alive before he opened his eyes, thanks to the flames in his shoulder blade. As sleep faded, he didn't move, lest he spark more pain. A bandage wrapped around his shoulder and chest, binding the wound tight. An extra pillow kept his weight off the sore area.

He blinked his eyes open. Eric sat in a chair close to the bed, his fist resting against his mouth. His features sagged with weariness. People had been in and out of his room earlier, all talking in low, somber tones. Haziness clouded the memories of what happened after the battle, but one fact had registered in his brain. He licked his dry lips.

"Hey." His voice croaked like a frog.

Eric stirred. "You're awake."

"Mostly."

"Should I ask what mood you're in?" Eric asked in a weak attempt to tease him.

Braylee raised his fingers in a dismissive wave. "I think you're safe."

Eric leaned forward in his seat. "How are you feeling?"

His back felt as if it was on fire. "All right for now."

The prince eyed him. "I can see clearly that you're in pain, Braylee. I can get Seria."

"Nay. Not yet." He didn't want to fall asleep again. "What about the rest?" He was not the only one injured.

"She's tending to them right now," Eric said. He settled back in his chair, his scrutiny never leaving Braylee. "Your family is on the way."

That distracted him from the pain clawing into his skin. "They are?"

"I figured you'd rest easier with your wife and daughters nearby."

A shallow sigh eased its way from his aching body. "I would. But I didn't expect... Thank you."

"It was the least I could do for you. You had us all worried."

"I knew I was in good hands."

Eric gave a weak nod and stared at the floor, a line breaking the space between his brows. Braylee set his discomfort and sadness aside.

"I'm sorry, Eric."

Eric looked up, and Braylee caught the flash of grief. His mouth worked for a moment before he replied. "I managed to say goodbye. I'm grateful for that."

As a Steward, Braylee's loyalty to the king was strong, and the loss was sharp. Calla would reel from the death of their leader.

But Aden was first and foremost Eric's father.

He opened his stiff fingers toward the prince, every movement sending sharp streaks through him. Eric grasped his hand with his own.

No words were needed. Eric sniffed. "Thank you, my friend."

There was nothing Braylee could say to lift the cloud of mourning that would cover Eric in the future. All he could do was walk through it with him.

Eric wandered through the halls, heading for the lower level. His brain and body had gone numb, operating on instinct alone. There was too much to do, too much for him to process. He needed to get the full report from Jervis and Aladee on how the castle had fallen prey, as well as deal with their prisoners. He was thankful he could rely on his captains to run things when he was incapable of thinking clearly.

The Stewards at the fort had to be notified, and his father's memorial service needed to take place in short order, but Eric could hardly bear to think of that. Beyond that, there was the kingdom's future that now rested solely on him. No longer would his father lead Paladin while Eric defended it from the Gateway. Which led to the big question hammering at him.

What should he do now?

His feet dragged as he walked the foyers which now rang with blessed peace, though coated with somberness as the news spread of the king's passing. He moved to the sitting area off the throne room, where Aden had hosted dignitaries and Steward officers over the years. His captains, save Braylee, would meet with him soon to go over the details. Braylee would be a part of future deliberations, but for now, he needed his rest.

The room was dark and quiet, drawing Eric in with its comfortable air, free of the activity throughout the large estate. He stopped short when Lena rose from her seat in front of the fire.

"I'm sorry," she said. "I know I'm not supposed to be in here—"

He held a hand up. "No need to apologize. You're free to go wherever you like. These are not usual circumstances." He wondered if he would ever feel at home in this building again.

She nodded, her gaze disconcerting in its directness.

Eric raised his head, remembering his duty as the prince. *King,* he reminded himself. Though the coronation would be put off—Eric wasn't ready to carry out the traditional ceremony—technically, he was now King of Paladin.

"Aladee told me what you and Seria did," he said, his voice thick. He coughed and continued. "I want you to know how much I appreciate what you did in helping my father."

She crossed her arms. "I'm sorry it did not prevent his death."

He shook his head, stiffening his spine. "That's not a burden you need to carry. Your efforts helped secure the castle. Gave me a chance—" He cut the rest of the words off, unable to say them without cracking.

Lena moved toward him, her steps cautious. "Are you all right?"

"I'm fine." He stared at the wall across the room. *Stay strong.* "I have a lot to see to in the next few days, so I'll probably stay for a few days beyond the wake—"

"Your Highness?"

He started at the nearness of her voice. She stood right in front of him.

"Aye?" he responded hoarsely, caught in her contemplation.

"Would it be appropriate for me to hug the Prince of Paladin in his bereavement?"

The question startled him. "Aye, of course." He expected her to give him a quick hug and move away.

But Lena raised up on her tiptoes and wrapped her arms around his neck, holding him close. His arms came up automatically around her back, but hesitation froze him for a moment.

Stay strong.

But her presence was comforting, and he was tired. The grief was a cold rock sitting in his heart, but in her warm embrace, it shifted, allowing him to feel again. His arms tightened of their own accord as his resistance melted, and he buried his face in the crook of her neck. Tears stung the back of his eyelids, and his throat ached with his loss.

"It's okay," she whispered.

He broke. His shoulders shook as she held him, grieving his father and worrying over a kingdom that he now reigned. Lena remained constant, a steady pillar of strength for him to lean on in his weakness. She said nothing more but stayed there with him as he regained control of his emotions. Finally, he drew back, already missing the warmth of her arms as they slid down. He didn't look at her, but he kept his arms loose around her waist. Nothing was said at first, but there was no awkwardness, only comfort.

He swallowed. "Thank you." He forced himself to look at her, swept up in the soft brown tones of her eyes, dim with tears of her own.

"I hope I didn't come across as forward. But it seemed you needed a hug."

His lips loosened as he let out a chuckle. "I guess I did." He searched her expression and found no trace of embarrassment or forwardness. Only compassion. And maybe something more, but he was afraid to hope.

All this time, when he had no idea where she was, she had been here. Wonder at his father's decision mixed with the grief.

"I don't know..." He frowned and tried again. "I don't know what's going to happen. What the future holds." She did not waver, not even when he caressed her cheek with his knuckles. "But I'm glad you're here now."

She didn't offer a reply, but her gaze held a promise that he grasped on to. He wanted to kiss her—oh, how he wanted to kiss her. But he held back, lest she feel manipulated in his state of emotion.

Voices sounded outside the room, and she retreated, their contact broken. But he did not look away, hoping she could see more than what a simple thank you could say. Her mouth curved up in a gentle smile.

Then the door opened, and they turned away.

39

Iniquity is purged by mercy and truth.
-The Sacred Code

The events that led up to the castle takeover began to come to light. Little by little over the course of the next day, Seria pieced together what had happened.

The infiltrators had gained access into the castle, thanks to Varon, over several days, staying holed up in empty, unoccupied rooms until they were ready. Jervis received a call of a riot, to which he and his men readily responded. When the time came for the infiltrators to strike, everyone was taken by surprise and overwhelmed.

But it was Naomi's unwitting cooperation that first allowed Varon entrance into the fortress. Seria's heart broke for the woman, having witnessed her reaction when Varon's true character was revealed. Naomi was a difficult woman, but Seria did not believe she had any knowledge of his plans. Varon had been killed when the Stewards took the castle back, but the damage was still done.

Eric and Braylee discussed it as she changed Braylee's bandages. His wife, Griselle, had taken their daughters to the kitchen for a midday meal while Seria worked.

"She should've known better," Eric said, pacing the room.

Braylee grunted in reply as Seria applied a new, clean rag against his wound.

Eric stopped and crossed his arms. Weariness rounded his shoulders and drew his mouth down. "Her actions were catastrophic and cost too many lives. Including the king's."

"What are you going to do?" Braylee asked between his teeth.

"She'll have to be punished, of course, most likely imprisoned. We can't have people working for us who bring the enemy right into our bedrooms." His voice was brittle, tight with pain.

Seria bit her lip as she finished tying off the bandage and helped the big man lie back on the pillow. He was healing well, though the location of the injury would make his shoulder hurt for a while and limit the use of his arm.

"Is everything all right, Seria?" Eric asked.

"Oh, aye, of course." She let out a nervous laugh. "He's doing very well. Griselle is going to have trouble making him rest."

Braylee winked up at her. "She's already threatened to leave if I don't listen to you."

"Then why the long face?" Eric asked.

She sighed, putting her things back in the basket before facing him. "It's about Naomi."

He frowned. "What about her?"

"It's not my place to question you, Eric, and I understand you being especially angry at what happened."

"But?" He shifted his jaw.

She played with the strings of her apron like she always did when put on the spot. But she had to say something. "I don't believe Naomi meant for any of it to happen. I was there in the kitchen when she discovered the truth. She had no idea what he was."

"That's no excuse for acting in a way that threatens the security of an entire nation."

"I agree. But she's not the first one to have been deceived by a Darkman."

Eric looked thunderstruck. His Adam's apple worked several times before he spoke. "That's not the same thing." His tone lacked conviction.

She dared to disagree. "I think it is. I brought a Darkman right into the Gateway, who then later walked into the fort. Which led to the infiltration of Shadowmen. That's how this siege happened, so I'm just as much to blame as Naomi."

He turned to the single window that looked out over a field of grass, his back rigid.

Seria glanced at Braylee, who gave her a reassuring nod before addressing Eric.

"Could it be that you're feeling more animosity towards this woman because it led to the loss of your father?" Only he would have dared to speak so openly to the prince.

Eric's head lowered, and he did not move for a long, heavy moment. "You're right," he said, hoarsely. "I let my own emotions lead me in this."

"You've got a heavy load," Braylee said, still ministering to the prince, despite being bedridden.

"I will step aside and let Captains Aladee and Jervis address it. I trust them to be more than just and fair." Eric exhaled and looked to Seria. "Thank you, Seria, for the reminder."

She offered him a smile of understanding. "After the grace you showed both Mason and me, I know what's in your heart. I wouldn't want you to act in such a way that you would regret later."

"Man is sometimes weak when their own hearts are on the line."

"Especially when they're walking in a state of exhaustion," Braylee added. "You need to get some rest."

"I agree," Seria said as she gathered her supplies on the wooden tray she had swiped from the servant's closet. She promised to send Braylee's family up and left the two men alone.

Griselle and the girls were sitting at the large table in the kitchen, although Eric had told them they were free to eat at the dining table.

"How is he?" Griselle asked when Seria entered.

"He's doing fine."

The younger girl clapped with a cheer. "Is he ready for visitors?"

"Aye. The prince is with him now."

Ella perked up and pushed her empty plate back. "I'm done."

Griselle exchanged a chagrined look with Seria before she followed her daughters from the kitchen.

Seria chuckled as she cleaned up their dishes. Braylee's family was delightful. The girls were adorable, and Griselle was exactly the type of

DARKEND

Quill & Flame
PUBLISHING HOUSE

woman Seria would have expected Braylee to have. She was both warm and strong, exuding a motherly and cheerful essence.

The obvious bond between the couple stirred a deep longing within Seria to share in a love like that. Her heart inevitably turned her thoughts to Mason.

She had not seen much of him since the day before when he told her about Braylee, but even in the few glimpses she managed to snatch, he seemed so different. He still sported that stubborn set to his chin, but there was a meekness about him that was not there before. A new maturity darkened his eyes, and she wondered how much of it came from his recent captivity, though she still knew very little about it.

A few other women were working to prepare the evening meal, but the room lacked the usual busyness. Seria missed the hustle and bustle. The quiet was too heavy and her hands too idle. It was a sharp reminder that she no longer had a patient to keep her occupied.

Aladee and Jervis were busy chasing down all the loose ends that had resulted in the castle siege. Lena had made herself scarce ever since Aden's death. Seria determined to find her as soon as she had a chance.

In the meantime, she cleared the lump that had formed in her throat and approached the other women. "Would you like some help?"

Mason headed for the rear castle doors, after spending all day helping to transfer the prisoners. Because there were too many to be housed in the tower, the Darkmen had been taken to a fenced-in courtyard in another location not far from Daymont. Which meant a lot of walking, and now he was tired and hungry.

He had just made it to the hall leading to the kitchen when screams pierced the air, interrupting his musing. His insides seizing, he bolted for the source of the sound. Had they missed an enemy soldier?

Following the screams to the kitchen, he pulled his sword. Multiple female voices cried out in distress, and another one tried to talk over them. Mason shoved his way through the doors.

"—only a raccoon, and if you'll get down, we can chase it out!"

Mason slid to a stop, quickly taking in the room. Two women were standing on the table, clutching each other and staring at something on the floor. A blonde woman—Seria—was sweeping at the floor behind a barrel.

"What's going on?" he asked, trying to calm his heart rate.

Her head came up. "Oh, Mason, it's you!" Relief slowed her frantic movements. "A raccoon snuck in here through the door, and it's causing a ruckus."

"It tried to bite us!" one of the young women exclaimed.

Seria let out a yelp and sprang to the side. A small, gray animal dodged around her. "Oh, stop it!" she yelled. "Don't let it into the hallway!"

Mason released the swinging door to close behind him, then waved his sword at the raccoon to divert it.

"Don't cut its head off!"

"I'm not trying to!"

The raccoon darted under the table, triggering more screams from the women.

"Oh, would you calm down?" Seria crouched down.

"Watch it, there it goes!"

"Where?"

The raccoon bolted past Seria, and she squealed, looking ready to climb the table with the others.

"I thought you weren't afraid of it," Mason challenged, trying to herd the animal to the open door.

"I don't want it running at my face!" She ran to his side to help force it out. "Come on, you confounded beast. Get out of here."

Together, step by step, they urged it closer to the door until it caught sight of the sunshine and ran to the safety of the outdoors. Mason secured the door and for the first time got a good look at Seria. Her hair was coming out of its bun, and she put her hands on her hips, panting.

Their eyes met, and he didn't have to read her thoughts to know they went to the same place he went. Back to that moment months ago when another raccoon snuck into her cabin during a thunderstorm.

She snorted and let out a loud giggle. Unable to stop the mirth that burst from his lips, he bent over, hands on his knees, and let it out. Before long, they were both out of breath, shouting with laughter.

"What are the odds?" Seria gasped, wiping her eyes.

"I think it's obvious," he said, standing up straight and trying to catch his breath. "It's you."

"What?" She poked a finger into his ribs. "You were there both times, sir."

He flinched and put his hands up. "I came to the rescue both times."

"Is that what you called it when the first one sent you flat on your back?" Seria's eyes danced with the memory.

"I was not myself," he returned.

She started to say more when something caught her eye behind them. He looked and almost laughed again. The two women still stood on the table, staring at them like they were mad.

"Do you two know each other?" one asked.

He looked over at Seria in time to meet her gaze.

"Aye, we do," Seria said with a sweet smile. The way she said it warmed his chest from the inside. Now that the raccoon was gone, it hit him that he was standing face-to-face with the girl he had longed for these past few months.

The other women scrambled off the table. One shuddered and rubbed her arms. "Ugh. I need to get out of here."

The other looked around as if expecting more varmints to materialize out of thin air. "Our shift is almost over, anyway."

Seria chuckled. "Go ahead, ladies. The stew is almost done, and I can tend to it until the next shift comes in."

They did not have to be told twice. Without so much as a goodbye, they hustled through the door.

"Well, Sir Racoon Tamer," Seria said, amusement ringing. "Would you like a cup of tea after your harrowing ordeal with yet another dangerous beast?"

His lips twitched before he could stop it. "Aye, Lady Varmint Chaser, I would."

Her laugh trailed her as she moved to a cupboard and pulled out the tea leaves. With nothing else to do, Mason watched her, not minding in the least.

Long gone were the rags she wore in Cadence or the men's trousers she had sported in Shales. In their place was a long deep-red gown, covered over with a black tunic. Her long, blonde hair was twisted in a thick knot at the back of her head that made her look like a woman, rather than the girl he had fallen in love with. Dark shadows highlighted her eyes, and she looked exhausted. But her green irises radiated peace and maturity, despite the sorrow that still traced her rosy features.

Never had she looked more beautiful.

"You look well."

"Thank you, but lately I feel like I've been dragged by a team of horses," she said, stirring the tea.

"You've had a rough go of it, from what I've heard."

The spoon in her hand slowed. "I'm thankful it's over, though I wish it would've ended better." She gave a quick shake of her head. "How's Sanjo?"

He rolled his eyes, already grinning. "I should've known you'd be more worried about that donkey than me."

"Not exactly." She drew the words out as she collected two mugs from a shelf. "But I knew him longer."

"You'll be happy to know your donkey is quite content and lazy, although he's developed an obsession with watching the ducks."

"Dear Sanjo." Seria poured two cups of tea and placed one before him before sitting across from him with her own. "Does he still get his carrots?"

"Now you're pushing it."

She cocked her head. "Something tells me you're stealing my donkey's affections."

"I could never do that," he said, crossing his arms on the table. "One glimpse of you, and he'd knock me down flat to get to you."

"I appreciate you looking after him."

Mason wrapped his chilly fingers around the steaming cup. "It's the least I could do."

She took a sip. "And what about your horse? Do you still have him?"

"I still have the roan, aye."

A frown turned her lips down. "Aw, Mason, do you mean you still haven't given that poor animal a name?"

"What name am I supposed to give him?"

"Any name but 'the roan.'" She shook her head. "Poor thing is going to have an identity crisis going through life without his own name."

He wrestled back the laughter building in his chest. Mercy. He hadn't felt like laughing like this for ages. "Fine. I'll call him Red."

"Good." She took another drink. "It's about time."

Their banter was much like it had been in their early days before his identity had been revealed. They had reclaimed it briefly during their nightly visits under the stars, but always with a level of tension that kept them from truly feeling free with one another.

More than ever, the truth sank deep that he had not been good for her then. Thank the Lambient she had figured that out before he did, or he didn't know what would have become of either of them.

Seria sobered. "It's good to see you here. Working with the Stewards."

"I didn't make it easy on myself at first."

"I would've been shocked if you had." Her tone was dry. "But I can see you've changed. For the better. I'm proud of you."

Nothing anyone at the fort could say would match the way her praise made him feel.

"I was worried about you when...when I heard you were taken." She reached across and squeezed his arm.

The simple gesture touched a part of him that he had feared was dead. He laid his hand over hers, reveling in the feel of her cool skin against his. Her touch and her words planted a seed of hope that he was afraid to even acknowledge, lest it dry up without a chance to take root.

"I made it out all right," he said, keeping his tone light. The last thing he wanted to do was give her a hint of the nightmare he went through. "I thought of you a lot."

"Did you?" She looked pleased.

"It was a good distraction."

She ducked her head. "I, um, I heard your voice a few times."

"You did?" He should've expected it, the number of times he had talked to her in his head. But when he remembered what it was he said, his neck heated. "What'd I say?"

Now she flushed, and he did not press her for more. The urge to entwine his fingers through hers almost overwhelmed him, but it suddenly occurred to him that he was breaking one of the stipulations of his sentence. He could have dismissed it, in light of the king's death, but it felt too disrespectful. For the first time, he wanted to do the right thing, even if it meant putting his desires aside. Even if it was torture releasing her hand. But he withheld the words he wanted to say and pushed to his feet.

"I better go check on my horse." He sent her an easy smile, so she wouldn't be hurt by his departure. That roan was a poor substitute for the company he wanted to keep.

"You mean Red?"

He laughed softly. "Aye, Red."

"Thank you for running to the rescue," she said with another grin. "And for the talk. I can't tell you how good it is to see you looking so well. Especially after..." Her face darkened. "I'm glad you're safe."

"You, too." As he moved away, he thought of her parting words.

His body may be safe at the moment, but his heart was in great danger. Because despite the distance between them and the time that had passed, he was still very much in love with Seria Gayle.

40

Trust in the Lambient forever, for in His might is everlasting strength and hope.
-The Sacred Code

The rockets announcing the passing of the king shook Eric to the core. Dressed in his formal red tunic and cape, he stood at the head of the column of Stewards, his eyes fixed on the pink and gold streaks feathering the morning sky above. Every boom, followed by a shower of sparks, echoed in his spirit, reminding him that his father was gone.

Silence covered the meadow just beyond the training fields where they gathered. Behind him, the Stewards were arranged by companies, the Reservists forming rows beyond them. A few citizens were there, as well as the royal staff. The atmosphere was somber, mournful, despite the glorious dawn.

As the last of the fireworks faded, Eric slowly turned to the crowd. He could feel every eye on him and sensed their sympathy. While he appreciated their support, he was afraid their compassion would break him. Now was not the time for him to show his weakness. Paladin had lost their leader. The citizens would look to him to lead them from here on out. He had to show them that he was capable and ready.

Even if the idea scared him to death.

Captains Jervis and Aladee Planks stood at rank, as well as Captain Nathan Bowman, who had come from the border to be here. Retired captains and officers gathered behind them, their posture stooped with age but their heads held up high.

Braylee had refused to miss the king's memorial service and stood between his wife and Seria, one arm in a sling under his cape. Before him, his two daughters watched Eric, their young faces shadowed with compassion.

In the back, almost hidden by the shadows being cast by Daymont's bulk, Mason hovered, arms crossed. Eric was surprised to see him, knowing his opinion of the king had not been too high. But he appreciated his attendance, nonetheless.

The casket where Aden's body lay sat on a platform in the middle of the field next to a pile of stone that would cover his final resting place. A few feet away was another carefully maintained pile of stones. The queen's grave.

He swallowed, finding comfort in knowing his parents were reunited after a long separation. Together they would dwell in the presence of the Lambient in the High Light. Eric was happy for his father. But, oh, it was hard to let him go.

A hymn was sung as Aden's body was lowered into the earth. Then the Steward chaplain of the chapel read from the Sacred Code, passages of comfort and reassurance of Aden's reward. Every word strengthened Eric's resolve to stand tall and honor his father in his last ceremony. His gaze wandered across the field and snagged with Lena's, brimming with understanding.

He squeezed his eyes shut and drew in a deep breath, accepting the strength she offered him. How was it possible to experience such a deep connection with no words spoken? Opening his eyes, he offered her the faintest of smiles to convey his appreciation. Then he turned his attention back to the ceremony.

The Stewards had the final moment in the service. As one, they raised their Beacons, their lights shining in the dawn until the cemetery was lit up like midday. The Reservists raised their swords, the blades reflecting the light. Another song rose from the choir, rising toward the heavens in celebration of the king who had served the Lambient his whole life.

Eric's heart swelled until it hurt. In the middle of his grief, a deep joy blossomed like a balm to his wounded soul. It did not ease the pain, but it brought an awareness that all was as it should be. His father had lived his life until it was time to step into death. And now it was Eric's turn to take up the mantle Aden had left behind.

As the prince, Eric was not required to say anything at the service. He was, after all, in mourning. But as the Stewards lowered their light rods, he readied himself to speak.

"I would like to thank you all for being so faithful to my father," he said, his voice thick. "I wish I could stay, oversee the running of Paladin within castle walls. But unfortunately, there is a war. And I must protect Paladin first before I can officially lead as king." His voice caught on the last word.

No one seemed surprised at his decision.

"But I will do all I can to ensure the safety of my kingdom, and when the war is over, I will do all I can to follow in my father's footsteps." He ended with a quiet "Thank you," and turned away, signifying the end of the service.

He was glad no one followed him. Needing a few minutes alone, he headed for the chapel. Taking a seat in the back, he sat there, silent, his mind going back over the years he had attended this very chapel with his father. This was where he first heard the ancient words of the Sacred Code before he was old enough to understand them. It was in this building he made the decision as a lad of twelve to become a Steward. And it was here that he first drew his Beacon.

The reverence of the building sank deep through his skin and into his spirit. He drew in a deep breath and bowed his head. "Thank you, Lambient, for the years You allowed me to share with my father," he whispered. "Let me be a worthy successor to his throne and lead my people according to Your will."

There was no audible answer. But a breath of peace brushed by the ragged edges of his grief. It was time to move forward.

He left the quietness of the sanctuary, stepping out into the golden morning. There would be more moments of grief, but for now, he had to look ahead. King Aden's death would not stop or prolong the war. If anything, it could accelerate its coming.

He strode through the castle halls almost without seeing them, the hollowness in his stomach driving him to the large kitchen. As he pushed through the swinging doors, memories of the many times he used to sneak in and steal pastries when he was a boy swept him.

Mason sat at the table, a mug of cider before him. He pointed his mug at him. "You as tired as you look?"

Eric took a seat across from him. "Probably."

Several women worked over the hearths at the far end of the room, but they gave him his privacy. A somber maiden brought a tray with another mug and a fresh pitcher of cider, along with a plate of boiled fish and some fresh slices of bread. Eric thanked her and poured a cup, relishing the spicy sweetness as it drained down his parched throat. Then he fell to the food, famished after two days of very little appetite.

True to his nature, Mason didn't talk, but sat quietly, looking lost in thought.

When he finished, Eric let out a breath and straightened. "I'm sure you're wondering what changes my father's death"—he almost choked on the word—"brings to your sentence, and what it may mean for your future."

"It doesn't matter." Mason sat up in his chair. "I'm staying with this till the end."

The declaration moved Eric more than it should have, stated as shortly as it was. Mason could have requested a leave. But his determination eased a little of the anxiety that had been growing like a stubborn weed.

They sat without speaking, draining their mugs.

"I must say, I did not expect to see you at the memorial."

The chair creaked under Mason's weight. "I admit I wasn't fond of him before, but I think I understand a little more the motive behind his judgment. In any case, I was the one in the wrong."

"I appreciate that you came, as well as everything you did in protecting the castle."

He frowned into his mug. "I'm sorry we didn't get here in time."

"We did." Eric squeezed his hands together. "My father was an old man with ailing health. As much as I'd like to deny it, his time here would not have been long anyway. And we managed to secure the castle, as well as give me a few minutes...to say goodbye. Your urgency and actions outside the walls helped provide that."

Mason gave him a long look, and if it wasn't for Eric's Beacon on his belt, he would suspect he was reading his mind.

"Did you know they were here?"

Eric did not have to guess who he was talking about. "I had not a clue. Although thinking about it, I should have. My father could be hard against wrongdoing, but he had a heart for those who needed a fresh start." He waved at the room. "Many of the staff and even knights are made up of former transgressors."

Mason's brows lifted. "Well, then I appreciate him even more."

Jervis entered then, scanning the room until he found Eric at the table. "Aladee gave me strict orders to make sure you have eaten."

Waving at the plate, Eric said, "You may assure your lovely wife that I'm keeping my strength up for the days ahead."

Joining them at the table, the captain accepted his own cup of cider. "It sounds like you have a plan."

Leaning forward, Eric wrapped his chilly fingers around his mug. "Nothing specifically laid out yet," Eric admitted. "But I cannot stay here long. Jader will find out soon about the loss of the king, and I have a strong feeling it will decide his next move."

"What do you think will happen now?" Lena asked.

Seria took her time in answering. Arm in arm, they climbed the hill up to the castle after a much-needed morning stroll after the service.

"Aladee and Jervis both said we have a place here," she said. "For the time being, I feel like I should stay."

"Prince Eric told me they will be evacuating the civilians out of the fort when they return. So, my family will be closer."

"That'll be a relief."

"Did you hear what happened with Naomi?" Lena asked as they topped the hill. When Seria shook her head, she continued. "She was sentenced to work in the mill."

"They removed her from the castle?"

"She refused to admit any wrongdoing. I think Varon's death put her in denial, even though several witnessed his actions as well as her association. Aladee offered her several opportunities to acknowledge her role. When she refused, the captains had no choice but to deem her unsafe as a castle resident."

"I'm sorry for her," Seria said. "I know what it's like to make a humiliating mistake that everyone knows about."

Lena squeezed her arm. "You've grown so much."

"I learned a lot, to be sure," she replied. "I'm trying to be more accepting of Lambient's will."

"That's not always easy." Lena studied the browning grass before her feet. "Especially when the heart is involved."

Seria studied her friend. Always in the back of her mind was Aden's suspicion that Eric cared for Lena. Could Lena return those feelings? "Is your heart involved, Lena?" she dared to ask.

At first, the only response she got was a sigh. Then Lena raised her head to meet Seria's eyes. "Maybe. But we're...leagues apart. And even if there was a chance, this war makes everything uncertain."

"Could it be the prince you're speaking of?"

Lena's cheeks tinted. "I sound as bad as Ella, carrying around a crush on the prince."

Seria laughed at the comparison. "Ella is a dear girl, but you aren't swept away by looks or titles."

"They don't hurt."

"For sure, and I think you'd make a lovely queen."

"Oh, stop it, Seria," Lena said, her face reddening even more.

Seria squeezed Lena's shoulders. "I mean it. And if the prince has any sense, he'll recognize that."

"I'm a civilian." Her smooth brow creased. "It wouldn't be proper, I'm sure."

"That's not necessarily true." Seria gave Lena a smug look. "I happen to know the queen was a civilian herself before she married King Aden."

Lena's eyes lifted to hers. The hope that glimmered there made Seria's heart ache, and she prayed she had not said too much. "Prince Eric is an honorable man. If he has come to care for you, he won't let his throne come between you."

They approached the large, wooden back door. Lena stopped and sighed. "In the meantime, I need to do the same as you and learn to wait on the Lambient's will. I think I'll start by visiting the chapel."

"I would join you, but I should check on Captain Braylee."

"How is he?"

"He's already getting around fairly well now but still experiencing some pain."

"I'm glad it wasn't more serious. I don't want to think how hard that would have been on Prince Eric."

Seria noted how carefully Lena still addressed Eric. "He was quite relieved to know his captain would recover completely. Braylee has already insisted he'll go back when the Stewards return to the fort."

A shadow fell over Lena's face. "Do you know when that will be?"

"I don't think they'll be here much longer." Seria shared Lena's feelings about the coming departure. She hated the thought of Mason leaving, especially with so much left unsaid between them, but there was a war going on. "Would you like some tea?"

"Nay, thank you." Lena's smile was strained.

Seria put her arms around her friend and hugged her tight. "It'll all work out, Lena." In her heart, she believed it.

Lena squeezed her back and took the worn trail that wound around the eastern wing to where the small, stone chapel stood in the inner courtyard.

Seria entered through the servant wing and took the hall that led to the kitchen door. Men's voices, low in serious conversation, met her ears just before she entered. Eric, Jervis, and Mason all stopped and looked up at her.

"Oh, I'm sorry." She backstepped. "I was going to fix Captain Braylee some tea. I can come back."

Eric waved her in. "Go right ahead."

She caught Mason's eye. He gave her a look that made her insides go soft. The same optimism she shared with Lena rose up, swift and strong.

Jervis winked as she passed. "That big ol' soldier still has you running for him?"

"If it was up to him, he'd be done with the whole thing," Seria returned.

Eric leaned forward and resumed their conversation, rubbing his face. "What we need is a fix on that Shadowpit."

Mason stirred with a frown. "I tried to pinpoint it," he said, scratching at the table. "I can give a general idea about the distance, but nothing very reliable."

"Nothing stood out about the terrain?" Jervis asked.

"Not really. I already told everything I know." His words were clipped, as if he did not want to be reminded.

"I sent scouts out after Mason returned," Eric told Jervis. "But they could not pick up a trail even from where we came across them."

"Shadowmen are very good at covering their tracks," Mason muttered.

Seria pretended she was trying not to listen, but she kept her movements soft so as not to miss a word.

"The only thing they found of interest was your tunnel, Mason."

Mason glanced at Seria, amusement glowing in his amber eyes. "Seria's tunnel."

She shrugged when the other two men's attention swiveled to her. "It was by sheer happenstance that I found it."

"We'll have to keep it under guard now," Eric said. "We can't have anyone else discovering it and getting access into the valley. It's fortunate you did find it."

"The tunnel," Mason said, soft and thoughtful.

Eric turned to him. "What about it?"

"There's something about it." He shook his head, looking hesitant. "Did you notice any strange heat when you were in it with me?"

"Not really. Nothing unusual."

Mason then looked to Seria. "How about you?"

"I never noticed it." By this time, she had forgotten about what she was supposed to be doing.

"What is it, Mason?" Eric asked.

"The fork in the tunnel. It..." Mason winced. "This is going to make me sound crazy, but it gets very hot and the second passage...it's strange."

Eric sat back and crossed his arms, clearly trying to follow Mason's reasoning.

"Every time I passed through it, it was almost as if my Shadowstone was responding to it." Mason flicked a look Seria's way, as if embarrassed to speak of the stone. "The same feeling I had in the pit."

Eric's features sharpened. "Do you think that tunnel leads to the Shadowpit?"

Mason thought for a moment. "Based on the traveling we did and the terrain, it's very possible we were right at the base of the Slate Mountains. The Shadowpit could be inside the mountains, connected to the tunnel."

Seria's pulse quickened. Had she been that close to the Shadowpit every time she used it for her silly fishing trips?

"Why would the army allow that tunnel to be so unprotected?" Jervis asked.

"It's hardly visible to the naked eye unless you know to look for it," Eric said. He slumped back. "It doesn't matter. That second passage was entirely too narrow. There's no way to get into it to even know for sure."

Seria inhaled sharply. When Mason looked at her, she opened her eyes wide, inviting him to read her thoughts.

His brows lifted. "Lena."

"What about Lena?" Eric's voice pitched a little.

Jervis tilted his head back. "Oh, I see."

The prince frowned. "I don't."

"Lena can walk through walls." Seria reminded as she approached the table. "She could get someone through that passage."

Understanding dawned, followed by uncertainty. "I don't want to put her in danger."

"Unfortunately, this is a dangerous time we're living in," Jervis said. "She's already faced it within the walls of this castle."

"If she's the key to finding it, you may not have much choice," Mason said. "I, for one, would love to see that thing gone."

An unspoken exchange passed between the two men. As she watched the play of emotions on Eric's face, she became certain about one thing. Eric did care for Lena.

"She wants to see peace in the Gateway as much as anybody, Eric," she said, forgoing the formality.

He squeezed his eyes shut. "I'll consider it. It would be foolish to miss an opportunity like this."

Mason's stiff posture relaxed, and his gaze found hers again. "Good idea."

For a moment, it was just the two of them again, working together to solve a problem. Only this time, there was no hiding, no secrecy. His look deepened, and she was gripped with the sudden desire to throw her arms around his neck and cry.

"I have those every now and then," she said with a little laugh to break the moment.

Aladee entered then, with a laughing Shayna in tow. The little girl had become fast friends with anyone who came to visit her papa.

"Oh!" Seria hurried to resume her task. "I plumb forgot what I was supposed to be doing. I hope he hasn't been uncomfortable waiting on me."

"Not at all," Aladee assured. "He says he's feeling quite strong this morning, even after the service.

Eric addressed the Stewardess. "I might need to borrow your husband for a while."

She exchanged looks with Jervis, who wrapped an arm around her waist. "We both know his duty to the Lambient comes first." Even as she said it, her hand slid around his shoulders.

Seria finished what she was doing and set all the dishes on the tray. "You want to walk up with me?" she asked Shayna, who had wandered to the corner where she worked.

"Sure." Shayna's dark eyes sparkled as she glanced at Eric. "Ella's gonna be sorry she didn't come down to help."

Tempted to laugh, Seria speared her with a warning look. "Don't you do anything that would embarrass your sister."

Shayna shrugged. "I was just saying."

"Aye, you were just saying." Seria took a muffin from a bowl. "How about you have a snack and not say so much?"

The little girl stuffed a bite in her mouth and giggled, leading the way to the door.

Seria slowed as she approached the table. The prince and captains were discussing their next plans, but Mason watched her. Something about the intensity in his look sent a trickle of hope through her.

"Maybe this will all be over soon," she said, keeping her voice low. "Especially if Eric can get into the Shadowpit."

Something flickered across his expression, but he only gave a short nod. "Aye." He looked as if he wanted to say more but only gave her a little smile as she left.

Shayna chattered in the hall, but Seria could not attend to anything she was saying. She took a deep breath and tried to calm her fluttering pulse. Even after all this time, Mason could sweep her away with a single look. The longing in his face was clear, and that left her almost dizzy with the possibilities. Did they still have a chance after all?

But even as hope took root, she tamped it down. The king had only just died. It was selfish of her to already think of what that might mean for her future.

Guilt fanned the warmth that had filled her cheeks, and she took a deep breath and tried to focus on the little girl's chatter. Mason still had a duty to the Stewardship. Now was not the time to let her heart get in the way.

41

*Moverik the Great managed to use his Gift and his connection to the
Shadowpit to control his subjects, even across great distances.*
-The Lost Record of Gifts

Jader lowered the Shadowstone and settled the chain around his neck
again. Wearing the stone was merely a precaution these days, ever since
that day Mason almost got a glimpse into his thoughts. It had startled
Jader at the time, but he should have known. The ability of a Reader was
the most powerful of all the Gifts. Nothing but a Shadowstone would
block its effects.

"All goes well in Calla?" Bruin asked.

Reminded that he was not alone, he turned to his commander standing at the end of the table and rolled the scroll where Feegan's words had
scrawled moments ago. "The king of Paladin is dead."

Bruin's craggy face eased into a semblance of a smile. "Then all went
as you predicted."

"Down to the letter," Jader said. "Our young rebel even tagged along."

"What of Feegan?"

"Oh, he escaped with nary a scratch." Jader led the way through the
halls of his castle. Only a few sconces were lit for the sake of his servants.
Even with his blind eye, Jader moved about in the darkness with ease.
"He even got a shot at Eric's favorite captain, though it was not a killing
shot. But he said he did not suffer as many casualties as he expected,
thanks to Mason's interference. Most of his recruits are still alive, though
locked away."

"Which will help us in the long run."

"Exactly." Jader moved through a meeting room to the balcony that opened up to the west side of his castle.

It was too bright for his liking, but his subjects would need the daylight to travel. He stepped out onto the balcony and rested his hands on the rails. Beside him, Bruin looked down at the sight. Hundreds of men and women stood in formation, rows and rows that stretched from one side of the yard to the other. Their black uniforms blended into a mass of humanity. Before the columns, a few of his Shadow Soldiers waited, ready to lead the recruits at the order to move.

"How many is this now?" Bruin asked.

Jader waited to answer, lest eagerness break his voice. "Four hundred and still counting." The summer and early autumn months had been well spent building his Shadow Army. Men and women of all walks had eagerly answered the call and embraced the Shadowstone. The soldiers below were among the most recent recruits and awaited their final test. Once completed, the rebel towns to the east would be ravished and his army stronger than ever.

The Gateway would never be the same after this war.

The power that coursed through his veins grew with every vow spoken and stone accepted. Already he could transport farther than he had ever been able to before. Soon, it would not matter where Mason hid; Jader would not be bound by time or distance.

He raised his head high. "Our Shadow Soldiers will be our greatest line of offense," he said. "The stronghold will be weak and in chaos by the time they strike."

"Along with thousands of Darkmen," Bruin added.

Jader could not stop his smile. "And Feegan's recruits will hit them from the Old Realm." The years of planning and strategizing had all come to this, and it could not have worked out more perfectly. Even Mason's pathetic conversion had not hindered him. If anything, it gave him an advantage.

"And Mason?"

"It is time to remind him who he works for while he walks about freely at Daymont," Jader said, turning away from the army down below. "Move them out immediately. I expect my first report by tonight."

Bruin gave a short bow and then strode from the room. His horse and provisions were already prepared for the long march to The Gateway.

Jader walked to a high-backed chair in the darkest corner of the meeting room. Easing down into it, he let out a breath.

We are nearly there. His connection to Shreil was clear and strong, and with every decision, he felt his master's approval. Soon, he would reign both sides of the Gateway as Shreil's most powerful hand.

He lifted his hand, snuffing out what little light had escaped into the room from the sunlight, and closed his eyes. All was still, as if the air itself was afraid to stir. Jader cleared his mind, drew from the dark lord's power, and reached out for Mason.

Braylee stared into the fire and sipped from his cold cider, his mind far away from the sitting room where he reclined on the davenport in the large library.

His left shoulder was wrapped, his arm secured to his chest. It was still sore, but it would not keep him here when Eric headed back to the fort.

"You're frowning again."

He stirred and looked at Griselle, who sat comfortably beside him. "What's that?"

She squeezed his knee. "I can tell you are miles from here. Are you worrying again?"

"Trying not to."

His oldest daughter sat curled up on Griselle's other side, her nose in one of the many books in the room. Shayna skipped into the room after another round of visits to all her new haunts. "Did you know there is a fountain in the throne room?" she asked.

"I did, and I hope you weren't snooping around in there," Braylee said. The girls had been given strict instructions to stay clear of the royal quarters.

"I just peeked in on my way to the kitchen."

He cocked a brow at her. "On the other side of the building?"

Shayna's eyes sparked with impishness. "I got lost."

Braylee groaned. "I'm sure you did, you little sneak."

"I didn't go in, Papa. Honest."

Unable to hold back his smile, Braylee pointed at her. "Be sure you don't."

Ella closed her book and plopped her chin in her palm.

"What's wrong, sweetheart?" Griselle asked.

The girl sighed. "I don't understand."

"Understand what?"

Ella shifted toward her mother. "Why Prince Eric has to go to war. Shouldn't he stay here?"

Braylee swirled his mug, watching the contents swish around, much like his thoughts. There had been a lot of talk that day about the prince's return to the Gateway.

"Prince Eric has a duty to his people," Griselle answered.

"But King Aden's death means that he should be king now. What happens to Paladin if the prince doesn't come back?" Ella looked distraught at the idea.

Griselle gave Braylee's knee another squeeze and took her time answering. "It is true that if Prince Eric doesn't return, we will have no king. But I think he is acting on a deeper principle than the need to lead his people."

"What's that?"

Cupping her daughter's smooth cheek in her hand, Griselle answered. "That of love, dear one. A king who loves his people enough to be willing to give his life to save them."

Shayna sat in a chair across from them, drawn into the conversation. "But what happens if he dies?"

Braylee winced at her blunt question.

"Paladin will go on. Even without an earthly king, Lambient will take care of us. So, I don't want either of you to worry about what will happen."

Ella frowned. "But I still don't want Prince Eric to get hurt or..."

"I know. We must pray for all the Stewards. They're out there doing the Lambient's work." At that, she looked to Braylee. "It's very important, and they need us to be brave and do our very best here."

After a long moment, Ella nodded. "I'll try."

Shayna piped up again. "I'm gonna be a Steward like Papa when I grow up. Then I can fight with Aladee."

One corner of Braylee's lips broke from their tense lines, and he regarded his spunky daughter. "That's Captain Aladee, young lady. And I'm sure she'd be happy to have you at her side."

Griselle rose. "How about some dinner, girls?"

Shayna dashed to the door. "I'll race you there!"

"No running in the halls," Braylee called. When she gave him a sneaky smile, he narrowed his eyes. "I mean it."

"I won't. Love you, Papa!" She had taken to telling him every chance she got, but he wasn't sure if it was because his injury made her feel more sentimental or to distract him from her antics.

"Love you, too, Spunky," he returned dryly.

He stood and caught Ella before she left, gathering her close with his good arm. "Don't you worry about the prince, sweet girl," he whispered. "He's got a lot of friends looking after him."

She gave him a look of complete trust and followed her mother and sister from the room.

Braylee strode to the fireplace, smoothing the whiskers on his jawline. His Beacon, strapped to his belt, glinted softly in the golden glow of the fire. His heart was torn between two places that he wanted—needed—to be.

At the sound of footsteps, he looked up, expecting to see Griselle coming back. Instead, it was Mason.

"Is this a bad time?"

"Not at all," Braylee said, waving to one of the chairs before the hearth. "Griselle just took the girls to get some dinner."

Mason stayed on his feet, looking at a loss for words.

"Is something wrong?"

"Nay, not really." Mason rubbed his hand over his hair. "I wanted to see how you were doing."

Sure there was something more on the younger man's mind, Braylee took the other chair. "I'm well, thank you. Sore, but it's nothing that will keep me out of commission." When Mason gave his sling a pointed look, he chuckled. "Griselle and Seria insist that I keep it on for now."

Mason took the seat across from him. "That's good."

"I never got a chance to thank you."

"For what?"

"You and Jervis got me inside pretty quick. Seria said I could've lost a lot more blood."

"You were targeted because of me." He wouldn't look at Braylee. "That Shadowman... He shot you because of me."

Braylee tapped the fingers of his good hand on his knee. "If so, that still wasn't your fault."

"Except—"

Holding his hand up, Braylee said, "Aye, you're still facing consequences from your former life, but you aren't responsible for the bad choices others continue to make, Mason."

"I wish I could believe that," Mason muttered, staring into the fire.

"I think your biggest challenge is forgiving yourself."

"Maybe." Mason stood. "I won't keep you, I just wanted to—" He cut off with a grimace.

"What's wrong?"

Instead of answering, Mason groaned and pressed his hands into his temples. "Submission begets..."

The faint whispers lifted chills on Braylee's skin, and he rose from his seat. "Mason?"

Mason's face went slack, his eyes red-rimmed, and he straightened. "Drop your Beacon."

Braylee wrapped his fingers around the rod's handle. "I don't think I will."

Nostrils flaring, Mason drew his sword from his belt. "You're going to die either way."

Backing away, Braylee raised his bound arm as much as he could, his palm extended out. "Get a hold of yourself, Mason."

But the young man stalked forward, his posture rigid. He swung his sword, and Braylee deflected it with his Beacon, then circled the chair, keeping it between them. "Stop!"

The command earned him another swing, and Braylee gritted his teeth, his heart thumping in his chest. "I don't want to fight you." But the fear that Griselle or the girls could return made him raise his Beacon, letting the light spill out and fill the room. He jerked his wounded arm out of the sling, sucking in a breath at the pain it jarred.

Mason faltered and shielded his eyes. "Drop it!" he tried again.

"I won't," Braylee said, holding it up higher and taking a step. "Fight this, Mason. This isn't you."

The light seemed to infuriate him, and Mason knocked the chair over. Braylee took that moment to jump forward and grab Mason's sword hand. As soon as Mason reached for him with the other hand, Braylee shoved the Beacon into it, then retreated, leaving his only weapon behind.

Mason let out a gasp, then there was a long pause as he stood there, frozen. The light flashed brighter, then faded into a soft glow in his hand. He blinked at the Beacon, then raised his head up to Braylee. The redness faded from his eyes, and he dropped his sword, stark terror filling his face. "What happened?"

Braylee let out a breath. "That's what I'd like to know."

42

You were once full of darkness, but now you are filled with the light from the Lambient. So, live as people of light! For His light produces that which is right and true and good.
-The Sacred Code

Eric shoved through the door of the library, the buzzing in his ears loud and grating. He stopped short and took in the room. Braylee stood in the middle of the space, his sling hanging loose from his shoulder. One of the chairs was tipped over on its side. Mason sat in the other chair, his hands clasped before him and his head down. His sword lay on the floor.

"What happened?" Eric asked. He had been on his way to the evening meal when his intuition ignited, and he felt a very real threat within the castle walls.

"We have a problem," Braylee said.

Eric's stomach twisted. "What?"

Mason stirred. "Me." His eyes were dark and haunted.

"What do you mean?"

"I heard Jader's voice in my head," Mason shuddered. "The Shadow Pledge. I heard him say it. And I can't stop it."

"What are you talking about?" Eric asked again, already dreading the answer.

"I turned on Braylee," he rasped. "I would've killed him if he hadn't stopped me."

"The Beacon stopped him," Braylee said, standing the chair back up.

Eric shook his head, trying to make sense of what he was hearing.

"Jader controlled you?"

"Aye." Mason looked defeated. "All the way from Ignadon."

"We don't know where he is," Braylee said.

"Does it matter? He wasn't in the room. I'm at his mercy, and he has none." Mason covered his face with his hands. "Which makes me dangerous. I could turn on anyone at any time."

Eric looked to Braylee, hoping for a denial, but received none. "Mercies," he whispered. He gave Mason a quick look. How could they be sure he wouldn't turn again?

"He still has my Beacon."

"What?"

Rubbing his wounded shoulder, Braylee said, "I could see he wasn't in his right mind. As soon as I had a chance, I forced it into his hand. That's what broke the spell."

Eric saw Braylee's Beacon sitting on Mason's leg. "That was a big risk you took. Surrendering your only weapon against a Reader."

Braylee leveled his sober gaze on him. "Lambient's power doesn't come from the weapon alone, Eric."

"Maybe not, but it's still pretty handy to have." Eric scratched his jaw. "This doesn't make sense. How can Jader gain control of you like that?"

"The Shadow Pledge." Mason lowered his hands. A muscle jumped in his jaw. "He controls everyone who takes it. I had no idea how deep it would reach, and when I took that Shadowstone, it also gave him access to my Gift." His face paled. "By the moon. Machlin."

"What happened at Machlin?" Braylee asked.

Mason folded in on himself. "They killed one another, and it's my fault."

"Talk to me, Mason." Eric hardened his voice to cut through Mason's despair.

"Jader told me to control them—the men of Machlin. To tell them...to kill each other." He gave Eric a wild look. "Everything is still a blur; I didn't remember until now. I didn't want to, Eric. I refused. But I couldn't stop myself."

"Dear skies above." Eric clasped his hands over his head and paced away, the ramifications hitting him like a hammer. "This is what he's been working for all these years."

"What are you thinking?" Braylee asked.

Eric spun back to them. "What little we know about Readers all points to the same pattern." He pointed to Mason. "Your headaches, the voices you hear on occasion, and the ability to control some people without looking them in the eye are typical signs of your powers growing. Your Gift will continue to multiply until you can control large numbers of people with naught but a few words."

Mason frowned. "How large?"

"Records show it could be in the hundreds. Maybe more." Eric watched as Mason processed the information.

Horror darkened Mason's countenance. "I could control hundreds of people for *him*." He fixed wide eyes on Eric. "He could use me to turn the tide of this war in his favor."

Eric worked to stay calm, though his heart began to drum in his chest.

Mason rose, looking ready to bolt. Braylee's Beacon fell to the floor. "We can't let him do that."

"We won't, Mason."

"Nay, I mean, you can't let him use me. You have to remove the threat."

"What are you saying?"

"I'm saying take me out if you have to." Mason's voice roughed in his fervor. "Don't let me be a tool in Jader's hand anymore. Kill me first before you let me hurt anyone else."

Eric drew in a deep breath. "We're not going to let Jader use you, and we're not going to kill you."

"You can't—"

"I don't have to kill you. We have another tool." Eric pulled his Beacon out and held it up. "You said this is what snapped you back. It's time you get your own. Then Jader won't be able to reach you."

Mason flinched and stepped back. "I can't."

"If this is about you not feeling worthy, you should know by now—"

But he shook his head, looking panicked. "I can't carry it, Eric, because it won't let me."

Eric's arm dropped. "What do you mean?"

Mason looked at the discarded Beacon on the floor. "It burns me."

"Burns you?"

"Since when?" Braylee asked, reflecting Eric's confusion.

"Since the beginning." Mason slumped in defeat. "Or almost that long. I'm not sure anymore. But I can't hold it very long without excruciating pain."

Eric dropped into the other chair. He had never heard of the Beacon harming any of its handlers. Why now?

"That's why you struggle to see yourself as a Steward," Braylee said.

Mason gave a miserable nod. "It's rejecting me."

"Nay. I don't believe it." Eric shook his head. "The light would not flow from your hands if Lambient rejected you."

"Then explain why it burns me."

"Because of that Shadowstone. Shreil is trying his best to hang on to you, and Jader is using every trick he has to keep you in his grasp. There's a battle between light and darkness within you, but Lambient has already won." He jabbed a finger at Mason. "You just have to believe it now."

Mason said nothing, and Eric refrained from pushing him. He knew as well as anyone how hard it was to act out what he knew to be true. He rubbed his mouth and thought for a minute. "Have you tried wearing it?"

Mason blinked and shook his head. "Nay. I haven't earned one for myself."

"Let's try it." He started to offer his own.

"Nay, Eric." Mason's breathing hitched. "Not now. Don't let go of that thing. I don't know what Jader can see through me. If you don't have it on you, and he gets to me..."

Eric stilled, appreciating Mason's very real concern. "All right, I see your point. But the Beacon still offers protection to every Steward who wears it, and it may be that having it on your person will protect you from his control." When Mason still hesitated, Eric pressed on. "It's worth a try, at least. If it doesn't work, then we'll know."

A long, strained silence stretched before Mason nodded. "I'll try."

Mason walked to the Steward chapel in a daze, Eric and Braylee on either side of him. The revelation of his Gift had left him reeling, scrambling to find some foothold in a mountain of fear. He had always confronted his problems with grit and sheer stubbornness. Never had he been this afraid of what the future held. After all these months and all the growth Mason had endured, Jader still had a grip on him. One Mason wasn't sure how to break.

Eric pulled the heavy wooden portal of the chapel and entered the sanctuary. His stride slowed as he walked the middle aisle, as if not wanting to disturb the peace. Braylee stood by the door, his Beacon back in place on his belt.

Mason followed Eric and stopped just inside, the quiet of the building surrounding him. Stone benches lined both sides of the aisle and stretched to the walls on either side. Rows of blue stained-glass windows shut out the view of a world draped in night, but he could imagine how the sun broke through the colored glass. It was the front that drew him in further, though. A crystal globe sat on a podium, sparkling in the light of the lanterns that arched around it. The Beacon Orb.

Eric started to reach for it, then stopped. He looked to Mason. "You pull one out."

"What?"

"You never got a ceremony, and the timing is all wrong now. But this is your moment to pull your own Beacon."

"But—"

"It's time, Mason."

Mason stared into the glassy sphere. It seemed to call to him, and something within him responded. "How do I do it?"

"Reach out and take hold of one end."

It sounded simple, but it didn't stop Mason's heart from pounding as he reached out and placed his hand on one of the smooth bumps. He could see now it was one of dozens of Beacons, pressed together with their tips pointing in so that they made the shape of a sphere. He gave a tug, and one slid easily out of the sphere and into his hold. It shone with a steady glow, and he stared into it in awe. For a while, he thought it wouldn't burn, but as soon as the thought took shape, it heated his fingers. He clicked it into place on the new belt Eric had given him. The light receded, as did the heat.

"If these were normal times, you would've had a ceremony." Eric's tone was soft, almost reverent. "The Grand Marshal would give a speech, and one by one the cadets would take their Beacons and their official place in the Steward Army."

Braylee joined them. "You may not have gotten an official ceremony, Mason Grey, but you are a Steward, no matter what the enemy says. Don't ever forget that. You have your own Beacon now. Don't be afraid to use it, to let its light fill you. That's the only way you will overcome Jader's hold on you."

Mason worked to believe it, but even the feel of the rod against his hip did not alleviate the fear spiraling through him.

He was a danger to everyone here. Prince Eric and his Stewards. The castle civilians. Seria. A jagged knife cut through him. Ever since defecting to the Steward side of this war, he had believed he would be the one to take Jader down. Instead, he had become Jader's greatest tool.

"It may be my strongest defense," he said. "But until Jader's out of the way, I'm still too much of a risk."

Eric crossed his arms. "What's on your mind?"

Mason gulped the fear and pride that tried to smother the words. This was bigger than his desire to be the one to defeat Jader. "You need to lock me up."

"Lock you up?"

"That's right." Some of the fear that seemed to freeze his insides melted into resolve. "You know wearing a Beacon isn't enough. It's too easy to lose in a battle."

At that, Braylee quirked a brow in Eric's direction. "He's got a point."

Eric frowned at both of them, and Mason pressed harder. "I won't risk everyone's safety or the fate of this war on a chance. Put me in the lowest, hardest-to-access cell you have. If I'm there, I can't cause harm, no matter what Jader does to me."

"And what if this war goes on?" Eric asked.

"Then I stay down there until it's done or Jader's dead." Mason narrowed his eyes. "I will not let my pride be used to destroy everything you've stood for."

After a long moment, Eric conceded. "All right," he said. "I don't like it, but it might very well be the safest place for you and the kingdom."

They left the chapel then and took the path around the back of the castle, their destination the tower on the other side of the training fields. The one that the Passions had used to house the most dangerous of criminals in years past.

A blonde figure appeared on the path before them, and Mason's heart dropped to his feet.

"Good morning!" Seria greeted, her smile cutting him like a whip. His feet dragged to a stop as she approached them. All the tentative hopes that had started to take root were yanked from that secret place where he held his fragile dreams and stomped on.

Thanks to the tentacles of the Shadowstone, he could never hope for a future with Seria. He would not jeopardize her safety for his selfish desires.

Seria's steps faltered as she approached. "Mason? What's wrong?"

Wild panic thundered in his chest. What if he lost control now? What would he do to her? He took a step back, resting his hand on the Beacon. The feel of it grounded him, wrestled the terror into a semblance of fear that he could manage.

Eric stopped beside him, a question in his sympathetic gaze.

"Don't go far," Mason said lowly.

Seria gave him a confused look as Eric and Braylee withdrew themselves but stayed within sight down the path. "What's going on?" Her head tilted in that adorable way that always made him want to smile. Now, he had to swallow back the tears that stung.

"I...have to leave."

"I see." Her expression fell. "Are you going back to the Gateway?"

The question pricked because he couldn't tell her where he was going. The fewer people who knew his location, the better. But he also could not lie to her. Not anymore.

"Nay." His head dropped. "I can't go back there."

"Why not?"

He stared at the ground, noting how dead and cold it looked after the warmth of summer had passed. "Jader can control me."

A soft gasp met his ears. "What do you mean?"

"When I made the Shadow Pledge, it allowed him into my head."

Her voice rose. "But you're a Steward now. He has no power over you."

Shame pounded him. He squeezed his eyes shut and forced himself to go on. She needed to know, needed to let him go. "He's already done it. Made me...give orders that led to the death of dozens. I almost killed Braylee in the library."

"That can't be," she breathed. "You carry the light of the Lambient. The Beacon protects you."

"I can't even wield the Beacon, Seria. It burns me every time I hold it too long."

There was a pause, and he could only imagine what was going through her mind.

"Does it still glow for you?" she asked.

"Aye, but—"

"Then nothing else matters." She drew nearer, though he still refused to look at her. "The only way that Beacon can glow is if you've surrendered your heart and will to the Lambient. You've done that, right?"

"Aye," he answered shortly. He had already gone through all this in the library.

"Then you can fight this. You surrendered your will to Lambient. You carry His light within you."

"What if it's not enough?"

"Then Shreil really is more powerful than Lambient."

Mason's head came up. "That's not what I said."

"But it's what you believe, Mason. The Sacred Code says forgiveness is for anyone who seeks it. But I guess your past mistakes are too much for Lambient to handle."

He fell silent, not sure how to respond. She didn't understand. Didn't she know how much he wanted to be able to shed this weight?

"Mason, look at me."

"I can't." What if he slipped and controlled her?

She startled him when she cupped his face with her hands so she could look deep into his eyes. "Mason. The Lambient forgave you. Now, you need to forgive yourself. That's what this is all about. Your problem is you still can't believe it. You can't believe that Lambient can see past your mistakes and into the man you want to be. He forgave you, Mason, now you have to accept it."

For just a moment, he let himself get lost in her green gaze. The touch of her hands was cool and soothing. "It's not that easy."

"I'm sure it's not." Her thumbs stroked the whiskers that lined his jaw. "But it doesn't mean I'm wrong. Once you let go of your fears and your guilt, neither Shreil nor Jader can keep their hold on you."

Darkness begets submission...

He sucked in a ragged breath and jerked away, breaking her hold. "Get out of here," he breathed. Shadowy fingers crept over his vision as Jader whispered in his mind.

"Mason—"

"*Get away!*" he yelled, grasping for the Beacon at his belt. As soon as the cool glass touched his fingers, the shadows started to recede.

A strong hand took hold of his elbow, and Eric spoke. "We need to go, Seria."

As Eric drew him back down the path, Braylee's strong presence on his other side, Mason chanced a glance over his shoulder. Seria stood alone, pale and stricken. "I'm sorry," he whispered shakily as they led him away.

43

Who among you fears the Lambient and obeys His voice and still walks in darkness and has no light? Let him put his trust in His name and stay firm upon his Savior.
-The Sacred Code

Clouds threatened to dump rain over the fort as Lionel moved about his route, checking on his men. The mood was somber and gray. News of the king's death had rocked the knights, and Lionel felt like his soul walked through constant sludge. His struggles seemed so trivial now. While he moped and complained about the path Lambient had laid before him, the Dark Army was striking. They had killed his king, wounded his captain. And they would take more, as much as they could to prepare the way for Jader's dark power to cover the land.

Excited shouting drew him back to the present. Jogging ahead of the crowd of curious spectators, he arrived at the gates at the same time a troop of soldiers rode in, their horses lathered and the men worn.

Dudley stepped before them. "Sgt. Nahm, what's happened?"

Nahm pulled his horse to a stop before him. "The Dark Army attacked us at Rackson." He leaned against his saddle horn, a deep scratch across his face. "They came just before high noon."

"They attacked at full light?" Lionel asked.

"We had received reports of a Gateway town falling under fire, but before we could ride out to check, they struck us."

"Shadowmen?" Dudley asked.

"Never saw any. Just Darkmen. A lot of them. We were outnumbered."

I'm sorry, Captain. There was nothing we could do."

"The fault does not lie with you." Dudley's gray brows slashed down. "We all knew this was coming. Were you pursued?"

"Only to the outside border of Rackson," Nahm answered.

"What about the other civilian towns?" Lionel asked.

Dudley chewed his cheek. "Let's send some of our scouts out there, see what they can find out."

The scouts rode out in less than half an hour, and Lionel paced the walls for their return, his insides twisting.

Was this it? The start of the war they had all anticipated? After the strike on the castle that resulted in the loss of the king, Lionel almost hoped it was. He itched to strike back against those who had threatened their kingdom, all in the name of darkness. But he also knew that war would bring more loss and death, and he wasn't sure he was ready for that again.

One by one, throughout the next few hours, the scouts returned, their reports all the same. Darkmen were attacking the Gateway towns that resisted Jader's rule. Hundreds of men poured into the civilian villages, burning their buildings and killing the people. It seemed to be happening simultaneously in the north and south.

Dudley was grave as he looked out over the shell of Cadence, into the distance. "There's no mistake what this is." He raised to his full height. "Contact the prince. The war has started."

Lionel left to send the message, his heart tripping in his chest. It was time.

Stopping at the well where he would send the news to those in Calla, he pulled his Beacon and looked at its pure light, remembering all who had carried this flame of commitment before him. Ollen had served his purpose, as had King Aden and Uralis. Lionel would do the same.

The message accelerated Eric's plans to leave the castle, and he met with all his captains in the meeting room to discuss their next course of action.

He sat at the right of the head of the large table, feeling his father's absence keenly. "We'll take your company along," he told Jervis. "We need to increase our number of Stewards at the fort. Captains Nathan and Aladee, you will remain here to guard Calla."

"Aye, Sire," Nathan responded, while Aladee nodded in agreement.

"How soon do you want to leave?" Jervis asked.

"In an hour. I wish to arrive at the stronghold by nightfall."

"Very well, if there's nothing else, I'll see that it's done."

Nathan and Aladee went with him to offer their assistance. Eric caught Aladee slipping her hand in Jervis's as they left. When they were gone, he looked to Braylee. "You're very quiet."

The big man folded his hands on the table. His shoulder was still wrapped, but the sling was gone. Though his mobility was a little slow, the worst of the injury seemed to be behind him. "Are you sure it's a good idea for you to go back to the front?"

Eric met Braylee's serious look. "You know I have to."

"War is not to be taken lightly," he said. "We can't assume anything. And Paladin needs its king. Now more than ever."

"Paladin also needs peace and safety."

"Your Stewards are more than willing to fight this war for you."

"I know. And I'm grateful. But I can't ask them to fight a war that I'm not willing to lead them in."

There was a long pause, then Braylee released a heavy sigh. "It's no more than I expected of you, but I wish it didn't have to be."

"There's a lot we could wish for, but it doesn't change the present situation." Anxiety gnawed at him. The attack on the castle was but one small step in Jader's greater scheme. The Gateway was where the brunt of his force would hit. And Eric had to be there. "Your family is welcome to stay here at Daymont while we're gone."

That drew Braylee up short. "What's that?"

"I mean it," Eric said. "I want to know they're here safe when war hits."

Braylee rubbed at his whiskers. "I appreciate that," he said, his voice suspiciously thick. "I would rest better."

"Good. Then it's settled."

After Braylee left him, Eric hastened to pack his small canvas bag and make sure Oakley was saddled and ready to go. With still one more stop to make, he headed out of the barn.

"Eric?" Seria's soft call stopped him. She emerged from a stone bench outside the little chapel. "I hear you're leaving shortly."

"Aye, I'm afraid so."

She cast her gaze around them. "I don't suppose...is Mason going with you?"

Her obvious worry drew him off the path. "Nay, he is not."

"Is he all right, Eric?" Her voice quavered. "He seemed so...distraught."

He took her hands in his. "I can't share everything right now, Seria, but rest assured that he is safe for now. I need you to trust me in this and not get carried away by your worry."

A wry smile twisted her lips. "In other words, don't go stowing away with the Stewards?"

The memory sparked a low chuckle. "That would certainly be helpful for all involved." He sobered. "Pray for him, Seria. He's committed to the Lambient, but Jader is just as determined. The battle within him is a great one."

She tilted her chin up. "I will pray for all of you."

He squeezed her fingers and released her. "I appreciate that."

"There's something else I want you to know."

"What's that?" he asked, looking up to gauge how much daylight he had left.

"Your father approved of Lena."

His head snapped back down. "What?"

Her eyes brimmed with both amusement and sincerity. "He told me himself that he wanted to make sure the future queen of Paladin was safe during this war."

He stared at her. How had his father known of his feelings for Lena all the way back in Calla?

Seria bit her lip. "Maybe this was a bad time. I hope I didn't overstep, but I wanted to give you something to look forward to when all this is over."

He swallowed and cleared his throat. "Nay, I appreciate it," he said hoarsely. "It does give me something to hope for. I need that right now, especially with him being gone."

"He was a great man."

"That he was. And I am eternally grateful for the care you gave him in his last weeks."

"I'm glad I was able to know him. I see where you got your charm."

His laugh loosened the tightness that gripped him. "Thank you, Seria."

She squeezed his arm. "Thank *you*, Eric. For everything you've done for me. And for Mason. And Lena. I mean, really, you've done a lot for everyone. For the whole kingdom, I'm sure." Her words picked up speed. "Especially with you going out and risking everything to defend Paladin." At his smile, she sighed. "I'm talking too much again, so I'll be quiet and let you go now."

Eric laid his hand on her arm. "Keep yourself well, Seria, and I'll see you when this is all over."

"You too, Prince Eric." She bowed her head, then took herself off to the castle, but not before he saw the tears brimming in her eyes.

His men would be gathering in the courtyard soon. For a long moment, he stood still on the path, his heart full. His mind moved from one face to another, friends and allies who had supported him these past long months. His dear father was gone to him, but his love and care would carry Eric on. And when the day came that he could return home, Lena would be here.

His heartbeat accelerated at the prospect of war. But his spirit was calm. Braylee was right. It was a risk for the king to lead the way into battle. But Eric knew he was doing the right thing. He had a host of Stewards at his back and the Lambient at his side. He would not fight alone.

Mason hated the waiting. The quiet didn't bother him so much, even if it did invite unwanted worries. But he was used to solitude.

The cell was dimly lit, but to his dismay, his vision still cut through the darkness easily. Another reminder that he still had not shaken the hold the Shadowstone had on him, despite the Beacon that remained attached to his hip at all times. He even slept with it.

But it was the waiting that made him want to climb the walls. Not knowing what was happening outside the tower left him feeling useless. After all his vain belief that he would be the one to undo all the wrong that Jader had done, he was stuck in a prison cell to keep from being used against his will.

The threat of Jader's control made him look at his Gift in another light. Never before had he considered the men and women he had commanded to do his bidding. The feeling of vulnerability and loss of control made him sick to his stomach, yet how many people had he controlled over the years without any thought of their well-being?

I'll never use my Gift for my own gain again, he promised the Lambient. *I'll gladly give it up. Just get me through this.*

Echoing footsteps drew him to the door. There were no other prisoners down at this level. Soon, Eric appeared in the shadows outside the barred door. "How are you holding up?"

"I wouldn't recommend this as a holiday spot," Mason said, trying to keep his voice light.

"I'm sorry we can't make it more comfortable for you."

He glanced at his belongings that had been brought to him earlier. His blanket covered the narrow cot, and an extra change of clothes sat draped over the straight-backed chair in the corner. One of the guards had even brought him a book to read. "It's better than I expected, honestly."

"I'm glad." Eric's too-casual tone unnerved him.

"Something's happened, hasn't it?"

With a sigh, Eric nodded. "I'm afraid so. The Dark Army has started attacking the Gateway towns."

Mason's fingers coiled around the bars. "The towns?" His mind worked to understand Jader's move. "Why the civilians?"

"Punishment for turning on him?"

"Maybe, but so late in the game, it seems a waste of time. Why not go straight to the fort?"

Eric rested his forearm against the barred window. "You think there's another motive?"

"There has to be. Those towns are insignificant. While he doesn't care anything for civilian lives, he usually has a reason. With Rackson, it was to draw the Stewards out and get me in the stronghold." He winced. "At Machlin, he was testing me to see if he could overpower my will."

"So, why now? And multiple ones at that?"

"He wouldn't hit so many unless he was getting something he wanted. Strengthening his army." Cold dread washed down his spine. "Blades, Eric. Shadowmen."

"What?"

Mason pounded a fist against the bars. "I'd bet my Gift that he's growing his Shadow Army. They're attacking as a final test to earn their Shadowstones."

Eric went grave. "How many are we talking?"

"I have no idea. To my awareness, he's never tested so many at once. But if he's about to hit the Gateway, he'll want as many Shadowmen as he can get his hands on."

"Mercies." Eric's arm dropped to his side. "Then we have no time to lose."

"I wish..."

"I know, Mason." Eric reached through the bars and dropped his hand on Mason's shoulder. "This will be over soon. I'll not leave you locked up like a common criminal."

Mason gave a harsh laugh. "I *am* a criminal, remember?"

"Not anymore." Eric's voice hardened. "You keep that Beacon on you. Next time I see you, you'll be a free man."

It took an effort to wrestle his self-loathing into a corner of his mind. "You be careful, you hear?"

"We will." He gave Mason's shoulder a hard squeeze then was gone.

Mason rested his forehead against the cold bars, his heart shriveling at being left behind. This was his fight. Jader had manipulated him all these years into hating the Stewards, fighting against them at every turn, and even killing them. But the truth had won out, and Mason now stood with them against the darkness Jader wielded against them. Yet when the time came that they needed him, he couldn't help them.

"Please be with them," he whispered into the still air. "Don't let Jader win in this. He can't win." Recognizing the pleading tone that had leaked into his words, he straightened and moved to the chair, dropping into it heavily.

The Beacon pressed against his hip, and he wrapped his hand around it, relishing the way it lit for an all too brief moment before the heat forced him to release it. Defeat weighed him down, and he dug his elbows into his knees, dropping his head. Despite all the counsel offered to him by Eric and Braylee and even Seria, the truth was too obvious to ignore. The Dark Steward was a failure.

44

The day is at hand, the night well spent. Cast off the works of darkness and put on the armor of light.
-The Sacred Code

Once at the Gateway Stronghold, Eric wasted no time in evacuating the civilians. The announcement was made his first morning back, and by that afternoon, the last of the carts and wagons rolled out of the fort, escorted by a squad of soldiers.

Eric made sure Lena's mother and grandfather were among the first to leave the fort. It would ease Lena's mind a great deal if her family was out of the line of danger.

Already he missed her steady presence—much more than the stash of honey tarts she had somehow managed to sneak into his saddlebag. She never said much, but her thoughtful hug stayed with him, and he brought it to mind every time he could sense the weight of the world on his shoulders. She gave him hope, something to return to.

But first, he had to survive this war.

Stewards filtered back throughout the Gateway to aid the towns that had been hit by the Dark Army, but the attacks on the Gateway had eased off, leading Eric to believe that Mason was right. Jader had used the towns to grow his power. His men brought back the survivors, and Eric made sure they were given aid, then sent them on to the Old Realm.

It kept his Stewards busy and him distracted from his grief.

Jervis took to his work without hesitation. He and Dudley had shaken hands at his arrival, reunited like old friends. The three captains worked well together as they prepared their men.

The Steward cadets were still there, most of them alight with the anticipation of fighting alongside their older compatriots. They were young and maybe too eager, but Eric needed them.

Only a handful of citizens remained behind. Barry, the stubborn blacksmith, insisted they needed him to tend to their horses, and he wasn't wrong. Nola also declared she felt safe enough surrounded by "her" Stewards, and besides, who would feed the men if she left? Marcus offered to stay with her so she would have help.

While Eric would have preferred every unprotected man or woman be out of harm's way, their work was essential. But every family with a child was expected to move on.

The lack of normal life happenings gave the setting an eerie feeling, one that carried over to his men. More guards were added to the night watches for both the front and back walls. Weapons were polished, sharpened, and repaired, and stayed within reach at all times. A feeling of tense expectancy covered every corner and filled every building.

The Dark Army was coming. The only question now was when.

The atmosphere of the castle was so much more subdued now. The beloved king was laid in his final resting place. The inhabitants of Daymont had seen the prince and his Stewards off with flags, scarves, and cheers, and now they were gone, back to defend the Old Realm against Jader's sinister plans. It all left a tense, uncertain feel in the air that made Seria feel like she should tiptoe through the halls that once echoed with voices and purpose.

She was more than happy to help settle Lena's family into their new quarters, though Calvin grumbled about being stuck in the prince's castle. But afterward, she still felt at loose ends without her patient—oh, how she missed that kind, old man! Finally, she made her way downstairs to the servant wing.

"Miss Seria, whatever are you doing here?" Charlin asked when she spotted her.

"I wanted to see if I could have my old job back."

Charlin's look became scrutinizing, and Seria could almost see what she was thinking. Why would Seria choose to go back to working in the laundry?

Seria turned her palms up. "I no longer have any work to do, and I can't sit idle."

"We can always use help if you're sure."

"Of course. I'm happy to help." And as Charlin directed her to move to a washtub, Seria felt the truth of her own words.

Being a healer didn't make her any more or less important than anyone else. She was loved and valued no matter what role she played. Her healing skills may be called into service again soon, but in the meantime, she would work wherever needed, even if it meant going back to washing laundry.

She was glad for her work, tiring as it was. Scrubbing, hanging, and folding laundry was time-consuming, but it was so automatic that it allowed her thoughts to run free. Sometimes that led to more anxiety, but she was learning to turn those worries into prayers.

The workings of the staff were back to an almost-normal status now, and Lena put out more baked goods than she had been allowed to before. It eased Seria's mind greatly to see her friend's heavy load lighten. Lena still put in a full day's work, but the endless kneading that left her tired and sore had lessened.

They met daily in the staff dining area for meals, and sometimes Aladee joined them. The captain stayed busy with training her Stewardesses and overseeing the castle, but she made time to check in when she could. It meant a lot to them both, considering how she must miss her husband.

"Do you get to talk to him much?" Seria asked as they finished their midday meal. "I mean, with the Beacon?"

"We try to connect every evening," Aladee said. "I am blessed that we both have Beacons to make it possible. So many wives do not have that advantage."

Seria thought of Griselle. The older woman had taken Braylee's departure with more grace and poise than Seria had thought possible. She made a note to visit with her later. The girls were a nice diversion from the worry.

Lena crossed her arms on top of the table. "It's hard not knowing."

"There's not a lot to know yet," Aladee said. "Jervis says that their sources confirm the Dark Army is on the move, but no one has any more than that. We must be patient."

Seria sat back with a sigh. "How I wish they could've found the Shadowpit. That would solve so many problems." Her thoughts flitted to Mason, who still felt the effects of the cursed pit.

"Aye, but unfortunately, finding it is only one part of the problem," Aladee pointed out. "We don't even know what it would take to destroy it."

A Stewardess cadet stepped into the kitchen to speak to Aladee, and Seria went back to her meal, mulling over what little she knew of the Shadowpit. Mason had never spoken of it in her presence, but when it was brought up, she could see his discomfort. It made her sick to think of the horrible things he must have experienced there. If only they could know how to do away with it.

Without warning, her mind flashed back to that day she hid in her quarters, watching through a crack in the door at the Darkmen who had taken over King Aden's suite. Their conversation drifted through her memories.

"We should take all the rods and toss them into Jader's Shadowpit...Melt them all to nothing."

Feegan's outrage at the man's ignorant suggestion had been swift. *"Keep your mouth shut about things you don't know about...Our enemy does not need your help."*

Seria let out a gasp. Was it possible the unsuspecting man had struck a nerve?

"What is it, Seria?" Lena asked.

Trying to make sense of what she had heard, Seria stared at her for a moment. Could it be so simple? "I only just now thought of something." She quickly recounted the conversation.

"Mercies, you're right." Clarity glowed from Aladee's face. "I remember that too. How did we miss it?"

"It's no wonder, the duress we were in. Do you think that could be the answer?"

Aladee thought about it. "It's a strong possibility. One that we should at least look into." She rose from the table. "I have to go see about something now, but I'll let Jervis know about it when we talk later. Thank you for pointing it out."

Seria finished eating and moved back to the laundry room to resume her work, but her mind was at the fort with the Stewards. She lifted a prayer that maybe this was the answer they needed. Maybe they could end this war before it started.

45

Darkness shall fall on the day of the Lambient and no light. It shall be very dim with no brightness.
-The Sacred Code

The scratch of wood across gravel notified Mason of his meal's arrival. Crossing the small room, he picked the tray off the ground. Steam wafted up from the dish—rabbit and potatoes, and a thick slice of fresh bread tempted him. Next to the dishes was a small, leather-bound book. "Thanks," he called.

"Did you finish the last one?" the Steward guard asked.

"Almost. I'll send it back with the tray."

"Sure thing."

Before the man could leave, Mason asked, "Any word from the fort?"

"Nothing new since the civilian evacuation."

Mason thanked him again and set the tray on the table. The reading material was a kind gesture to help pass the time, but it did not ease the anxiety that mounted with each day.

After downing the midday meal, he sat on his cot. It would be at least an hour before he saw or heard from anyone else. The inactivity ate at him. He was accustomed to action, not sitting. Even praying did not bring the comfort he needed. He begged the Lambient to take his Gift from him, thus removing the threat he was to the cause. But Lambient was silent on the issue.

The quiet drove him to pace the small confines of the room. After several laps, he slowed, listening. It was *too* quiet. No voices down the hall. No clink of metal as the guards shifted or changed duties.

Shadows gathered in the corners of the cell. His skin crawled. He moved to the door and peered out of the small opening. The narrow hall before his cell stretched out before him. The lanterns that should be burning on either side of the walls were dim. "Hey, what's going on?"

Only his echo responded.

Darkness tinted the edges of his vision, and a cold whisper hissed in his mind. *Darkness begets submission.*

"Nay," he rasped, leaning against the door and shaking his head. "You don't control me as long as I carry the Beacon."

"Impressive." The familiar voice behind him turned his veins into ice. Like a man lost in a nightmare, Mason turned, his breath frozen in his lungs. Jader stood in his cell, tall and stately in his long, crimson robes. His dark eye bore into him, cutting through his skin. "The way you talk, one would be almost convinced you believe yourself to be a Steward."

"I am." A knot of dread threatened to choke him.

"Come, Mason." Jader's pale eye twitched. "You know as well as I do by now how untrue that is. You swore yourself to Shreil. There is no turning back."

"Where's the guard?"

"Not a concern for you, so do not trouble yourself."

Anger flooded him, sizzling hot against the cold apprehension. He didn't even know the man's name, but he had treated Mason decently. "How did you get in here?" he demanded.

Jader raised his head proudly. "You shall see for yourself soon."

"I won't be used by you again."

A chilling smile curled Jader's lip. "You have no say in the matter."

"That's not true as long as I have—"

"This?" Jader held a hand up, Mason's Beacon dangling from his fingertips.

Mason looked down at his empty belt.

This isn't happening.

"Let us get to business, shall we?"

"Nay!" Mason clenched his fists, furious that Jader had made his way here, of all places. He swung his arm back, ready to plow his fist into

Jader's thin, snarky face.

"Darkness begets submission."

Mason's limbs froze. He fought against the control, but despair clouded his mind, just like the gray cloud lining his vision.

The words kept coming.

"Submission begets power." Jader's pale eye twitched as he drew nearer. "And power begets victory. And by this night's end, I will see victory."

Mason's heart seemed to melt within him as all the fight drained. No matter how much he wanted to, he could not resist Jader's control.

Nor did he want to anymore.

Prison Courtyard
Calla, Paladin, Old Realm

Jader watched with satisfaction from a shadowed cove of trees as his newly liberated Darkmen filed through the open gates of their prison. Nearly two hundred men walked free from the courtyard where they had been contained. Feegan stood beside him, his chest thrust out as if he were responsible for the breakout.

But the man to be credited soon joined them, his red-rimmed eyes intense in his focus. The Calla guards had been controlled to release the prisoners and now lay dead, killed by the very ones they had freed.

"That's all of them, my lord," Mason said, coming to a stop before them.

"Good." Jader turned to Feegan. "The next phase is up to you, Captain. Do not fail me."

Feegan bowed low. "I shall break through the back gates, Emperor Jader, or die trying."

Jader tapped his foot at the tiresome dramatic flair. "We do not want to keep you waiting, Captain."

"Of course. I shall see you on the other side when victory is ours." Feegan clicked his heels together, then strode to a copse of trees where his horse was tethered. Soon, the sound of hoofbeats announced his departure. Scores of silent soldiers followed him on foot. They would take a longer route to avoid drawing the awareness of the Stewards at Daymont and to pick up more recruits at nearby towns where Feegan and the other Shadowmen had generated support.

Jader looked to Mason. "You have done well, my boy. Now it is time to put you in place for your next task."

"As you wish."

A black cloud surrounded them, taking them from the courtyard and depositing them in a dark, quiet corner of the Gateway Stronghold. Jader thrilled at the power that allowed him to not only transport himself but take another human with him. No one was around, thanks to Eric Passion's recent evacuation. His worry over the insignificant civilians had left his fort empty, allowing Jader's arrival to go unnoticed.

"Here is where you must be careful," he told Mason, keeping his voice low. "No one must know you are here yet, or your work will be prohibited."

"I understand." Mason's keen eyes were already peering all around them.

"Give the recruits time to march from Calla. Just before sunset, that is when you will act."

Mason nodded, and Jader swelled at the submission. All his work and planning were finally paying off. The level of control his Shadowstone granted him over his subjects was satisfying in its own right, but to have a Reader under his total authority meant absolute control. And that was what would bring about his victory this very night.

"You know what to do. Your assignment boils down to this. Kill the prince. Destroy the Stewards."

"Aye, my lord."

"Then I shall leave you to it." Jader stepped away from his scout and allowed the cloud to wrap itself around him again, pulling him from the fort and settling him in a large field miles away. A hundred feet away, thousands of soldiers lined up, his Dark Army, ready to march at the call.

Bruin waited for him. "Is all in place?"

"Perfectly," Jader said. "Mason will do his job well, and soon, the

Stewards will face opposition on all sides."

The commander raised his head to the skies. "It'll be sunset in a couple of hours."

"It is time to march our army forward, Commander Bruin. I shall meet you there."

Bruin bowed his head and strode to his horse. Once mounted, he rode to the front of the lines. "Move out!"

Jader's shoulders rose and fell as the sound of feet moving rhythmically filled the air. The Passion reign was about to end. The time for darkness had begun.

46

The Gift of sight can peer straight into the heart of a man, as well as cut through distance and nightfall.
-The Record of Gifts

Lionel leaned his elbows against the outer stone wall, his mind wandering as he scanned the empty town of Cadence and the forest beyond. The sun hung low in the west, and shadows stretched out from their corners.

Something was about to change for everyone in the Gateway. He could sense it as well as every living soul within the boundaries of the fort. Everyone moved about softly, as if their footsteps would arouse the enemy and start the war.

Dudley stepped to his side and mimicked his pose. "How's everything looking?"

"The same as yesterday," Lionel said. "Nothing's moved as far as I can see. Not even a leaf."

"The air is pretty still," Dudley said. "Makes me wonder if Bruin isn't involved."

The thought had not occurred to him. Lionel looked up at the purple sky with more trepidation. Could this be the calm before the storm?

"You've been quiet lately."

He shrugged. "I've made enough of a fool of myself recently. Figured I'd do better to keep my mouth shut from now on."

"Son, there isn't a soul on this earth that hasn't done the same." He gave Lionel a direct look. "But that doesn't mean you don't still have something to offer. Don't let past mistakes shut you off from growth."

Leaning back against the wall, Lionel crossed his arms. "Do you ever get tired of being left behind?"

"What do you mean?"

"The last several missions the prince went on, Captain Braylee always went with him. You're First Captain. Does that bother you?" He winced as soon as he asked and waved the question off. "Forget it."

"If you mean, do I feel like I'm missing out on doing my part, nay, I don't." He stared out into the distance. "I've put a lot of years into this service, and I'm nearing the end of my journey. While I would never choose to sit in a rocking chair for the rest of my days, I'm content to finish out my days in one place. See, wherever I serve, I'm doing my part. Even if it's small." He looked at Lionel again. "I'm not trying to impress anyone. Just serve the Lambient in whatever way I can."

Pricked by Dudley's words, Lionel scuffed the ground with his boot.

"Besides, the prince and Captain Braylee make a solid team. They work together as well as Uralis and Braylee ever did. I don't need to push my way in just to prove something."

"That's been my problem," Lionel said. "I've always felt I needed to prove something."

"You've already proven yourself, but if you're referring to the times you were not at the forefront of the action, remember that we all play a role. If everyone is the first to go to battle, then there's no one behind to hold the fort."

For the first time, Lionel pondered the possibility. Maybe he had put too many expectations on himself. Dudley was content to do what he was asked, even if it meant that he missed the glorious moments that others experienced. And there was no one Lionel respected more than the crusty old captain.

"Well, if no one else has told you, I think you do a decent job," he said, lightening his voice.

Dudley shot him a scowl. "Don't you be patronizing me now, boy."

Lionel raised his hands in surrender. "I wouldn't think of it. But I do appreciate you being straight with me lately. I was losing my way there for a while."

"We all do once in a while." Dudley looked back out into the twilight.

Lionel started to say more, but the older man stood up straight, his posture tense.

"What is it?" Lionel asked, staring out into the duskiness, but seeing nothing.

Dudley's jaw hardened. "They're coming." He pulled his Beacon out and sent out the highest alarm.

Lionel could feel the buzz of his light rod on his belt. Two long pulses and a flashing light.

"Get ready, son." Dudley's face had lost all humor. "I'll go to the watchtower, see if I can get a better view." He turned to go, then stopped short with a deep grunt.

"Captain?"

His back bowed, Dudley slowly swiveled back, a crossbow dart sticking out of his stomach and blood flowing down the front of his tunic.

"Captain!" Lionel caught him and eased him down to rest against the wall.

Dudley shuddered and tried to speak, pointing in the darkness. "Sh-shadowman."

Lionel jerked his light rod up and peered into the darkness. Fury sent him to his feet, his sword out and ready. "Who's there?" When there was no reply, he shouted, "Show yourself, coward!"

The labored breathing of the man beside him drew him back down. "Easy, Captain." He pulled his dagger and cut a piece off his tunic, all the while looking around him. He could see shapes of Stewards approaching along the wall. "Someone get over here!"

"Lieutenant, what happened?" Zakkias ran up and gaped at the bleeding captain.

"Shadowmen," Lionel bunched the rag around the bloody arrow sticking out of Dudley's body and shifted to move him. "Help me get him out of here."

"Nay." Dudley put his hand over Lionel's, stilling his movements. His eyes, awash with pain, pinned him in place. "The army. They're here." He flinched and hissed between his teeth. "Duty first."

The captain's order pierced him, and Lionel rose to look out. He could see faint pinpricks of light in the distance now, bobbing torches twinkling in a large, shadowed mass. But there was no way to tell how many in the failing light.

His jaw clenched, Lionel stepped to the edge of the wall and looked out at the ground level, where soldiers milled about. "Everyone at arms!"

Indecision pulled his gaze back to the captain. Relief dimmed the fierceness of Dudley's glare, and he gave a small, pinched smile, his skin pasty. "I'll be fine, son."

"Stay with him," Lionel directed Zakkias, then ran down the wall to the gate towers, barking out orders as he went. "Get in position!" He almost didn't recognize his own voice. Sharp and authoritative.

The gatehouse was straight ahead when there was a deafening roar, and the ground before him disintegrated into a wall of rock and rubble. Lionel was thrown in the air, hit the ground hard, and all went black.

Eric barreled out of the chapel before the alarm had receded from his Beacon. He had spent the last hour there trying to calm the thrum of nerves that had beset him all day. "Who lit the alarm?" he called out.

All around him, Stewards were on alert, hurrying to previously planned locations. Someone ran to the bell and clanged. They were trained for this, ready to act.

Braylee was already heading in his direction. "I haven't seen Jervis since the evening meal. Dudley's at the outer wall." An alarm of that magnitude could only be sent by a high officer, and three of them were here at the fort.

BOOM!

Everyone ducked and looked to the west. A cloud of smoke billowed into the darkening sky.

"The outer wall." Braylee's voice was grim.

Eric straightened, his breathing uneven. "Lambient, help us."

Before he could make a move, another Steward ran stumbling toward them. "The Shadowmen..." he panted. "They've escaped." Then he fell and lay still, blood pouring from the knife embedded in his back.

Eric knelt to check on him, but he was already dead. Murmurs sounded, as sober awareness spread across the faces of those standing within earshot.

Captain Jervis appeared on horseback, leading Oakley, already saddled. "I just got word from Aladee. The Darkmen prisoners have escaped Calla and may be headed this way." His scowl deepened. "And Mason Grey is missing."

The ground shifted underneath him. Mason was behind locked doors and under heavy guard. How could he have gotten out? Eric feared what his absence could mean.

"An attack on all fronts," Braylee said. "From without and within."

It was happening. Jader had waited long enough. This was the night that would go down in history.

Eric took Oakley's reins. For a brief moment, fear gripped him. But he wrapped his fingers around the hilt of Lavrynth, shutting the worries down. His sword warmed against his skin, reminding him of the power and blood that ran the length of the silver blade. It was greater than any power of darkness Jader possessed over this fort or Mason.

All around him, men looked up at him, their expressions reflecting the same determination that rumbled within him. He swung up on the gray's back. Hardening his features, he slid Lavrynth from the sheath. "They brought the war to us, gentlemen," he said. "So, let's give it to them."

47

You cannot fight darkness with darkness.
-The Sacred Code

All Mason knew was darkness. A cyclone of black, gray, and a sickish green swirled in his head, blocking every thought and reason. He remembered nothing—felt nothing—but Jader's words and the compulsion to heed them. He kept close to the walls of the buildings scattered throughout the fort as he headed for the corner block near the barracks. When the signal was given, the Reservists would all gather there and await orders. Mason would make sure they helped turn the tide in Jader's favor.

The storm inside him pulsated and grew, blocking out anything that tried to distract him, to pull his thoughts from his mission.

Kill the prince. Destroy the Stewards.

But a voice seemed to whisper through the noise, small and still. A tiny twinkle in the middle of the gloom swirling in his mind. It slowed his movements.

Kill the prince. Destroy the Stewards.

The order sounded loud and clear, grounding him back in the present. He moved on. But as he drew closer to his destination and his first task, something pricked at his subconscious, something he felt he was forgetting.

The company of Reservists poured into the square, their gray breastplates flashing in the evening light. Mason waited until they were all there, hundreds strong, restless and murmuring. He kept to the shadows for a moment, unseen and undetected. His pulse spiked. He knew what he had to do. He stepped into view before the troop. They stopped and looked at him, their expressions ranging from confusion to uneasiness to distrust.

"What are you doing here?" Hiram asked, a deep scowl etched on his rugged face. "I thought you stayed back in Calla."

Mason started to give the order, but something made him hesitate. He stood immobile, his insides churning. Sweat dripped down from his temples.

Hiram frowned and took a step closer. "What's wrong with you?"

Kill the prince. Destroy the Stewards.

Jader's command overrode whatever tried to stop him. He raised his head and spoke so they could all hear. "Leave your post now and attack the Stewards." His words slurred in the effort to get them out.

There was a loud chorus of "At once" throughout the ranks. Only a few seemed to hesitate, looking confused.

Hiram cocked his head, his movements sluggish. "What...do you mean?"

It did not surprise Mason that his Gift had not reached everyone the first time. Until his power was fully developed, Eric said his control would be inconsistent.

Eric...

The name struck a chord, stirring up images that he couldn't see. Blurred faces. Familiar but disjointed voices. A girl's smile teased at him, green eyes that seemed to see into his soul. That still, soft whisper breathed into his ears again, into his spirit. Then...

Kill the prince. Destroy the Stewards. He swallowed the lump that had formed in his dry throat. There was only one voice that mattered. And he couldn't fight it.

As Hiram stared at him, Mason shook the strange feeling away and looked the militiaman in the eye. "You will kill the Stewards."

Hiram dropped his chin, his confusion melting into compliance. "At once."

Seria pulled a brush through her hair, her mind miles away. Lena sat on the other bed, looking just as distracted.

As it often did, Seria's mind turned to Mason. Their last meeting still weighed heavily on her, though she tried her best to do as Eric asked and not worry. But her heart squeezed every time she remembered the tortured look on Mason's face as he was led away. His harsh behavior had stunned her, even hurt her, until she gave herself time to think about it.

Mason was scared and trying to protect her. Because Jader still had some kind of hold on his mind.

Seria shuddered at the thought. How awful it must feel to be in the grip of one so wicked.

Lambient, please, be with him. Seria lowered the brush to her lap. *Help him overcome this. Help all of them to defeat this darkness Jader is trying to bring into the world.*

There was a knock on the door. At Lena's call, Aladee entered.

"Why, hello, Captain," Lena greeted.

"I wish this was a simple social call, but I'm afraid it isn't."

Something about the Stewardess's appearance made Seria uneasy. "Have you told Jervis about the Shadowpit yet?"

"Aye, but we have another problem.

Dread spiraled through Seria's stomach. "What is it?"

Aladee licked her lips. "The Darkmen prisoners have escaped."

"Oh, no," Seria breathed, even as Lena gasped.

"Someone released them at some point within the last couple of hours."

Her limbs suddenly weak, Seria sank onto her cot. "Who?" she asked hoarsely.

Aladee looked reluctant to answer. "I believe it was Mason."

Lena's eyes widened. "How?"

"Jader," Seria croaked. "He said Jader could control him."

"Aye. That's why we were holding him in the tower."

Shock rolled over her. "He was imprisoned?"

"By his suggestion and agreed upon by the prince," Aladee answered. "They believed it was the only way to keep him and everyone around him safe."

"But he still got out," Lena said.

Aladee winced and circled the room. "I don't know how, but it's as if he disappeared. Which is why his absence was not noticed for some time. And by then, our guards in the courtyard were taken down and the Darkmen freed."

"Where are they now?" Lena asked.

"It looks like they're heading to the Gateway."

Seria's eyes slid closed. *Oh, Lambient.*

"I don't think there is any immediate threat to the castle, but I would feel better if you remained here for now."

Seria nodded. Even if she wanted to, she had no energy to argue.

"Thank you." Aladee gave them an encouraging smile. "I'll come back to check on you later."

Lena and Seria exchanged sober looks when she was gone, but neither of them said anything. What could be said at that moment? No words would change the course of events.

Seria buried her face in her hands. *Oh, Mason, come back to us.* A muffled sob slipped out. *Come back to me.*

Eric spurred Oakley to a strong canter as they rode across the inner bailey for the gates. Braylee and Jervis were positioned on either side of him, with scores of Stewards behind them.

They were almost to the gates when a volley of arrows rose from both sides of the courtyard and landed within their ranks. Eric drew Oakley up short and looked back. Horses and Stewards hit the ground, struck with arrows.

"Incoming!" Braylee shouted.

Another wave of arrows rose, but Eric shot his hand out, deflecting most of them from his men. Battle cries cut through the noise as scores of men ran out of hiding, swords in hands, blocking the path to the gate.

"What is this?" Jervis asked, his eyes wide.

Eric shared his confusion. Where had these fighters come from? There were too many to be the escaped Shadowmen.

Fighting commenced all around them as the new arrivals attacked. Eric dodged a long sword, swung his blade down over the man's weapon, and kicked him in the head. In that brief moment, he caught sight of the gray breastplate.

It can't be.

"They're Reservists!" he called out. He raised a hand, pulling multiple weapons from the hands of the militiamen. "They're our men!"

But there was no stopping the militia from their assault, forcing the Stewards to reciprocate. Eric's heart sank lower with every man who fell. He tried his best not to fight his own men, but his Gift was limited, and he was forced to use his sword time and time again. And they kept coming. It seemed their entire Reservist Army had been turned against them.

Pushing Oakley to Braylee's side, Eric caught his eye. "Mason has to be here."

It was the only logical explanation, but even as he spoke it, the question of "How?" pulsed through his mind. They had left Mason locked safely away in the king's tower miles away.

"*Fire!*"

He whipped around, catching glimpses of red against the black silhouettes of scattered structures. Multiple buildings were on fire throughout the fort, adding to the chaos that already surrounded them. Where was Mason?

Eric scanned the area, trying to distinguish the shapes in the gathering dusk. "Beacons up!" he called.

One by one, the Stewards turned to their Beacons, shining their lights against the militiamen that came at them and blinding them. Many of the Reservists retreated, fleeing the beams that stung their eyes. But the Reader was the only one who could turn their minds back around. Which meant Eric had to somehow track him down.

48

Lionel groaned as he blinked back into consciousness. Pinpricks of pain ran up and down his body, and a spot on his back throbbed, but he was alive. Bracing himself against the pain, he pushed himself up and looked around in the dusty haze. Chunks of stone lay in scattered heaps around him. And bodies. At least half a dozen men were covered in the rubble. Where the large, wooden gates used to hang, a huge gaping hole yawned. On either side, the wall still stood, damaged and unstable.

The explosion that had blown them apart had been caused by someone from within. The Shadowman who had shot Dudley, perhaps.

Lionel coughed to clear his lungs and jumped to his feet. "Report!"

Voices called out to him, assuring him that others still lived. He stumbled to the gap in the wall and looked out. The Dark Army had not reached them yet, but the row of torches leading them grew ever closer. "Prepare the cannons!" he shouted, looking for a way up the remainder of the wall. The gate towers were gone, but he still needed to see what was out there.

"Cannon one is destroyed!" a man replied.

Someone else chimed in. "Cannon three has sustained damage."

"Then get cannon two ready!" Lionel yelled, climbing a flight of stairs still standing.

"Already on it."

By the time Lionel reached the men, Sgt. Nahm was there and had the cannon loaded and aimed. "Fire when ready!"

It only took a moment to light the wick.

"Stand clear!" Nahm said, and everyone took a step back. The slim cannon kicked back and let out a loud boom. Lionel watched the fireball arch through the sky and land in the middle of the approaching troops.

"Again!" He ran a short distance down the wall. "Archers, at the ready!"

Dozens of men scrambled up to where he stood, their bows in hand and arrows already nocked. Many were too wounded to make it to the top, cutting their number down by a third. The cannon went off again before they were in position.

Lionel gave the order, and arrows flew through the air, disappearing into the dark mass heading their way.

He lost track of time as he continued the onslaught. Despite the dead-on aim, the army continued to advance. But now, he could see glimpses of forms under the shimmering torchlights and the flames of the cannon fire. Hundreds—if not thousands—of Darkmen advanced. There was no way to tell how many Shadowmen were mixed with those. Taller shapes began to take form behind them, rolling closer and closer until he could make them out. Trebuchets, launch engines big enough to hurl devastating projectiles into the midst of the fort.

Where were the rest of the Stewards? They should have gotten here by now. Lionel could not hold a damaged wall for long with one cannon and a fraction of the guards.

"Fire again!"

Even as the explosion went off, a sinking realization came over him. The Dark Army was getting closer. He ground his teeth, staring out at the shrinking distance between them. "Get the wounded to the inner gates," he directed.

He called for another round of defense while his men assisted their injured comrades to the gates. But they could not fight them off in their condition. Not without every man under his watch dying and Jader's army getting through the inner gates. He took a deep breath and called out over the noise. "Fall back to the inner bailey!" Then he looked to Nahm. "Fill it up as much as you can, light it, and get out of here."

"Aye, sir," the knight said, grimly.

Lionel was the last one on the wall when the fuse was lit. The explosion almost deafened him, but he stood his ground to see the shot make its mark. Then he ran for the steps and followed his men across the killing fields, to the gates beckoning to them. All the while, he prayed he had not made a mistake.

The ground exploded a hundred yards from the small, rocky ledge from where Bruin overlooked the thousands of men at his command. They were nearing the gap in the wall, but the Steward cannon fire had slowed them down.

He cursed loudly at the lack of response on his side. "Find out why those trebuchets aren't going," he bellowed to one of his runners.

The runner reeked of apprehension, but he did not dare to argue. Ducking his head, he crouch-ran through the lines of men.

The large missile weapons were awkward, but they were lighter than cannons and easier to transport. But they did no good if they didn't work.

Bruin adjusted the thick cloak hanging at his back, ensuring it was fastened around his neck securely. His men all wore matching garments and leather gloves. They would need them soon. With every minute, they drew closer, but their progress was too slow to satisfy him.

The runner soon returned and huddled on the ground. "Lt. Staten said the trebuchets have jammed, sir."

Bruin narrowed his eyes at him, enjoying the elevation he had over the man. "Both of them?"

The man would not look at him. "It appears so."

"Is Lt. Staten aware of his job in this war?"

"I assume so, sir."

"Then maybe you best remind him that Emperor Jader will arrive here soon for a status report."

The skinny man ducked his head. "Aye, sir."

Bruin fisted his hands as the man ran off. Idiots. They stood on the brink of the greatest victory anyone had ever known, and they couldn't run a blasted trebuchet.

Jader appeared on the ledge beside Bruin.

"My lord." Bruin gave a slight bow. "I assume everything went as planned inside?"

Jader looked more than satisfied. "Indeed. Our inside man has done a beautiful job. My Shadowmen are loose within the fortress, and he has removed one of the Steward captains." He gave a low chuckle. "Prince Eric thinks he is strong, but his reliance on his leaders makes him weak. Once they are all removed, he will fall."

"And the Reader?" He had to bite back his scorn.

"As obedient as a well-trained dog." Jader's eye glittered with his success. "By now, he will have their Reservists turned to our side. The Stewards will be too busy fighting their own people to withstand us."

Bruin had to share Jader's pleasure. With the exception of the weapons malfunction, everything was working out just as Jader had planned. By the end of this night, they would have control of the fort and, by extension, Paladin and the Old Realm.

Jader lifted his head high. A stiff breeze blew his russet hair back, and up ahead, clouds billowed. "It is as I said, Bruin. Despite Mason's immersion into the Stewardship, Shreil's power still reigns supreme. I told Aden as much years ago, before Calla's War. And now his son will realize the full impact."

A loud creak sounded, followed by a spring releasing, and one of the trebuchets launched a spiked, metal ball into the air. It landed well within the fort on the other side of the damaged wall. What little concern Bruin harbored melted away. He looked up at the darkness hanging over the fort. A shape shifted within the depths, fangs flashing, claws reaching. He smiled.

Darkness always overpowered light.

49

Let your light pierce the powers of the dark.
-The Sacred Code

A sober Aladee returned later that night. "The fort is under attack from the west."

A strained silence filled the little room. The Dark Army had reached the Gateway.

Trembles overtook Seria's body. "So, the war begins, and the Shadowpit is still inaccessible." With that pit, every Shadowstone would power the enemy against the Royal Army fighting to protect the Gateway.

"There is little we can do about it now but pray," Aladee said, even as her voice shook a little. "Captain Nathan and I have our troops ready here. You need to be ready for anything, just in case. The castle is on full alert."

Just in case the Dark Army broke through the fort. Daymont would be next. Seria's eyes met Lena's as she fought back the tidal wave of fear that wanted to drag her into a sea of despair.

Then an idea struck her. It was crazy and impossible, but maybe it wasn't. "What if we could get to the Shadowpit?" she asked before Aladee left the room.

The Stewardess turned back to her. "We, who?"

Seria motioned to the three of them. "Us."

"Miss Seria, why on earth would you believe that even a possibility?"

Standing to better face the tall woman, Seria pressed her case. "I know exactly where the tunnel is at. You have a Beacon." She pointed to Lena.

"And she could get us in."

Aladee frowned, though her gaze drifted.

Lena spoke up. "Seria, how could we make the trip undetected? There's a whole company of Darkmen running loose."

Aladee paced the floor, chewing on her nail.

"They may not notice three people traveling as much as they would a whole company. We can keep to the woods as much as possible. And I have something else that can help us." Seria ran to the trunk under the small window and pulled out a dark cloak. "Crue gave me the one Mason gave him, so I have two of these. And Lena, you have one. They're Darkmen cloaks. They'll help camouflage us in the darkness."

"It's crazy and dangerous," Aladee finally spoke, coming to a stop in the middle of the room.

Seria paused before arguing. Her last wild idea had led to her stowing away in a Steward cart and igniting the anger of the prince. She would not do anything like that again. But now that the idea had taken root, she could not shake it.

"But...I do know a path we could take."

Both Seria and Lena stared at Aladee.

"You do?" Seria gripped the cloak to her chest, trying to ignore the way the smell of the cloth made her think of Mason.

"I do. But we would have to be very careful."

Seria looked to a dumbstruck Lena. "Lena? What do you think?" Her friend's Gift was a vital part of this scheme. If she could not handle such a dangerous mission, there was no point in even talking about it.

Lena shook her head slowly. "I never imagined that I could do anything. But this..." She hugged herself. "What kind of chance do we stand?"

"I have no answer," Aladee said, her expression firm. "But if there is a chance, it will come at a cost."

Seria flinched as the reality of what she'd suggested sank in. If they got in, even if they were successful enough to destroy the pit, there was no assurance they would walk out.

Lena's soft voice pulled her back to the present. "I'll do it."

"Are you sure?" Seria asked after a pause.

Lena set her feminine features in determined lines. "As long as that Shadowpit remains, Jader will always have his power."

"I believe Lambient will go with us," Aladee said. "I cannot promise what the end result will be, but He equips His people to do the work that is needed."

A tremor ran over Seria's frame. They were going to do this. She had never harbored thoughts of going anywhere near the war, but if she could do this one thing to help end it, she would go as far as she needed to.

"We need to do it right away," Aladee said. "Now."

Seria pulled her father's breeches and tunic out of her trunk, along with the sword Mason had given her. She ached with the memories.

Please, Lambient, keep him safe. Keep them all safe.

Aladee called Rossi to the room to disclose their plans. The woman's eyes widened.

"How perfectly bold and brilliant," she said. "I only wish you would allow me to go."

"I need you here. You know the part the Stewardesses play in protecting Paladin. You must lead them in my absence."

Rossi put her fist over her heart. "I will, Captain. Do you need me to do anything now?"

"You could get three horses ready. And Lena will need a suitable set of clothes and a sword."

Narrowing her eyes, Rossi swept a searching look over Lena's slight frame. "I'll take care of it." She left to carry out her task.

After she dressed and pinned her hair back, Seria attached her sword to her belt and bent over a map with Aladee and Lena, doing her best to point out the location of the tunnel.

"It might be easier to reach it from this side of the bluffs," Aladee said, tapping the canvas. "We could cut through the mountains here. Can you walk us through that many layers?" She looked to Lena, who nodded.

"It takes very little effort on my part."

"Good. This is probably one of the narrowest areas of the Slates, as well as being hidden by the bluffs surrounding the gap."

"But you and Seria have to be sure to keep hold of me. I don't know what would happen if you let go."

Seria didn't want to even imagine it, and from the way Aladee winced, neither did she.

Rossi had Lena's supplies delivered while Aladee gathered her own provisions and informed Captain Nathan that she would be leaving the premises. The horses were saddled and ready for them by the time they stepped out into the cool evening. Rossi stood by as they tied their bags behind the cantles and mounted.

"Take care, Captain," she said. "We'll see to things here."

"I know you will." Aladee turned her horse around and looked at the other two women. "Let's go."

Before moving to follow, Seria gave Rossi a grateful smile, hoping she'd have a chance to get to know the other woman more after all this was over. She felt the two of them would have a lot of fun together. "Take care, Lieutenant."

"You too, Miss Seria. And Lambient be with you all."

As they left the grounds of the castle behind, the wind whipping their hair in their faces, Seria's mind moved to the Stewards in the Gateway. To Mason. Her heart beat with certainty that she was on the right path. Though she had no idea if this mission would end in success or failure, she was willing to try. For her friends in the army. For the prince. For the man she had once hoped for a future with. And for the Lambient most of all.

50

There are only five Readers known in history, and Moverik is deemed the most famous. Of the other four, two were slain to prevent their powers from fully developing, one disappeared without a trace, and one went insane under the weight of his power.
-The Lost Record of Gifts

"Someone's coming through the gates!"

At Jervis's call, Eric spun Oakley around to the gates, expecting to see dark forms storming through. But the red breastplates told him it was his Stewards. The men who had been at the outer gate, many of them aiding the wounded.

"The Dark Army is coming!" Zakkias shouted, blood streaming from a cut near his eye. The man he supported sagged against him, his arm torn and bleeding.

"What happened?" Eric asked, jumping to the ground to help.

"Someone from the inside blew the gate up," Zakkias panted as they led the wounded man away from the fighting. "Lt. Lionel called a retreat."

Eric's heart sank. "What about the captain?"

"Dead, sir."

Eric could not stop the sense of loss that hit him. Dudley had worked for his father since before Eric was born. But there was no time to grieve him.

More men arrived, battered and grim, but still holding their swords in a firm grip. At the very back ran Lionel, his arms and legs pumping at full speed. "They're coming!"

"Shut the gates!" Eric ordered, even as he ran for the steps. The battle between the Stewards and Reservists was still going on but had broken up into smaller chunks, scattered throughout the fort.

Someone made it to the gate tower and cranked the massive portal closed while Eric found a position on the wall and looked out, Braylee and Jervis flanking him.

Other Stewards took positions up and down on both sides of them, alert and waiting for orders. Distant yelling became a deafening, soul-chilling clamor, but Eric could not make out the approaching company.

Lionel caught up. "They're at least a thousand strong with who knows how many Shadowmen among them, and a couple of launch engines." He hesitated. "I couldn't hold the wall, sir. Everything happened so fast."

"You getting the men back here saved many lives."

"It was Dudley who spotted them in time to send the warning. But not in time to…"

Eric bowed his head. The Stewards had lost another great leader. "I don't know how we'll win this war without him."

"To which he would say, he's not the deciding factor in a win or loss," Braylee said gruffly, his face twisted in his sorrow.

"You're right."

The longer they stood there, the louder the clamor became, and soon, Eric could see signs of the Dark Army's presence. Fires broke out here and there, and the sound of breaking glass and splintering wood cut through his ears.

"Here they come," Braylee murmured.

They could see the Darkmen storming the streets now, brandishing torches and swords that glinted in the gray darkness, destroying anything in their rabid path to the next wall. It would not take them long to direct their attention to the next gate.

He turned away from the destruction below, but the sight on the other side sickened him. The Reservists still raged against his Stewards, pulling much-needed numbers from where they needed to be. "Jervis, I leave you in charge of the defense of the wall for now. We'll deal with the problem on the ground."

Oakley stood where Eric had left him, his eyes wide and feet dancing. Eric took hold of the reins and deliberated his next move.

Lionel followed him. "Dare I ask what happened here?"

"Our Reservists have been turned against us, but not by their choice."

"How?"

Reluctance made the answer drag. "I believe Jader has somehow taken control of our Reader."

Lionel went taut. "How do we counter that?"

"The same way we beat Jader. With the Lambient's light."

Zakkias ran up, gesturing above them. "Sire, something's happening!"

They all looked up. The sky bulged and blackened, shapes forming and disintegrating faster than it took to make them out. Eric stared, chills running up and down his spine.

A smoky apparition tore away from the rest, taking form as it lowered itself to the ground. Fangs gnashed as a dragon-like head appeared, its eyes black and empty, and a thunderous roar erupted from its maw. Oakley reared in terror, nearly ripping the reins from Eric's hand. Eric kept his footing, but there was no stopping the trepidation that rushed through him.

Jader's shadow creatures.

All around him, men cried out. Fear was rank and rampant as more creatures took shape, their razor-like claws striking. Even the militiamen cowered away.

"Lambient above, help us," Eric breathed.

"What is it?" Zakkias asked, his eyes swallowing his face.

"Nothing but monsters created out of shadow." Eric had no idea what they were capable of, save emitting terrible fear, but he hoped they were mere apparitions that could not cause physical harm.

The dragon dove straight down at the men on the ground, its movements so quick and smooth they had no time to prepare for it. It tore through the middle, covering the bulk of the men in a blanket of darkness. It flipped back up, and its tail whipped out, catching Eric across the chest. He hit the ground hard, sucking the oxygen from his lungs. Oakley let out a panicked squeal.

So much for a mere apparition. These things were created for one purpose. To destroy.

Every bone protested as he rolled over and tried to clear his vision. He could not tell how many there were. Five? A dozen? They seemed to hover in one place yet be everywhere at the same time. Tasting blood, Eric pushed himself up and took stock of the situation. Men were down. Horses fled. Beacons shone as Stewards valiantly tried to beat the shadows back.

One monster struck a shed, and it splintered into a thousand pieces, its barbs catching in the clothes, leathers, skin, and hides of man and beast. Then it turned on him, its eyes narrowing like a cat's before it attacked. Eric jerked his Beacon up and out, striking him with the light whip. An explosion of white sparks scattered like fireworks. It let out a howl of pain and recoiled, but it did not retreat. If anything, it grew angrier.

What little energy Eric had left after the light whip drained from him. His knees buckled, but Braylee's strong grip on his elbow kept him upright.

The creature rose on its back legs and bellowed, emitting plumes of black smoke. The battle cry rang out over the valley and echoed back from the mountains. It was answered by the rest of the dragons, and they scattered, taking their awful presence throughout every corner and leaving the courtyard heavy with fear and shock.

The Reservists recovered first and resumed their mindless assault.

Eric's spine snapped straight. "Lt. Lionel, get the wounded to the infirmary. Then report to Captain Braylee at the back wall."

When Braylee's dark gaze met his, Eric said, "I need a strong leader back there when the rest of the Darkmen show up."

Braylee acquiesced and ran to where Beast was tethered. Eric handed Oakley's reins over to Lionel. "He'll get you there faster."

"But, sir—"

"Go, Lieutenant. There's no time to waste."

Lionel relented and led the horse away. He called several men to help start moving the wounded to the infirmary, where Luron would be ready for them.

Eric took his sword in one hand and his Beacon in the other. Then he marched back out into the battlefield and held his rod up to throw a beam of light, cutting through the middle of the throng.

A militiaman came up behind him, but Braylee, riding by on Beast, knocked him out with the hilt of his sword before he rode down through the center. When he was gone, the crowd around Eric surged again, and he fought on, wrenching swords out of the hands of the men, blocking and ducking. But too many of his men had already fallen. If this went on, every man in the Reserves would have to be killed, and that possibility twisted inside him like a knife.

Another explosion rent the night, and in the distance, one of the barracks went up in flames. Fires dotted the main street of the fortress. Men ran and fought in every direction.

Above, another dragon flew by, swirling and writhing. Eric tightened his grip on Lavrynth and chased after the monster as it soared through the middle of the courtyard, deeper into the stronghold. He lost track of everyone else as he ran, and he had no idea what he was doing, but still, he ran, his boots pounding the ground.

Then its big head swiveled and spotted him. He slid to a stop as it rotated in the air and struck. Eric could feel the hot air against his face as he dodged the razor-sharp claws. The dragon passed him by and continued its course. Ahead, there were more shouts and cries.

This time, he did not pursue. His lungs throbbed within his chest, and his legs trembled, ready to collapse with every step. The monsters were everywhere, and his men were scattered. Flashes of Beacons lit up in the fog as they tried to defend themselves, but the beams did not hold them off for long.

Urgency pounded through Eric's head. There had to be a way to destroy them, but his mind and body were exhausted fighting the despair the dragons seemed to carry with them, which must be Jader's purpose.

In a brief respite, he leaned back against a stone wall, his mind racing for solutions. Shadow creatures terrorized from the sky. The Dark Army came from both sides. Shadowmen, loose and unseen, destroyed any part of the fort they could. The Reservists had been turned against their allies.

So much had gone wrong in such a short amount of time.

One thing at a time.

He had to find Mason. With the militiamen fighting their every move, they would never be able to focus on fighting their real enemy. And perhaps Mason could lead Eric to Jader himself.

Where are you, Mason? Eric had no idea where to start, unsure that Mason was even here at the fort. He might have controlled the army from a distant location, though Eric had a strong feeling that wasn't the case. But the chance of stumbling across him was too small to hope for.

So how was he to find him?

An idea came to him, and he latched onto it. Maybe he could reach out to his mind, the same way Mason had done to him more than once.

Fight him, you stubborn soldier. You're a Steward, not a Shadowman.

He waited, but there was nothing. Not a reply or a premonition. For all he knew, he was talking to empty air. But if Jader had control of Mason's will, he would not come running at Eric's beckoning. Not without Jader's approval. It would have to feel like a chance to act on Jader's behalf.

He drew in a deep breath and prayed for wisdom. Then he spoke out loud. "I'm going after Jader, Mason. If you want to stop me, I'll be at the chapel." He ground his teeth together. "You want a fight, come and get it."

It was dark and almost quiet in the corner of the large room where Mason waited. In the distance, he could hear the results of his actions. The Reservists had started a separate mini-war within the walls of the stronghold. And Jader's monsters had been unleashed.

Soon, the Dark Army would break in on both sides, and the Stewards would be crushed between them. Jader would be pleased.

A feminine whisper brushed against the shadows clinging to his mind. *Mason, come back to us.*

He blinked. Breathing became difficult, and he struggled to remember what he was doing.

The war had started. The Stewards were defending the Gateway against Jader's Dark Army. But Mason stood against them. Didn't he?

Something stirred within him, too faint to identify. *Come back to me.*

Hazy memories tried to take shape, but it was as if they were covered with black smoke. He struggled to see through it, trying to understand what they were trying to tell him.

Another voice, hard and passionate, echoed between his ears. *Fight it...you're a Steward, not a Shadowman.*

He winced at the pain it sparked. It felt so familiar...but before he could grab a hold of it, Jader's command once again filled his mind.

Kill the prince. Destroy the Stewards.

Mason hardened himself against the memories trying to invade. They didn't matter. All that mattered was following Jader's orders.

The other voice returned. *I'll be at the chapel. You want a fight, come and get it.*

Ah, yes, he recognized it now. The prince. Jader's greatest enemy, and therefore, his, as well.

He raised his eyes to scan the spacious room where he waited, dark and empty, ransacked by the Shadowmen who moved about freely in the fort. Curling his fingers into fists, Mason answered the challenge out loud. "Gladly."

51

Where the light is, darkness hasn't a chance and must flee.
-The Sacred Code

Braylee rested his hands on the wall, maintaining a calm appearance, though his insides tensed. "Here they come."

The noise grew as the escaped Darkmen from Calla approached. Jeers and shouts proceeded the appearance of hundreds of soldiers, all wielding swords, bows, even clubs. This army may not be as trained as the rest, but they were still dangerous.

Braylee kept his men in position and watched as the enemy drew closer. Behind him, he could hear the shadow creatures raging about. The Stewards stirred in uneasiness, but their expressions were resolute.

"Incoming!" someone shouted. Dozens of arrows arced through the night sky, some lit with flames, and landed behind the walls. Most fell harmlessly, but a few struck. Cries rang out as men dropped to the ground.

"Return fire!" Braylee barked.

The response was immediate. The archers aimed straight and true at the front line, but the Darkmen carried shields both in front of them and above their heads.

"Hold!" Braylee glared down at the mass. They were too protected for arrows to do any good. "Fire the trebuchet."

The long-reaching projectile launcher would do more damage than their bows could at this point.

Large metal-tipped arrows were shot from the engine arms. It hit the front of the crowd, scattering men in every direction. But those behind them kept coming, walking over their dead or wounded comrades.

"Captain!" Gann's sharp call drew Braylee around. His heart sank at the dozens of gray-clad soldiers advancing in their direction from within. The militiamen had reached the back wall.

"Third unit, take defense position," he shouted as he took his sword. He met Gann's eyes. "Stay up here and keep the engine firing."

A great shout filled the courtyard as he jogged down the steps. The Reservists attacked without any hesitation, and the Stewards reacted in full force.

"Beacons!" He pulled his rod and used it to blind the young man rushing at him. Others followed suit, and the area was lit like midday. The militiamen faltered and retreated, but it would not last.

Gann shouted out another warning from on top of the wall as the approaching Dark Army fired again.

"Watch out!" someone else cried.

A deafening roar assaulted Braylee's ears before a shadow creature dove at him. He ducked and watched it soar away.

"What are we going to do, Captain?" Dakim asked, his eyes wide. "We can't hold them all off."

Braylee concealed his dismay as several cadets stared back at him. The young soldiers had been positioned here with the assumption they would not be on the front lines of defense. With another army approaching from the rear and their own Reservists turning against them, the front lines were now blurred.

He set his jaw. "We're going to hold them off as long as we can. No matter what."

The fear on the boy's face melted into cold acceptance. He gave his companions a nod, and they responded. "Aye, sir."

The chapel was ransacked. Every room in the small building lay in ruins. Smashed lanterns were scattered across the scorch-marked floor. Drapes hung in slashed tatters from the blue and green stained-glass windows. And the Beacon orb was missing, most likely taken to ensure it would offer the Stewards no help this night.

Stepping through the door of the meeting area, Eric cast the light of his Beacon around. Not sure if the damage had been done by Mason or other Shadowmen, he was cautious. Darkness edged the walls, the windows black and imposing.

His heart thumped wildly in his chest, and his ears rang with the sound of steel and shouting. Everything in him itched to go back out and fight. To defend his men. But he waited, his muscles rigid and his ears tingling for a footstep he would not be able to hear in the dark.

But his intuition rose to the forefront, and he stopped to listen, stretching out with his mind more than his ears.

Something shifted in the air, and adrenaline shot through his veins. Diving to the side, he felt the hiss of a blade that barely missed slicing into his neck. He rolled a few feet away and regained his footing. The light rod eased the shadows back until Mason came into view.

Eric sucked in a breath. Jader's control was evident in the emptiness of Mason's expression, the cloudiness of his red-rimmed eyes. And Mason's intention was clear as he raised his sword. Once again, he was under Jader's authority.

But one thing stood out to Eric that brought both optimism and dismay. The Beacon did not affect Mason as it did before he became a Steward. But while that proved to Eric that the light still resided within him, it also meant he would not be hindered by the light rod. He snapped it back onto his belt and put out a restraining hand. "Mason, wait."

But Mason struck again, silent and pale.

Eric backstepped to avoid the blade. "Stop! This isn't you."

"I told you to kill me."

Although Eric could hardly recognize the man before him, the statement gave him hope. It was the same thing Mason had told Eric after learning what Jader could do through him. Maybe there was part of him still remembering who he was.

Mason attacked again, putting Eric on the defense and preventing any more talk for several moments. They inched their way through the middle aisle of the stone benches. He swung Lavrynth, sweeping another strike to the side. "Fight this, Mason. You don't belong to Jader anymore."

"Shreil is my master."

"To blazes with Shreil!" Eric burst out, sidestepping to put a pew between them. "He doesn't have the power to take what belongs to the Lambient."

Mason kept coming, kept swinging that blade without hesitation. He shoved a chair out of the way as he stalked Eric around the room.

Eric gritted his teeth as he deflected another blow. "I don't want to fight you." He blocked a blow to his left. "You're a Steward. An ally. A child of the Lambient."

"Stop!" Mason's shout exploded from him.

The outburst only fueled Eric's attempts as he worked to keep space between them. He reached out with his mind for a candlestick sitting in a corner, flinging it in the air. Mason threw his arm up to block it, his face darkening as he stepped up on another bench. Taking advantage of the spare moment, Eric used his Gift to flip the heavy seat over.

Mason hit the floor hard and jumped back to his feet with an animalistic growl.

"Fight him, Mason!"

"It's useless to fight." The Reader snarled and kicked another chair away, backing Eric into a corner. "You will die tonight."

His insides churning, Eric stood his ground as Mason attacked. Their swords crossed time and again as Eric did his best to hold Mason at bay. Their blades locked at one point, their gazes crashing. Eric ground his teeth. "You are a *Steward*, Mason."

Mason's brows slashed over his clouded eyes. "I'm a Shadowman."

"Nay! You held the Beacon, you swore yourself to the Lambient. He lives in you." He shoved against the blade with his own, pushing Mason away.

For a brief moment, Mason's expression cleared. He hesitated and blinked, and optimism flickered. Outside, a dark dragon flew by the window, its shriek echoing into the room, rattling the dishes and the chairs. Mason stiffened and stepped back, readjusting his grip on the hilt.

"Darkness always overcomes light."

Eric set his jaw and grabbed his Beacon. "We'll see about that." As Mason moved to attack again, Eric shot out a blast of light that hit the other man square in the chest.

Mason screamed and dropped his sword, retreating. Eric followed his steps, keeping the rod pointed at him, the light centered at Mason's heart.

The pain was excruciating as shards of light pierced every cell in Mason's body. He let out another guttural cry as it shot into his head, clearing the gray cloud that had blocked him from thinking and feeling.

Memories rolled before his eyes. Holding the lit Beacon in his hand for the first time. Fighting Bruin with Eric at his side. Throwing his Shadowstone over the cliff. Surrendering his life to the Lambient.

There was another pulse of light, pushing back the control that Shreil tried to hold sway over him through Jader. It burned like fire as it ran through his limbs and receded. He fell to his hands and knees, sucking in huge gulps of air. The light receded.

A stillness surrounded him. Then muffled footsteps. "Mason?"

Eric's soft call drew his head up, and regret slashed through him. "What have I done?"

Eric crouched on one knee before him. "Whatever you did tonight, it was not by your own will."

He dropped his head. "I should've been strong enough to fight it." A shudder passed over him. "I let him in."

"You're human, Mason. You will fail, but Lambient's grace covers our failures."

"I don't deserve it," Mason rasped. "I can't forget."

There was a pause until Mason began to wonder if Eric saw that he was right. He could not be completely forgiven, or he would not have let Jader take over his will.

"Mason." When Eric said nothing more, Mason raised his head again. Compassion and confidence radiated from Eric's gaze as he continued.

"I forgive you."

The three words stabbed at him, making his heart bleed over the wounds that remained in his soul.

"For every act of violence, hatred, and anger you ever committed against me and my kingdom." Eric pointed to the door, passion igniting his speech. "Those men out there, fighting to serve the Lambient—some of them may struggle, but many of them also forgive you. And Seria."

The name brought a lump to Mason's throat as he remembered the light and love in her eyes.

"Seria forgave you for the wrongs you committed toward her. And my father...I know that in his heart he forgave you, or he would never have given you a chance to stay here."

The lump grew tight and uncomfortable, and he tried to swallow.

"And the Lambient." Passion seeped into Eric's words and he rested a hand on Mason's shoulder. "He's the one who gave us the strength and grace to forgive. So, of course, He would have enough to forgive you. So, who are you"—he jabbed a finger into Mason's chest—"to hold on to your own guilt?"

Mason hung his head, speechless. His eyes stung as he tried to accept the truth.

Eric held his Beacon out. "Take it, Mason. Let it remind you again that you are forgiven."

"I can't." Mason looked up again. "It burns." Another reminder that he was not what he should be.

"Then let it burn!" Eric's voice hardened. "Let it burn every doubt from your mind and burn into your very soul until you are on fire with His light. By His strength, we can do anything, even fight Shreil himself."

He stared at the Beacon, his spirit yearning for its touch.

There was another roar outside, and Eric cast a glance at the window. "Unfortunately, I don't have time to wait for you to realize what you already know." He put the rod on the floor and stood. "I need you to reverse your control on the Reservists before my men all kill each other."

Mason stared at the rod for a moment longer.

"Mason."

Urgency propelled him to his feet, picking the light rod up as he went.

He watched it glow, soft and gentle, as if reassuring him that it was still there for him. Taking a deep breath that cleansed him of the last few nightmarish hours, he holstered it and asked, "Where are they?"

"At this point, everywhere. But the majority of them are in the inner courtyard. That's where you should head first."

"Where are you going?"

Steel entered Eric's eyes. "I'm going hunting for dragons."

52

The Lambient will be sun and moon to me and enlighten my darkness.
-The Sacred Code

The Gateway, Old Realm

Aladee led the way through trees and bluffs closer to the base of the Slate Mountains. They kept their voices low and their ears alert. So far, they had not run into any trouble, but Aladee had taken every precaution on the trip, keeping to the woods and out of the open.

They paused at the edge of the woods and stared up at the mountains before them. Aladee pointed. "I'm thinking that's the narrowest stretch. Your tunnel should be right on the other side."

Seria looked back, half expecting to see Darkmen on their trail. "How do we get there without being seen?"

Aladee glanced up at the sky. There was no sign of the moon or stars. Only blackness. "I don't think we should take the horses. We can go quieter on foot."

Seria wrapped Mason's cloak tighter around her and glanced at Lena, who looked peaked and tired under her covering.

"I'm fine," she assured.

They left the horses untethered.

"They'll be better off," Aladee said. "They'll wander back home on their own if they need to."

The implication that they might not return made Seria want to run back to the castle. Instead, she patted the mare's neck before following

Aladee to the wood's edge. The Stewardess took her time in looking around, making sure no one was near before she stepped out and motioned for them to follow.

"I'll have to keep my Beacon down unless absolutely necessary," she murmured.

"I'm sort of used to the dark by now," Seria said. After hours of riding, her night vision was clear.

They made their way across the meadow, keeping their steps soft. Seria tried to block out the anxious thoughts and focus on what was ahead. If they could get to the Shadowpit, they could help bring an end to this terrible war.

Aladee's stealth and Lena's calm did much to steady her nerves, but her throat and mouth were still dry with trepidation of the unknown. Every time her fear reared its head, though, she would remember the men in the fort and whisper a prayer for them. Especially for Mason, whose mind was no longer his own.

Aladee pointed to the south, where the Slates opened up, though she couldn't see the breach from here. "The bluffs around the gap keep us out of sight. The gates into the fort are right on the other side. That's where the Dark Army will be gathering on this side."

Even with her night vision, Seria could barely make out the dark land masses. She wished she had Captain Dudley's Gifted long vision, but maybe even he was limited by the dark.

They reached the foot of the mountains without mishap. Seria leaned back against the rock and drew a deep, relieved breath. They had made it safe thus far with no problems. It almost seemed too easy, as if trouble awaited them at the next step. But she shook the thought away and listened to what Aladee was saying.

"I used to live not far from here when I was a girl and played around over here a lot. There's a bit of a cleft in here." She took a step and seemed to disappear from view. Seria pushed herself off and peered into the crack. It cut into the mountain several yards.

"Oh, that makes it easier," Lena said, stepping inside the fissure. "Not as many walls to go through."

"That's why I thought this scheme of yours might work," Aladee said, her smile flashing in the dark. "I figure we should come out not far from where the bluffs begin on the other side."

"Right where my tunnel begins." A thrill of victory went through Seria. But she quickly reminded herself that jumping ahead would only breed impulsivity.

"Are you ready?" Aladee asked.

Lena moved forward. "Let me test it out first."

"Be careful," Seria whispered as her friend put her hand on the mountain and eased her way inside.

They waited, silent as a gravesite, for several minutes before Lena ventured back out, her cheeks glowing.

"I didn't go all the way through, but I could feel the density lessen the further I went. I believe you're right, Aladee. This is a narrow track, and I don't think I'll have any trouble getting us through."

"All right, make sure everything is secure before we go," Aladee said, tightening her belt. "We don't want anything to slow us down, especially since we don't know what's on the other side."

Seria and Lena followed her lead in checking their clothes. Then Lena took Seria's hand, Seria held Aladee's, and they moved forward. The Stewardess held her sword tightly with her free hand.

The same chilly rush went through Seria's body that she experienced every time Lena took her through solid walls. But this time, the sensation did not lift as they walked straight through the foundation of the mountain. Seria gaped at the patterns etched in the rock, amazed at how solid it was. Yet they moved through like water through a curtain.

The minutes ticked by, and Seria's heart beat with every step. What would be on the other side? Would it be guarded? Or was the entire army positioned around the Gateway Stronghold? The mountain was cold, settling in Seria's chest like a knot she couldn't unravel. It made it hard to breathe, and Seria was struck with a new fear. Would they run out of oxygen here?

But soon, Lena came to a stop and looked back with a finger to her lips. Seria and Aladee nodded her on. Lena eased her way out, then tugged Seria with her. Seria almost stumbled as she stepped free of the rock, sucking in a lungful of pure air, sharp and cold.

Aladee moved forward, her Beacon up. They were surrounded by a cluster of thick bluffs that reminded Seria of short, squat men sitting around a table. They had come out on a wide shelf of rock that sloped steeply down. Seria remembered passing beside it on her trips to her fishing site. They were not far from her tunnel.

"We'll have to find an easier way to ground level," she whispered. "It levels off a little further down."

They moved with cautious steps, shrouded in deep shadows, though Aladee allowed a dim glow to illuminate their steps. The night dew had gathered on the stone, so the going was slow and treacherous.

The shelf narrowed so that they had to walk single file. Aladee drew up shortly and extinguished her light. Seria held her breath. Then she heard voices drifting in the night air.

Nay, please, not now.

But they drifted closer, the volume unchecked and the tones unconcerned.

Aladee's silhouette backtracked and stepped close to Seria's side. "We can't go this way." Her murmur was barely detectable.

Though she wanted to argue, Seria knew better than to question the Stewardess's direction. Getting caught would do nothing for their mission.

But there had to be another way. Maybe Lena could get them through from here. She would have to wait to suggest it until they were further from the marching voices. She shivered at the idea that they stood so close to enemy soldiers and eased away.

There was a soft gasp and the sound of gravel crunching. Lena slipped on the wet rock, and Seria reached out to grab her. But in the darkness, she missed a step and her whole body lurched forward and over the shelf. She threw her hands out to grab something, but there was nothing to break her fall.

The only thought on Seria's mind was the need to keep her friends safe from danger, so she bit back her scream as she fell over the edge.

53

*The Reader known as Moverik was recorded to have controlled an army
of five thousand men to overthrow the ancient city of Kain.
-The Lost Record of Gifts*

The effects of Jader's attack were evident with every turn Mason took.
There was too much fire. Too many bodies. And it was too late to undo
what he had done. But he could stop good men from killing good men.

As he drew closer to the inner bailey, the clash of swords rang out over
the crackling flames. Ignoring the stitch in his side, he pushed ahead. The
courtyard came into view, full of gray-clad Reservists and red-armored
Stewards, all fighting each other. He ran right through the middle of
them. "Stop!" he bellowed, throwing his command out as far as he could.
"Stand down! Put your weapons down!"

For a long, agonizing moment, it seemed his command fell on deaf
ears. But then one, two, and more militiamen stopped and released their
swords. The noise level dropped, and the Stewards hesitated as their
opponents quit attacking. Mason let out a breath. Not one Reservist
within view resisted his control. A few cheers sounded up and down the
ranks, but he didn't quite feel like celebrating.

Zakkias trotted over to him, his youthful face streaked with sweat and
his sword with blood. He gave Mason a grateful look. "It's good to see
you, sir."

"Is that all of them?"

"I don't think so. A lot of them scattered throughout the fort."

Jervis's voice sounded from the wall. "Incoming!"

There was a loud crash, and a plume of dust billowed upwards. He and Zakkias exchanged quick looks. The gates shuddered but held. The Steward cannons returned fire.

Jervis appeared at the top and gave them all a quick, surmising look. "Every man in position! It's time to turn our fight to the other army."

Dozens of knights moved in every direction, their focus sharp and sure. Many ran up the steps to assist the archers. Others took up positions throughout the courtyard. A few helped the wounded—both Stewards and militiamen—to the infirmary on the other side of the Great Hall.

Mason took in the scene on the ground, the way the men moved into position, with no hesitation as they faced the gates and readied for the enemy to penetrate the fortress. The Reservists all stood still, compliant as the Stewards confiscated their weapons. Regret sliced through him at how lost and unsure they looked. Even now, after he released them from their unwitting opposition, their minds were not yet their own.

Something moved in a dark corner across the yard. Jeck raised his crossbow, aiming it up at Jervis, still standing in clear view at the top of the stairs.

"Jervis! Get down!"

The crossbow released a dart, and Jervis dropped before Mason swung his bow and fired. Jeck fell with a heavy thud. Mason ran for the steps, Zakkias on his heels, but Jervis was already back on his feet before they cleared the top.

"What was that?" Jervis asked.

"A Shadowman just took a shot at you." Relief sharpened Mason's tone. Jeck would no longer be a problem.

Zakkias spoke up. "Mason took him out."

Using his sleeve, Jervis wiped sweat off his face. "Then I thank you. They're doing everything to bring us down from the inside out."

At a screech up above, they all ducked.

"It doesn't help to have those devils flying around our heads," Jervis growled.

Another explosion rent the air, this time from the inside. They all turned to see a red blaze tinting the dark night.

Mason slapped his hand against the wall. "Enough is enough." He reversed his steps and headed down.

"Where you going?" Jervis called.

He paused. "I may as well put these confounded Shadowstone abilities to good use."

"Jader's not going to take you reversing his orders very well."

"I'm more worried about fixing the mess I made here." He was halfway down the stairs before he noticed Zakkias was still following him. "What are you doing?"

"You could use someone to watch your back."

Mason waved him off. "I don't think my back is anywhere you want to be close to right now."

"I'll take my chances."

Once they reached the bottom, Mason tried to shake him off again, but Zakkias cut him off. "I'm going. Sir." There was nothing but respect in his demeanor, but the address set Mason back. He had no seniority, couldn't technically give the Steward orders. But the determination Zakkias displayed took away his desire to. If he got the young man killed, he would never forgive himself, but something told him Zakkias would not avoid the risk of dying anyway. Not on this night.

"All right, fine. You can stick with me for a while."

Seria slid and rolled all the way down the slope, landing in a heap at the bottom. She let out a groan before she could stop herself.

"What's this?" a voice startled her from the black night.

With trembling arms, Seria pushed herself up to her knees and strained to make out her surroundings. "W-who's there?"

Several figures approached, all wearing black. They fanned out, blocking her in against the bluff.

"That's what we'd like to know," a woman spoke up, though Seria could not see her. "What are you doing out here?"

Seria's mind spun with her options. She couldn't scream for help, or Aladee would come running, and that would prove to be disastrous.

Instead, she blurted out the first thing that came to her mind.

"I w-was looking for M-Mason."

There was a pause. "What do you want with Mason?" an unseen voice asked, deep and chilly.

With no idea what she was doing, and hoping against all hope that using his name would not put him in any more harm, she forced herself to speak again. "He said I'd find help here." Jader had once made an attempt to capture her. Maybe her connection to Mason would keep her alive. At least for now.

A shadowy figure appeared before her, gradually taking form until she could see a man's face inches before her own. A purple-black stone rested against his chest. She flinched and backed away, but his cold fingers gripped her elbow, digging into the bruises starting to form after her fall.

Amusement spread over his countenance but did not touch the dead look in his eyes. "You wouldn't be the little wench that got our boy into all kinds of trouble now, would you?"

His words shot alarm through her. Oh, mercies, she hadn't made things worse, had she?

"We can't let her walk out of here," someone said.

"Oh, no," the man said, tightening his hold. "We'll hang on to her."

"Kill her," the woman said sharply.

"Now, Dreeya, don't get ahead of yourself," he said. "We'll take her with us."

"To the pit?" The other man sounded incredulous.

A small measure of victory trickled through the river of fear trying to drown her. Maybe this would work out for the better.

"You know the emperor is gonna wanna see her." He jerked her toward him. "Make sure she's alone."

Cold terror cut through her as the man dragged her with him, and she fervently prayed that Aladee and Lena would not be discovered.

Dozens of people surrounded her, visible, so not Shadow Soldiers. But the man who held her had faded from view again, and it was as if the night itself had captured her. Her heart fluttered in her chest like a bird caught in a trap. They were taking her to her original destination, but what on earth would she do then? She was alone, held hostage by who knew how many. And the Stewardess with the Beacon needed to destroy the pit had disappeared.

Lambient, help me. Her muddled mind could not come up with anything more to say.

They marched through the darkness for a few minutes before they stopped and turned to enter a dense stretch of thorny bushes. The vines reached out to snag her tunic and trousers as she passed. Then they came to a wall of rock with a crack in it. The man shoved her ahead into the narrow crevice. They walked silently on, venturing deep within the mountain. Despite the chill of the autumn air, sweat formed on Seria's brow and her back, making her hair and clothes stick to her.

The air grew thick and foreboding. With every passing moment, Seria felt heavier, as if leaving any memory of light and freedom behind. She fought the despair that made every step feel like she was slogging through mud. She would not let it drag her down into its depths. With every stride, she repeated what few lines she knew from the Sacred Code.

He will guide my steps. The Lambient delivers those who call on Him. Light overcomes the darkness.

The words fanned the flickering flames of the faith she had held on to since a young girl, sitting at her parents' feet, learning about the Lambient. The same faith that had sustained her after their brutal murder.

She may be surrounded by the enemy, without the friends she had started with on this journey, but she was where she was supposed to be. And she was not alone.

The path made a sharp curve to the left, and a red-tinted sheen reflected off the rocks. Her captor pushed her on until they stepped out of the narrow passage and into a soaring, open space.

Seria's heart skipped a beat. A wide cave spread out before her, its ceiling high above them. Indeed, it seemed the mountain itself was hollowed out by the cave. Pointy rock pillars jutted from the floor and ceiling like jagged teeth.

Her blood drained from her face at the huge pit that gaped in the middle of the cave floor. The source of the red glow. From where she stood, she could not see inside it, but the crimson smoke and light that rose from its depths sent terror streaking through her.

She had made it to the Shadowpit.

Around the pit, several dozen dark forms milled about, talking quietly, their stances alert. Behind her, even more soldiers filed out, joining their comrades around the pit. Seria's knees weakened at the sheer number of men and women that surrounded her. There had to be at least a hundred people in the cave.

"Hey, Balt. Whatcha got there?" someone called from within.

The man forced her on and positioned her so that she was the center of attention. The stares and jeers pierced her skin like needles.

Balt chuckled. "This here gal is none other than Mason Grey's little filly."

Murmurs rose from the crowds around her, and she wrapped her arms around her quaking middle. *Stand tall. Don't fall apart. You're not alone.*

"I still say we should've killed her," a dark-headed woman snarled. Seria recognized her voice as the one Balt called Dreeya. She was a hard-faced woman with a dangerous glint in her eyes. "Jader's not going to be happy you dragged her here, of all places."

"She won't be here long. Just long enough to be useful."

Seria tried to block out the discussion of her fate, but a huge rock of fear lodged in her windpipe, making it hard to breathe. She scanned the cave around them, looking for another exit. There were cracks and jagged cuts in the wall, but no opening wide enough for her to get through. The only escape was through the narrow passage she had come from.

Steam poured out of the hole on the rock floor and gathered, draping the air in an ominous chill.

"You're awfully interested in our Shadowpit, girlie." Balt's voice jerked her head around. "Wanna closer peek?"

Before she could answer, he grabbed her arm, dragging her to the pit, and held her inches from the edge. She could not stop herself from flinching back.

The hole was roughly round, glowing from a lava-type substance at the bottom. Purple veins ran up and down the sweating red walls of the pit. But it was the essence that terrified Seria more than anything. Despite the heat emanating from its depths, it lifted chills on her arms and in her heart. Icy cold fear wrapped its fingers around her.

A rumble echoed, and everyone turned to the entrance in time to see another score of men and women clad in dark leather entering, led by another Shadowman.

"Ah, Naman." Balt clapped his hands. "We're all here now." He shoved Seria toward Dreeya. "Chain her up until Jader tells us what to do with her."

Instead of grabbing her arm, Dreeya dug her fingers into the hair at the back of Seria's head. A sharp tip of a dagger stuck into her side. "Let's go, Seria Gayle."

Her heart sped up at the use of her name. She was right in surmising her connection to Mason would keep her alive for the time being. But the hatred this woman displayed weakened her resolve.

Dreeya forced her to a small cutout where metal shackles hung down from the rock ceiling. "How perfectly romantic that you get to be chained in the very spot where your lover spent his time," she spat.

As her wrist was enclosed in the cold metal, Seria tried not to picture Mason here and prayed for his safety. He was the reason she was here. He and every other man and woman who fought against Jader's evil.

The sound of the shackle locking around her wrist echoed in Seria's ear like a death drum. Dreeya stretched her other hand out and locked it to a second cuff on the other side. Then she stood back and stared at her. "You're not worth the trouble you caused." She turned her back and joined the others.

Seria squeezed her eyes shut and tried to slow her breathing and calm her racing mind. The Shadowpit was here, but she could not accomplish what she needed to on her own. She needed a plan.

Opening her eyes, she looked around at the scores of soldiers, all waiting around for something. The entrance to the cave was to her right, about twenty feet away. Once she freed herself from the cuffs, she could find the right moment to run and hopefully get out before anyone could catch her. Then, if she could find Aladee and Lena, they could come back as soon as the way was clear, and Aladee could destroy the pit.

Her plan had fallen to pieces, but she refused to be defeated.

54

Mason had never seen anything like the dragons Jader had unleashed. The black monsters slithered and writhed everywhere he looked, sending shivers down his spine with their screeching cries. Though they attacked periodically, they chose to hover above, spreading fear and chaos wherever they went. Stewards faced them with their Beacons, but the lights did not penetrate their thick, smoky exterior.

His heart pounded wildly in his ribcage like a prisoner yelling to get out, and he reined back the horror that made him want to stop where he was and bury his head. But he could not afford that luxury. He had to find the Shadowmen before he handed over a victory to Jader.

He and Zakkias ran through the streets in the direction of the biggest fire, keeping their eyes peeled for more rogue Reservists. The closer they got to the blaze, the more his heart sank. As they rounded a corner, his fears were confirmed. It was the barn that housed the officer's horses. And Sanjo.

He slowed his pace, unable to pull his gaze from the sight. The barn was engulfed, angry red flames eating away what was left of the wooden walls. A part of him wanted to run and try to save the animals. But reasoning stopped him. It was too late. There was no way any of them survived that blast. All he could do now was try to stop further destruction and bring down the ones who sought to destroy all that was good.

I'm sorry, Seria. His chest aching, he ran closer, hoping to find tracks that would lead him to the one responsible.

"Master Mason!" The familiar voice made him stop and spin around. Through the smoky darkness, Crue appeared, waving them over.

"Crue!" Mason stared at him. "What the blazes are you still doing here?"

"I didn't leave with the last group." The boy squared his shoulders. "I wanted to stay and do my part."

"Blades, boy, do you have any idea how foolish that was?"

"There are other boys here." Crue cast a quick look to Zakkias, who wisely stayed quiet.

"Soldiers, Crue. You're not ready to fight yet."

"I caught him setting fire to the barn!" Crue pointed to a man whose arms and feet were wrapped around a tree and tied. The man had a large knot on his temple and a murderous scowl. "I knocked him out with a rock and got the animals out before it blew up."

Sure enough, behind Crue, several animals milled about nervously in a large pen. He searched through the restless herd until he spotted a gray, swayback donkey plodding toward him. "Sanjo."

The donkey nosed his outstretched hand, the feel of the soft muzzle stirring up the embers of hope that had been dying out throughout the night.

"Where's Barry?"

"Some of the horses got away. He thought the soldiers might need them, so he's out looking for them."

"Crazy fool." But Mason could not stop the admiration from softening his words.

Zakkias returned from investigating the man's binding. "He's tied good and fast. He's not going anywhere."

Mason gave Crue an appraising look. "Rescued the barn animals and took down a Shadowman in one night."

"I expect we'll see you in the Steward ranks someday," Zakkias added.

Crue ducked his head. "One got away."

"Did you see what direction?"

Crue pointed in the direction of the two large buildings in the center of the fort. "I caught a glimpse of him going that way before he disappeared in the dark."

Mason scanned the ground, searching for a trail no one else would be able to spot. There—his enhanced vision caught a set of footprints, heading where Crue had said.

"Thanks, Crue. You were a huge help." He pointed at him. "But don't you go taking any more risks than you need to, got it?"

"Aye, sir."

Mason left him there and headed after the tracks, Zakkias staying behind him. The screams of the dragons made his skin tingle.

The farther he went, the more other footprints crossed the trail. Tracking a Shadowman was hard enough without the help of extra boot marks.

Not far from where he stood, a Steward fell face first, an arrow in his back. Swinging his crossbow up, Mason checked all around and dashed to check on him, but the man was already dead. And there was no sign of anyone else around. Shadowmen. Hiding in the dark, taking shots at Stewards while the shadow creatures had them distracted.

Across the street from where he crouched, the door to the mess hall swung shut. Maybe Mason wouldn't need the trail anymore. He looked back at Zakkias and pointed. The knight gave a single nod and let Mason lead.

Making sure his crossbow was loaded with darts and the Beacon was in place, Mason ran for the mess hall. It was time to bring this Shadowman to light. He stepped to the side and flung the door open, waiting for a shot. Zakkias pulled his Beacon and entered, casting its light around the long room. The stillness within beckoned Mason, and he ducked inside.

None of the lanterns burned, and distorted shadows stretched from the rows of tables, throwing a dizzying pattern on the wooden floor. Darkness edged the walls, the windows black and imposing. Every so often, the roar of Jader's shadow creatures echoed.

No one was in the dining room, so Mason led the way to the kitchen. Motioning for Zakkias to wait, he eased the swinging door open, stepped inside, and looked around. The sight of the empty working area made him wonder where Nola was keeping.

He started to leave when he heard a soft *clink*. In the far corner, Marcus riffled through the cutlery.

"Marcus?" He lowered the bow. How had he missed him?

The young man did not look at him. "Hello, Mason." After the flat greeting, he went back to his sorting, pulling a large knife out and setting it aside.

"What are you doing here?"

Marcus selected another knife and studied it. "Just cleaning up."

The odd behavior sent an eerie feeling slithering across Mason's shoulders. While chaos unleashed its fury, why would Marcus choose that moment to clean the kitchen?

"Where's Nola?"

Instead of answering, Marcus turned with the knife. "It's amazing how many weapons one can find in a kitchen, isn't it? Right under the noses of everyone."

Mason's hair stood on end. "Marcus, what are you doing?"

The shadows in the corner thickened, shrouding them both. Marcus finally looked at Mason in the eye. "I'm doing what you were supposed to do."

Every muscle clenched. Mason noticed for the first time how Marcus blended in with the shadows. He took a step back.

Impossible.

Marcus's face hardened. "It's no wonder you don't recognize me. You were too wrapped up in your own ego." He clenched the knife, another one in his belt, and advanced. The shadows seemed to follow him. "You couldn't be bothered to know who all was following you into the fort that night. So long as we helped you get your Shadowstone."

Everything fell into place then, and Mason's blood froze in his veins. Marcus was one of the Shadowmen who had infiltrated the fort with him the night of Bruin's storm. Hiding in plain sight.

"Where's Nola?"

"Out of the way."

"If you've hurt her—"

"What?" Marcus pulled on the chain around his neck. "I think you're forgetting something. You have no power over me."

He stared at Marcus. "You're the one who let Jeck out."

Amusement flickered. "Him and everyone else."

Blazes. Mason shot visual daggers at the man, angry that he had lived and worked among them for so long for the sole purpose of this. Worry for Nola and apprehension for everyone else tightened its grip on him, but he remembered the Beacon and who he was fighting for.

Tension mounted as they stared one another down. Marcus moved first, flinging his knife. Mason dodged the blade and let out a wild shot that flew past the other man's ear.

Zakkias burst in behind Mason, his Beacon already up. Marcus gave a snarl and tossed another knife. Mason stumbled back to miss it, and when he looked, Marcus was gone, escaped through the back door.

"Are you all right?" he asked.

"I'm fine," Zakkias said, already crossing the floor to look out the door. He shone his light all around, then shook his head. "I don't see him."

Mason joined him, ready to follow the Shadowman again, when something thumped on the other side of the room. They both swiveled to a tall cabinet in the corner. Stepping to the side, Zakkias reached for the handle and waited for Mason to give the signal. As soon as Mason was ready, his crossbow up and aimed, Zakkias flung the door open.

Nola stared up at him, gagged and bound.

"Nola." Mason holstered his bow and reached to help her out. Relief poured over him like rain, and he worked on the tight knot that bound her hands behind her back.

Zakkias slid the gag off her. "Nola, are you hurt?"

She spluttered in her outrage. "That fool Marcus threatened to kill me and then threw me in the cabinet!" She rubbed her wrists. "When I get my hands on that boy, I'm going to strangle him. That's what I'm gonna do. Acting like he's a clumsy oaf when he's working with the Shreil himself!"

Mason exchanged amused looks with Zakkias. "It's a wonder he didn't kill you, Nola, so just calm yourself."

"I think he was too scared of her," Zakkias said with a chortle.

She rolled her eyes and waved her hand at him. "Pshaw."

The building rumbled as another shadow creature screamed its way past. Nola shivered. "Gracious. I can only imagine what's happening out there. All I could do was sit and pray."

The reminder sobered Mason. "You need to stay here, Nola. Out of danger."

She didn't offer any argument, but she grabbed a pan and a wooden mallet as she headed for the large pantry at one end. "You two be careful out there now, you hear?" She paused before closing herself up. "Lambient be with you."

Zakkias gave a soft chuckle and moved to a window to peer out. "If only she could share that attitude with the men." A blood-chilling shriek echoed in the night. He sobered with a shudder and looked back at Mason. "A lot of us won't last the night."

Mason could not bring himself to cushion the very real possibility of death. Not to this young soldier who had already experienced the loss of a beloved company. They were at war, and Jader was not going to lose without taking as many men down with him as he could. "Maybe, maybe not," he said. "Either way, we do what the Lambient has already done once."

"And that is?"

"We lay our lives down to defeat Shreil." Steel hardened his voice as he drew his sword out, the metal hissing against the sheath. "And we take Jader down with us."

55

The Lambient, my Lord, will enlighten my darkness.
-The Sacred Code

"Watch out for Jader." Mason's warning played over in Eric's mind as he strode through the streets. *"He can appear where he wills."*

The very idea was hard to believe and left his skin crawling as he kept his eyes moving, watching for him. If that was true, the threat Jader presented had just multiplied.

The path before him darkened as a shadow creature passed over him, heading for the back wall. He tightened his grip on Lavrynth and followed it. Up ahead, he could hear the mayhem the creature caused. Men shouted, beams of light flashed, and unearthly roars shook the ground.

Running now, Eric reached the wall, where pure madness had taken over. Militiamen clashed with the Stewards; a few men from both sides lay on the ground. On the wall, a few knights remained, looking and pointing out into the distance. And in the sky, the shadow creature swirled and writhed in the air, overseeing it all. Braylee was in the middle of the fray, trying to hold back a Reservist. Lights flashed as the Stewards used their rods to hinder the militia.

Eric started to reach for his Beacon before remembering he had given it to Mason. Instead, he thrust his hand out, yanking the swords from the hands of the militiamen, an easy enough feat with only twenty or so men. The Stewards quickly overpowered them. "Bind them!" Braylee ordered.

"Mason is undoing the control as fast as he can," Eric assured them.

A look of exasperation crossed Braylee's face. "Where's your Beacon?"

Eric gave him a sheepish grimace. "Someone needed it more than I did."

A bellow sounded, piercing their eardrums. Eric spun as the dragon dove from the sky. "Watch out!"

The creature cut right through the middle of them, knocking men down on both sides. Then it turned and charged again. Eric and Braylee jumped out of its path, rolling back upright to confront it.

The dragon reared up before them, its empty eyes narrowed in on them. Black flames emitted from its gaping mouth, and it stretched wide wings out, beating hot air back at them.

Other shadow creatures gathered behind it, their sights set on the two men before them.

"I think we made it angry," Braylee said, spreading his feet apart.

"Maybe a little."

The dragon in front lashed out, its teeth snapping. Eric retreated, and Braylee threw a beam from his Beacon. The Stewards behind him regrouped and added to the glow. The creatures hissed and dodged the light, but it did not hold them back for long.

Fear tried to take hold, but Eric pushed it back. That's what fed these monsters. He needed to be stronger.

"By His strength..."

Lavrynth's hilt warmed in his grip. The silver blade turned white, its pure light seeping into Eric's core. His blood surged through his veins, connecting with the blood of his ancestors and the Lambient's power woven through the sword.

Of course. How could he have not thought of it before?

Eric raised his head, staring the shadow creature straight into its black soul. "You have no power here." He took a step forward, energy thrumming through him. "Be gone!" He shot his arm up, the tip of the sword pointing at the monster's chest. White light burst from the blade like lightning, striking the shadow creature. A monstrous scream split the air.

Splinters of light broke from the sword's streaming light and pierced the other dragons. They all writhed and shrieked as the light drove its way into their cores.

Eric gritted his teeth and struggled to hold the sword steady with both hands as power flowed through it. He couldn't hold it for much longer, his earthly body not strong enough to withstand that kind of power. His lungs seized, and his muscles shook.

Then Braylee stepped to his side, adding his Beacon to the flow of power. One by one, more Stewards joined, until it was nothing but a massive, roiling blaze of light, consuming the shadow creatures. There was a loud *POP*, and then they were gone. All that remained was black smoke, drifting lazily back to the sky.

Eric's arm dropped, and he slumped to the ground. All around him, Stewards laughed and cheered.

Braylee clapped Eric's back. "Are you all right?"

Waving a limp hand, Eric said, "Fine. Just give me a moment."

"Good. Because we're not done yet."

Eric looked up. Fire burned in various locations throughout the fort. On the far side, the Dark Army still raged. And somewhere out there, Jader still roamed.

A familiar gray horse rode in, and Lionel dismounted before them. "What happened?" he gestured up at the sky. "That was…I don't know what that was!"

"That was Lavrynth sending those shadow creatures back where they belong," Braylee said.

Eric rose to his feet with a groan, arms shivering from the exertion. "Lavrynth and a couple dozen Beacons."

"Hopefully, that's the last we'll see of them tonight," Lionel said. "Those things were wicked."

"If they do come back, we'll know how to beat them again."

"Your confidence never ceases to amaze me, Braylee."

The big man shrugged. "I've seen too much to have doubts now."

It was a lighthearted comment, but it stuck. "You're right, my friend." He looked around. "We need to get some of these men to the infirmary." He called for the cadets to help with the transport.

Braylee turned to Lionel. "You stay here, Lieutenant. I'll come back and check in with you shortly."

A look of uncertainty flickered, then a short nod. "Aye, sir." He climbed the steps to assume his role.

"Where are you going?" Eric asked, already knowing the answer.

Braylee did not even bother to look at him as he assisted a man to his feet. "Someone's got to keep an eye on the prince who can't even hang on to his own Beacon."

"Aren't you the one who said the light within is greater?"

"More or less. But it's a lot easier to walk in the dark with the other one."

Eric let out a laugh. "Can't argue with that kind of logic."

Seria fought against the exhaustion and discomfort weighing her limbs down. The essence that rose from the pit surrounded her, making it hard to breathe. But she pushed through the dark thoughts that crowded her mind and pondered her next step.

Getting out of the chains.

For a long time, there was no chance to work on getting loose. She attracted too much interest, and many of the soldiers stared at the girl they blamed for Mason's treachery. Others drew near to leer at her, turning her stomach with their hungry gazes. But Balt made it clear she was to be unscathed until Jader had a chance to see her for himself. Eventually, they lost interest in the girl chained to the ceiling.

Snippets of conversation drifted to her. Talk of the Dark Army breaking through the first wall of the Gateway Stronghold. Of Shadowmen on the inside. Of strange creatures made by Jader's hand running wild.

It all tried to poke holes in the wall of confidence she had built in the Lambient and his Stewards, as well as her own self-assigned mission. Would all of this be for naught? Would Jader emerge on the other side of this war victorious?

She slammed the doubts down. As she told Mason days ago, Lambient would always be victorious over Shreil's dark power, no matter how bleak it may look now.

Checking to see that guards and Darkmen were occupied, she wriggled her right wrist and curled her fingers in to reach the pin tucked into the edge of her sleeve. Pulling it out with her fingertips, she worked it into position and slipped it into the lock. It was difficult to do with one hand, but her father had trained her well, all under the guise of fun and games. She thanked him now for his wisdom.

The pin shifted, and the tiny click seemed to boom in Seria's ears. She stifled a cry of relief and worked the cuff loose. Her chest lightened, and she bit back the urge to laugh. It was too soon to slip out completely, so she had to bide her time until the cave had emptied.

At Dreeya's approach, Seria curled her fingers around the pin and the shackle, keeping it closed.

The Shadowwoman appraised her with a hard look. "So, you've got it into your silly little head that Mason has changed for you?"

Seria blinked at the unexpected statement. "Nay. I don't believe that."

Dreeya scoffed as she circled her. "I don't know what he sees in you. I've never seen a more pathetic sight. You're nothing."

She's trying to rile you. Seria waited until Dreeya came around to the front. "I've never claimed to be much. But I know I'm not nothing."

Crossing her arms, Dreeya smirked. "Let me guess. Your *Lambient* loves you just the way you are."

"That's right. And even more, He loves you."

"Don't go there, missy. I don't want to hear it."

"Why not? It's true." Seria tried to see past the harsh exterior to a woman who may have been hurt in the past. "He does love you. And He's ready to accept you, just like He did Mason."

Dreeya stepped closer, her eyes snapping. "Let me get one thing straight with you. I don't need His forgiveness. I've chosen my master. He's done more for me than your Lambient ever has." Bitterness laced her words.

Arching her aching back, Seria pushed on. "Is that why you wear that rock?"

"This rock gives me power."

"Except the power to be free."

A sneer twisted Dreeya's features. "I am free. Free to live outside of the bonds of your Sacred Code."

Seria lifted her chin. "And yet you are bound to Jader."

There was a slight pause before Dreeya let out a harsh laugh. "That's funny. You speak of freedom and bondage while you're chained to a cave."

"My body may be bound, but my spirit is free."

"Pretty words for a girl devoted to a man who doesn't love you."

Seria pressed her lips together.

"You know that, don't you?" the vicious woman asked. "He's using you to get what he wants. Mason Grey has never allowed himself to fall for a girl, and he certainly wouldn't start with the likes of you."

A small trace of sympathy reared its head. "I see." She cocked her head. "He must have hurt you too."

A vein popped out on Dreeya's neck, and she seemed to physically force herself to stay calm. "Mason is a traitor." Then she sneered. "But Jader's not done with him yet."

Seria raised her chin but stayed silent. Dreeya was a Shadowwoman. She would say anything to break Seria down.

Dreeya's look of triumph threatened to cut through Seria's resolve. "He's back where he belongs, working at Jader's side. I told you; he was just using you. Nothing can change his loyalty."

Stay calm. The command did not stop the spike in her pulse rate.

"Not so smug now, are you?" Dreeya reached for Seria's freed hand and pried the pin out of her fist. Then she clicked the cuff shut again and walked away, leaving Seria alone in the dark.

56

Zakkias pointed out a possible trail leading to the back wall, where
Mason suspected more rogue Reservists were hiding. When they arrived
at the courtyard, Mason spotted a squad of subdued militiamen in a
corner, their hands bound, guarded by a Steward. Mason studied them,
getting a feel for the state of their will. "They may come around on their
own soon."

"Where did you come from?" Lionel enquired from the top of the
steps, his face stormy.

"You don't want to know."

Lionel's eyes narrowed. "Do I want you here now?"

"He's with us, Lt. Lionel," Zakkias spoke up.

Mason held his suspicious gaze. "If not, then maybe you'll get that
chance to kill me after all."

Lionel relaxed. "I can only hope."

"Sir, they're bringing a battering ram!" Sgt. Gann called out from
above.

They all ran up the steps and looked out. Sure enough, a swarm of
Darkmen ran for the gates, shields hoisted up above their heads. At the
front of the crowd, a wooden beam poked out, topped with a thick metal
cap with a vicious-looking point.

"Oh, that's not good," Zakkias breathed.

"Secure the gates!" Lionel hollered down to the soldiers below, then to the men on top, "Fire the trebuchet!"

The engine launched its deadly projectiles. Down below, men grabbed posts and braced them against the gates to hold them.

"Here it comes!" Gann shouted.

The massive beam slammed into the gates, sending vibrations through the walls that shook Mason's bones. The men regained their hold and blocked the gates again.

"Don't you have cannons on this side?" Mason asked.

Lionel gave him a wide-eyed look. "They didn't exactly expect an attack by their own people when they built this wall."

"At least the shadow creatures are gone," Gann said.

Mason swept the skies. "What about that?"

"Prince Eric destroyed them with that sword of his."

"Well, it's about time we had some good news tonight." His comment was punctuated with another blow to the gates.

"We could use some more," Lionel muttered and then shouted more orders. The creaking sound of the trebuchet mixed with yelling and the whizzing of arrows.

"Can you control the Darkmen?" Zakkias asked. When the older men all looked at him, he shrugged. "It worked for the Reservists."

"Aye, why don't you work some of that power against them?" Lionel jabbed a thumb at the militants.

Mason looked out at the mass. He wasn't sure how far his voice would carry, but even if he could stop a few at a time, it would slow them down.

He climbed a stone block so he could look out further and cupped his hands around his mouth. "Stand down and surrender!"

No one swayed from their objection. Not even one. He tried again, louder. Still nothing.

"Well, that's that, I suppose," Lionel said.

Steward archers fired nonstop, hindered by the shields. And the battering ram hit again.

Darkness begets Submission.

The words exploded through Mason's head, sparking a sharp pain that ran from temple to temple. He let out a cry and grabbed his head.

"Mason!" Zakkias cried, catching him by the arm to steady him.

"What's happening?" Lionel's voice was sharp.

Mason dropped one hand to the reassurance of Eric's light rod and sent a silent plea up. *Get him out of my head!* He gritted his teeth, grabbing Zakkias's shoulder to keep from falling to his knees. "Jader's trying to get inside my head again."

"Well, tell him to shut up," Lionel barked. "We're busy."

The suggestion was so absurd that Mason let out a shaky laugh. "Aye, I'll just do that."

Strangely enough, the grasp for his mind receded, leaving in its place voices. Too many voices, all swirling around like leaves in a whirl-wind. He caught snatches of Eric talking and a whisper of Jader. Alarm slammed through him. "Where's Eric?" he asked.

"He and Captain Braylee left shortly after the shadow creatures were destroyed," Gann said.

"I have to go."

"Are you sure?" Lionel asked. "You look like you've just encountered one of those monsters on your own."

He heaved a breath. "I'm fine." It wasn't a lie, exactly. Physically, he was fine. The headache was gone, but the sense that Jader was close would not leave him. "I need to find Eric."

"You're not going to do something stupid, are you?"

"I don't plan to."

"Good." Lionel slapped Mason's shoulder.

There was nothing more to say, so he headed for the steps. Zakkias moved to follow, but Mason stopped him.

"Nay, Zakkias. You stay here."

"But—"

"If that army breaks in, Lionel is going to need good men to depend on. Besides, you can't do for me what the Lambient can." He would not risk Zakkias's life if he met up with Jader or, worse, lost control again.

The younger man must have seen that Mason was determined to have his way this time. "Be careful, sir."

"You, too."

The Steward moved back to join Lionel and Gann at the wall, and

Mason moved on. His insides quaked at the idea of seeing Jader again, and fear that he would fall prey to his power once more became a noose around his neck, strangling him. He wasn't strong enough to fight it. But where he was weak, Lambient would be strength for him. And for now, that was all he could count on.

Eric stepped out of the infirmary and glanced over in time to see Braylee flex his recovering shoulder. "Are you wishing you had stayed home?" he asked.

Braylee gave him a direct look. "I have no regrets."

They left the wounded in Luron's capable care and headed back to the front, always on the lookout for Shadowmen.

"As much as I would rather know you were home safe, I'm glad you're here. I feel better when you're at my side."

"You would've made out all right," Braylee said. "But my first duty is to Lambient, so I'm where I'm supposed to be."

The buildings around them cast deep shadows, prime hideouts for those who could blend with them. It was quiet here in the civilian corner, though in the distance, the sounds of battle interrupted the stillness. Fires dotted the view, creating an orange tint wherever he looked.

Ever since Eric had disintegrated the shadow creatures, the sense of danger grew, making his skin crawl. It rose with every step until he came to a stop, his nerves buzzing.

"What is it?" Braylee asked, his voice low.

"We're not alone."

WHIZZ!

Eric threw his hand up, diverting a dart before it hit him in the chest. Braylee raised his Beacon, exposing three dark figures rushing at them. Sensing another approach from behind, Eric pivoted and raised Lavrynth to block another man's sword.

There was no time to brace for the attack. The light of Braylee's Beacon revealed at least five Shadowmen surrounding them.

Braylee struck first, grunting as his blade met his opponent's. Eric faced off with two of them, Lavrynth glinting as it struck again and again. Every chance he got, he yanked at their weapons, but he couldn't hold them off and fight too. There were too many, but he and Braylee persisted, back-to-back.

One man fell to the ground, holding his hand over the gaping wound in his gut. Another caught Braylee's blade across the neck and crumpled in a lifeless heap. But they made their marks too. A searing pain shot through Eric's leg when a sword tip caught him above the knee. Blood trickled from a cut on Braylee's temple.

Eric swung around to block another blow, but his wounded leg buckled, and he dropped to one knee. Braylee stood over him and deflected the blades. Two Shadowmen teamed up and overpowered him, knocking his sword from his hands. Eric gathered himself to jump up, but an arrow appeared in the center of one of the Shadowmen's chest.

"Got him!" Dakim's triumphant shout could be heard on the other side of the street. Several young voices cheered him on.

Without warning, a swirl of black fog formed around Eric, and a chill snaked down his back as he forced himself to his feet.

"Eric." Braylee's warning drifted through the haze.

"I feel it," Eric answered. Just *what* he felt, he couldn't tell. Was this Jader's darkness falling?

Everything seemed to slow down, like a bad dream Eric couldn't escape from. The Shadowmen still hovered nearby, barely seen in the haze, but they did not attack. Their stillness unnerved him. What were they waiting on?

Then he heard Jader speak, soft and aloof. "Kill the others."

Before Eric could decide if the order had been spoken out loud or in his head, the Shadowmen disappeared into blackness as they went after the cadets.

That snapped Eric out of his stupor. "I guess I shouldn't be surprised you're still in the business of killing boys."

"I told your father years ago that his faith in his light was sorely misplaced." Jader's voice seemed to come from everywhere, echoing in his head and whispering in his ears. "Now he is dead, and your kingdom is crumbling around you."

"You won't win," Eric ground out.

"I already have."

The darkness grew thicker, and Eric's lungs seized as it swirled around him, a funnel of fear and evil. A cold presence at his back ramped his defenses up. But even as he turned, catching a glimpse of Jader's pale eye flashing in the darkness, he knew he was too slow to evade the black spear coming at him. His body flinched in anticipation of the deadly strike, already regretting that he would not see the end of the war.

Suddenly, Braylee was there, shoving his way between Eric and the wicked blade.

"Braylee, no!"

But it was too late. Jader's spear plunged through his dear friend's chest.

For a moment, everyone froze. Eric stared at Braylee, paralyzed by the horror of what he was seeing.

A savage grin lit Jader's face as he yanked the spear out.

Braylee stumbled against Eric, who wrapped his arms around him. "Nay! Braylee!"

This wasn't happening. It couldn't happen. Not to Braylee.

Braylee's weight pulled them both to the ground, and Eric dropped to his knees, still holding him. Panic was a monster screaming inside Eric's head, blocking out anything around him. "Lambient, help us," he panted.

But the life continued to drain from Braylee's strong body, and Eric was helpless to stop it. "Braylee, hold on," he whispered, as if that would prevent the inevitable.

There was no regret in Braylee's fading eyes, though his voice was silent. He reached up and touched Eric's face, then went limp. The Beacon he clutched in his other hand flickered, then went dark before rolling to the ground beside him. A blade pierced through Eric's soul, shattering it and leaving him empty, numb.

"Nay!" Eric bowed his head over his friend, a crushing weight of grief breaking him. Not Braylee. Not after all they had been through together.

Awareness of Jader's presence prickled, and he looked through a wall of tears to where Jader stood, looking amused, the bloodstained spear in his hand. Rage coated Eric's sharp grief, white-hot and justified. He snatched Braylee's Beacon and his sword and rose to his feet, overcome with the flame of retribution.

He shot a blast from the Beacon, which Jader deflected. But Eric stalked the emperor, Lavrynth hot in his other hand, and brought both the blade and the rod down on Jader's spear. Jader spun the pole and jabbed the point at Eric's torso. Eric jumped back and then attacked again.

Everything else faded until all Eric could see was Jader. His limbs moved of their own accord, his mind zeroed in on the single purpose of taking Jader down. The emperor moved with more speed and grace than one his age should be able to, but Eric's fury gave him strength, pushing Jader back. But before he could take advantage of his retreat, Bruin made a sudden appearance, his long sword cutting between Lavrynth and its victim. His gray eyes sparked as he forced Eric away.

A tendril of black smoke shot out from Jader's spear and wrapped around Lavrynth, jerking it from Eric's grasp.

Eric stepped back and swept his Beacon up to knock Bruin's blade to the side, but Bruin countered with a solid punch. Knocked off balance, Eric stumbled to the side and searched through the shadows for his sword. The cold tip of Jader's spear bit into his ribs, and he sucked in a breath. Bruin stood close on his other side, blocking his escape. Shadows crept along the ground, encircling Eric in a cold grip.

Jader's good eye glittered. "So falls the last of the house of Passion."

"No!"

The shout cut through the haze, and through the darkness surrounding them, Mason burst, brandishing his sword, his face a storm of fury.

57

For ye were once a servant of the darkness, but now are ye as a flaming light of the Lambient. Walk as children of the light.
-The Sacred Code

Mason swung his weapon full force at Jader, who quickly spun out of reach, but Mason did not let up, adrenaline spiking through his body, buzzing through his skin, as he jabbed, blocked, and pushed, forcing Jader into a retreat. For the first time that Mason could remember, anger showed itself on Jader's face.

Before Bruin could intervene, Eric pulled Lavrynth back to him and directed his offense at the commander.

The brief glimpse he had gotten of Braylee lying on the ground slashed at Mason, driving him on. To let up for even an instant would give Jader an advantage.

The black spear spun, the blunt end grazing Mason across the temple. He stumbled back and shook the stars from his eyes, but Jader had already put space between them, his eye almost black with rage. "Your stubbornness is getting tiresome."

Mason spread his feet out. "You will not kill him."

"I do not have to." Jader's tone sharpened. "You will kill him for me."

"I won't," Mason growled. He dropped his hand to rest on the Beacon at his belt.

Jader walked forward, his stride confident. "You belong to me."

Mason could feel the tug on his will, but he resisted. "I belong to the Lambient."

"You are a Shadowman," Jader sneered. "A child of darkness."

Shadowy fingers stretched from the fog and reached for Mason, chilling the steel that ran up his backbone. He lifted the light rod, gripping it with white knuckles.

Darkness begets submission.

The Beacon began to warm, stirring up the same doubts he had wrestled with ever since the very first time it lit in his hand.

"Let it burn every doubt from your mind and burn into your very soul until you are on fire with His light."

He clenched his jaw, wrapping his fingers tighter around the rod. He would not let it go again, even if it killed him. It glowed a brilliant white, shooting warmth up his arm and through his chest and the rest of his limbs. Truth pulsed through him, breaking through the dry soil of his spirit and uprooting the lies he had believed for too long.

Forgiven. Accepted. Loved. The words reverberated within him like a drum, driving out the last of the whispers that desperately tried to get his attention. His mind was clear.

"Not anymore," he said, his voice laced with iron. "I am a child of the light, Jader. I'm a Steward." With that, he shot his hand up, and light blasted from the Beacon, straight at Jader.

A great puff of smoke mushroomed from the spot where Jader had stood, but the emperor was gone, vanished before the Beacon could strike him.

Mason spun to where Eric and Bruin fought, but before he could assist, a black cloud surrounded Bruin, taking him from harm.

The coward.

Mason dropped his arm, stunned at what he had just done. Weariness made him feel heavy and clumsy as he spun a slow circle, checking through the darkness all around them to make sure Jader was not hiding. But when the black haze lifted, they were alone.

His attention fell on Eric, who now cradled a very pale and still Braylee against him. A band tightened around Mason's chest, cold and sharp. He made his way slowly to them, his heart trying to deny what his mind told him. Braylee was gone.

As Mason lowered himself to a knee, he gazed down at the man who had saved him from captivity, challenged his pride on the dueling fields, and then pulled him out of Jader's control at Daymont. But for Eric, he was a friend. A confidante. A brother.

He could not help but question Lambient. Why did good men have to die for evil men? Braylee. Ollen. Liam. It wasn't fair. Mason had wasted his life, with nothing to show for the years he spent serving Jader. Braylee had devoted his life to the right. He had the respect of countless people for his good character. He had a family waiting at home for him.

If Mason had gotten there sooner, maybe he could have prevented it. But he was too late. Again. Sorrow drew his head down. "I'm sorry." It was all he could manage.

The prince raised his head, his face wet with tears. "It should've been me," he croaked. "It was meant for me."

Braylee made his choice. The statement blazed its way into Mason's mind. *So that others can do the same.*

He drew in a sharp breath as it sank into his consciousness and forced himself to speak. "He knew that. That's why he did it."

Eric shook his head, his Adam's apple bobbing. "Everyone...I can't..." He closed his eyes and shuddered.

Mason could sense the crushing weight of grief and responsibility that dug their talons into the prince. "Eric..." He hesitated, not sure what to say. What words of comfort did he have to offer someone who had put his faith in the Lambient for most of his life? There was nothing he could say to ease the grief, he knew that as well as anyone.

But Eric had been there for him earlier that very night. It was Mason's turn to do the same. So, when Eric looked at him, he reached out and took his shoulder. "I know I can't fill his shoes, and I wouldn't even try." His voice broke, and he cleared his throat. "But will you let me help you finish what you both started?"

There was nothing encouraging or even comforting in the request, but Eric stared at him, as if gripped by the request. After a moment, he blinked and drew in a ragged breath. Some of the acute grief faded, though pain still lingered in his eyes. He looked down at the man in his arms, and another tremor went through him as he laid Braylee back on the ground.

"I don't know if I'm strong enough," he admitted.

"You don't have to be. Let Him be strong for you." Hearing Seria's words spoken out loud by his own tongue sent a pain through him. How she—who deeply loved her friends—would grieve for Braylee. So many people would.

Eric gulped and ran a hand over his face, taking a moment to gather himself.

A distant crash made them both look up. Jader was not done yet. The war still went on around them.

A muscle popped in Eric's jaw, and his spine straightened. "This ends tonight."

"Let's do it then."

Looking down at Braylee once more, Eric adjusted the limp arms across the still chest and reached for the Beacon. "I need to borrow this for a while, my friend," he whispered. "Thank you, Braylee. For your service. And your friendship."

Mason rose with him, his own emotions whirling within him. Rage ignited by justice heated his blood. It was not a blind vengeance he sought now. This was a cause that men died for, the best of the best. And if Mason was about to die fighting for it, then he would lose his life willingly.

Jader and Bruin stepped out of the black fog into the warm comfort of the Shadowpit. Ignoring his commander, Jader stepped to the edge of the chasm and stared into it, letting it soothe the hot edges of wrath that sliced through his calm. Anger was dangerous, impulsive. He would not allow it to lead him now, not when all he desired was right at his fingertips.

The purple veins in the hole sparkled back at him, reminding him of the power lent to him by the one who created it. Shreil had graced him many years ago when he discovered the Shadowpit as a young militia-man, desperate to prove himself, and found a way to utilize its power.

He would not fail Jader now.

Turning from the familiarity of the pit, Jader caught sight of a blonde girl chained to the rock wall, gawking at him with wide, terror-stricken eyes. Jader's lips tightened. "Balt."

The Shadowman in charge of the security of the cave hurried to his side. "Aye, sir."

"What is this?"

"We caught her roaming around here."

Outrage colored his vision. "How is that possible?" The entrance to the cave was sealed by a force Jader had put in place himself. No one could find it on their own.

"N-nay, I meant we found her outside. So, we brought her in here for you."

"You brought an outsider in *here*?"

Balt's stammering tried what was left of Jader's patience until Dreeya spoke up. "This is Seria Gayle."

Jader regarded the girl again. "Is that so?" He approached her, enjoying the way she recoiled, and then straightened as if to resist him.

"So, you are the girl who turned our boy's head." When she stared back at him silently, he reached out to stroke her jaw. She jerked her head away. He smiled. "I can see why he thinks himself infatuated. You are quite spirited, I hear."

Where once rage had simmered at Mason's defection, now amusement flowed. This was an interesting and satisfying twist.

"Your timing is impeccable, I must say." He rubbed the long scar on his face. "Your Mason has grown quite stubborn. Your presence will assure his cooperation."

Her eyes widened, then she frowned and clamped her mouth shut.

"You do not believe me?" He chuckled. "You have made him weak." He moved closer, taking in her flushed complexion, the brightness of her eyes, the faint freckles across her cheeks. "Much like those pathetic Stewards. At this moment, your so-called strong prince is weeping over his beloved captain's dead body."

His words hit their mark, and she paled. "That's not true."

"I assure you, it is. I saw to it myself."

Her breathing accelerated, and she blinked rapidly. Her reaction gratified him.

"The prince is nothing without his Stewards. Without his captains to lean on, he cannot stand on his own. He is helpless and weak."

"You're the one who's weak," she spat, fire shooting from those green eyes. "He's stronger than you'll ever be."

"You have much to learn, my dear."

"I'm not your dear." Her cheeks reddened again, and she pulled against her chains. "And you're going to learn what the Stewards can do by Lambient's hand."

He took a step closer, silencing her. "Your disposition is admirable, Seria Gayle, but misplaced. The Stewards are already defeated. And now that you are here, your Mason will ensure my victory."

Her pert chin raised high. "He won't help you."

A low chuckle escaped him. The girl was feisty, if ignorant. "You overestimate his loyalty. He will do anything to protect the girl he claims to love."

"His devotion to the Lambient is greater than anything he feels for me. He will never bow to you."

Growing tired of her nonstop chatter, Jader turned away. "We shall see." He met Bruin's amused gaze. "This night is still ours."

58

*The ability to move things without touch can be used with great power but
is also very taxing on both mind and body.*
-The Record of Gifts

Eric dragged chains of exhaustion behind him as he limped the streets of
the fortress, aiming for the front wall. The cut on his leg throbbed, and
his side bled where Jader's spear had caught it. But through all that, his
mind seemed disconnected from his body, watching from afar as he tried
to pull himself from the depths of grief to the present task.

How was he supposed to take the burden of leading his army to
victory when he had no father to encourage him? No king to serve? The
captains he had relied on for months were gone, leaving him on his own.
In the face of the evil surrounding him and the loss encompassing him,
he felt so small and weak.

But not alone.

A pulse of light flickered in the numb stone where his heart should be.
Texts from the Sacred Code filtered through his memory.

I am in the midst.

Where darkness dwells, My light shall shine.

I never leave My children.

The Lambient's light will shine on.

He could not go on by his strength alone. He was too shattered, his
heart torn and bleeding. He had no hope for himself, but he found a
semblance of peace knowing he had the Lambient with him.

And beside him, Mason strode with long, purposeful steps, determination hardening his jaw. The former Shadowman, a Reader who had once been Jader's tool and Eric's enemy, now a Steward fighting against the same shadow Eric resisted.

Throughout the fort, his other Stewards fought with him. Lionel. Captain Jervis. Those overeager cadets he fervently hoped were still alive.

Nay. Eric was not alone.

The reassurance shot a tiny root into the cold, rocky soil of his grief, and a bud of hope emerged. It was not much, but it was enough to keep him moving. The inner wall loomed before them, shaking in the onslaught of the attack without. It would not hold for long, and then the Dark Army would come in.

He painstakingly mounted the steps to scope out the damage to the wall. As soon as he and Mason reached the top, another cannon blast hit it. Eric grabbed the short wall to keep from tumbling off the side and peered out. What used to be the outer bailey was filled with soldiers in black, carrying torches and ladders. The first several rows shot out a never-ending rotation of arrows. The Stewards responded with their own volleys, firing straight into the mass. Every few minutes, their cannon would fire with a deafening *boom*. It always hit its mark, but with so many enemy soldiers out there, they just walked over the dead and kept coming.

"There's at least a thousand Darkmen out there."

"With several hundred Shadowmen," Mason added.

Eric stiffened. "Hundreds?"

"From what I can tell, aye. Waiting on the edge of darkness."

His blood chilled at the thought of that many agents of darkness running loose within the walls.

Captain Jervis emerged from the thick dust, his dark face streaked with sweat and dirt. "We're holding them off, but their trebuchets are causing problems."

A tall launch engine stood in the middle of the masses, its long arm ready to deal another blow. Men labored to load massive chunks of stone into the sling. Further out, a dim shape rose, rattling closer on a large cart pulled by two large oxen, slow but powerful. The massive weapons did not cause as much damage as cannons, but they did enough.

"Another one." Jervis groaned and smacked the wall. "Our cannon already took one out. I don't know how much more our wall can take. They're using our rubble against us."

The first trebuchet snapped up, flinging a chunk of rock straight for the wall. Eric shot his hands out and steadied himself. Summoning his Gift, he let it build in his arms, flow to his fingertips. The weight and speed of the projectile tore into his strength, and for a brief moment, he doubted he could hold it. But then it slowed and held in midair. With a deep grunt, he pushed against it, sending it crashing back into the weapon and crushing it.

"Got it!" Mason exclaimed, catching him by the arm as he rocked back on his heels.

"But I couldn't do it again," Eric panted. The effort had taken a lot out of him mentally and physically.

"Then we'll work on that last one," Jervis said.

"What about the Reservists?" Eric asked Mason. They still stood at the side of the courtyard, out of range of the Dark Army's attacks, but still immobile.

"They're not themselves yet," Mason said. "I could control them to fight…"

It was tempting, but Eric shook his head. It wouldn't be fair to send men to their deaths without any say in the matter.

Mason's relief was evident. "It shouldn't be long before they have their full faculties back."

"Any chance you could control *that* army?" Eric pointed to the Darkmen.

"I already tried," Mason said with a scowl. "Something is blocking me."

"Or some*one*."

"Brace yourselves," Jervis called out.

The second trebuchet launched another shot, but it fell short of the gates.

"It won't be long before it gets into range," Jervis said.

Eric looked out at the ranks of Stewards on the ground level, waiting. Their weariness was evident in their stooped postures. The night had been long already, and the army had not even broken through yet. Despair was beginning to make itself known.

He left Jervis where he was and descended the stone steps. His men watched as he took position in front of them. The yelling on the other side of the wall was punctuated by Jervis's calls to his men on the top.

"It's been a long night," Eric called out. "You've fought well, but we're not done yet. We've lost men. Good men." He had to stop for a heartbeat to gather himself. "We owe it to them to keep going. They didn't lay their lives down so we could lose heart now."

Men straightened, raising their heads as new strength poured through them. Jervis shouted out a warning just before the wall was struck by another blast. Everyone flinched, then regathered themselves, steel entering their faces.

"But above all, we fight for the Lambient." Eric raised his voice. "His Code, His way, His light!" With that, he lifted Braylee's Beacon high, followed by the rest of the men. "We will not surrender to Jader!"

A cheer sounded from the throng.

"We will not back down before Shreil!"

Another rousing response.

"And we will not succumb to the darkness!"

The roar was deafening, rising to fill every corner of the battered fort.

Eric held Lavrynth before him, strength and boldness filling him. "Let's fight!"

Seria struggled to silence the beast of terror that roared in her ears. She'd been unable to take a full breath since Jader had appeared before her eyes. The cuffs rubbed against her tender skin, reminding her that she was still a prisoner.

Denial and grief raced to take the lead over her emotions. It couldn't be true. Braylee couldn't be dead. Not the captain who always stood so sure and strong by the prince's side. But a sinking feeling that Jader had not made it up ripped her denial to pieces.

Poor Eric. The loss of his closest friend would devastate him, cut through him like a gaping wound. But regardless of what Jader believed, it would not destroy him.

Seria pushed past the terror and grabbed hold of the same faith that had sustained Eric for most of his life. The same faith she prayed would keep Mason if Jader used her capture to tempt him.

The emperor was still there, staring into the abyss like a hungry man. It unnerved her, the way he soaked in the darkness. Finally, he raised his head and looked to Bruin. "Commander, it is time."

Bruin retreated into the shadows, out of Seria's vision.

Jader addressed the crowd. "Ladies and gentlemen, if you will." He raised his hands in invitation.

Seria watched with bated breath as dozens of men and women lined up before him. Several Shadowmen waited at Jader's sides, holding small wooden boxes.

"This ceremony would look much different if we were not forced to defend our rights," Jader said. "If we were not at war. Nonetheless, the essence is the same. You will pledge your oath and receive the ultimate weapon known to man. Then you will go out to fight in the greatest war that will ever be in our history."

Horror seized her as she realized what was happening. *Oh, Lambient, it can't be.* She scanned the silent crowd in dark clothing and mail. There had to be at least two hundred standing there, waiting.

Chills raced over her skin.

Jader was raising another army of Shadow Soldiers.

59

Have no fellowship with the vain works of darkness, but rather oppose them.
-The Sacred Code

A cannonball struck the inner wall of the Gateway Stronghold, sending the gates flying open with a shower of splintered wood and chunks of stone. Mason threw his arm up to shield himself from the shrapnel.

"Arms at the ready!" Eric shouted, even as he forced the gates to swing back with his Gift. It would not hold the enemy back for long.

The two of them stood with the knights, waiting. Behind him, Mason could feel the determination that cloaked the Stewards. But suddenly, the weather turned. Bitter cold bit through Mason's skin and froze his breath. His fingers tingled gripping the cold metal.

He looked to Eric, and together they said what was on their minds. "Bruin."

The gates were shoved open by the mass of adversaries. This was it. There was no stopping the stampede of Darkmen and Shadowmen flooding through the demolished gates. All of them wore gloves and heavy cloaks, ready to fight in the freezing temperatures that would hinder Eric's army.

His toes already stinging, Mason bounced on the balls of his feet, then sprung forward, straight into the throng.

At first, he and Eric fought side by side, their swords swinging almost in unison. The bedlam was deafening, the echo of steel crashing against steel soon swallowed up in battle cries and agonizing screams. All around Mason was a blur of Steward red and Darkmen black. Hundreds of men struggled to stay alive as the two armies converged.

Mason ducked, spun, dodged, jumped, and blocked. His hand melded to the metal hilt, and his legs moved of their own accord. The exertion heated his body from the inside, coating his back with sweat, raising chills on his skin. For every Darkman that fell, another took his place. They filled the courtyard, streaming through the fort like a river. Fires erupted on all sides as the Darkmen carried out their intention to destroy the stronghold and everything in it.

Mason lost track of Eric in the mayhem. His mind cast to Crue and the blacksmith at the livery. To Nola in her hiding place in the kitchen. Braylee's wife and daughters in Calla. Lena at the castle. And Seria. All were counting on them to protect them, to drive the Dark Army out of Paladin.

He gritted his teeth and cracked his Beacon across the face of a Darkman, then swiveled to miss the dagger of another. Everywhere he looked, there were bodies. Friend and foe. The throng pressed in, pushing the Stewards back. Flaming fireballs and heavy rubble flew on every side, forcing Mason to duck and dive. Bitterness sat in his stomach. The Darkmen were using the very Gifts Lambient had created to bring His army down.

An explosion rent the air, tossing him like a discarded rag. He landed hard on his back and, with a groan, rolled to his hands and knees. Scanning his surroundings, he found himself in a dark corner, tucked away from the fighting. The small, scared boy in him wanted to hide there, but the soldier wouldn't let him. He pushed himself upright and took stock of the situation.

The prince was across the bailey, surrounded by Stewards and Darkmen. Mason picked his sword up from the ground and headed that way when movement caught his peripheral. A Darkman stood in the shadows, his bow up and aimed at Eric.

"Areem, don't!" Mason shouted.

There was no flicker of acknowledgment, but the young man seemed frozen in uncertainty. Mason ran at him, slamming into him and wrenching the bow from his hands. Areem scrambled to his feet and grabbed his dagger. "Don't come any closer!" His hand shook, fear shouting from his dark eyes.

Mason put a placating hand up. "Put it down, kid." But just like with the rest of the Darkmen, Areem did not obey.

A glimpse into his thoughts, however, revealed his terror, now that he was in the middle of the war. He could kidnap children from harmless civilians with a company of ally soldiers at his back. He was even willing to shoot a boy in the back to please his leaders. But to come against an army of knights who possessed greater skill than he and be expected to lay his life down for a leader who cared nothing for him threw his fear back into his face and revealed how unprepared he really was.

"I–I don't—I don't know what to do!" His breath puffed out in quick, white clouds in the cold.

"Listen to me—"

Areem shook his head wildly. "I can't hear you!"

Mason tensed when Areem raised his hands, but the boy reached for his own ears and plucked out two small bits of wax. He threw them to the ground almost defiantly and stood like a frightened cat, ready to bolt. "Are you gonna kill me now?"

"Not if I don't have to." Mason pointed his sword down. "But you're gonna have to make a quick choice on which side you're going to stand on."

Areem shot a fearful look around, and Mason moved closer. "Listen, Areem. I was wrong. Jader wants only destruction for the sake of his power." He had to rein back his fervor, but if there was a chance Mason could save Areem from the dark path he had trod for so long, he had to try.

For a moment, it looked as if Areem would refuse. But then he dropped the knife. "I don't want to die."

Mason could see that he was genuine. All his bravado and ambition had drained from him. Self-reproach for his own recent actions had kept him awake for too long. "That's probably the best decision you've made yet."

The younger man did not seem so sure. "They'll kill me," he said. "Just for talking to you."

"Not if I can help it."

60

Great strength is given to the people so that they may defend the helpless.
-The Record of Gifts

The gates at the back wall shook under the weight of the battering ram, weakening with each heavy impact. "Hold your place!" Lionel shouted.

The Stewards continued to fire back at the enemy, but the Darkmen would break in soon. Lionel clenched his teeth against the cold so hard they ached. His inadequacies loomed as he fought to hold the enemy out.

"Sir, I don't think it'll hold much longer!" a corporal shouted from below.

Where was the prince? If Lionel let the enemy soldiers in, he would carry that failure for the rest of his life. But there was no one else to take the lead here. So, Lionel pushed through his self-doubt and did what he could. "Get the men ready to fight," he ordered.

There weren't many stationed at this wall unless he wanted to count the Reservists still too stunned to stand with them. Most of the knights were taken up with the fighting further in the fort. Even some of the cadets had disappeared. The sound of a multitude of voices and cannon fire could still be heard in the distance behind them.

He turned back to the throng of dark soldiers below, yelling and firing their flaming arrows up at the Stewards. They had had no deaths on this side, though a few Stewards had been hit by the wild shots coming from below. But their time was about to run out.

"Sir!" Zakkias pointed. "There are more coming."

"By the moon," Lionel breathed, stepping to the spyglass. They could not take much more of this. The cold was already slowing them down, hindering their movement.

He peered through the glass, catching sight of scores of riders and people on foot, advancing quickly. Flashes of light at the front led the way in the dark night. Torches? Holding his breath, he waited a few more heartbeats as they drew nearer. Snatches of red capes on the horsemen lit a flicker of hope. Not torches. Beacons. "It can't be."

"What is it, sir?" Gann asked, trepidation lining his question.

Lionel stood up straight. "Skies above, those are Stewards."

"What?" Gann looked through the glass. "You're right! They're leading a host of civilians."

"Reinforcements." Optimism took hold. Maybe this night would not end in failure.

But then Zakkias pointed. "They've been spotted."

Sure enough, many of the soldiers at the rear turned to cut the Stewards off, easily outnumbering the reinforcements.

"Cover them!" Lionel shouted through numb lips.

A volley of arrows shot from the top of the wall, many of them bouncing off the shields. Some hit their targets, but most did not reach the mass that surged for the coming Stewards.

Lionel pounded his fist against the wall. The reinforcements were going to be cut down before they would even reach them. But just before the two masses met, a volley of arrows flew from the bluffs clustered around the wall. Each one met its mark, and dozens of Darkmen fell.

"What was that?" Zakkias exclaimed, looking ready to jump from the wall in his excitement.

Lionel grabbed the looking glass off its stand and raised it to his eye, scanning the shadowy bluffs. A few moments later, rows of heads appeared, aiming their bows and letting their arrows fly with unnatural accuracy.

Victory nearly took his breath away. "Stewardesses!"

Zakkias pumped his fist and let out an ear-piercing *"All right!"* He turned to the men below. "The Stewardesses are here!"

Cheers and disbelieving laughter rose as Stewards and Reservists both celebrated.

Lionel watched the fight unfold before his eyes, calculating the position of each group. The Dark Army was caught off guard and scattered, turning their anger on those who had intervened. The civilians were engaged in a fierce fight at the rear, and the Stewardesses continued to shoot. The battering ram was abandoned.

"Let's go. We can catch them in the middle." He mounted the prince's horse and called out a few orders so the ranks with him would position themselves in the most strategic locations to overwhelm the Darkmen.

"Sir!" Hiram's voice drew him around. The militiaman stood tall, though his hands were still bound. "We would fight too, please." His eyes looked clear, his stubborn jaw jutted. The other Reservists gathered around him.

Lionel did not take long to make up his mind. "All right then. Cut them loose." It was swiftly done. "Open the gates!" Lionel called.

The damaged gates dragged as they opened. The shrill squeak of hinges that Lionel had dreaded only a few moments before cut through the air. But it did not signal a defeat. Rather, it was a step toward victory.

The Stewards ran out in full force, followed by the Reservists, their weapons up. In less time than Lionel expected, the battle was upon them. Dark soldiers fought back, malicious and hateful, but they were losing ground.

Feeling a cold sting attack his confidence, Lionel pulled his Beacon from his belt. "Watch out for Shadowmen!"

A shield of light went up, protecting them for as long as they could against the Shadowstone's attack. It would not hold it back for long, but maybe long enough.

More beams cut through the darkness as the Stewardesses and Steward reinforcements joined in. Soon, a web of crisscrossing light rays surrounded the enemy, blinding them. Lionel noted in amazement that the militiamen and civilians did not seem to be hindered by the brightness of the Beacons and continued to battle the enemy soldiers. Maybe the Lambient had stretched out His hand to assist them in the dire moment.

A fuzzy form took off running from somewhere to his left, and Lionel pursued him on horseback. A gray-headed man in black clothes spun around, his Shadowstone up and aimed at Lionel.

The sting of the stone took his breath away, and he froze long enough for the man to relax and raise his crossbow with a smirk. Then an arrow pierced the Shadowman's chest, and he hit the ground, gaping in shock.

Lionel caught his breath and looked behind him. A redheaded Stewardess stood behind him, her bow still up at her shoulder.

"Sorry to interrupt, but I had a little score to settle with that one," she said, a hard set to her square chin. "That was the Shadowman who killed the king."

Looking down at the dead man, Lionel felt no pity, only disappointment that he had let him overpower him so easily.

Soon, the Dark Army disintegrated and ran for the cover of the woods beyond. Some still fought until they were overpowered and struck down. Scores of bodies lay around them.

Lionel waved his arm over his head. "Let's get inside before they regroup!" He led the way back into the fort and pulled his horse to the side as everyone streamed inside.

A bearded Steward rode to meet Lionel. "Captain Hurshel Neems," he said with an outstretched hand, "at your service."

Lionel could not stop the smile that stretched across his face. "Lt. Lionel Percy. I cannot tell you how happy I am to see you." He waved a hand to include the civilians and the Stewardesses. "All of you."

"We heard things were looking grim in the Gateway," the redheaded Stewardess said as she joined them, swinging her bow over her shoulder. "Thought you could use some help. I'm Lt. Rossi."

Inclining his head in a courteous bow, Lionel said, "Indeed. That gate was not going to hold up much longer."

The Stewards were in the front of the company, all on horseback. About a hundred civilians followed them into the courtyard, most of them on foot. The rest of the Stewardesses rode in at the rear.

When the last were safely inside, Lionel looked up at the gateman. "Get them closed!"

A sickening crack pierced his ears before the gatemen called out, "The gates are too damaged! The pulley won't reverse."

Urgency quickened Lionel's movements as he slid to the ground. This part of the battle may be won, but it did not lessen the danger outside. "Let's push them closed!" He ran to the gate closest to him and threw his weight against it. Others joined him, and the massive plank inched forward.

"Oh, honey, I can handle that," Rossi said, nudging him aside. With nary an effort, she singlehandedly pushed it closed, then proceeded to do the same with the other.

Lionel gaped at the redhead, his reasoning scrambling to surmise that the woman was Gifted. She chucked his sagging chin as she passed him. "Don't leave your mouth hanging open, handsome. You might swallow a bug."

Shaking himself, Lionel cast a warning scowl to Zakkias, who grinned like an idiot, before addressing Hurshel again. "I believe most of the threat is centered at the inner bailey."

"Well, then." Hurshel gathered his reins. "I think your Reservists and my civilians are more than enough to hold this wall now. Why don't you lead these good Steward knights where the need is?"

Lionel stood a little straighter. "Where'd you get them all?" he asked, eyeing the throng of men and even some women.

"From the towns in Paladin," Hurshel answered. "People who were getting tired of the uprisings. When we"—he motioned to the group of senior Stewards gathering around them—" decided we would not stand back and watch our kingdom break, we found a lot of good men and women willing to join us. Some of them are even Stewards."

"They came to the castle earlier tonight," Rossi added, moving her horse alongside Lionel's. "That's when we made our plans."

"I am mighty glad you did."

His heart lighter than it had been all night, Lionel climbed back in the saddle and took his place at the front of the mixed company of Stewards, all looking at him expectantly. "Let's get to the inner courtyard!"

61

The power that the Shadowpit possesses is not a Gift of the Moon, but rather a tool created by the lord of darkness, Shreil, and utilized by his followers.
-The Record of Gifts

The blare of a horn pierced the night, sending alarm ricocheting through Mason. He exchanged quick looks with Areem and bolted to the edge of the alley.

There was a slight lull in the fight as many looked in the direction of the Great Hall, the mess hall dark and silent beside it. A horseman appeared, riding out from the middle of the two tall buildings with his sword raised over his head. He was followed by a troop of Stewards and Stewardesses, streaming around both halls.

"I don't believe it," Mason breathed, recognizing Lionel upon the prince's horse.

The fighting spread out as the dark soldiers took to evasion and defense. The war of the Gateway had culminated in the stronghold that had stood in the gap for so many years. For a moment, the tide seemed to have shifted. The reinforcements bolstered the fighting Stewards and pushed back against the wave of Darkmen.

But then the air sharpened, and snow swirled in the biting wind. For the Dark Army, it wasn't so bad, protected by their winter gear. But Eric's army, already cold, faltered in the storm, especially those on horseback, hit by the wind and snow. Many of them deserted their saddles and took to the fight on the ground.

The coldness seeped into Mason's boots, numbing his toes and the tips of his fingers. Icy air clung to his lungs. He jerked back around. "Areem, where's Bruin hiding?" The commander would not ride into this battle until victory was near.

Even as he hesitated, the answer flashed through Areem's eyes. "On the edge of the gap," he said, shakily. His defection made his fear of the Darkmen very real. "He and Jader are watching from the northern bluffs."

The bluffs. The ones that surrounded the entrance to Seria's tunnel—the same tunnel that led to the Shadowpit.

Excited voices nearby drew Mason back around and out into the open. Dakim and several cadets clustered together, pointing at the new arrivals.

"What are you boys doing way out here?" Mason asked, stepping out of the alley. "Aren't you supposed to be guarding the back wall?"

Dakim's hair lay limp on his head, his eyes wide in his sweaty face. "We didn't mean to go so far, but the prince was in trouble, so we stopped to help." Dakim waved a hand. "And somehow, we ended up out here."

Struck by another idea, Mason startled Areem by grabbing his arm and pulling him over. "You stay with them. You'll be safer with them than lurking in the shadows."

Some of Areem's usual pride tightened his jaw, but Mason cut him off before he could argue. "If those Darkmen find out that you ran, you're a dead man. And if the Stewards catch sight of you, they'll assume you're the enemy, which also means—"

"I'm a dead man. I get it."

"Good. Then stay here and out of trouble." He looked at Dakim. "And if he gives you any trouble, knock him out and hogtie him, but don't let the Dark Army get him."

"I will, sir," Dakim said with a serious nod.

Areem rolled his eyes but did not resist.

"Where are you going, sir?" Dakim asked.

Mason peered through the whirling snow. Several horses danced about in agitation, abandoned by their riders. "I'm going after Bruin."

Seria lost count as men and women stepped up to receive their Shadow-stones. The purple rocks glimmered as the soldiers hung them around their necks with chains of gold. It seemed Jader's ceremony would never end. Finally, after the last one, Jader raised his hand. Complete blackness fell, and Seria bit back a whimper. Jader's voice drifted through the darkness. "Submission begets darkness. Darkness begets power. And power begets victory."

There was a long pause, broken by murmurs and moans, and then someone said, "I can see in the dark!"

A chorus of triumph rose before the darkness was lifted. Seria felt sick as she stared at the crowd. Shadow Soldiers. Every one of them.

Jader tilted his head back. "My Shadow Soldiers, you are a late but welcome addition to my special forces. The time has come to join the army in the Gateway. You will replenish my numbers, and together, you will destroy the Stewards!"

They cheered, and then Bruin ordered them to fall into ranks. He pointed a man and a woman out. "Zell and Rayken, you two stay here with Dreeya and the others. Balt and Naman will stand guard outside."

The group bowed in acquiescence and moved to their positions.

Jader moved back to stand in front of Seria. "Have no fear. This night is about to come to an end."

Seria pressed her lips together, refusing to speak to him.

Jader spoke to Bruin. "I'll leave you on the outskirts. When you come across our rebel Reader, you know what to tell him."

"Aye, sire."

They left her then and stood before the recruits. Jader raised his hands, and a cloud of black smoke appeared around him, gathering at the feet of his new soldiers. Little by little, it swelled until it consumed them, and Seria could no longer see any of them. Then it dissipated, and she let out a gasp.

All of them were gone.

She tried to wrap her mind around what she had witnessed. But one fact prevailed above all the rest. The cave was almost empty. There were only five soldiers left inside.

Dreeya cast a vicious look at Seria before she moved to confer with the man, Zell. They huddled close and whispered. Rayken rolled her eyes and took a seat on a thick stalagmite to sharpen her dagger.

Seria's heart jumped. There was no better chance to make an escape and hopefully find Aladee and Lena outside. Keeping an eye on the dark group, she worked a second pin from the hem of her left sleeve and into her grasp. Then she started picking the lock.

62

Eric pulled his blade from a Darkman's torso and let the body fall. He gave a quick look around, his breath freezing in the cold air as he paused to get his bearings. Everywhere he looked, turmoil ensued. Bodies lay strewn about, and the air was riddled with cries of pain and anger. Snow blew into his eyes, biting at his skin. His feet felt like blocks of wood.

The Steward reinforcements had done much to boost his morale, but the dip in the temperature put a chill on it. The sting of cold covered his skin and stiffened his fingers. His lungs blew out short puffs of white, frosty air, squeezing to get a full breath. They were still at the mercy of Bruin's Gift, and the Dark Army did not back down. Their capes and gloves kept their movements smooth and forceful against the Stewards, who fought the cold as much as enemy soldiers.

They had their sights set on the prince of Paladin, but Eric's knights put themselves in the gap between the enemy and him. It pained him like a blade to the gut that they risked their lives for his. And every time one fell, that blade dug a little deeper.

He utilized his Gift every chance he got, wrenching weapons away and slinging objects at his adversaries. But the effort drained him, as well as the nonstop physical motion. Every lift of the sword, every sidestep, every twist and turn sent waves of exhaustion over him until he was sure he would be carried away with it.

The constant onslaught from the Shadow Soldiers did not help. Men and women hid among the ranks of Darkmen, using their stones to weaken the Stewards. Eric suspected they had yet to see the full force of the Shadow Soldiers here. How much longer could they hold up?

He stood in the eye of the storm, unnoticed for the time being, surrounded by darkness. It was not Jader's darkness, fortunately, but it was deep and cold regardless. For a moment, he remained there, heartsick and weary. And he prayed that it would end soon.

Not far off, Lionel held his ground with that dogged stubbornness he carried. His determination fueled Eric's flagging strength, and he straightened. Sensing a presence behind him, he tensed, then relaxed. "Marcus, what are you doing way out here?"

"Trying to help," Marcus answered, stepping out of the shadows, looking wan and strained. The heavy cloak over his shoulders was covered in dirt, torn in multiple places near the hem.

"Are you all right?" Eric asked.

Marcus's gaze darted around them, and he stepped to Eric's right side. "It's just...a lot."

"Aye." Eric looked back at the fighting, readjusting his hold on the hilt of his sword. "It is." He couldn't stand here any longer. Not when every life in the fort was in danger.

The skin on his neck prickled, and his awareness sharpened. As instinct took over, he stiffened, readying himself for an attack. But it was on his right that the walls of defense went up. He turned to Marcus, his sword already coming up, and blocked a dagger swing that would have slit his throat.

The younger man recovered quickly, stepping out of reach of Eric's sword and raising his own. The uncertainty on his face was replaced with malice. Marcus's eyes glittered. "Not so much of an idiot now, am I?" he sneered.

"What is this, Marcus?" Eric snapped.

"Hold it!" A sharp voice behind him stopped him short, silencing the questions. Keeping Marcus in his line of sight, he took a careful glance over his shoulder. A Darkman with a low ponytail and a fierce expression approached, his crossbow up and leveled.

A cold spear of fear hit Eric in the chest. He was about to die here. Surrounded again by the enemy. Recognizing the fear as the work of the Shadowman, Eric resisted the mental attack and reached out with his Gift, but both men had a steel-like grip on their weapons.

"Good timing, Karsch." A slow grin stretched Marcus's lips. "I'm about to give Prince Eric here the same royal treatment I gave that old geezer captain."

"You killed Dudley?" Eric rasped.

"Thought it was time he started retirement."

The Darkman stopped a few feet from Eric, his eyes narrowed. "Looks like you could use some backup."

"Nay, just a witness that I was the one to kill the prince of Paladin," Marcus said, lifting his sword. There was a quick *swish!* and Eric flinched. But it was Marcus who fell, a short arrow embedded in his chest.

Jerking, Eric gawked at Karsch, who spoke to the dead man. "I wasn't talking to you." Then the Darkman bowed his head to Eric. "Your Majesty."

For a moment, Eric wondered if he was hallucinating. Before he could decide, Lionel jumped before him, his blade and glower zeroed in on Karsch.

"Nay, Lionel, wait!" Eric shouted, halting the swing of Lionel's sword.

Karsch dropped his weapon and put his hands up.

"Who are you?" Eric asked, still trying to figure out the man's motive.

"My name is Karsch Webber." His gaze was clear and steady. "I'm the one who contacted Lt. Kullen about the Reader in Machlin." He reached under his cloak, hesitating when Lionel aimed his sword at him.

"Watch yourself," Lionel warned.

Karsh shook his head. "I'm no enemy." He pulled his cloak back and pulled a glassy rod from his belt.

Paralyzed with shock, Eric stared as the Beacon lit up.

Lionel's sword drooped. "What...? *How?*"

Pushing sweaty strands of hair back off his face, Karsch said, "You're not alone in this fight. There are other hidden Stewards here." He motioned to a gray cloth tied around his bicep. "This is our mark."

"But what about us?" Eric managed. "You could all get killed by your own allies."

"We could. But it was a risk we took so we could enter with the enemy. It's enough for us to know the Lambient sees our deeds, whether it's to die in the line of battle or" —a smirk appeared—"jam their launch engines for as long as we can." The strength that seeped from his persona was proof enough even without the Beacon.

Eric's jaw hung open, an incredulous laugh escaped him. "Thank the Lambient. I am more grateful than I can say."

Rapid hoofbeats interrupted the conversation, and Mason rode up on Oakley. "Eric, I know where—" He stopped short, confusion clouding his face at the sight of the Darkman with the Beacon. "Karsch?"

The covert Steward grinned. "You are not the first Darkman to find the Light, Mason Grey. Although you may be the first Shadowman that I know of."

Though he looked like he wanted to say more, Mason resumed his address to Eric. "I know where they're at."

That sobered Eric. "Where?"

"At the bluffs. I think I can get us there."

Eric knew what he wasn't saying. Mason's Shadow abilities would allow them to slip unseen through the crowd. "Let's go." He swung up behind the saddle on Oakley's broad back and looked down at the other two men. "Keep going." It seemed such a lame line in light of all they had already done, but they nodded.

Mason eyed Karsch. "I hope I get an explanation later."

Karsch saluted with the Beacon. "Count on it."

The ride through the fighting humanity was surreal. Mason's cloaking hid them from both Darkman and Steward, though Mason warned that Shadowmen would still be able to spot them, and an occasional Beacon flash caught them as they passed. Eric's perception and Gift worked together to shield them from any hits.

They passed through the inner gates and into the bailey. The wreckage appalled Eric. Fire and destruction had razed his fort to a shell of what it used to be.

They were nearing the wrecked outer wall when a familiar presence loomed over Eric, cold and taunting. A quickening of his senses compelled him to follow after it. "Wait, stop here."

Mason pulled Oakley to a halt. "What's wrong?"

Eric ground his teeth. "Jader's here. Waiting for me."

There was a pause. "What do you want to do?"

He took a moment to consider his options. It was quiet here in this courtyard, but shadows gathered at the edge, as if waiting for him. He slid down to the ground. "I'll give him what he wants." With the noise of battle battering him, he leveled a look at Mason. "You need to stop the army."

Mason grimaced. "Their ears are plugged."

That was news to Eric, but he dismissed it. "That shouldn't matter. I heard your voice in my head from miles away."

"But I tried. It doesn't work."

"Mason, think about it." Eric rested his hands against Oakley's warm neck. "Lambient gave you that Gift, and it could be that he gave it to you for this very moment."

The Reader stared back at him, a muscle in his jaw popping. "I'll give it another try."

"And keep trying until you get it."

Mason regarded him silently, his eyes dark. "All right," he finally said. "I'll deal with Bruin."

"Be careful. He's itching to kill you."

"Last time I checked, you weren't on Jader's good side, either."

"I'll see you soon." The promise felt forced, but he refused to let doubt cloud his thinking now. He patted Oakley and stepped away. Mason gave him one more long look, then urged the horse on.

Eric watched them run through the demolished gates. Then he took both weapons in his hands and turned to face the darkness.

63

The Gift of the Reader is sometimes falsely believed to have been created by Shreil, but, like all others, it was designed by Lambient, though the purpose of the Gift is often debated.
-The Record of Gifts

Eric pursued the shadows through the courtyard as they shifted and drew him in further, and a strange premonition warned him he was walking into a trap. But he ran on anyway.

Then it stopped to hover and swirl, disorienting and dizzying, but Eric kept his eye on the silhouette forming in the center. His Beacon lit as he narrowed the gap between them. "Jader!"

The form turned. Even in the shadows pressing in all around them, Eric could see Jader's pale skin and that white eye twitching.

"I knew you would be foolish enough to follow me," Jader said.

"This ends tonight," Eric ground out. Blood roared in his ears, and his skin prickled with the heat surging through him. One of them was about to die, and he would do everything in his power to make sure it wasn't him.

But he was willing to die if it meant stopping this man and his evil.

"You are correct." Jader took slow, even steps forward. "It does end tonight. But I do not think it will end as you so naively hope."

"You've already lost." Eric held his ground as Jader approached. "You lost your Reader. Your army failed to get through the back gates. Even some of your own Darkmen turned out to be Stewards."

A vein in Jader's neck ticked. "Setbacks, foolish prince, do not mean defeat. The Reader is still firmly in my grasp."

Even as a sliver of doubt stuck him, Eric rejected it. Jader would use every bit of mental manipulation to tear him down if he could. Eric had to be stronger. He *would* be stronger.

As if sensing his hesitation, Jader smiled. "You are so confident in your Stewards, young prince, but at your death, your kingdom will have no ruler. They will be ripe for change."

"Not from you. They will never follow you."

"Your people already have." Jader's scrutiny did not waver, his good eye boring into Eric's skin. "You know this. The militants at the back wall were made up of *your* people. The riots. The unrest. That is the message your loyal people have sent you."

Eric gave a quick shake of his head. "A few loud complainers don't represent the majority."

Instead of replying, Jader looked down at the weapon in Eric's hands. "I suppose that is the sword you used against my shadow creatures."

"It's the same weapon that defeated you before," Eric shot back.

Jader rubbed the scar that ran down his face. "Is that what your father told you?" He walked along the edge of the circle of darkness, looking as if he were out on a stroll. Eric rotated with him, not about to turn his back on him. "Your father lived in the same state of denial you do. Belief in a light that was extinguished long ago when your Lambient lay dead in a pool of his blood."

"That blood still flows, Jader."

"In that sword?" Jader gave a soft huff. "That sword is nothing but a piece of metal. It holds no threat to me."

"It put a stop to your monsters."

"My young prince. Do not assume that because you poked at Shreil's darkness you made any kind of victory." He came around the front again and extended his hand, drawing a long tendril of smoke that thickened until a spear of black metal formed in his grasp. The same one that had killed Braylee a short while ago. The memory of it piercing Eric's beloved captain's chest staggered him.

The darkness swirled around Jader's pale face. "'Tis useless to fight me." He pointed his spear, and Eric swiveled away from the wicked dart that shot from the end. His pulse raced, and he adjusted his stance, Lavrynth held before him.

So, the spear could shoot darts. Wonderful.

"I told Aden Passion years ago that he would learn what my power could do."

"My father defeated you," he said, trying to ignore the way the cold seeped through his boots.

"Your father empowered me." Jader mocked. "My so-called exile put me where I needed to be, allowed me to be a tool in Shreil's hand." He shot another dart that Eric dodged by a hair.

Eric set his jaw, tired of the taunting. He did not wait for Jader to speak again before he went on the offense, striking with both weapons.

Jader deflected the attack with ease, once again unleashing the skilled fighting skills he hid beneath his fancy robes. His movements were fluid as he blocked Lavrynth and then angled to bat the Beacon away with the other end of his weapon.

Eric was taken aback at the skill with which Jader fought. A sickening feeling told him he was grossly outmatched. The only way he would walk away from this was by the power of Lambient alone.

Spinning to avoid the sharp edge of the spear, Eric reared the hand holding the Beacon back and gathered all his strength. Then he snapped it forward, letting the light whip out, reaching for Jader. But Jader shot out his own lash from the spear that grabbed hold of the whip and shot sparks all the way through to Eric's hand and through his body. He cried out and released the rod as the black whip jerked it away and tossed it aside.

Stunned, Eric shook the sensation off and gripped Lavrynth with both hands. He was still not weaponless. This sword would do the work.

Jader looked eager to continue. "Shall we continue, or would you like to surrender now?" One corner of his mouth curled up. "I might be persuaded to keep you alive—"

"Never," Eric spat. "I'll die first."

"So be it."

A cold wind bit at Mason's exposed skin as he led Oakley through the gates, over the footbridge, and into the empty town of Cadence. The dozens of small huts stood untouched under the night sky. Unbidden, his gaze moved to the south, where Seria's ramshackle little cabin rested. Memories plucked at him, stinging his heart, but he could not lose himself to those now. Seria's safety, and the safety of an entire realm, depended on the end of this war.

Snow dusted the ground, making the way treacherous. The bluffs, gathered in a cluster where the Slates met the wall, were naught but an easy walk from Cadence. Mason could picture Seria making her way to the tunnel, her arms swinging by her sides, and Sanjo ambling behind her.

Why was everything pointing to Seria?

Maybe because you're about to die, and you're wishing for one more moment with her. He dashed that thought away, even as a cold awareness settled like a rock in his gut.

Echoes of the battle going on in the stronghold drifted to his ears, and he thought of all the men and women still fighting to defend it, praying they would overcome the darkness. All the time he and Oakley circled the empty town of Cadence, keeping close to the stronghold wall that met the bluffs, he wrestled with the prince's challenge.

His thoughts churned along with the tension in his stomach. Jader had spoken of the Reader, Moverik the Great, who had gained control of thousands for Shreil's service. Could he send his silent words into the minds of the Darkmen? It had worked with Eric. Even Seria had heard him calling to her from Machlin. But could he send a command the same way?

It was worth a try at least.

He tugged Oakley to a stop at the last rock formation before he reached the bluffs, where Bruin would be hiding. Not sure what to expect, he climbed off the tall gray. There was no guarantee this would work, but he had an advantage Moverik didn't have.

Lambient, I've abused this Gift you've given me. Please help me use it now for You.

He closed his eyes and reached out with his mind, targeting only those who worked under Jader's will. The mental strain wore on him, making him weary before he even spoke the order. He drew in a shaky breath and spoke silently.

Surrender now.

He waited for something, a physical zing or the sound of silence from the fort. But there was nothing but a dull ache in his head. Mason ground his teeth and rubbed his chilly hands together. The immobility had allowed the cold to seep into his bones.

This had to work. The Stewards could not fight both the plummeting temperatures and the Dark Army.

He repositioned himself, clenching his fists. He said another prayer around the pain building in his head and tried again.

Stand down. Surrender your weapons.

Lights flashed, and drums pounded. Voices screamed in his ears. His knees buckled, and he dropped to the ground. He forgot where he was, lost in the wilderness of his mind, and willed himself to keep going, to push past the agony. It felt like his skull was splitting open. He had no idea how long he knelt there, holding his head as if to hold it together.

Throwing his Gift out in one last ditch effort, he released a groan that turned into a drawn-out yell. The effort might kill him, but he couldn't give up. Not when the noise of the battle made it clear the Darkmen were still working under the authority of Jader.

An invisible blade sliced through his forehead, ripping a pained cry from his chest. For a moment, he thought he was being torn apart. In desperation, he reached for the Beacon at his belt. Piercing light shot through his body, and the voices grew, drowning out every other noise. Blank faces swam in his vision, gone before he could comprehend what was happening. Then there was a snap, and it was over, leaving him sucking in cold air.

Someone nudged his back. He swung his arm out to fight them off and punched to his feet, grabbing for his sword. Oakley tossed his head and gave an annoyed snort.

Mason slumped. "Sorry, boy." Wiping cold sweat away, he listened. Nothing had changed. Defeat nearly brought him down to the ground again. After all that Jader had believed his Gift would accomplish, it had failed him.

It's not up to you now.

The whisper stilled him, reassuring and confident. He drew in a shaky breath and stood tall. He had done all he could do. Lambient would have to do the rest.

A hard gust of wind took his breath away. Oakley let out a squeal and spun away, galloping back to the gates. Mason let him go and braced himself, gathering all the stamina he had left.

"I was wondering how long it would take for you to come." The snide voice froze him to the spot for a moment.

Mason clenched his jaw. "Then you know why I'm here."

Bruin's form emerged from the shadows, his cool gray eyes glittering with the challenge. "If it's to stop me, then you should have brought help."

A scowl twisted Jader's usual composed features, and the emperor stopped his offense. For the space of several silent heartbeats, he stood like a statue, cold and hard.

Eric heard the change in the air too. "What's the matter, Jader? Lose control of your army?"

Jader's hate-filled gaze shot to Eric. "Do you believe for a moment that I rested all my chance for victory on one man?" he asked, severe and chilly. "Your Reader is but a tool, one who will be dealt with soon enough." He thrust his hand out, and darkness fell.

Eric stiffened, blind to everything beyond the nose on his face. His Beacon was lost, but energy hummed through Lavrynth's hilt, grounding him in the moment. His sword carried the blood of his ancestors and Lambient. It would not fail him. This was the purpose for which it was forged and handed to Eric's forefathers.

A shift in the darkness allowed him to see Jader dimly through the shadows, and he suspected the lord of darkness was toying with him. Jader slid his hands along the surface of the spear, biding his time. His patient amusement infuriated Eric. This man had taken so much from so many people. He was the one responsible for his father's early death, the lives of countless people on both sides of the Slates, the boys of Handan, the loss of his dear friend.

A roar built in his chest as he tightened his hold, letting the power surge through him. It did not matter how black the darkness around them lay. Lambient's light was always brighter.

The blade glowed white hot, simmering with the righteous anger that pounded through Eric's veins. As he swung the blade at the dark emperor with the last bit of strength he had left, a roar ripped from his throat, carrying his outrage to the blackened skies above.

Jader raised his spear to meet the sword in midair. It struck the blade with a force that rocked Eric's bones and sent him flying off his feet. He landed on his back, the impact forcing air from his lungs. Rolling over to get his feet beneath him, he tried to shake the shock away and lifted his sword. Horror slapped him in the face with a cold hand as he stared at Lavrynth.

The blade was broken.

64

The Lambient promised that He would dwell in the thick darkness.
-The Sacred Code

Lionel was surrounded by Darkmen, trying his best to hold them off, despite the sharp cold that slowed his movements and made breathing difficult.

Karsch had disappeared into the throng with a promise to keep working behind the lines. Rossi was in the middle of the frenzy, tossing men aside as if they were rag dolls. One man approached her from behind, a club in his upraised hand. Lionel grabbed a crossbow from a dead Darkmen and fired. The man fell at her feet without a sound.

The stout Stewardess swiveled and caught sight of him. "Watch out!"

He ducked as she plowed her fist at someone behind him with a hard *THUD*. "Where've you been while we've been defending your fort?" she demanded.

He waved at the dead man at her feet. "I just saved—"

"Lieutenant!" Zakkias yelled. Lionel swiveled to look, then wished he hadn't.

Another troop of Darkmen headed their way, their swords glinting and their steps unhindered.

Rossi stepped to his side, bumping him. "We can take them," she said with a stubborn tilt of her jaw, but Lionel caught the exhaustion in her tone.

There weren't many allies left where they remained, though the ones who remained fought with grit and persistence. Jervis's booming voice could be heard in the distance, and the Reservists fought on their side again. But the extreme cold and sheer number of enemy soldiers was about to do them in.

Lionel spread his feet apart, weapons ready, and steadied himself. If this was how he was going to die, he would go down fighting.

The Darkmen came at them as one, raising their swords with a mighty cry, ready to cut down the few that still stood in their way.

But they didn't.

The whole band of thirty or so men stopped short, as if running into an unseen wall, dropped their weapons, and raised their hands in surrender.

"What the—" Rossi exclaimed. "What trick is this?"

It was the same everywhere Lionel looked. Darkmen threw down their swords and gave up. He met Rossi's wide eyes. "What happened?" she asked.

"If I had to make a guess," he said, "I'd say Mason found a way to control the whole confounded army."

Zakkias gave an incredulous laugh. "Is it over?"

At that moment, deep, black darkness fell, dousing every lantern light, torch, and flame. With it came another layer of cold, this one settling into one's soul.

"Not yet," Lionel answered.

The Stewards' rods glowed here and there, spread out over the courtyard as they were, but the shadows hung like thick curtains all around them. Lionel sensed more than saw or heard the approach of multiple Shadowmen in every direction, unleashed by the darkness that did not hinder them. He tensed and brightened his rod, bracing for another attack. Shadow Soldiers appeared at the edge of the Beacons' light, more than Lionel could count. Their presence cut short the jubilation and turned the atmosphere toward fear.

Zakkias hissed between his teeth, the light of his Beacon casting sharp panes on his strained countenance. "There's so many," he gasped.

The Stewards outnumbered the Shadow Soldiers, but a host of hundreds was a force none of them had encountered before. And with the winter storm blasting at them, it all threatened to overcome the weary knights.

Lionel had already seen high moments throughout the night. The destruction of the shadow creatures. The reinforcements at the back wall. The surrender of the entire Dark Army. But he was tired. His soldiers were weary and cold. And the Shadowmen had the added benefit of Jader's darkness. But then he remembered the hidden Stewards, and he pressed against the despair.

"Hold steady," Lionel said, though his own heart threatened to pound its way from his chest. "There's not as many as it seems."

"You're right," Rossi agreed, her eyes alight. "It matters not how many Shadowmen come at us, light will overcome darkness."

Lionel gave her a quick look. "Aye, but—"

She clutched her rod like a torch. "He's always greater!"

"Lieuten—"

"A thousand will fall at our sides!"

The darkness swarmed in on all sides, robbing him of a response to Rossi's exuberant declaration. Even Rossi moaned against so many Shadowstones. But then, all around him, dozens more Beacons lit up in the hands of Darkmen who came running from the edge of the yard. Their beams caught the Shadow Soldiers in the middle, who were forced to disperse their attack to face the new threat.

"*Now,* what's happening?" Rossi demanded.

Lionel's body weakened with relief. "I tried to tell you, but you wouldn't hush up long enough for me to get it out." He flashed a grin at her stunned expression. "There are hidden Stewards among the Dark Army."

A pained cry drew them around. Zakkias was on his knees, clutching his chest, apprehension incapacitating him. Before Lionel could move to assist, Rossi stood before the young knight like a mother bear, her eyes blazing as she raised her Beacon against the pair of Shadowmen who held Zakkias in their grip, their stones glowing and sparking. A waft of black smoke drifted out toward the light Rossi held. She wavered under the two men's invisible attack, but she bared her teeth and held on.

Lionel's blood heated. "Hey!" As soon as the Shadowmen cut their attention to them, he whipped his Beacon out in front of him. A coil of light lashed out, straight at them. One of the men fell like a rock.

Rossi recovered quickly and swung her Beacon like a club at the other, sending a wave of white fire that knocked him flat on his back.

Zakkias gaped from his knees. "You just used the light whip, sir!"

Lionel helped him to his feet. "I'm having trouble believing it myself."

"I'm sorry, sir." Zakkias rubbed his chest. "I couldn't—"

"No need to apologize for being human, Private."

Rossi swept them both with an annoyed look. "Should we invite anyone else to this little heart-to-heart? The Shadowmen trying to kill us, maybe?" She stomped back off into the fray.

Zakkias offered Lionel a slight shrug and followed her.

Lionel exhaled, his limbs weak and shaky after the exertion of the whip, and shook his head. "And I thought Seria was bad."

65

The Gift of the Reader is known as the rarest and most powerful of the Gifts.
-The Record of Gifts

Bruin came at Mason with unhinged fury, striking right and left and never leaving himself open. It was all Mason could do to block and dodge. There was no chance to strike back. He backstepped as Bruin came at him, then realized he would be blocked in by the abutting stone. With a quick left feint that had Bruin's blade smashing against the stone, he dashed out of reach. Even with Jader's power that now blanketed the valley, Mason's vision easily cut through the darkness.

"You're good at running," Bruin growled, stalking him. "As soon as you get what you want, you run off."

Anger flared. "When have I ever gotten what I want, Bruin?" he snapped. "I lost my brother as a child and was taken in by a power-hungry tyrant who only wanted me for my Gifts."

"You stayed long enough to get the benefits of the Shadowstone, then betrayed us for a useless power that will fail you."

"It hasn't failed me yet."

"You know nothing about power, you fool." He struck again, cutting the verbal exchange short and bringing his blade down against Mason's so hard it rattled his bones.

Mason spun out of reach of the sword and spoke in the lull to catch his breath. "It ever bother you that Jader sends you to do all his dirty work while he sits in his fancy castle in Ignadon?"

"Trying to distract me by running the emperor down?" Bruin smirked. "Don't bother. Nothing you say will sway my loyalties."

A whirlwind of snow swept around Mason, stinging his face and hampering his sight. He heard Bruin's soft footsteps and dove out of the way, barely missing a blade to his scalp. "Can't fight me without cheating, can you?" he asked, shielding his eyes from the snow.

"You mean to tell me you haven't used your Gift tonight to your advantage?"

Mason bit back an answer. Talking Bruin down was not going to work. The commander was too smart to let his emotions take over his actions.

The snow accumulated around him, accelerated by Bruin's hand. The white storm clashed against Jader's black veil of darkness until everywhere Mason turned was a blur of gray.

Bruin's shape appeared before him, his sword arcing before Mason could stop it. He jerked back to miss the brunt of it, but the tip sliced across his chest. Pain flamed along the long cut, and he stumbled back, pressing his hand against it. Warm blood seeped through his clothes and stained his fingers.

Another soft footstep snatched him back to the present, and he grabbed his Beacon, aiming it blindly at where he thought Bruin might be. An angry grunt assured him he met his mark, and he blinked through the storm to see Bruin stumbling back.

The Beacon warmed Mason's cold fingertips, and he clung to it, craving its heat. Not giving Bruin the time to regroup and go on the offense again, Mason ran at him, both weapons flashing in the grayness.

Bruin brought his sword up in time to block Mason's hit, but the light rod flashed in his face. Another quick spin of Mason's sword, aided by the rod, and Bruin's sword flew out of his hand. The big man's iron-hard fist crashed into Mason's jaw, forcing them apart again, though Mason kept himself between Bruin and his weapon.

"That's it, Bruin," he said, pointing both weapons at him. Exhilaration raced through him, slowed only by a heavy note of caution. When Bruin's lips curled up, the note quickly became an alarm.

"Did you really think you would find me here alone, Mason?" he asked, his expression as icy as the weather that numbed Mason's feet.

Fuzzy gray forms took shape as they surrounded him. Shadow Soldiers. At least ten of them, their purple stones hanging around their necks, winking at him in victory.

Mason tried to breathe, tried to keep his stance loose and poised. But it was as if he was frozen to the ground.

Bruin straightened to his full height. "How funny to think you believed that you had the upper hand. The only reason you're not dead yet is because Jader still has use for you."

Angling his head to get an idea of where each soldier was positioned, Mason pushed back the burning fear that tried to engulf him. There was no way out of this. One man—especially a fledgling Steward—could not take on a dozen Shadowmen.

My life is yours. The prayer seemed fitting. It was one of the last things Ollen had uttered before his death. It was what Eric lived by. It was the oath every Steward carried with them to their deaths as they fought the darkness of Shreil.

He braced himself for the attack that would end this fight, and as the Beacon lit up in his hand in preparation, he had but two wishes.

First, he wished that he had been able to do more to aid the Royal Army in winning this war. And second, he wished he could have spent his last moment with Seria.

Bruin moved in closer, and Mason eased back, mindful of the soldiers behind him. He didn't try to stop Bruin from retrieving his weapon again. What was the point?

"Look at you," Bruin said. "Standing like a martyr, ready to die for your god." A look of contempt twisted his whiskers. "You're pitiful. As weak as those Stewards you've thrown yourself in with. But you're not going to die. Not yet."

"I won't bow to Jader," Mason said. "Not ever again."

"Oh, I think you will, though it may not be for the reason you believe."

Mason stared back, immovable. Nothing Bruin said would weaken his resolve. But Bruin's next words shook him to the core.

"Your precious Seria is in our possession. You will surrender to Jader's will, or she dies."

Click.

At the release of the lock, Seria held her wrist in place and checked to make sure the soldiers were occupied before she inched her arm down. At a glance from Dreeya, she grabbed for the loose cuff and stood still. If anyone looked closely, it would be apparent her wrist was not enclosed.

Zell murmured something in Dreeya's ear, distracting her from what Seria was doing. She sidled up next to him, letting him slide his arm around her waist.

Seria waited another long moment before trying again. Keeping her movements slow and careful, she slid her free hand over to the other cuff and worked the lock. Every movement was torture, and her ears roared with anxiety. Another click and she was free. She grabbed hold of the two shackles again to regroup and catch her breath. One phase was done. On to the next.

Seria gathered herself and eyed her sword, tossed haphazardly against a rock not far away. She would grab it on the way if she could. *Hopefully, before they cut me to pieces.* She rolled to the balls of her feet, cleared her mind, and counted.

Dreeya glanced back at her just as she dropped her arms and ran for the exit. "You little wench!" Dreeya shouted as several of the Shadow Soldiers jumped to intercept her. Zell cut off her course to the exit, and she slid to a stop.

He laughed. "That was pretty impressive, but where did you think you were gonna go?"

Dreeya was not so amused. It would not take much to push the furious woman to cause bodily harm.

Fear lodged in Seria's windpipe as three of them surrounded her. The other two watched from across the cave.

"Listen," she said, shaking all over. "Jader's deceived you. He doesn't care about any of you."

Dreeya exchanged leers with Zell. "Are you trying to save us now?"

"I believe everyone deserves a second chance." Seria's voice scraped across her dry tongue. "If you'll help me, I'm sure the prince will offer grace. The Lambient is forgiving. He will—"

"You listen to *me* now." All humor fled Dreeya's expression, leaving nothing but ice. "I don't need grace or forgiveness, not from the prince or your Lambient." Her eyes narrowed into slits. "I scratched and fought for every step that led me here, spitting, clawing, and killing every person who dared to stand in my way, including those who brought me into this world."

Seria's stomach turned, revulsion chilling her to the bone.

"So don't fool yourself into thinking you can convert me. I'm a Shadowwoman, and that is what I will be until the day I die."

"Oh, Dreeya," Seria breathed. "You really are awful."

The Shadowwoman let out a bark of laughter. "Am I supposed to feel guilty now?"

Through the entire terrible conversation, Seria inched closer to her sword. As soon as she could reach it, she snatched it up and aimed at them, with no idea what she was going to do. She could not hold off a cadet, much less three Shadow Soldiers.

Zell sniggered, and Rayken rolled her eyes, her stance relaxed.

Dreeya smiled. "Oh, honey. Surely you don't think you're going to fight us."

Movement behind the dark soldier caught Seria's eye, and she swallowed a gasp. Aladee stepped out of the rock wall, her sights set on the Shadowpit, her bow in her hands.

Seria kept her eyes trained on Dreeya so as not to betray Aladee's appearance and spoke up to cover her movements. "Nay, I'm not that foolish."

"Hey, stop her!" Zell shouted.

Dreeya whirled around as Aladee took off running for the pit. The Shadow Soldiers rushed to head her off, but Aladee whipped her bow up and downed two of them before they could cut her off. Then Dreeya was upon her, forcing her to drop the bow and pull her sword.

Seria's captors turned away, and she took advantage of their distraction to swing at Rayken. The flat part of the blade caught the Shadowwoman on the back of the head, and she fell like a rock.

"Oh, gracious! I killed her," Seria exclaimed.

Dreeya let out an enraged shriek, and Zell hastened to join her. With her friend in danger, Seria ran after him and struck at his upper leg, slicing a gash through his thigh.

He roared and turned on her, his eyes wild. "You filthy hussy!"

Seria tripped as she retreated, dropping the sword. Her heart pounded as Zell stalked her to a wall, his murderous intent clear.

Then a hand grabbed her clothes from the back, yanking her inside the rock wall. Lena pulled her free and into a narrow crevice.

"Oh!" Seria exclaimed. "I'm so glad you're here! Give me your sword."

Lena blinked at her. "You're not going to try to fight—"

"Gracious, no! I'm going to poke at them and draw them away from Aladee. Now *give me your sword*!"

Lena handed it over without another word and eased her out of the rocks again.

"Sorry for yelling at you," Seria said as she dashed away.

Aladee and Dreeya were locked in a fierce fight, their swords slashing the air and crashing together. Zell had abandoned the spot where Seria had disappeared, limping back to the duel to assist Dreeya. Seria ran at him, but he turned before she reached him.

"Where did you—" He cut off the question with a growl. "Enough of your tricks, little girl." He stopped short when Lena appeared a few feet down and picked up Seria's discarded sword. "How..." His eyes narrowed, and he reached for his Shadowstone. "You girls have bitten off more than you can chew."

A cold hand of terror grabbed Seria, clamping around her middle and making it hard to breathe. Lena went stark white. Seria had never experienced anything as terrifying as the hold the stone held over her.

Aladee kicked Dreeya in the stomach, knocking her away long enough to shoot a blast of light that caught Zell in the back. He let out a yell and released his stone.

Seria went limp, catching herself on the cave wall with a shaky hand. Lena gasped and shuddered.

Rayken stirred, rising to her hands and knees with a groan. Lena ran over and whacked her on the head with the hilt of Seria's sword. Before Seria had time to react, there was movement at the entrance. Balt ran in with another Shadow Soldier.

There was nothing like the terror that latched on to Mason at the very idea of Seria being in danger.

In his mind, he was sitting in her cabin, watching her stir the stew. Tranquility wrapped around them like a hug, and her smile sent beams of light straight through his spirit. There was peace and contentment there. But then reality sank in, and the snow destroyed the image.

Bruin could be lying, using what he knew to be Mason's greatest weakness to break him down. But as he stared into Bruin's cold face, Mason somehow knew it was true. Seria's life hung in the balance of Mason's choice.

His heart pounded like a war drum, and indecision froze his feet to the ground, squeezing the life out of him. How could he make the choice that would lead to Seria's death? How could he live with himself?

Trust me.

The soft words floated over the wild flood of desperation. A harsh truth tore his heart open.

He could not betray Lambient. Not even for Seria's life. Readjusting his hold on the Beacon with shaking fingers, he set his jaw and faced Bruin, who watched him like a cat toying with their prey. "I won't."

A flash of surprise tightened Bruin's craggy features. "You would sacrifice the woman you claim to love just to keep from surrendering?"

"Nay, Bruin. I surrender everything to the Lambient. He's the one I serve."

Bruin's fury could be seen even through the raging snowstorm. "If that's the way you want it. I'd rather see you dead anyway."

Mason settled his weight back, staring Bruin down despite the circle of Shadowmen closing in on him. He waited for them to use the stones and the cold grip of despair that would follow.

When it came, he held on to the Beacon like a lifeline, drawing on its strength and warmth like a dying man. His lungs, already struggling in the thin, cold air, emptied, and a sharp pain hit him in the center of his chest. His sternum felt like it was being crushed under the pressure. His legs buckled, but he locked his knees.

Bruin strode forward. "But know that your girl will die."

Hot rage surged, and he let out a yell, running forward to meet Bruin halfway. With the power the Shadowstones held over him, though, the tall man had the advantage and batted his sword out of the way, knocking Mason off balance and sending him to his knees in the snow. The crush of the stones intensified, and he gasped at the sharpness of it. It weighed him down, making it impossible to rise. Bruin's feet appeared before him, the tip of his sword catching Mason's chin and forcing him to look up.

"I told you I would kill you."

Mason gritted his teeth, waiting for the blade to slice into his neck.

But a shout startled Bruin, and the invisible grip that held Mason lifted. As the sword swung away, Mason lay heaving in the snow, his whole body tingling with relief. He looked up in time to see Stewards he did not recognize on horseback. Riding from the direction of the New Realm.

The Shadowmen shifted away, drawing swords and readjusting their hold on their stones to hold the newcomers off. But the knights kept on riding as if unaffected, their Beacons splitting the darkness.

Bruin cursed and punched his fist forward, sending a violent wind that knocked some of the men off their horses. Others held on, despite the animals' panic.

Mason pitched to his feet, his weapons still in hand. "Bruin!" he shouted, pulling his attention away from the Stewards.

The commander sent the sharp wind at him instead, but Mason raised his Beacon as a shield, and it absorbed the impact. Then he strode forward. "You threatened someone I love," he snarled.

Bruin sneered, even as he positioned himself to meet Mason's wrath. "It's not the first time."

Something snapped within, and Mason attacked, fury lending power to his strokes. The big man did not falter, but in his black rage, his defenses went up like impenetrable walls. Behind Mason, the Stewards clashed with the Shadowmen, their fight mingling with the wind that roared all around, echoing against the Slates. But Mason blocked everything out but the man before him, who was just as determined to be the victor.

Every clash of swords sent shockwaves through his arms. The cold sapped his energy, but he forced himself to keep moving, to stay one step ahead. Images pounded through his head in rhythm with his swings. Liam. Seria. Braylee. Shon. Eric. Ollen. The children at Joshun. The families of the Gateway. The years he lost serving the Dark Army.

All of the devastation and destruction that Jader brought at Bruin's hand fueled his anger.

But Bruin was still stronger, and he pushed back, forcing Mason to retreat, speeding his movements to keep up. Bruin struck, and Mason swiveled in time to block him, locking the blades against a boulder. Bruin used the moment to send another punch, but Mason ducked and pummeled into Bruin's stomach. They fell back against a massive rock, and Mason ended up pinned beneath Bruin's solid form. Bruin pulled a dagger and drove it down. Mason dropped both weapons and grabbed his wrists before the blade could plunge into his chest, groaning with the effort.

A gleam of victory pierced through Bruin's glare as the tip edged closer.

Mason drilled his stare into Bruin's, aware that Bruin was about to overpower him. But a sense of peace and confidence poured through him. "Fall back, Bruin," he ground out, his hands shaking to hold Bruin's back.

Something flickered in Bruin's expression, almost too subtle to catch.

A fire grew within Mason, and his Gift responded. The words rising up in him were not his own. It was as if Lambient spoke through him. "Fall back under the very Gift you wielded for darkness."

Bruin's face went slack, and his weight lifted, releasing the pressure. Mason shot forward and reversed the blade, sinking it into Bruin's chest. The commander stumbled back, eyes glazed over, and fell against the bluff, gasping.

The air crackled with energy, and the snow increased until Mason was nearly blinded by it. He moved back, staring as Bruin slumped against the rock. The weather was out of control. The snow turned to sleet, then hail. Wind screamed. A lightning bolt struck the snowcapped peak up above them, sending a shower of ice and rock tumbling down.

Mason ran for cover as the avalanche slid down over the bluffs. A strangled cry rose from underneath that was quickly muffled by the roar of the collapse. Mason quickened his pace and shouted to the Stewards still fighting. "Watch out!"

He dove for the ground and rolled over to see the mountain fall on top of Bruin. Snow and dust billowed into the air, and then an eerie silence fell. Powerless to move for the moment, Mason dropped back into the snow, his mind grappling to comprehend what had happened. Mason's last words, backed by Lambient Himself, had overpowered Bruin's Shadowstone.

And now Bruin, the great commander of the Dark Army, was dead, buried by his own storm.

66

The Shadowpit echoed with the chaos. Two more Shadow Soldiers, including Zell, lay dead on the ground, but Aladee now held off Dreeya and Balt. Seria could see her strength was waning.

Rayken had regained consciousness, and Lena narrowly evaded her grasp by darting back into the wall, throwing the woman off for a brief moment before she turned to Seria. She held Lena's sword with trembling hands as the Shadowwoman approached her. Just before she reached her, Lena appeared again, knocking Rayken across the head with the sword hilt.

"You're getting quite good at that," Seria panted, then ran for the three-way fight, tripping over her own feet in her hurry.

Get it together, Seria, before you fall on your own sword.

She reached the fight and swung without aiming. It slashed across Balt's back, and he let out a yelp before falling to his knees. Seria stared down in horror at the blood that gushed from the wound. Aladee and Dreeya continued on as if nothing had changed. The Shadowwoman's fury ignited her frenzy, but Aladee's passion kept her in step. Seria stood over the man, hoping he would stay down, and watched the women fight.

At one moment, Aladee slipped, leaving her left side wide open. Dreeya took the chance to strike, but Aladee pulled back and slammed her heel into the woman's stomach. Then she bolted for the Shadowpit, the Beacon in her grasp. Hope burst through Seria's fear like the sun on a rainy day. But it was quickly replaced by fear when she glanced back in time to catch Rayken stepping behind Lena.

"*Lena, look out!*"

The smaller woman jerked, but not in time to miss the blow of a rock against her temple.

Seria screamed as Lena crumpled in a heap. Rayken left Lena there and dove into Aladee. The Beacon flew out of Aladee's hands as she rolled with the Shadowwoman, already fighting to get on top. Without waiting to think it through, Seria ran for the Beacon while it still glowed on the cave floor. She snatched it and dashed for the pit, praying she could get there before it went out.

But Dreeya jumped in her path, crouched like a panther, lithe and coiled. Seria drew up short, and the Beacon went dark.

Defeat and fear swirled in a black, foggy circle around Eric. Jader stalked the ground like a cat before its prey, his vicious words breaking through the walls of Eric's resistance. "Your father once told me that he would see me and my power defeated." His expression sharpened. "And yet he is the one who is dead. And I still stand." Fury and hatred leached into his voice, rolling off his thin form.

There on his knees, blind and helpless, Eric could not argue with him. Braylee's Beacon was lost. Even Lavrynth had failed him. He could feel the dark fingers of despair and defeat dragging his soul down in a blackness he could not pierce.

"You believed you had the power to stop me. Now look at you. You are useless without your leaders." The words landed with a solid hit to Eric's confidence. "Your marshal. Your captains. Your father. You are nothing without them."

Eric squeezed his eyes shut. How could he lead his people? All he did was get the people he loved killed. Brave Stewards and Reservists.

Innocent civilians of the Gateway. Helpless boys of Handan.

His failures and his losses pressed down on him, squeezing the life out of him.

Jader's voice, almost soothing in its even cadence, wrapped around him again. "There is no one to stand by you now. You will die. And everything you stood for and fought for will fade away. It was all a waste." By the nearness of his speech, Jader must be a few feet in front of him. "You see the truth now in what I say, young prince. Your light has failed."

Eric gritted his teeth and braced himself against the cold ground with his hands, shaking his head in a feeble resistance. His body trembled as Jader's dark power clamped its hold on him. Wind and snow beat at him, chilling his skin.

The light within you is greater...

Eric forced the promise echoed countless times through the ages out in a weak whisper. "Than the darkness without."

A faint hint of hope lit the bleakness. Braylee's assurance had not relied on his Beacon but in the Lambient alone. That was why he was able to hand it over to Mason the day Jader had controlled him.

"There's always a light." Eric raised his head, forcing himself to speak past a rigid throat. By the Lambient, he could somehow see through the darkness to meet Jader's cold stare. "Behind every cloud, the sun shines. In the darkest night, the moon is still there. The stars still break through. You can't stop them."

"How poetic," Jader crooned, turning his spear to point at Eric. A wisp of smoke snaked from the tip and struck Eric where he knelt. He clenched his teeth, fighting the urge to cry out as a sharp chill exploded through him as he resisted the power Jader held over him.

The emperor pulled the spear back, and Eric fell forward again, quaking. His hand clenched, wrapping around something hard. He slid his fingers across it. A bow. Empty and discarded without the arrows.

His breath quickened as a strong revelation unfurled for him like a scroll.

Eric could not defeat Jader. He would never be strong enough to fight the power Shreil wielded through the man who had surrendered himself to the darkness. But the Lambient's light resided within Eric, powerful even without the tools He provides. In the Lambient's hands, he could do anything, strike down any enemy, defeat any power that rose.

He struggled to his knees, bringing the bow up with him. Settling it at his shoulder, he pulled back the string and aimed it at Jader.

Jader's low chuckle drifted through the fury of the squall. "You will need more than an empty weapon to fight me."

"I have all I need," Eric said, holding steady, waiting. The wind whipped around them, angry and harsh. Snow stung his eyelids until he thought they would bleed.

And then, suddenly, the wind died, and the snow dissipated.

Jader stilled and flicked a glance into the darkness. Eric felt the slight shift of his attention and reached out mentally for Braylee's Beacon. It flew into his hand and pressed against the string. As soon as it lit up, illuminating the space between them, Eric released the string, driving it forward with his Gift. The Beacon shot forward and pierced Jader's chest.

The emperor jolted as the rod embedded itself in his sternum. Light radiated from the site, streaking down Jader's limbs and through his face. The staff in his hand puffed into nothingness, and the darkness lifted around them.

Eric did not move from his position, holding Jader's stunned stare as he dropped to his knees. They were eye to eye, and Jader released a strangled breath as his hands tried to pull the Beacon out.

Time seemed to slow down as the dark lord fell forward, his blood spilling on the ground as he lay still and silent. Then sweet air rushed into Eric's lungs, and he exhaled as warmth stole back into his body.

67

Darkness ends when the Light shines.
-The Sacred Code

Everything in Seria withered at the sight of the dark Beacon. The noises faded into the distance as her failure stared at her, mocking her. Aladee would die fighting the Shadow Soldiers. Lena could already be dead. They had accomplished nothing.

Dreeya sniggered. "You risked everything to save your precious boy, and for what? To die for him?"

Indignation stirred what was left of Seria's fight. "I didn't do this for Mason," she said, her voice steady. "I did this for the Lambient. And if it means I die before I carry it through, then I'll die knowing I gave my life for Him."

Her words carried a strength she thought had drained from her in the last few hours. But she meant them. It no longer mattered how she was remembered. Lambient knew her intention, and that was enough for her.

Dreeya's face twisted in disgust. "You're pathetic."

Warmth shot through Seria's hand from the rod. The Beacon glowed, immersing her in its comforting light. It grew brighter until Dreeya stepped back, squinting against it. But Seria soaked it in, wonder and joy wrapping around her like the arms of her father.

The Lambient had seen her.

Movement pulled Seria's gaze up in time to see the Shadowwoman coming at her with a dagger. But an arrow shot past Seria, burying itself into Dreeya's stomach. The woman pulled up short, her eyes bulging before she fell in a heap at Seria's feet.

"Throw it in, Seria!" Aladee cried, already nocking another arrow as Rayken bolted for Seria.

Her breath stuck to her lungs as Seria ran, the Beacon buzzing in her grasp. Rayken fell to Aladee's arrow, crashing into Seria's legs. She stumbled, righted herself, and kept going, sliding to the edge and throwing it in before she could think about it. Everyone stopped short, staring at the Shadowpit for what seemed like an eternity. Seria held her breath, afraid that after all the struggle, it wouldn't work.

But then a shrill whistle pierced the air right before a blast of white light burst straight up from the pit. Seria was thrown back, and the ceiling above crumbled. Chunks of the cave fell all around, pelting her. She tried to regain her footing when the floor rocked, throwing her off balance. A boulder broke from the ceiling above her and fell amidst a shower of debris, trapping her left hand beneath it.

A scream tore from her as agony ripped up her arm. As the cave fell apart around her, she shifted to her knees and tugged at her arm. Every move was torture, but it held fast.

"Seria!" Aladee shouted from across the floor. Balt abandoned the fight and fled for the exit.

Lena stirred from her spot but did not awaken completely. Seria blinked through the cascade of falling rubble. "Get Lena out of here!" she cried, biting back the pain.

Aladee fought to reach her, but the pit stood between them, still hot and volcanic. "Seria!"

"Get Lena!" Seria repeated. There was no way Aladee could reach her in time, and even if she did, the boulder was too heavy, too locked in place. She could not let them die with her.

All around them, cracks split the wall. Aladee was forced back. She shielded her eyes with her arm, still looking for a way through.

"Go!" Seria screamed. "Please, just go!" Her plea ended in a sob. "Save Lena!"

The Stewardess dashed for Lena and lifted her in her arms. She cast one last conflicted look back before she ran through a crevice that had formed in the wall she had come out of. Seria begged Lambient that they would get through, that Lena would regain consciousness so she could pass them through. Whatever they needed to survive.

The cave shook and rumbled around her, breaking apart at the seams. There was no way out. Seria bit back the cries as she pulled helplessly again, to no avail. They had done it. The Shadowpit was destroyed. But Seria would die along with it.

Eric blinked and tried to gauge his surroundings. The moon lent a silvery glow to the devastation all around. The broken gates came into view, where the first assault had fallen. Bodies of Stewards lay amidst heaps of bricks and stones.

Graulik Jader was dead, his staff gone and his power broken.

In the distance, a whistle sounded, followed by a loud blast that startled Eric. Through the thick dust, a familiar gray horse cantered, his ears up and nose quivering. Eric pushed to his feet and caught Oakley's reins. His muscles complained as he swung up, but he forced himself to sit upright and urged the horse outside the fort through what was left of the gates.

Mason was still out there with Bruin.

There was no hint of snow, and in the east, a hint of dawn's light edged the star-studded sky. But it was the bluffs that gripped his notice. A massive pile of rocks lay at the base of the Slates, as if a chunk of the mountain had fallen in on itself.

A group of men milled about, their swords in their hands, pointing to the site. Eric hurried that way. To his amazement, Sgt. Mavis Derron and Lt. Kullen Hendrix were among them. On the ground, several forms lay, clad in Shadowmen attire.

"Where's Mason Grey?" Eric asked as he drew near.

Kullen pointed to the pile of massive rocks that had spilled from the mountains, and Eric sucked in a breath. But then a figure rose from the ground. He moved slow and stiff, and Eric urged Oakley closer and jumped off.

"Mason, are you all right?"

His clothes were filthy and torn, his shoulders rounded in exhaustion, and dried blood caked across a wide cut on his chest. But he was alive.

Another shrill whistle sounded, and a blast shook the mountain. Mason grabbed his head with a cry. At the same time, Eric's intuition flared, buzzing over his skin and making his ears ring. "Mason, what's going on?"

A stricken look crossed Mason's face. "They're in trouble!"

Anxiety clamped down on Eric's lungs, and he somehow knew. Aladee. Seria. *Lena.* "They're in the tunnel."

Without another word, he ran for the opening, Mason coming up behind him. The ground shook beneath him, slowing his progress. A narrow beam of light shot straight up to the sky, and one of the lower peaks crumbled in on itself. His lungs failed him.

Skies above. What had happened?

A bedraggled figure appeared in the opening and struggled down the incline, stumbling under a heavy load. It was Aladee, carrying a limp Lena, shouting something Eric could not make out in the noise. He met her at the bottom and took Lena into his arms just as Aladee collapsed. His heart clenched at the nasty purple bump on the side of her head. "What happened?" he asked as he lowered her to the ground.

Mason slid to a stop beside them, his eyes wild. "Where's Seria?" His voice did not even sound like his.

Aladee pointed back. "She's still in there!" Tears raced down her dark cheeks. "You have to hurry. I couldn't reach her."

"Dear Lambient." He didn't wait to hear more but bolted for the tunnel, ducking through the cascade of rocks that slid down the mountain.

"Mason, wait!" Eric watched him run headlong into the tunnel. Lena and Aladee needed help. But Seria was still trapped.

"Stay with her," he ordered Aladee, who stirred enough to support Lena's head in her arms. A violent tremor shook the ground as he tried to stand.

Then, with a deafening and sickening crash, the opening into the tunnel caved in.

68

I have put my trust in the Lambient that I may not fear the end.
-The Sacred Code

Please let her be alive.

Mason repeated the plea as he ran through the tunnel, his heart throbbing at the idea that she could be hurt. He would not even consider the worst. The tunnel had collapsed behind him, leaving no way of escape, but he ran on. He came upon the fork, noting immediately that the narrow crevice had split apart. It no longer held the same draw it did before, but a strange energy pulsed from it. He looked up as the entire structure shuddered and plunged through the opening before it was blocked by falling rocks. Then he darted through the widened path.

The foundation trembled under his feet, knocking his hopes against his fears. That he would survive the war only for Seria to lose her life, was unthinkable.

Please.

He caught sight of the opening at the end and quickened his speed. "Seria!"

The Shadowpit looked nothing like it had when he was chained here. Many of the stalagmites had crashed to the floor, breaking into pieces. Cracks ran down the walls like black veins. The pit itself glowed with an angry red fire, shooting a geyser of white sparks into the air every few moments that brought more of the cave down.

"Seria!" His voice pitched as he peered through the chaos. She was here somewhere.

"Mason!" Her weak call sounded from near the Shadowpit, and he bolted for her, tripping over something soft. He halted at the sight of Dreeya's sightless eyes staring up. A trace of sadness for the bitter woman's end stirred, but he did not give himself time to dwell on it.

"Seria!"

"Over here!" Her reply was broken, laced with pain and terror.

The pit spat another blast upwards, and Mason narrowly avoided a massive stone landing on top of him. He raced around the edge, scanning through the dust and angry red glow for the woman he loved.

There. Crumpled against a boulder, her face streaked with tears and her hair caked with dirt. "Seria!" He hurried to her, looking her over for signs of injuries.

"Mason, what are you doing here?" she cried, her right hand wrapped around her swollen left arm. The other hand was hidden under the heavy boulder. She was trapped.

"Getting you out of here," he said, realizing the situation. He ran his hands down her bruised arm and gave a tentative pull. Her cry of pain stopped him.

She shook her head. "There's no time."

"I'm not leaving without you," he rasped. "It will hurt, but I've got to move this rock."

Her head bobbed, her breathing already shallow and accelerated. "Do it."

He pressed his hands against the boulder. "This is gonna hurt."

She squeezed her eyes shut, her jaw clenched.

Mason hardened himself against the pain that moving the rock would inflict on her and pushed. Her scream pierced him, but there was absolutely no give. Not in any direction.

At another rockfall, he threw himself over her until it settled.

"You're going to be all right," he panted, shoving the end of his sword under it for leverage. But it still didn't budge. There was no way to move it. And the cave was falling in all around them. He turned back to those wide eyes that reflected what she already knew.

"Oh, Mason," she breathed. Her skin was gray, mottled with the agony she must be in.

"We'll be all right."

The Shadowpit hissed, readying to shoot another geyser up. The next one might bring the rest of the pit down on top of them.

He moved closer, careful of her arm, and pulled her against him, sheltering her as much as he could from the falling debris. "Tell me you didn't come here on my account."

"I had to come. For everyone." In her obvious pain, her voice came out thin and brittle, missing the spunk he was so used to hearing from her, but even so, it was filled with assurance. She drew back to look up at him, putting her free hand on his cheek, fresh tears spilling. "But if it meant saving you, I would do it all again. It can't hurt you anymore."

He buried his face in her hair as she clung to his neck. At long last, they were finally together, but was it to be the final time? His heart splintered, shattering into pieces and piercing the dream that would never be realized. Except for the one fragment of comfort that he was right where he wanted to be.

She pushed him back. "But I didn't do it so you could get yourself killed here." A bit of her old fire colored her tone, and he almost smiled.

He looked her in the eyes, seeing the mourning in her gaze as assuredly as he felt it in his chest. This might be the end. "Seria, I'd die a thousand deaths to spend my last day with you."

"Remember that night we went fishing?" she asked, so softly he almost missed it. "When we talked about our dreams?"

He couldn't speak, but his arms tightened around her. That conversation had played out in his mind many times since that night.

"I'm sorry you never realized your dream of a home," she continued, as if she did not notice the way the world was collapsing around them.

He leaned over her so the rocks could not hit her and whispered in her ear. "My home is you, Seria."

"And you're mine."

A shrill whistle split his ears, and she tensed against him. His breathing quickened as he looked back at the Shadowpit. Angry red flames lined with a purple light licked at the lip of the hole. Mason braced himself for the final onslaught.

"I love you, Seria." He pressed his lips against her temple, glad she did not seem to be afraid, though her bravery broke him. But if she had to die here, he would make sure that the last thing she knew was his love.

"And I love you." Her free hand knotted in his shirt, cold fingers grazing across his cut. "I'm so proud of you. I'm just sorry—"

He kissed her forehead, then looked down at her. "If your face is the last thing I see, Seria Gayle, then I'll die a happy man."

Another blast shot up, sucking the oxygen from the cave. Mason dropped on top of her as a roar of cracking stone surrounded them. Everything shook, knocking the rest of the cave down. Pain went through Mason's body as he was struck by dozens of falling rocks. Seria went limp beneath him.

Something bashed against his skull, and a dull ache draped over him. Groggily, he looked up, his vision fuzzy and dizzying. He swung his heavy head to look back at the pit, wondering if it was over. In his disorientation, the rocks seemed to float. Everything slowed as a hazy fog filled his mind.

Then a massive white blast erupted, stabbing his eyes as it spilled from the pit like a volcano. Pain rocketed through him briefly.

Then there was nothing.

69

On that day, the Lambient will bind the wounds of His people and heal their hurts.
-The Sacred Code

Eric stood on the balcony of his sitting room in the Great Hall at the Gateway Stronghold and watched the gentle rain shower that fell. For the first time in a long time, he did not have to wonder if Bruin had anything to do with the weather. This rain was natural. Peaceful. Cleansing.

Bracing one hand against the railing, he drew the cool, autumn air in, tempted to step outside and let the rain soak him, penetrate his skin and sink into his weary spirit. Two weeks since the Gateway War had ended, and he still felt battered.

Evidence of the battle remained. All of the gates were ruined beyond repair. Piles of the outer wall lay in ugly heaps, reminders that even the mightiest of structures could be broken down. Many of the civilian homes and businesses were gone, burned by the Dark Army. The Steward Chapel had been ransacked, its benches demolished and the copy of the Sacred Code ripped to shreds. But all of that could be replaced or fixed. Nothing would bring back the lives lost that night. So many good people.

Captains Braylee Wright and Dudley Nells had been taken to Calla and laid to rest, their Beacons beside them, with great honor, along with the many other Steward and Reservist casualties.

It was easy to feel small and forgotten in the wake of such loss. Indeed, each morning, Eric woke with a bleeding heart, the wounds still deep and raw. But he found that every day, some of those wounds were closing up, scabbing over. The scars would never go away, but little by little, healing was taking place.

Maybe one day, he would wake up without thinking of all that had been lost.

Men and women moved about in the streets below, each one attempting to pick up a remnant of life from before the war. The civilians had not been granted their return yet. There was still too much damage and not enough shelters. But soon.

For now, the Royal Army worked to repair the damage. The Beacon Orb had been found in a charred shed, blackened by soot but otherwise unscathed. There was a sense of relief that filled the cracks of grief, a release that allowed them to breathe again.

The war was over. Jader and Bruin were gone. New life could begin, but at such a cost.

There was a physical ache in his chest that the king was not there to see this hard-won peace. His hand rested on the hilt of Lavrynth, reforged by Barry and shining like new. It would always be a link to his father.

A soft knock drew his head around. For an instant, he expected to see Braylee entering the room and held his breath at the absence that stabbed at him.

Lena opened the door at his call, dwarfed by the tall portal. "You asked to see me?" she asked, her voice soft.

He tilted his head to the window, and she joined him. While he studied her profile, she looked out at the rain.

"It's lovely, isn't it?" she asked.

"It is," he said hoarsely. When she turned to look at him, he gently grazed the faint bruise on the side of her head, the last physical sign of her ordeal. "How are you?"

"I am well."

He moved his hand to her jawline. The timing was not proper, but he could not wait another day. The last two weeks had been spent healing and burying the dead. Eric and an entourage of knights and friends had only returned to the Gateway the night before from Calla, where they had traveled for the memorial service. There had been little time for him to talk to Lena alone during that period. But if recent events had taught him anything, it was that long life was not guaranteed any of them. Life was harsh and hard. Young people died along with the older generations. And Eric did not want to live another day without this gracious, brave woman.

She softened at his touch, and a faint pink tinged her cheeks at what she must have seen in his eyes.

He wrapped an arm around her and pulled her to his side, his heart sighing when she leaned her head against him. They watched the activity outside for a while, then he cleared his throat. "I hope you are aware, Miss Lena Carwright, that I fully intend to make you my queen."

She tipped her head to the side, and brown eyes shone up at him. "Do you think your people will approve?"

"I think they will fall in love with you. As I have." Then he lowered his head, acting on the desire that he had carried for months, and kissed her. Her lips were as soft and giving as the woman who offered them. Her hand slid around to his back, small and warm and gentle.

When he broke the kiss, he held her, resting his chin on her head. She hugged him back, a gentle presence that breathed comfort into the aching places of his broken heart. No words were needed as they simply enjoyed the peace and one another's company before another knock drew them apart. Eric kept hold of her hand, however, as he granted entrance.

The door opened again, and he smiled at the young woman, her long blonde hair sweeping over her shoulder. "What are you two up to in here?" Seria asked.

Eric chuckled at the pretty way Lena flushed. "Nothing I wouldn't do in public," he assured, kissing Lena's hand.

A serene light filled Seria's face. "I am thrilled to see you both finding happiness."

"I think we're all due for some happiness," Lena said.

Eric gave Seria an appraising look, ending with the bandage that wrapped her left hand. "You're looking well, Seria." He spoke the truth. Her skin had regained its rosy color after she was rescued from the cave.

"I am well," she said, as her good hand brushed the bandage. "In truth,

I have no right to complain."

Though Seria's hand would never be the same, her acceptance touched Eric. "Luron is chomping at the bit to have you at his side again."

She blinked at him. "With this?" She held her broken hand up.

He shrugged, forcing nonchalance into his response. "Why should that stop you? You still have a wealth of knowledge about the healing arts along with a heart of compassion for your patients. I suspect maybe even more so now," he added, softer.

She stared at him for a long moment, hope flaring in her eyes. "I had almost given up on that part of me. But if it's still possible..."

He reached out to rest his free hand on Seria's arm. "Just because we surrender our dreams to the Lambient, doesn't mean He won't give them back, even if they look different than we expected."

Her eyes filled with tears, and she sniffed. "Then you can tell Luron I'll be happy to help."

He gave her arm a squeeze and released her. "I am eternally grateful that you both stand before me," he said, tightening his fingers around Lena's. "As well as for what you and Aladee did at the cave."

A shadow dimmed the brightness of Seria's eyes, but it did not erase the peace on her countenance. "I'm glad it's over."

"As am I," Lena added.

Crue's head appeared around the edge of the door, his brows raised in question. Eric waved him in. "Aye, Crue, come on in."

The boy disappeared and returned a few moments later, leading Mason inside. He spoke quietly and stayed at the ready as Mason moved carefully into the room, still recovering from the injuries he took in the Shadowpit. He lowered himself to the chair Crue took him to and offered a nod at the boy.

Seria's face lit up, and she looked as if she wanted to jump in and help, but after exchanging quick looks with Lena, she waited. When Mason was seated, she walked over and put her undamaged hand on his shoulder, which he clasped in his own. Crue gave everyone a respectful nod and left without a word.

Giving the arm of the chair a solid pat, Mason turned his face to the couple. "Now would you like me to tell you how Lena feels about you, Your Highness?"

Eric laughed out loud. "Nay, thank you. We managed without you." That Mason was able to find humor in his situation did much to ease his concern.

Mason settled back against the chair with a half grin. "Suit yourself."

Lena gave him a quizzical look. "Should I even ask?"

"Nay, you should not," he said with a wink. Then he swept the other two a quick look and headed for the door, tugging Lena after him. "Well, we have things to see to, my dear."

"We do?" she asked.

He gave her a pointed look and glanced at the other two. "We do."

"You know I can still see your not-so-subtle looks, right?" Seria asked, her voice dry.

"And I don't need to see them," Mason said low with a hint of laughter.

"Who said I was trying to be subtle?" Eric stopped at the door and looked back. "And by the way, if you were uncertain, the restrictions of both your sentences have been lifted." He waggled his brows at Seria before he left them alone.

"You're enjoying this too much," Lena said, a smile teasing her prim lips.

"I think it's time they have a piece of that happiness you were talking about earlier."

Her face softened. "Have I told you that I love you yet?"

"Nay. I was beginning to think I would have to take Mason up on his offer."

"Then let me say it now." She reached up and kissed his cheek. "I do love you."

At the bottom of the stairs, Eric drew short. Braylee's widow stood in the foyer with her daughters. "Griselle. I did not expect you to be here."

She drew herself up as tall as she could. "I wanted to be here. As did my girls. Braylee would not have missed this day, and I felt we should be here in his place."

"Thank you," he croaked. That they had traveled from Calla to be here touched him beyond words.

Her plump cheeks creased in soft lines. "He considered you a dear friend."

Eric dropped his head, trying to regain his composure. Lena's hand slipped into his, and he held on to it like a lifeline. He swallowed. "That means a lot."

Braylee's daughters held their mother's hands, sober and quiet. Eric crossed the room and knelt before them. "I want you to know that I loved your father. Like a brother." His voice caught. "And I miss him every day. I'm sorry I could not get him back home to you."

"It's all right," Ella said. "Papa was doing what he was supposed to do."

"There was no one better than your papa."

"Everyone loved my papa," Shayna said, eliciting quiet chuckles.

"That's because of that big heart of his," Lena said.

Eric stood to his full height and took Griselle's hands. "If you wish, you have a home in Daymont for as long as you need."

Griselle's eyes widened. "Oh, Prince Eric, I don't know what to say."

"I hope you will say that you will stay there." It was the very least he could do for the family of the man to whom he owed so much.

She looked down at her girls, who both offered a slight nod. "Then I speak for all of us when I say we would be happy to stay. I thank you, Prince Eric." Then she clapped her hands. "Well, now, we don't want to hold up the ceremony. Come along, girls."

Ella paused at the door. "Papa knew you'd be a good king," she said, shyness tinting her voice. "And I think so too."

Eric gave her a wink, and then she slipped out after her mother and sister.

"Are you all right?" Lena asked.

"I don't know how I'm going to get through the ceremony after that," he said with a weak laugh, swiping moisture from his eyes.

"You've got a lot of friends here. You'll do fine."

As they moved to the door that led to the Great Hall, another wound in his heart began to heal.

70

What the Lambient has lit, no darkness can overcome.
-The Sacred Code

Seria still could not believe they had survived the cave-in. The look on Mason's face when he realized he could not free her would forever be etched into her memory, along with her grim awareness that he would not leave her. It made her love him more than she ever thought possible. A sweet ache filled her as she watched him now.

If it had not been for the timely arrival of Eric and his Gift, they would have been crushed beneath the rocks of the Shadowpit. Dozens of Stewards had pitched in to dig them out, but it was Rossi, with her unnatural strength, who had made the biggest difference. Seria would be eternally grateful for those beautiful souls who had saved her and Mason from certain death.

Mason turned his head in her direction and stood. "You're still here, right? You've been gone too long, and I need to hear your voice."

"I'm here," she said as she moved around the chair to stand before him. Her heart squeezed at his blank stare. The loss of his eyesight had been a harsh blow. Luron said that it was the blast of the Shadowpit, and it was uncertain whether his vision would ever return. Though something twisted within her at the faint white scars that outlined his eyes, they didn't detract from his rugged good looks. Looking at him now for the first time since their separation, her heart pounded for a different reason.

They had not talked much since the war ended, yet not for lack of trying. Both had required extended care in the infirmary along with many others injured. But not long after Mason first awakened, he almost brought the building down trying to find her. It was only after she went to him and assured him she was well that he could rest and receive the care he needed.

And as soon as she recovered, Seria had traveled to Calla with Eric, Lena, and the Stewards for the memorial services. Mason had insisted she go since he could not, still healing from the injuries he had sustained at the cave-in. The days apart had seemed to drag. Though she was thankful she had been able to honor the fallen Stewards in their final ceremony, she was, oh, so glad to be back. With him especially. "How are you feeling?" she asked.

"Ever the healer, aren't you?" Mason quipped. "Better now that I'm upright, though I'm still pretty sore. I've had enough of infirmary care to last me a lifetime."

"Are you angry...about your eyes?" She almost didn't ask the question, but he could not see what she was thinking by looking at her anymore.

His head dropped slightly, and she could almost imagine he was staring at the floor as he contemplated his answer. "I wanted to be at first," he admitted, massaging his forearm. "But I've spent so many years being angry and bitter. That's not the way I want to live my life anymore." One corner of his mouth quirked up. "At least this way, I won't see into people's private thoughts anymore."

"What about your other Gift?"

"I decided during the war that I didn't want to force people to act outside of their own will, so it's a blessing, really. I still get whispers of voices in my head sometimes, but the control seems to be gone." A peaceful smile lit Mason's countenance. "I truly believe Lambient did this for me."

Her eyes stung. The man who stood before her was so different from the one she dragged into her cabin so many months ago. He had gone from a vengeful, embittered soldier to a warrior of strength and faith.

"I'm sorry about your hand," he said, nodding in her direction.

Seria glanced down at her damaged appendage. It still pained her more than she cared to admit, but she was thankful it had not cost her their lives. "I am well."

"Are you?" he asked. "Truly?"

"I confess, I've had my moments," she said. "But Braylee told me once that doing the right thing sometimes means sacrifice, but it's always worth it."

He stepped closer. "And is it?"

"Aye." There was no doubt or hesitation in her answer. "Sometimes we're left scarred, but that doesn't mean we're broken. I'll still be able to serve as a healer." Wonder filled her that she could fulfill her dream.

He reached out to take her hands in his gentle grasp, his touch featherlight over her bandage. "This hand will always serve as a reminder of what you did to end the war. Of how close I came to losing you."

She stepped closer when he gave a soft tug. Her heart raced in her chest as she stared up at his beloved face. Scarred and worn now, but to her, it appeared so much stronger and even more beautiful than before.

He released a nervous chuckle. "It feels like I'm doing something wrong, being here with you like this without chaperones."

"I know what you mean," she said with a laugh. Their whole relationship had been built on secrecy and lies. For the first time, nothing stood between them to keep them apart. The very thought took her breath away.

His hand framed her cheek. "I may have lost the ability to see you, Seria, but I will never forget your face. You were the spark of life and light that pointed me to *the* Light."

She sniffled. "I thought you told me you weren't good with words."

A grin lightened his expression. "I learned from someone who never seems to lack for them."

She gave him a light smack. "I take back what I said."

He did not look the least bit repentant, but when he sobered, she bit her lip. He might not be able to view anything through those amber eyes of his, but she could still see the intensity rolling in their depths.

"Do you think you could spend the rest of your life with a blind man?" he asked, sliding his hands up to her shoulders.

The question took her breath away, filling her with a joy and lightness that made her feel like she could float up and out the window. She cleared her throat of the lump that threatened to break her voice. "Only if you think you could love a girl with a crippled hand."

"I've never stopped loving that girl."

"We're not the same people we were back then."

"I like us better this way." His brows furrowed. "I don't want to go back. I didn't know how to love you then. It was a selfish love, unwilling to sacrifice my wants or admit my faults." His fingers caressed her arms. "But I've learned a lot about love since then."

"Me too. I used to think it was wild and exciting, highlighted by passionate kisses." Her cheeks warmed at her admission, but again, she reminded herself that she had to speak her thoughts out loud. "But the Planks showed me something different. As did Braylee and his wife in the short time I spent with them. You could not miss how deeply they felt for each other and supported one another."

"That's what I want with you. Something solid and lasting." A teasing glint lit his eyes. "But I do hope I still get a kiss every now and then."

She threw her head back and laughed, joy blossoming in her like a flower that had been denied the chance to bloom. "You're still a scalawag, Mason Grey."

"But do I still get my kiss?"

She brought her good hand up to his whiskered jaw. "Aye, you'll still get your kiss."

He wrapped his arms around her waist. "Starting now?" he asked, his tone low and husky.

Her heart was ready to abandon her body, taking her air with it. She answered by leaning into him and raising her face to his. Their breath mingled for a brief moment before he lowered his head.

This kiss did not hold the same sparks of abandon and danger as before, nor did it carry the reserve of caution and secrecy. This one was full of hope and promise, of two lives bent and broken by life but coming out stronger. Of two paths that had carried them apart for so long but now merged into one, and two hearts that had strayed from what was right yet beat in the rhythm of truth now.

Seria slid her arms around him as he pulled her closer, both lost in the moment, finally free to share what had been out of reach for so long. It carried no less passion, though perhaps it was more mindful of what they had come through to get here. This was a kiss fueled by a deeper, more thoughtful love than what they had experienced before, inspired and blessed by the love of the Lambient.

The world of literal darkness was not one Mason had ever prepared himself for. But strangely, he found that he could still *see*. Images formed in his mind so clearly, that it was as if he was seeing them through his damaged eyes. He knew there was a chance he would never regain his sight, but even if he never did, he had no regrets. Despite the loss, his spirit was at peace. If he had to lose his sight, his hearing, or his limbs to save Seria, he would do it again. And if it meant that his Gifts could never be used for selfish gain again, he would gladly give them over to Lambient.

Besides, how could he complain about the cost when he held the woman he loved in his arms? After months of emotional and physical separation, she was here. There was freedom in this new stage of their relationship, a rightness that assured him he could pursue it without guilt. "We should probably head to the hall," he murmured against her hair. "Prince Eric said he wanted us there early."

She nodded against him and stepped away, though he could sense her reluctance. "Do...do you want me to help you?" she asked.

"If it means I get an excuse for holding your hand, then absolutely." When her cool palm pressed against his, he wound their fingers together. "Thank you for asking, though."

"Lena's grandfather did not like to be treated like less than a man just because of his poor eyesight," she said as she led him through the door. "I want you to tell me if I ever start to hover too much."

"I'm sure you will," he teased. When he heard her annoyed grunt, he grinned. "It's always been your way to help in any way you can. I appreciate that, and I'll need it a lot in the weeks to come, I'm sure. But I'll let you know if it's too much."

"You better."

The prince's coronation—held in the Great Hall—was the most beautiful and meaningful service Seria had ever attended. Watching her dear friend take his place as king of Paladin filled her with pride and joy.

Eric had insisted it be held at the fort, rather than the castle in Calla, as a symbol of new beginnings in The Gateway. Seria suspected it also had to do with Aden's absence at Daymont during this pivotal moment in Eric's life. How the old king would have loved to see his son now, the strength that he had shown during the war and the aftermath.

She leaned over at times to whisper all that Mason could not see. The bright red and polished silver mail was such a contrast to the mud-and-bloodstained armor the men had worn during the last stand.

Jervis Planks and Mavis Derron stood at Eric's right and left as the new First and Second Captains. Seria had been on hand when Mavis approached Mason earlier to admit and apologize for his role in the Handan massacre. Her heart had warmed at the way Mason quickly extended forgiveness.

Head Councilman Gaynor led the oath, and Eric's voice did not waver as he repeated it, though it dropped once or twice in emotion. "I promise as King of Paladin and Leader of the Royal Army to defend the helpless, uphold what is right, preserve what is good, protect the innocent, regard the pure, honor what is just, and maintain what is true."

And then the crown was set upon his head, Gaynor said a prayer of blessing over him, and the Stewards lit their Beacons.

Seria could not stop the cheer that escaped her, which was quickly joined by dozens of others. Eric reddened at the applause, looking quite majestic with his long red cape draped over his shoulders and Lavrynth at his hip.

But Eric did not wish to be the sole recipient of honor where it was due. After the ceremony concluded, he took time out to point out the brave deeds of those who had helped to hold the fort against Jader's dark forces, including the Stewards that had hidden within the Dark Army.

Karsch had already accepted a position within the Royal Army and now wore the colors of a sergeant. Kullen and the remaining Steward spies were given credit for all their dangerous work in enemy territory. They would no longer work covertly in the Gateway, and many of them made plans to go back to the Old Realm, though some opted to stay where they had built homes for themselves. Hurshel and the other senior knights were recognized for their assistance in securing the back gates. They would resume their retirement but promised to always return if their services were needed. Seria was amazed at the deep, long-lasting loyalty the Stewards possessed.

Because of their bravery, Dakim and the cadets were instated as full-fledged Stewards without the usual trials. Dakim was quick to acknowledge Mason's help in his training. Mason grinned and waved it off. Special tribute was paid to Captains Braylee and Dudley, and Seria had to wipe away tears as the Stewards had a moment of silence for the great leaders who had fallen. And then, to her shock, Eric called Seria, along with Lena and Aladee, to the front of the crowd to recount how they had entered the Shadowpit with the sole purpose of destroying it. Her face flamed as cheers filled the courtyard. Lena's cheeks flushed, but she held herself proudly. Like a queen, Seria could not help but notice.

Aladee acknowledged the praise with a composed demeanor until Jervis engulfed her in a bear hug from behind, eliciting a surprised laugh.

Mason was noticeably absent from the accolades, which Seria suspected had more to do with his personality rather than lack of appreciation. Mason never liked a lot of attention, and Eric was considerate enough to respect that.

After the formal ceremony, everyone moved to the mess hall, where Nola and her crew had a glorious spread of food and drinks prepared. "And Lena managed to make some honey tarts for the occasion," Serie told Mason. "But I doubt any of us will get to enjoy them if Eric has his say."

She helped Mason take a seat on a bench at one of the long tables. "How are you doing?" she checked, setting a dish of roasted pheasant and vegetables before him.

"I'm fine," he assured, taking a whiff of the pleasant scent drifting from the table. "What'd you get me?"

She could not help but tease him. "Stew."

He got quiet, and she somehow knew he was transported back to her rickety shack when all she had to offer him was stew and oats. "With or without potatoes?"

She sat down beside him and bumped his shoulder with hers. "You'll have to eat to find out."

Others took seats around them, the conversation flowing like rushing streams after long-awaited spring rains. The sound of hope filtered through the chatter as everyone put the struggles of the past few months aside, even if but for a few hours, and focused on the future. New homes. Upcoming weddings. Changes that promised growth.

Mason was quiet through most of it, as usual, but he seemed content to sit beside her and take in the discussions.

"I hear Shayna is planning to join the Stewardship," Eric said to Griselle.

The two girls had opted to sit with the cadets for the meal, where Ella was rapt with admiration as the boys boasted of their deeds in the war. It seemed the teen's source of infatuation had shifted.

"She's talked of very little else, especially since Braylee's passing." Griselle shook her head. "She's determined to work with Captain Aladee someday."

"She'd make a wonderful Stewardess," Seria said.

"I fully expect she will one day take her place in the Royal Army," Aladee said. "But I'm afraid she will have to be satisfied with working under the new captain. I'm stepping down."

"What?" Seria exclaimed, her fork thumping against her plate. "Whatever for?"

"Because Jervis and I are expecting our first child."

Seria squealed, startling Mason, and she and Lena both jumped up from their seats. A glowing Aladee stood to accept their wild hugs.

"Congratulations, Jervis," Eric said.

There was no missing the pride and joy on the captain's dark face. "Thank you. We couldn't be happier. Especially since Griselle has offered us her home."

Griselle folded her napkin and set it beside her empty plate. "I have no need of it anymore, and it would please Braylee to no end that you can start your family there as we did."

"I greatly appreciate it," Aladee said as the women settled back at their places. "I'll miss working with my ladies, but I am looking forward to a mother's life at home. Besides, I have no doubt Rossi will excel at the job."

"Speaking of a good job," Jervis said. "Might I recommend a certain young lieutenant for a captain's position?"

"I already offered it to him," Eric said, his arm stretched out behind Lena on her chair. They already looked so natural together. "He turned it down."

Jervis's brows shot up as he sought Lionel, seated beside Zakkias. "After all you accomplished at the final stand?"

"For now," Lionel said. "I'm honored, of course, but I requested some time to lean more into my duties and position as a lieutenant. I don't want to waste the opportunities I have now in my rush to advance."

Seria stared at him. Lionel had grown since she had last spent time with him. Gone was the begrudging young man who chafed to be in the middle of the action. In his place was a soldier who had matured and grown wiser.

Lionel looked down the length of the table. "Allow me to extend my congratulations, Lt. Rossi. I mean, Captain."

She responded from the other end. "I appreciate that. Just make sure to keep yourself out of trouble." She stood to leave. "I won't have time to save your pretty head again."

Seria bit her lip and waited for Lionel's outrage. It was swift to arrive.

"Save my head—hey, what's that supposed to mean?" Lionel slapped the table and jumped up, jostling Zakkias as he stalked Rossi. "I seem to remember saving *your* pretty little head, *Captain.*"

"Well, that's interesting," Aladee said as Seria and Lena dissolved into giggles.

"Maybe we should leave him here when we head back to Calla," Eric said dryly.

"I think that would disappoint both of them," Zakkias murmured, and the whole table burst into laughter.

The voices rose and fell all around Mason in a pleasant clatter of words and phrases he could not always make out. The hiss and crackle at the hearth cast a comfortable warmth to the large room, a sharp contrast to the bitter cold that had gripped the fort a short two weeks before. And the smells of the roasted meat and spiced cider teased his nostrils.

The crowd did not bother him like it used to. Maybe it was because here he felt surrounded by friends. Maybe because it felt like home.

The evening passed in fellowship and laughter, and though Mason enjoyed it, after a while he began to feel restless. As if sensing his mood, Seria leaned over to him. "Want to get some air?"

"That sounds great."

By the time they stepped outside, the rain had passed, leaving a fresh scent of wet grass. Mason was glad for the peace, thankful for the merriment inside. The final stand had resulted in the victory they had all fought hard for, but that did not change the losses, and sometimes those pressed in close.

There were so many who should have been here to celebrate this day, men who had fought for it much longer than he had and had not lived to see the result of their sacrifice.

Frakes, the Steward who had offered him reconciliation, had been slain in the first onslaught at the front gates. It pained Mason that he had lost the chance to really know the man. Hiram had fallen in the defense of the back wall. While he had been a thorn in Mason's side, his bravery and loyalty to the king could not be faulted. Gann had been killed defending the prince, his body surrounded by a half dozen dead Darkmen. Two of the cadets had been lost when the Darkmen infiltrated the fort. Those deaths hit Mason particularly hard.

And the captains.

He tightened his hold on Seria's hand. Braylee was the one who had pulled him out of that dark place in Machlin. And Dudley had taught him a lesson about broken arrows and broken men. He would never forget the captains and the impact they had, each in their own way, on his life.

He drew in a deep breath of the cleansing air, letting it wash over the sorrow. There would be plenty of time to grieve. Now was a day of rejoicing, and he did not want to weigh it down with regrets and sadness.

Eric and Lena joined them on the porch.

"What will happen next, Eric?" Seria asked. "I mean, Your Majesty."

"We've come through too much to hold to formalities now, Seria," he replied, a smile in his voice. Then he sighed. "I expect a lot of rebuilding. A lot of healing."

"Will the fort stay in place?" Mason asked.

"It will, though it will have a new purpose. A true gateway between Realms now, and not a barricade. But there will be a lot of work to make it that way."

His hand settled on Mason's shoulder. "I found something of yours while I was in Calla." A long, slim item was placed in Mason's hand, cool to the touch at first, then warming.

His Beacon.

A light flickered before him, then grew. To his astonishment, he could see it. Not just in his mind but there in front of him, the radiance of the Lambient piercing through the vision dimmed by the blast. It filled him with hope and reassurance. The Lambient had not forgotten him.

"You know a Steward isn't supposed to lose his Beacon," Eric said his tone light yet wistful.

A tight chuckle broke free as Mason lowered the rod. "I've heard that."

Eric cleared his throat. "I hope you're ready to go back to work soon because I need your help."

"Mine?" As much as Mason would like to take his place with the Stewards, surely Eric did not mean that. What could a blind soldier do?

"You're still a Steward, with or without your vision," Eric said. "We train for more than sheer strength but hearts that will turn toward a noble cause. You have shown that to be possible." He paused, as if thinking. "There are a lot of former Darkmen out there who may be looking for a new direction. Young men, like your friend Areem, who may realize they've followed a lie and aren't sure where to go from here. We need an ambassador, of sorts. Your testimony could go a long way to bridge the gap."

In the weeks since the war's end, the idea had never occurred to him, but now Eric's proposal fanned a growing inclination to lead those who had gotten lost in the dark, as Mason had so many years ago, back into the light. This work would give him the chance to mentor more young men like Areem, Dakim, and Crue, the right way this time.

The warmth of the Beacon assured him that his job was not done. He gave a single nod, hoping his appreciation would be depicted in the simple gesture.

But Eric was not done. "I assume you and Seria both wish to marry soon and reside in the Gateway?"

Seria's arm brushed Mason as she stepped closer. "We've not talked about it, but you're probably right," she said.

"I understand," Eric replied. "However, a position like this will allow for frequent trips to Daymont, which I know would delight Lena, as well as myself. So, you will have the Planks' old quarters when you're in Calla."

Mason caught Seria's gasp. "But that's reserved for officers," he said.

"I can't think of anyone more deserving than the man who defeated Bruin Pralus and the woman who destroyed the Shadowpit."

Mason had no words. It was all so overwhelming, so humbling. While he was at peace with the loss of his sight, he had not expected a chance for a new life that allowed him to not only provide for Seria but continue to serve in the Steward Army.

Eric's voice shifted away as he addressed Seria. "I didn't want to mention this earlier until I talked to Mason, but this also opens a chance for you to work alongside the castle's healer as well. He was most impressed with your skill and is interested in incorporating your methods into his practice."

When Seria answered, Mason could hear her smiling through her words. "I would love to work with him and show him how to mix my mama's teas and tinctures."

"Good," Eric said, sounding more than pleased with himself.

There was a pause, then Seria asked, "What are Areem's plans?"

"He's going back home," Mason answered, glad for the shift in conversation. "Said he's seen enough soldiering days, and he wants to touch base with his family again."

"Oh, that's wonderful!"

Mason could not agree more.

"I still have trouble believing it's over," Lena said.

"It will never be over completely," Eric said, "though this battle has ended. As long as Shreil exists, there will always be darkness. Evil men will crave power, and the fight for good over evil will go on." His words swung up, as if he was staring up into the sky. "But Lambient is constant, and His truth will last forever."

A contented hush settled over the group. Mason could not see the scenery, but he could feel the stillness that surrounded them and the coolness of the breeze that brushed his cheeks. Autumn would soon fade into winter, but for now, the hint of late-season flowers drifted in the breeze and crickets sang their chorus. Happy voices drifted from the doors behind them.

It was good to be alive.

"How about a walk?" he suggested to Seria.

"Sounds lovely."

"We'll be back soon," Mason promised as Seria tucked her hand in Mason's arm, letting him lead, though she directed their path away from where destruction had laid waste to the courtyard. Instead, they strolled through the quiet streets.

"How long do you think they'll wait before an official announcement?" he asked.

"Hmm. It wouldn't surprise me if it came out as soon as they were back in Calla."

"Are you happy with the living arrangement?" he asked, wanting to be sure. "We don't have to accept Eric's offer."

"I love the idea," she said. "I can think of no one more suited to lead those lost in the dark to the light of the Lambient."

"And you will be a healer in both the Gateway and Calla."

She pressed her cheek against his shoulder. "And the man who dreamed of having a home of his home will now have two places he can call home."

He grunted at the irony, then kissed her hand. "I told you; my home is you."

"And you're mine."

The assurance was simple, but it resonated with her sincerity. Seria did not expect much to make her happy. Indeed, she appreciated the simple things.

"We do have one thing we forgot about," he said as an earthy smell tickled his senses.

"What's that?"

"Your old donkey." As if on cue, Sanjo's bray met them at the fence Seria stopped at.

She released his arm and cooed at the beast. Soft rumbles sounded from Sanjo's chest. "Thank you for taking care of him."

"I don't know how you put up with him," Mason said, crossing his arms on the top rail. "The most demanding animal I've ever met. I can hardly stand to be around him." A soft, fuzzy chin rested on his arm, and warm breath hit his cheek.

Seria snorted. "I'm sure it was torture for you."

Mason scratched the wrinkled nose. "You're not making this very convincing, you old beast."

Sanjo only huffed.

Turning so he could lean back against the fence, Mason placed his hands around Seria's waist and shifted her closer. He yearned to be able to see into those life-filled green eyes again, but he cherished the images engraved in his memory.

"It's not going to be easy for us, you know," he said.

"You mean your blindness and my crippled hand?" Her hair slid over his hand, and he could picture her cocking her head.

"I was thinking about your awful temper." At her gasp of laughter, he rushed on. "And your stew. I'm sorry, Seria, but I don't know if I can live off that for the rest of my life."

"Mason Grey! How dare—"

He clasped his hands behind her back. "But I might know of a boy who would be willing to give us a hand for room and board."

"Hmm. Could it be the same boy who is winning the heart of my donkey?"

"It might be. He's already stolen Red's affection from me. That horse could care less if I came around."

Eric had surprised him by bringing his roan back from Calla. Crue later informed him the horse had resumed his space in the barn as if he had never left. Beast had been left in Paladin. Mason thought it fitting that, after losing two masters, the bay had been turned out to pasture, where he could eat to his heart's content for the rest of his days. Oakley, of course, remained Eric's loyal mount.

Seria slid her arms around Mason's neck. "I would love to have Crue stay with us."

"He's a good worker. A good boy."

"Hard to believe you're the same man who couldn't figure out why I thought so much of Byron."

He winced. "I had a lot to learn." Looking back, he hardly recognized himself anymore.

"Did you know Byron's family moved back to Cadence?"

The statement brought him back to the present. "They did?"

"I talked to Keeli and Michael a few days ago. They both admitted life had been more difficult under Jader's rule, and they wanted to try again here. Keeli's working in the kitchen with Nola."

"That's nice," Mason murmured. "I'll have to pay them a visit."

"They'd like that. Especially Byron."

Mason rested his forehead against Seria's. "I'm still expecting to wake up and find this all a dream."

"It is, but not the kind that goes away in the morning. This is the kind you get to live. I can't wait to raise a family with you. We'll raise a whole squad of Stewards, and I've already got all their names picked out."

He leaned back. "Is that so?" Anticipation sparked at the idea of Seria as a mother.

"That's right." She tapped her finger on his shoulder and counted. "We'll have a Braylee and a Dudley, Shon and Aden and Ollen—" She stopped short, as if unsure how he would feel about naming a son after another man who had loved her.

But he kissed her cheek. "Maybe he'll be the firstborn."

"Nay, that won't do," she said, her voice dropping. "Our firstborn will be Liam."

Mason had to swallow twice before he could speak. "Only if the next one is named Shasta."

"Oh, Mason. I do love you."

"And I love you, Seria. Nothing will ever change that."

He found her lips with his and hugged her close. As her arms wrapped around his neck, he thought again of the tumultuous journey that had brought them to this place. None of it mattered anymore.

Nay, that wasn't true. He would not be the man he was without the hard knocks and losses that had shaped him. He had not always responded well and many times had made things worse by acting on his own desires. But he wouldn't go back and change anything now. He was a better man because of it, ready to love Seria the way she deserved.

Teeth nipped at his side, and he jerked, cutting the kiss short.

"Sanjo!" he scolded, giving the long head a gentle shove. "I thought we were friends now."

Seria's laughter was pure happiness. "He's just reminding you that you're not the only man in my life."

"Noted, you old bag of bones." He ran his hand over the spiky mane. Seria leaned past him to give the neck a firm pat.

"Come on, we better get back before the new king comes looking for us."

Mason laughed and slid his hand down her arm, entwining his fingers through hers. Together they walked back to the hall where their friends waited. Their old lives were behind them, but they moved forward with confidence and hope into this new life spreading out before them.

The Gateway War was over, but a new era was beginning.

AUTHOR'S NOTE

We did it, readers. We've journeyed through the Gateway with Mason, Seria, Eric, Braylee, and so many other beloved characters who have become so real to me. Even though this journey is over and the series is complete, I hope this story will live on in your memory and your heart. I hope it made you smile, cry, and laugh. I hope you found hope, beauty, and inspiration in the pages. I hope in a subtle way, it turned your thoughts to the real Light of the world.

By now it is clear that this is a story of redemption. Mason's journey from darkness and deceit to light and truth has been both a joy and a challenge to write. But my hope is that by following his journey, readers can find victory in their own.

After holding this story so close for so many years, it feels strange to let it go and be done with it. Now it's yours as much as mine.

Thank you, friends, for sticking with me through this beast of a story that had to be told and for supporting me during the writing and launching of every book.

If you enjoyed the books in this trilogy, even a little, I hope you will consider leaving a review. I appreciate every one. And feel free to follow me on Instagram @crystalgrantauthor. I'd love to connect. God bless you, friend!

Until we meet between the pages again,
Crystal D. Grant

ACKNOWLEDGEMENTS

Mom and Dad: thank you for all of your love and understanding during this time of writing, editing, and launching this series, as well as passing on your love of words and reading.

Richard: thanks for all encouragement and support; you have no idea how much your words mean to me. And thanks for coming through with another awesome title!

Holly: this book would not be what it is without your input. Thank you for all the hours you put into reading my early draft and brainstorming with me.

Emily: I am thrilled I get to do this writing journey with you. I appreciate you and your input more than I can say. Thank you for loving my story!

AJ: what more can I say but THANK YOU. You have been my cheerleader and friend through this whole process, and I could not have done it without you.

Brittany: Darkend is a better story thanks to your thoughtful insight; thank you for the work and enthusiasm for this story.

Meghan and Stephany: Darkend is clean and shiny thanks to your editing and proofreading prowess; thank you both for all the finishing touches.

C.A.V.A. girls: Thank you so much for your love and friendship. I thank God for putting you in my life.

The Quill & Flame family: I'm so glad we have such a supportive group of people, all cheering each other on and celebrating every book release and success story. Thank you and God bless each of you!

The Gateway Keepers: Thank you for the enthusiasm, support, and excitement you've shown for The Gateway Trilogy over the last three years. I couldn't have done it without you.

My local ACFW chapter: I am so thankful for each and every one of you. You are truly a blessing to me.

ABOUT THE AUTHOR

Crystal Grant is a self-labeled old soul who enjoys simple pleasures like freshly baked cookies, scented candles, and anything with fur or feathers. Whether reading, writing, or editing, she loves to dive into stories that settle deep into her mind and heart. As a hearing-impaired, homeschool graduate, Crystal found her voice in writing about characters who find their faith in order to overcome insurmountable obstacles. Elementary teacher by day, she strives to instill a love of books and learning within her young students. Crystal is the award-winning author of The Gateway Trilogy, which includes *Shadowcast* (2024 Christy finalist) and *Lightshed* (2025 Carol finalist). When she's not dreaming about stories that sweep her away to another time and place, she watches classic movies and TV shows that do the same. Crystal currently resides in southeast Missouri, where she is always looking for space for another book or coffee mug.

DISCUSSION QUESTIONS

1. Mason had turned from the dark ways of Jader and surrendered to the Lambient, yet still struggled to accept the forgiveness extended to him. Do you think that is a real issue people may struggle with, even if they've turned their lives around? What are some ways young converts can combat this?

2. "The Light within you is greater than the darkness without." How would you interpret this phrase? How can it relate to your spiritual life?

3. Despite Mason's rejection of the Shadowstone, he found that he was still susceptible to Jader's control. What real-life struggles could this be compared to?

4. Aden believed that wrong choices should still have consequences, even if someone has already admitted their wrong and repented. Do you agree with Aden? Why or why not?

5. What character struggle did you relate to the most?

6. "Just because we surrender our dreams to the Lambient, doesn't mean he won't give them back to us." Do you think our dreams on earth matter to the Lord? Why or why not?

7. Mason and Seria both ended up permanently incapacitated in some way by the end. Did that surprise or disappoint you? Why or why not?

8. Braylee chose to go with Eric into battle, even though he had a family back home that he loved. Do you agree with this choice?

9. Which character is your favorite? Why? Who was your least favorite character? Why?

10. What would you have changed about this story? What would you keep the same? Why?

11. What do you think was the most prominent theme or message of this book?